Wildflower Brides

Four Romances Blossom Along the Oregon Trail

ANDREA BOESHAAR
CATHY MARIE HAKE
SALLY LAITY
PAMELA KAYE TRACY

BARBOUR
PUBLISHING

Cover art: GettyOne

Illustrations: Mari Goering

ISBN 1-7394-3203-6

All Scripture quotations, unless otherwise noted, are taken from the King James Version of the Bible.

Published by Barbour Publishing, Inc., P.O. Box 719, Uhrichsville, Ohio 44683,

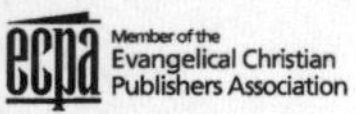

Printed in the United States of America.

Wildflower Brides

INTRODUCTION

The Wedding Wagon by Cathy Marie Hake
Bethany Handley arrives in Independence, Missouri, with a trousseau-laden trunk, a heart full of hopes, and two ribbon-wrapped packets of letters. One is from her best friend from boarding school, Penelope. The other is from Penny's brother, Joshua. One of Josh's last letters contained a thrilling proposal—for Bethany to wed him in Independence, accompany him across the Oregon Trail, and help him establish a new medical practice in the Willamette Valley. Faith fills in the gaps until Josh and Bethany learn marriage is just like their journey. They must discard old expectations that weigh them down and find simple joys to share with each other.

A Bride for the Preacher by Sally Laity
It is Emma Harris's dream to follow her father in doctoring the needy. Then when her father announces plans to take the family west, she reluctantly hopes there might be a place for her in the new territory. She isn't interested in traditional routes of marriage. . .until she nurses a certain preacher's fever while camped in the Black Hills.

Murder or Matrimony by Pamela Kaye Tracy
Pinkerton agent Bernard Williams always gets his man. . .only this time Bernie is after a woman. A field officer for over five years, Bernie has a reputation as a stickler only outclassed by Allan Pinkerton himself. At first, Bernie's sole preoccupation is uncovering the secrets Megan Crawford hides, but soon Bernie realizes that matching wits with the feisty female as well as battling with the Oregon Trail is wreaking havoc on his oh-so-organized routine. As Bernie digs into Megan's past, his gut feeling changes from: I'll have her in handcuffs before Independance Rock to I'll put a ring on her finger by Devil's Gate.

Bride in the Valley by Andrea Boeshaar
Dillon Trier, a hearty Missourian, is determined to carve out a life for himself in the Willamette Valley on land he can call his own. However, his only means of getting to Oregon is to drive the tyrannical Orson Millberg's second wagon and endure the unwanted attentions of his haughty daughter, Lavinia. In spite of his irksome situation, Dillon takes note of Penny Rogers. Her sunny disposition and spunky personality coax Dillon out of his shell. Better still, Penny is just crazy about him too. But when tragedy strikes, will it be the end of the trail or a happily ever after?

The Wedding Wagon

by Cathy Marie Hake

Prologue

Baltimore, 1860

"Miss Handley."

Bethany startled from her daydream and accepted the letter. Most of the other girls in the airy parlor were sharing snippets from their missives, and one girl got yet another box from her mama; but Bethany expected nothing. The bold script on this envelope made her heart flutter. "Thank you, Mrs. Throckmorton. Please excuse me."

Ignoring the other girls' pleas to stay and read the post aloud, Bethany hastened to her bedroom with less decorum than might be seemly. She rounded her four-posted bed with the candlewicked spread and sat in the window seat. Carefully, she opened the envelope and withdrew the letter. Joshua used plain white stationery for his other three letters—each two pages long. This envelope was ivory vellum and contained but a single sheet.

My Dear Miss Handley,

Over the past five years, I feel I've had an opportunity to get to know you by way of my sister's letters. In no way did Penny's tales of the escapades, wit, and friendship you shared prepare me for the vibrant young lady I met when you joined our family for Christmas. The missives we've exchanged since then have deepened my regard for you and assured me of your Christian commitment.

If there is no man who claims your heart or hand, I would be delighted and honored for you to consent to become my bride. I will endeavor to be a steady provider and thoughtful husband. The life of a physician's wife is not an easy one. Above that, instead of offering an elegant bridal trip, we would set out to traverse the Oregon Trail. I know I ask much of you. Nonetheless, I am a man of faith, and I hope you will find it in your heart to accept my proposal.

Should you be willing to be my helpmeet, join me in Independence on April eighth. We can wed at once, then spend the first days of our union settling the last-minute details for our adventure. In the event you hold other dreams and plans for your future, I wish you every happiness.

Very truly yours,
Joshua Rogers

Tears filled her eyes. Ever since Penny became her roommate and shared all of her stories and letters from home, Bethany had desperately wanted to belong to such a family. During the Christmas season, she'd been their guest and met Joshua for the first time. The cheerful holiday season and the warmth the Rogerses—especially Joshua—extended to her counted as the happiest days of Bethany's life.

"Oh, Lord, You're giving me everything I could ever want. I'll have a husband and finally be part of a wonderful family. Thank You for this."

Bethany kept Joshua's letter beside her as she sat at her writing desk. She dipped her pen in the crystal ink well and began,

Dear Dr. Rogers,

Thank you for your lovely proposal. I'd be honored to become your wife. I cannot think of a sweeter home than a wagon or a finer roof than a canopy of stars. . . .

Chapter 1

"Ouch!" Bethany cringed as Penny shoved another hairpin into her light brown curls. "The Indians won't have a chance to scalp me—you're getting the job done before we even leave civilization!"

Penny giggled and shoved one last pin in place. "There. Independence will never see a lovelier scalp."

Bethany looked up at her friend's beautiful blond upsweep and refuted, "Your hair always looks wonderful."

"Spoken like a true friend. Let's get you into your gown. I don't doubt Mrs. Throckmorton measured the seams within a half breath."

"She did, but Letty was a dear. She added on a tiny bit so I wouldn't have to be laced so miserably tight." Bethany slipped into the white satin gown with Penny's help and let her fasten the seemingly endless row of satin-covered buttons from hips to neck. She glanced at her reflection in the oak cheval mirror and fussed. "We cut the skirts much narrower so it wouldn't take up so much space in my trunk."

"You're so wasp-waisted, we could have had you wear a pillow slip for a skirt, and you'd turn every man's head." Penny's light blue taffeta gown rustled as she stood back and bobbed her head in approval. "We only have a few minutes. Where are your mama's pearls?"

"Here. Uncle Bartholomew sent them."

As Penny draped the luminous strand around Bethany's neck and fastened it, she muttered, "You'd think the old goat could have delivered them himself."

"I'm glad Uncle sent them. Had he come, he might well have given them to some other woman. I doubt he would have recognized me."

Bethany didn't even feel a pang at that fact. Orphaned at six, she'd spent the next five years trying, and failing, to be invisible and silent under the strict eye of Uncle Bartholomew's housekeeper and a stern governess. While they both went out to a Temperance League meeting one afternoon, Bethany took it upon herself to sled down the stairs on a silver tray. Skirts flouncing, stockings drooping, and one braid unraveled, she ran straight into her uncle. The very next day, she'd been shipped to Mrs. Throckmorton's Ladies' Academy. Fortunately, the headmistress valued loving-kindness as much as decorum and education.

"Well, your mama's pearls are your *something old*, and the dress Mrs. Throckmorton and the girls made you is your *something new*." Penny pulled a gold and crystal hat pin from her own sash. "I brought this to help keep your veil in place. It'll be your *something borrowed*."

"Oh, Penny! It's the one your papa gave to your mama—"

"On their first anniversary," Penny completed with a smile. "She would have wanted you to borrow it, I'm sure."

As they settled the sheer veil in place, Bethany confessed, "It feels scandalous, wearing a blue garter."

Penny laughed. "For all of our escapades, that makes you feel disreputable? What about the time we—"

A knock on the door interrupted them. "Ladies, it's time to go."

❧

Joshua stood at the altar and could hardly believe the vision beside him was real. Bethany handed his sister the bridal bouquet of Star of Bethlehem, phlox, flax, and violets he'd had delivered to her hotel, then knelt beside him so they could share Communion. The back of her gloved hand slid beneath her gossamer veil so she could partake of the elements. *Lord, bless our union. . . .*

He spoke his vows with assurance that no other woman could please him more. From the moment he'd met her, he'd lost his heart. Two weeks at Christmas and a few letters since were scarcely the courtship she deserved. Joshua thought about proposing and sending for her once he'd gotten settled in Oregon, but he was too smitten to wait. Then, too, he feared someone else would capture her affections if he delayed.

So here Bethany stood by his side. She turned to allow him to slip his mother's wedding ring onto her finger. In accordance with tradition, she'd split the glove along the fourth finger to make it possible, and he noted with pleasure that his bride's hand was both warm and steady. The flower-etched band fit perfectly. "With this ring, I thee wed and pledge thee my troth."

She looked up at him through the veil, so he could see her tremulous smile and wide green eyes. *This beautiful woman is my wife.*

"You may greet your bride."

Joshua carefully lifted the veil and tucked it back over her glossy curls. She blinked; but since her cheeks turned a fetching pink, he suspected it was more from nervousness than the light. Settling one hand at her tiny waist, he cupped her cheek with the other and kissed her for the very first time.

Before he even drew back, Penny intruded and gushed, "Now we're really sisters!"

His father embraced Bethany. "Welcome to the family, Dear. You're to call me 'Papa' from now on."

Josh watched his bride's smile warm. In that instant, he felt an odd twinge. He wanted the warmth of her smile to belong to him. *What if she just married me to be with them? She has no family and Penny always said—*

Bethany turned back to him. "Thank you for the flowers, Joshua. They're lovely."

"As are you." He stepped into the space beside her that his father had vacated and barely touched the delicate lace on her sleeve. "Your gown does you justice."

"Mrs. Throckmorton and all of my friends helped me."

He chuckled softly. "You had three weeks. From what I've heard, the redoubtable headmistress could have marshaled an army and led it to victory in that time."

Her gloved hand covered her lips as merry laughter bubbled out of her, and her eyes sparkled. "In half that time!"

With a few loud, bright flashes, the photographer took their portraits, and the wedding party moved to the hotel's dining room. Josh wondered if Bethany regretted not having a huge wedding with pews full of guests, but her easy conversation and cheerful attitude convinced him she didn't find their special day a disappointment.

Penny could take the credit for that. He'd never paid much attention to the fripperies and silly details of these affairs. The pricey ladies' academy obviously taught those essentials, because Penny had swept into Independence and arranged for the church, music, the bridal suite at the hotel, and a special wedding supper. She'd even selected a new suit for him in honor of the occasion. In the end, Josh tended but one detail: Penny insisted Bethany wouldn't want fancy hothouse roses. Though Josh had seen brides carry lilies, he associated them with his mother's funeral, so he went out and gathered a bouquet of fresh wildflowers that very morning. When he'd seen them in Bethany's hands, Josh knew he had chosen ones that suited her—bright, pure, and fresh.

Josh rose from the table and extended his hand. "May I have a bridal waltz?"

"Why, I'm honored to accept. Thank you." Bethany beamed as she took his hand and let him lead her to the floor. Others noticed her attire and veil and left the floor as the chamber orchestra struck up a waltz.

"Doct—I mean, Joshua, this day has been perfect," she said as she gracefully followed his lead.

He spun her and relished her graceful moves and the way they made her satin gown whisper. "I worried it would be a disappointment to you."

"A disappointment? Oh, never!" She swayed to the music in his arms and flashed him an impish smile. "If anything, I'm relieved. I'd be embarrassed to make a big fuss when I've no family to fill my half of a church or reception. If you feel we're missing out on any important customs, I'll be sure to tie flowers and strings of old shoes to our wagon when we depart."

Josh drew her closer and chuckled along with her. Her lightheartedness and ready laughter captivated him at their first meeting; and each time they were together, he grew to appreciate her sense of humor. He gave her hand a little squeeze and teased, "I hear shoe leather is too precious on the trail to waste like that."

"Far be it from me to be a wasteful wife."

"Or a barefoot one," he added.

Bethany turned a beguiling shade of rose. "Oh, Penny didn't tell you about that, did she?"

"About you being barefoot?" He had no notion what she referred to, but she'd sparked his curiosity.

"Truly, Joshua, I normally wouldn't be so bold as to be caught in public in such a state, but it was the price of vanity."

He chuckled and repeated, "Vanity?"

Her eyes glittered with humor, and her beguiling smile demonstrated the ability to laugh at herself as she confessed, "I'll never again waste money on shoes that are too big."

"Even if they're beautiful?"

"I assure you," she winked at Penny and Papa as he swept her by their table, "those slippers weren't worth it. Penny and I spent over an hour scrubbing the mud off the hem of my dress after that debacle."

"Where are those shoes now?"

She let out a small gasp. "You're naughty. You didn't know the story, after all."

"You can't leave me wondering."

"Very well. I doubt those lovely Italian leather slippers are still stuck in the mud. Most likely, someone happened by and declared they were an answer to prayer."

He smiled down at her. "Bethany, my dear, I'm sure you're right. I firmly believe in answered prayers."

Chapter 2

Oh dear. I didn't think Uncle Bartholomew's wedding gift would be a problem." Bethany emerged from behind the dressing screen wearing her new bottle-green-and-gold-striped dress and hastily slipped her snowy nightgown into the top bureau drawer. "Are we having our first fight?"

"It's hard for me to tell. You hid behind the screen until you were buttoned up suitable for church, and now you won't look me in the eye." When she summoned the courage to glance at Josh in the mirror, he patted the mattress in a silent invitation to come sit beside him.

Too embarrassed to share that perch since it was the site of last night's intimacies, Bethany sashayed to the raspberry velvet settee and tilted her head in a counteroffer for him to join her. To her relief, he was mindful of her sensibilities and didn't even comment about the fact that her heated cheeks must match the furniture.

Josh padded across the floor in his stocking feet and sat beside her. "I confess, you surprised me."

Bethany couldn't hold back her laughter. "No doubt, I'll do

plenty of that over the next fifty years or so. Seriously, though, Joshua—Uncle Bartholomew insisted."

"We were going to share the wagon with Papa and Penny."

"The wainwrights already made and delivered the wagon. I even chose a beautiful shade of emerald and had them paint it."

"Pretty or not, it'll still need a team of oxen."

"Of course it will. They're in the stable with the wagon."

Josh's brow knit, and his eyes sparked with an emotion she'd not seen yet as he said, "You've taken to arranging a lot on your own."

Bethany laid her hand on his muscular arm. "Don't you see? This way, we'll start out with a little home of our own, and we can take more essentials."

Looking less than convinced, he cast a glance at the trunk in the corner of the bridal suite. "Just what essentials are we supposedly missing?"

"Oh, I started with 'Ware's Guide to Emigrants' as a foundation and composed a list of necessities. Some things are already packed in the wagon."

He pulled a folded list from his shirt pocket. "I think we'd better compare lists. Mine is from Marcy's *The Prairie Traveler*."

Bethany twisted to the side, opened the reticule she'd set on the table, and pulled out a list at least five times as long. "Yes, well, that list was written by a military man. He simply didn't expect to have to set up a decent home at the end of his trip. I've pared this down to the barest essentials."

"Let's have a look." He took the slip and began to read. His very stillness amazed her. The men she'd seen at church or the fathers who came to visit their daughters at the academy often rattled coins in their pockets, drummed their fingers, or jiggled the foot they crossed over the opposite knee—but Josh had a way of settling onto a seat and looking completely at ease and in command. At Christmas time, that instilled a sense of calm in her. Now, it made her nervous. She'd never sat alone with a man, yet she was married to this one!

At first, he nodded in agreement with the items she'd listed. As the seconds ticked by, his expression became guarded. Finally, he turned and gave her a look of disbelief. "Calling cards!"

"They weigh nothing and take almost no space. I know every inch has to count, so I selected dishes and pots that all nest together. What did you think of the furniture?"

"Two chairs, not four. The bench and table are fine. Papa and I already lost the battle with Penny about the quilts." He winked. "I'm not going to waste my breath and go down to defeat again."

She eased back a bit on the settee. "I'm so glad you've agreed to the wagon. Since Uncle had his man procure it, it never occurred to me to ask you."

The corners of Josh's mouth pulled tight for a moment. "We're a team now, Beth. I'll always expect you to consult with me."

They went down the list, and Bethany tried to compromise. She would have anyway, but after unsettling Josh with the wagon, she wanted to ease his concerns. She sacrificed her barrel of straw-packed china and crystal. Wishing to show her cooperative spirit, she even agreed they'd bedroll beneath the wagon instead of using military camp cots.

"I'm not sure why you're taking a cookbook. You'll be making beans, biscuits, side meat, and mush."

Bethany shook her head. "Oh, no. Mrs. Collins's *The Great*

Western Cook Book was a wedding gift from the girls at the school. They've been helping me research what will store and pack. We made jerked beef, dehydrated vegetables and fruit, and found other things to take so we'll have nice meals. You might have noticed I don't list salterus because I'm taking something new called Rumford baking powder. I bought some foods already, but we'll need to buy others at the mercantile here in Independence."

"Penny bought some supplies, but she was waiting until you arrived to get most of the provisions."

Sliding her hand over his, Bethany tried to choose her words carefully. "I know it's a delicate subject, but I'd rather discuss it with you." Encouraged by his approving nod, she continued, "Since. . .funds. . .have become a temporary issue for Papa and Penny due to your father's reversal of fortunes, I thought perhaps you and I could beg their indulgence because it's our honeymoon and shop for the supplies ourselves."

He smiled. "That would suit. Papa's pride has him spurning my assistance, but I doubt he could refuse you anything."

"Perfect!" Bethany drew another item from the reticule. "Here you are."

"What's this?" Josh took the folded envelope and about choked when he looked at the letter of credit inside.

"My inheritance. The family attorney wired the funds to Mrs. Throckmorton once I received your proposal. I'm so relieved to give it to you. Carrying it made me nervous."

"It's a very substantial legacy. We'll endeavor to be good stewards. Did you have any hopes or plans for this?"

"I thought we'd use it to buy our supplies."

"Sweetheart, I can more than afford to provide for us. God's been very gracious to me. After our tithes and offerings on this, why don't we save the remainder and use it to build a nice house in Oregon or fund our children's educations?"

His reference to children made her cheeks grow warm. Eager to change the subject, she insisted upon Joshua showing her everything in his trunk so she could determine whether he had all he'd need, then was mortified that he insisted on inspecting the contents of her trunk. To her relief, he simply dipped his head when she held her hand against one drawer and choked out, "Small clothes."

"I'm pleased at how practical you've been," he praised, studying her dress. "Pretty, but not too many frills."

"Hopefully, the green and gold won't show dust or grass stains too badly." She looked down and pretended to brush away a speck of lint. "Everyone at the academy was so excited. They sewed clothes for me, and we figured out just how to use every last inch in the trunk. I don't think I could wedge in another thing."

"Not even another pair of Italian leather slippers?"

She buried her face in her hands as laughter bubbled up.

Josh took her wrists, kissed the backs of her hands very tenderly, then winked. "I'm teasing, but I'm not. I really do think you need another pair of shoes. Since I don't know how many pairs of stockings you have, we're going to get you a few more pair."

"Me? Oh, I don't think I'll need any. Quite the opposite; I was trying to find a diplomatic way of telling you I think we still need to stock up on essentials for you."

"I followed the list." He patted his pocket.

"That list was designed for an army man, not a doctor or

family man. I'll make a deal with you: I'll get another pair of shoes and see to completing your necessities, and you can obtain more medical items to pack. One of the advantages of taking our own wagon will be that you can have a better supply of implements and pharmaceuticals."

After room service delivered their breakfast, they dined over by the window and watched the streets bustle with folks all preparing for their westward treks. Bethany added cream to her tea and asked, "Do you think we ought to buy a milk cow to take with us?"

"Have you ever milked a cow?"

"No." She waited a beat and added, "Just a goat."

He chortled softly, then leaned forward. "Papa already bought one and named her Lady Macbeth because she's almost all white and has reddish brown spots on her forelegs."

A school bell clanged nearby. Josh consulted his pocket watch. "We're supposed to be at the meeting in fifteen minutes."

"I'm eager to meet all of our traveling mates. Aren't you?"

He rose and pulled out her chair so she could rise, then bent down so his breath brushed her cheek. "Not especially. The most charming one is already in my wagon."

Josh sat next to his bride and looked at folks in their square of benches. For the past twenty minutes, their guide, James "Rawhide" Rawson, had outlined their route and set out the rules for their train. He'd then divided everyone into three groups of twelve wagons apiece. Each group was to get acquainted.

Though Bethany sat with her knees pressed together primly, she folded and unfolded her hands in her lap. Just about everyone else seemed to be in motion, too. They crossed and uncrossed legs, fiddled with clothing, and gawked around, but Josh sat motionless. He could focus better when he stayed still, and he'd learned while sitting at his mother's bedside as her health faltered that tranquillity tended to be contagious. Whenever he sensed others needed calming, he purposefully acted restful. As far as he could tell, half of these folks were far too eager and needed to settle down; the other half were nervous enough that they needed to calm down. He shot Bethany a quick look and decided she fit into the latter category, so he slipped his hand over hers and gave her a reassuring squeeze as he suggested, "Why don't we get going on the introductions?"

A spry, fiftyish woman stood and bobbed her head at everyone. "I'm Willodene Haywood. Y'all just call me Granny Willodene." She cast a glance at the collection of children all wiggling in the middle of their square. "I reckon we'll never keep straight whose young'uns are whose today. May as well let 'em go out and frolic. You biggers mind the littlers. We're all gonna be together, so best you all learn to play nice." The children obediently traipsed outside.

Following Granny Willodene's example, folks introduced themselves. The Greens, Schmitts, and Barneses were all farming families, looking for a brighter future. Clearly, Orson and Eulalie Millberg counted themselves a cut above the rest of the travelers—they brought a little Irish maid along and hired a sturdy, taciturn man named Dillon Trier to haul their prissy daughter's piano in a second wagon. Rawboned Mr. Sawyer announced he'd be happy to use his carpentry skills to help folks out with their wagons if problems came up. The three Cole brothers looked brawny as oxen, and Josh thought the pharmacist, Mr. Harris, might be a nice companion for his own father and a professional ally for himself. He'd not paid attention to the man's daughter, but Bethany whispered, "Emma has such a shy, sweet smile." Young Parson Brewster, who performed their wedding, came over and took a seat. Bethany perked up a bit, and Josh suspected she subtly nudged Penny. He quelled a smile. Penny had played matchmaker for them; it would serve her right if Bethany returned the favor. Mr. Crawford, a book and Bible salesman, looked to have his hands busy with a wife, sister, and kids in tow. With Papa and Penny's wagon and theirs, the full dozen were accounted for.

Josh thought everyone in their circle looked hale. Both of the other circles belonging to their train had folks who hacked with consumptive coughs. He made a mental note to stock up on more eucalyptus and cherry bark.

Once their group finished the round of introductions, the menfolk seemed antsy to get out and see to matters. On the other hand, Josh noted how the women kept chattering and working at getting to know one another. The division seemed pretty clear: Most of the men were eager; most of the women worried about what lay ahead. He didn't want Bethany to fret, so he shot her a bolstering smile.

"Rawhide" banged on a post and gained everyone's attention. "Enough of the palavering. Weather's looking good, the prairie grass is four inches high so the oxen will have plenty to eat, and the mud on the trail's hardening. Since everyone has already mustered, we'll leave Thursday at daybreak."

"At least give us one more day—make it Friday," Mr. Millberg demanded in an officious tone.

"Nope." Rawhide turned his head to the side and spat a stream of tobacco into a brass spittoon. Without missing a beat, he added, "Friday's the thirteenth. Call me a superstitious heathen, but I ain't gonna set out on a day like that, and if we wait 'til Saturday, another train will set out ahead of us. Their livestock will eat the grass and foul the water."

"That part I agree with," said Parson Brewster diplomatically.

Rawhide smacked his gloves on his thigh in acknowledgment. "All of you are to bring your wagons and beasts to the edge of the west pasture by noon tomorrow at the latest. The Coles and I will guard them for you. Remember—pack for survival, not sentiment."

Bethany hopped up and tugged on Josh's arm. "We'd better hurry! He just cut our time in half."

Chapter 3

Careful!" Josh drew Bethany closer as they walked down the rowdy streets of Independence, back toward the hotel. They'd just finished wedging the last of their supplies into the wagon. "I have to hand it to you, Bethy-mine. You jammed more into that prairie schooner than I could have believed possible."

She smiled up at him. "I think we work well together. It felt right, making those difficult choices as a team."

Accompanied by his big yellow mutt, Parson Brewster came toward them. He hefted a small crate of supplies and said, "We'll move out at dawn tomorrow. I'm inviting everyone to meet by my wagon for a quick word of prayer before we start."

Josh gave Bethany's hand a squeeze. "My wife and I will be there."

The next morning, he held her hand again as folks gathered together to ask God's blessing on their journey. The feel of his strong hand clasping hers and the first golden rays of sunlight made Bethany feel this adventure was blessed. Afterward, she scampered to their wagon while the men listened to a few last-minute details from the guide. She quickly attached the ribbon streamers and bunches of wildflowers she'd gathered to the back and sides of the wagon.

Penny brought over a sign that sent them both into giggles. Josh came over, took one look, and chuckled as he tacked it over the dish box. *TIED THE KNOT AND UN-AFRAY-ED.*

It temporarily covered the golden caduceus Bethany had painted on the wagon. "A traveling shingle of sorts," she'd told Josh with a shy smile. His pleasure at that tiny gesture warmed her heart.

The second Penny had seen their pretty-colored wagon, she'd dashed off to the mercantile and returned with a bucket of paint. That wagon now sported a coat of blue paint, and several spatters dotted the wheel spokes, giving them an odd likeness to robins' eggs.

Penny glanced ahead at her wagon, then back at the other wagons. She moaned as she read the crudely lettered "Oregon or Bust" the Cole brothers had painted on their wagon's canopy.

"Sis, don't you dare say a thing to them," Josh teased. "They just might start admiring the blue paint job you did and hire you to—"

"Bethany," she interrupted, "let's walk together."

"No, my bride's going to ride with me this morning." Josh slipped his hand about Bethany's waist and snuggled her to his side. "We've been racing about for the past few days. It's time to take a breather."

"I'd like that," Bethany whispered.

The road away from Independence was so wide, the wagons lined up twelve abreast to leave. Folks shouted out with glee as Rawhide gave the order to set in motion.

"This is going to take some getting used to." Josh braced

Bethany as she nearly slid off the seat after another jolt. They'd been riding almost half an hour, and every yard brought another bump.

"I read the ride would be jarring."

"You like to read a lot?"

"Oh, yes. Do you?"

He smiled at her. "When I have the time." Josh looked at the oxen again and said, "Papa grieved at selling off the library, but the books were too heavy to bring. All I have are Marcy's *The Prairie Traveler*, my Bible, and a half dozen medical books."

"Your father has a whole library memorized. I've never known anyone who could recite so many pieces. It's enthralling."

"I suppose it's not uncommon for an English professor to know so much, but he and Penny both have the gift of oration."

He shot her a quick glance. "I saw a few books in your trunk. What were they?"

She waved her hand dismissively. "Nothing much. Whoops!" She jounced into him. "You're going to need to doctor yourself for all the bruises I'm causing, crashing into you!"

Josh didn't press her about her choice of reading material, though he felt a stab of curiosity. The fact of the matter was, he and his bride needed to get to know one another. He moved on to a new topic. "When did you milk a goat?"

"When I was twelve, Mrs. Throckmorton arranged for me to spend Christmas with some of her relatives. I learned all sorts of wondrous things about animals. Other than last December with Penny and Papa and you, it was the best Christmas I remember."

Penny and Papa and you. She stuck me last on the list.

"I thought Lady Macbeth was easier to milk this morning."

Josh squinted to look past the oxen to the rear of his father's wagon. Papa had roped Lady Macbeth to it. "She's ambling along nicely. With all of this dust, she won't be white by noon."

"Neither will the milk." Bethany twisted backward and pulled a jar from a small bucket she'd hung behind their seat. As she let him peep beneath the wet dishcloth, Bethany chirped, "All of this jostling will turn it into buttermilk!"

"I've never had much of a liking for buttermilk, but I relish buttermilk flapjacks."

"Do you mind if I give one of the families with lots of children the extra buttermilk, then make flapjacks later in the week? I have a menu all worked out for the next two days."

"Fine." He braced her as she turned to put the jar away. "Hold tight. Bump ahead."

Bethany pivoted and slipped her arms around him. The sweet scent of her honeysuckle perfume made him hold her even closer. Charmed by her self-conscious giggle, Josh brushed a kiss on her cheek and patted her before he let go. "Best put on your sunbonnet, Sweet Beth. The sun's starting to sneak over the top of our wagon."

As she tied the ribbons in a jaunty bow beneath her chin, his bride said, "I didn't know you disliked buttermilk. I recall from Christmas that you have a hearty appetite and prefer apples to cranberries. Tell me more about what you do and don't fancy."

"Everything you put in the food supplies looked good to me. You brought stuff I've never seen before."

"Oh, when I came back from Christmas without Penny because she was going on the trail, Mrs. Throckmorton used her upcoming adventure as a school project. We researched food, weather, and geography. Once you wrote and proposed, the cook went to the shipyard and train station to select the freshest fruits and vegetables from Florida, the islands, and South America. Everyone helped me preserve them. Mrs. Throckmorton and the girls have been like my family." She gestured ahead. "But now Penny and Papa and you are my real family."

Josh nodded. He didn't say a word.

❧

Bethany almost wished she'd walked with Penny, after all. Conversing with Joshua wasn't very easy. For the past four days, they'd had plenty to talk about and do. Now that they were all set and traveling, she came to a disquieting realization: She'd married a man she barely knew. She drew her cocoa-colored kerseymere shawl about her shoulders—as much to hide her shudder as to fight the April chill.

"Cold?"

"A little." She forced a smile. "I'm interested in hearing about what you've planned to do, once we reach the Willamette."

"Each family is allowed to claim one hundred twenty acres. Papa and I will each claim land. We thought to build cabins close to the shared property line so you and Penny can help each other and visit."

"Wonderful!" She paused, then wrinkled her nose. "What about your medical practice? You'll be away from town."

"Not necessarily. We'll not be in a big city, but townships are springing up everywhere. Choosing a good location shouldn't be overly difficult. I anticipate I'll be called away at times, so I wanted our cabin close to others so you'd have help."

"You're most thoughtful, Josh, but you needn't fret. I'm quite independent."

"Are you, now?"

She heard the challenge and amusement in his voice. "Yes. Why don't you teach me how to drive this thing?"

"There'll be time for that later. The wainwrights designed a clever seat here, but we can ride my horse or walk alongside to spare the oxen."

"Did you get new shoes for your pony, as you did for me?"

His chuckle lightened her mood. "Yes, but I won't expect you to eat grass. I had a friend go to Chicago and do some horse trading for me." As Bethany looked at the two, black-splotched white horses, Josh continued, "The one on the left is Tincture. He's Papa's. Ours is named Tonic."

"With names like that, they ought to stay in the pink of health."

"I hope so. That Tennessee walker of Orson Millberg's is a beautiful beast, but he'll end up in bad shape because he's accustomed to eating hay and oats. My friend got Papa and me these Indian paints because they're content to graze on the grasses."

"I hope you'll be content with grasses, too." She darted a look from beneath the brim of her sunbonnet. "I brought oatmeal, rice, barley, corn, and wheat."

"All that's fine—but I do like my flapjacks."

They spoke in fits and starts all morning. The awkwardness waxed and waned. Realizing her groom had sharp wit, Bethany tried to use humor to draw him out. By the time the wagons stopped for lunch, she was relieved to have Penny and Papa to help carry the conversation.

Papa threw a rust red blanket on the ground near a patch of violet and yellow wood sorrel, and Penny brought buttermilk. While Josh delivered their buttermilk to the Sawyers, Bethany set out the fried chicken, cheese, and apple tarts they'd gotten as a boxed lunch from the hotel.

Up ahead, a small ruckus drew their attention. Rawhide stayed mounted, glared down at the Millbergs, and waved at their maid. "Miz Katie, you put that chair right back in that wagon. You folks can sit on the ground just like everyone else. Noontime stops are necessities. Eat simple, rest up."

Mrs. Millberg huffed and her daughter fussed about her frilly pink dress while Mr. Millberg scowled and rumbled, "Now see here. These are ladies—"

Rawhide interrupted, "Are you implying the other women in my train aren't ladies, Millberg?"

Papa leaned forward and helped himself to a chicken leg as he quoted under his breath, " 'Twas yet some comfort, When misery could beguile the tyrant's rage, And frustrate his proud will.' *King Lear*, Act IV, Scene 6."

Penny whispered, "Oh, I thought that was from *Taming of the Shrew!*"

Bethany dropped her chicken wing as her composure slid toward mirth.

Josh snatched it from the blanket. "Fly, little bird!" He tossed it toward the parson's big yellow hound that lay in the grass.

"Josh!" His name came out in a shocked interruption to her laughter. "You wasted food!"

"No," he said as he handed her another piece of chicken. "I paid a pittance for your priceless laughter."

Rawhide gave them only a short rest before he spat out a wad of chewing tobacco, then rumbled, "Oregon ain't coming to you. Best get a move on. Want to gain as much distance as we can while folks and beasts are fresh."

By nightfall, they'd traveled to the Methodist Shawnee

Mission. For the first time, Bethany saw Indians. The men bought feed for their livestock and a few of the women started to cook supper.

Josh insisted, "I'll arrange for supper for us. It's been a long day. I want you to rest."

Penny limped up. "Rest? Oh, that sounds heavenly. My feet are beyond sore. I'm inviting Papa and myself along. The honeymoon is over for you two."

"You're welcome to join us." Josh tugged Bethany away from the wagon wheel she leaned against. "But the honeymoon isn't ever going to end."

The honeymoon isn't ever going to end. . . . Josh's words echoed in Bethany's mind as he held her arm and led her back to their wagon after they'd enjoyed a delicious roast beef supper at the mission. All around them, folks unfurled bedrolls beneath their wagons. She smiled at him. "I guess this is our first night to have a canopy of stars."

Penny soaked her blistered feet in a bucket while they listened to some of the other travelers sing and fiddle.

Bethany continued to stand by the campfire. She longed to rub her aching hips, but that simply wouldn't do. Papa stood and swept his hand toward the chair in a gallant motion. "Thank you for the offer, but I prefer to stand."

Josh refilled his blue-speckled graniteware coffee mug and shot her a look. He sidled closer. "Wagon jounce you a bit too much?"

She felt her cheeks go hot and confessed under her breath, "I'm liable to lose either my molars or manners if I sit down."

"Feel like a naughty girl who got a spankin'?"

Straightening her shoulders, Bethany declared, "I have no

idea what one of those would feel like."

Josh nodded his head knowingly, but his eyes sparkled with the impish humor she'd learned he exercised with endearing frequency. "I suspected as much. You must have been a very spoiled child."

Bethany made a show of looking about the wagon train as she declared, "I see all of the children have been tucked in. I suppose since I already have cinnamon rolls for our breakfast tomorrow, I'll turn in now, too."

Papa chuckled. "You napped along with the children while we crossed the Blue River, too. Fast as it was moving, I expected the roaring water to wake you up, but you slumbered on. Josh promised you'd already bought enough flour, but we stopped at Fitzhugh Mill and bought one hundred pounds more of flour and fifty of grist corn."

Bethany stumbled and Josh steadied her. She laughed as if she'd been clumsy. . .but fear welled up in her throat.

Chapter 4

All too early the next morning, the crack of a gunshot sounded as the train's wake-up call. Bethany crept from their quilts beneath the wagon so she could start breakfast. Chilly air had her making coffee and oatmeal to go with the cinnamon rolls.

"Delicious oatmeal, Sweetheart," Josh said as she refilled his mug. He smiled and leaned closer. "Do we have any hot water?"

"A bit to do the dishes."

"Good. Dip your hanky into it, then sneak it to me." When she started to ask why, he silenced her with a quick kiss before whispering, "Tell you later."

Josh wandered off as soon as she handed him her mug. Inside, the soaking hanky steamed in the morning air. A few minutes later, he sauntered back, tossed back another mug of coffee, and hitched up their oxen.

As he handed back her handkerchief, he murmured, "I needed it to draw a splinter out of Dillon Trier's hand. It's not a big deal, but his boss, Millberg, is so disagreeable, we want to keep quiet about it."

She whispered, "You trust me to keep a secret?"

"Trier doesn't mind you knowing as long as his boss is kept in the dark. I owe my patients their privacy, Beth. Many's the time you won't understand what's happening. I'll expect your blind trust on those occasions."

Bethany nested the dishes in the dish box mounted on the rear of the wagon, then tucked her hands into the pockets of her apron. "If it's all the same to you, I think I'll walk today."

Josh studied her for a long moment, then said, "Fine, but we get to eat supper alone then." He tapped her nose playfully. "And don't leave your shoes in a mud puddle along the way."

As she walked along, Bethany thought of Josh each time she saw wet patches of earth. This was the first day since their wedding that they'd been apart, and though she'd felt awkward with him yesterday, she missed him now. Plans for a nice, private supper filled her mind. What would make him happy?

Happy. He'd bent over backward to make her feel cherished. Guilt speared through her as she wondered how he'd react when he discovered her fear of water. Would he be understanding, or would he be mad? Deep in her heart, she knew she ought to have told him about this weakness of hers; but Bethany had feared he'd not wed her if she confessed how she dreaded water, and she couldn't let him leave her behind.

Penny chattered about the other folks on the trail, and she caught Bethany's attention when she dropped her voice and said, "Mr. Millberg has the looks and temperament of a troll!"

Bethany choked on her laughter, then said, "Our guide surely took care of him yesterday. Why, the way Mr. Rawson championed all of us ladies—I think he's quite clever."

Penny shuddered.

"You needn't fear him. Josh told me he researched the

guides, and I trust his judgment implicitly. Rawhide's capabilities and character truly impressed him. I'm going to think of our guide as a tattered knight."

"Knight? He's as superstitious as a Saracen! If you want to talk about knights, I'm positively surrounded by them. Will you think me too bold if I invite any of the men over for supper?"

Bethany shook her head. "Not tonight. Josh and I want to have a supper for two. Maybe tomorrow night. Mrs. Throckmorton would suggest Josh or Papa extend the invitation, though."

"Invites for what?"

Bethany and Penny both spun around at the sound of that deep voice. Penny stumbled and landed in a flurry of skirts and petticoats with a shriek.

"We're discussing supper, Mr. Rawson," Bethany stammered.

He crossed one wrist over the other on his pommel and leaned forward. "Call me Rawhide. And call me for supper, too. I'm obliged for the invite. See you just after sunset."

After he rode off, Bethany helped Penny up. "You'll have to handle him tonight."

Penny clung to her. "You can't expect me to entertain that heathen alone tonight!"

"Papa will be with you—"

"Papa will wander off and start reciting Shakespeare. Josh is the one who's vouching for Mr. Rawhide. The least you two can do is help me. You'll have plenty of other nights to share a private meal. After all, we're family—you have to stick by me!"

Penny was right. . .but Bethany felt her heart hitch. Would Josh be disappointed? Maybe not. He'd sent her off quite easily this morning. She spied a stem and white flowers and yanked a wild onion from the ground next to where Penny had fallen.

"See? That is a sign." Penny folded her arms resolutely. "I'm sure of it."

Bethany looked at the onion pensively. Surely Josh would agree that his sister needed their support. "With this as a start, what kind of menu do we serve to a Saracen?"

❧

The next morning, Bethany moaned when she lifted the lid to the Dutch oven. Last night's stew and fry bread turned out quite creditably. Josh hadn't said a word about them dining with his family and Rawhide, but she'd sensed tension in his shoulders, and he'd jiggled his leg instead of sitting still. Nonetheless, he'd said a kind word about the food. Unfortunately, her luck hadn't held out. The top of the breakfast biscuits still looked gummy, but the bottoms. . .

"Ma'am," the bass voice of one of the Cole brothers whispered over her shoulder, "them biscuits of yourn are burnin'."

The lid clattered and dropped onto the ground. "Oh. Yes. Oh, my."

"Ain't no need to fret." The big, black-haired man stooped, used the edge of his unbuttoned brown shirt to lift the lid, and shook off a few leaves. "Lookie here." He swiped her favorite crimson potholder, took the Dutch oven, and flipped the biscuits onto the inside of the lid, then neatly slipped them back into the oven upside down. "Iffen you settle coals atop the lid, they even up the heat so's the biscuits cook easily."

Bethany stared at the charred biscuit bottoms and chewed her lower lip to keep from crying. She knew her face must match the hot pan holder. Suddenly, the raised lip on the Dutch oven's lid made sense.

"Betcha ain't cooked none on an open fire."

"Just supper last night," she confessed thickly.

The black-haired giant leaned forward and rested his hands on his knees so he'd be at eye level with her. His voice rumbled softly. "You'll learn. My ma, she taught me. I reckon a smart lady like you'll pick it up right fast."

"Thank you, Mr. Cole." *Whichever one you are. . .*

"Ain't nothing. I was fixin' to start our vittles. Just need to reheat last night's cornmeal mush and coffee. Iffen you don't mind me sharin' your fire, I'd be much obliged."

Five minutes later, Bethany watched as Josh tucked bacon into a singed biscuit and gamely ate it. Papa and Penny exchanged a look, said nothing, and ate the unburned portions of their biscuits. Bethany intentionally served herself the worst of the batch. Bad enough, she'd burned them—the least she could do was suffer the consequences. Both of them looked like lumps of charcoal. The first bite tasted so dreadful, she sneaked the bacon out of them, then secretly dumped both into the fire as she reached for the coffeepot.

Mr. Cole turned out a neat breakfast and deftly slipped a wedge of fry bread into her apron pocket. Looking innocent as could be, he offered, "Doc, iffen you wanna take yore missus up to see Blue Mound today, I'll drive your rig awhile."

"I'd like that. Thanks."

Later, Joshua cradled Bethany across his lap as Tonic crested the peak of Blue Mound. She gasped, and his arms tightened as they stared out at the expanse of prairie ahead of them. "Land! Hundreds of miles of land." *And not a river in sight. . .*

"Ready to cross that?"

"The books said the trip takes six months, but it looks like we'll take an eternity to traverse that."

"We'll make our way across together." He turned her face to his and brushed a kiss across her lips.

Bethany whispered against his cheek, "The adventure of a lifetime."

"Rawhide groused about folks coming up here for a peek. I wish we had longer to gaze out, but if we hurry back, Bert Cole said he'd jump from driving our wagon to driving Papa's so he and Penny could view this, too."

As they rode back toward their green wagon, Bethany rested her head on his shoulder. He relished the feeling of her leaning against him, as if she fully entrusted herself into his care. Still, he needed to say something. "About supper last night—we were supposed to dine alone, and you invited a guest."

"I'm so sorry! Penny's terrified of Rawhide, and she insisted you wouldn't mind protecting her from him. I didn't know what else to do."

He stayed silent. If he complained about helping out his family, he'd certainly set her off. Besides, she'd almost paid him a compliment by saying he was capable of protecting them. Seeing as she'd apologized, he let the matter drop.

"Josh? I hate to ask, but how did you know which Cole brother is which? I can't tell them apart!"

"There's a space between Bert's front teeth. With Beau and Buck being identical twins, I'm as lost as you are."

"You're good at noticing little details."

"It's part of being a doctor." He dipped his head and whispered, "It's part of being a husband, too. This honeysuckle perfume of yours sure appeals to me."

"I confess, I dabbed it on to disguise the scent of those biscuits I incinerated."

"And here I thought you were being biblical."

She gave him a baffled look.

"I saw you reading Leviticus last night." He couldn't hide the chuckle in his voice as he teased, "So I figured you were inspired this morning to give a burnt offering."

For an instant, she winced, then her expression changed to carry a playful air. "I was just practicing for tomorrow. Since it'll be Sunday, I want to be sure to char them to perfection."

"I suppose we'll be healthy, then. One of my medical texts recommends charcoal for digestive complaints."

"Only thing is, you're complaining and won't digest," she muttered. "Mrs. Throckmorton always gave me peppermint for such maladies. I like her medicine better."

"I like this medicine the most." He dipped his head and kissed her sweetly.

❧

Sunday, after they spent part of the morning listening to a fine sermon on perseverance and had a quick noon meal, the wagon train set out. Penny started to plan a supper menu aloud.

"Actually," Bethany felt her cheeks go hot, "since our plans got scuttled because you were afraid of our guide, I'm going to insist that you're on your own tonight. Josh and I are going to celebrate our one-week anniversary."

That evening, Bethany lit a candle, stood back, and smiled. She'd covered the table with a white linen cloth and put a fistful of Johnny-jump-ups and poppy mallow in a tin cup. Her cornbread turned out perfectly. When Josh came around the wagon, she singsonged, "Happy anniversary!"

He'd just seated her and taken his place when Megan Crawford ran up with her arm about her nephew, Jeremiah.

"Doc, I'm sorry, but this can't wait."

Later, while Josh carried Jeremiah back to the Crawford wagon, Bethany took a deep breath and picked her beautiful Irish linen tablecloth out of the dirt. Josh had swept supper clean off the table so he could lay the twelve year old there to set his badly broken arm. By the time Josh came back, she was prying cold cornbread from the pan to serve with the rest of the stew. Two hounds had slunk over and feasted out of the bowls that got knocked off the table. Yesterday's burned biscuits, now a ruined anniversary supper. . . She tried to tamp down her disappointment. Either her dreams were going up in smoke or to the dogs.

Chapter 5

Josh watched his wife and sister walking in the distance. They'd joined the other women and children, keeping free from the dust the wagons kicked up. Penny and Bethany chattered like two magpies on a clothesline. He didn't want to begrudge his wife and sister their friendship, but it irritated him to feel as if he had to keep walking a tightrope between being a newly wedded man and an amiable son and brother. Everyone else seemed more than satisfied with how things were going. Everyone but him.

Indeed, most of the folks had settled into traveling quite nicely. Farmers sat at the campfire at night, remarking on how they'd normally be plowing and planting, so this felt like a pleasant holiday. Little girls plucked fistfuls of wildflowers; and the women had taken to harvesting handfuls of watercress, wild parsley, and wild onions. Boys threw rocks and played with slingshots. Because the wagons jounced so badly, most of the men walked alongside the wagons and occasionally cracked whips in the air to direct the oxen instead of riding on the hard, wooden seats.

Why doesn't Bethany walk with me?

The temperature dropped to freezing last night. They'd awakened to frost on everything. Instead of complaining, Bethany cheerfully whipped the cream she'd skimmed from the milk she'd gotten from Lady Macbeth last night, added in a bit of sugar, and whisked it with a few drops of cherry extract. They all ate their ice cream atop buttermilk flapjacks for breakfast. Remembering how she'd recalled aloud how he held a particular fondness for those flapjacks made him feel guilty for being surly about her skipping along with his sister.

He wondered what Bethany planned for supper. The first few days she'd cooked over the fire, she'd incinerated most of their food; but after a week and a half, she'd grown quite adept at making delicious meals.

They'd decided after the first few days that a morning prayer together would have to suffice, rather than lengthy devotions. With him needing to hitch the oxen and her seeing to breakfast, matters were too hurried for much more. In the evenings, they'd sit side by side and have their Bible reading time. He'd thought she might enjoy starting with the story of Noah—it struck him as fitting. As a matched pair, they were on a journey to a new life. It was the only time he'd noticed she didn't seem to enjoy their spiritual time together. Every once in awhile, he thought he caught a flicker of discontent on her face; but just as he got ready to ask, she always managed to say something perky that proved he'd simply misread her.

Marriage wasn't quite as easy as he'd expected it to be.

❧

"So much for honeysuckle perfume," Bethany sighed as the sun set the next day.

Josh took one good look at his wife and sister and burst out laughing. "Gloves?"

Penny peeled off her elbow-length, once-white glove. "This is never going to wash clean!"

Bethany pulled off the other filthy glove from the pair of once-elegant ballroom gloves they'd obviously shared and nudged the basket of buffalo chips down at her feet. She cast a wry look at Penny. "If Mrs. Throckmorton could see us now!"

"She'd have a fit of vapors!"

Josh looked at the dried plate-sized chips, then at the gloves, and chuckled. "Would she be more upset about your gloves or about what you've collected?"

Bethany waggled her finger at him. "If you make fun of us, Joshua Rogers, you just might have to cook supper over those stinky things yourself!"

He twitched his nose. "Beth, the honeysuckle still wins as my favorite—but one of your suppers will, no doubt, smell terrific."

Penny spun her glove around like a slingshot and launched it at him. He caught it as she declared, "Mrs. Throckmorton always said the way to a man's heart is through his stomach!"

"I researched her academy carefully before I recommended Papa send you there. I knew she was a wise woman."

"That does it." Bethany went up on tiptoe and gave him a hug. "You're forgiven for teasing us. I didn't know you're the one responsible for Penny being my roommate!"

He hugged her back. "Do I get a kiss for making her your sister?"

Bethany pulled away and sashayed toward the wagon. Her words floated back to him. "No, but you'll get apple crisp for dessert!"

❧

The evening after they traversed a hilly limestone region and crossed the toll bridge over the Wakarusa, Penny kept hovering. Some of the time, having family here was a blessing, not a burden. For now, Josh wished Penny would realize he and Bethany were entitled to some private time. More than a bit irritated, Josh finally groused, "Sis, we want to have devotions."

"Perhaps we could all join the others for awhile," Papa suggested. "It's early yet."

Josh shoved his hands in his pockets and balled them into fists. He'd just about run out of tolerance.

"I don't think I could sleep quite yet," Bethany confessed, ruining his plan to take a stand.

Soon, they all joined the others. Folks loved to hear Papa do recitations. He'd just finished Hamlet's soliloquy and beckoned. "Penny, come do Ophelia."

"Oh, great," Penny muttered. "I get to go die again."

Bethany whispered, "Want me to send that handsome Dillon Trier to rescue you?"

"I could only wish!" Penny sighed and took her place at the campfire. As she began, Rawhide tapped Josh's shoulder. Bethany grabbed his hand. "Do you need my help?"

Hours later, Bethany held Mrs. Wentworth's head as she got violently ill. Afterward, she blotted the poor woman's blue-tinged face and looked at Josh. He knelt quietly between two little boys who were curled double from stomach pain. None of the three of them stood a chance of surviving until morning. Mr. Harris was dosing two other children with some paregoric. With a miracle, that pair might pull through.

"Doc, we brought some tonic," one of the Wentworth men

said. "Dr. C. V. Girard's ginger brandy. Says right here, 'A certain cure for cholera, colic, cramps, dysentery, chills, and fever.' "

"Fine. Give her a tablespoon."

"Here. I'll hold her head; you spoon it in," Bethany said. "It sounds like just what she needs. You're a very loving son, Mr. Wentworth."

Josh marveled at his wife's reaction. He'd plainly told her the woman wouldn't last another two hours. Instead of running from the face of death, Bethany wanted to comfort both the patient and her distraught family. In the midst of this travesty, he held onto the solace that she'd left the evening entertainment and willingly joined him here. Indeed, he'd truly married a helpmeet.

The next morning, after the assemblage listened to the pastor's brief prayer and sang a hymn, Rawhide stood between two of the graves. "Folks," he let out a beleaguered sigh, "Mrs. Wentworth and them boys drank tainted water. Let this be a lesson—no drinking, fishing, or washing downstream from where the animals water. Indians go by that dictum, and they fare middlin' well. I said it back in Independence, and I didn't want to have to repeat myself. Now let's move out."

Too weary to walk, Bethany rode next to Josh. She rested her head on his shoulder and sleepily murmured, "Deuteronomy 1:21 says, 'Behold, the Lord thy God hath set the land before thee: go up and possess it, as the Lord God of thy fathers hath said unto thee; fear not, neither be discouraged.' "

He kissed her temple. "Thanks, Sweetheart. I needed to hear that." As she drowsed, he pondered on the verse and wondered what discouragements and fears they'd need to overcome before they reached their promised land in Oregon.

❧

The mighty Kansas River's current churned by. The Pappan Ferry consisted of two very flimsy-looking canoes lashed with poles. One at a time, the wagons were taken across the two-hundred-yard expanse for four dollars apiece. The animals swam, and for the last trip, the ferryman put a set of boards across so the "raft" could carry the last group of folks across. He collected a dime from each passenger as he allowed them aboard.

"I've got hold of you, my Beth." Josh cupped her waist and swung her onto the raft. Excitement filled his voice as he said, "Come stand here. You can watch the last of the oxen swim across the river."

Bethany could scarcely make her feet move. When the raft bobbled, Josh balanced her and tugged her to the spot he'd indicated. The river rushed by; yet in contrast, her mouth was so dry, she could scarcely swallow.

Josh slid his arm about her waist and nestled her closer. She huddled there, desperate to draw strength and courage from him. He looked down and grinned. "Such bright, shiny eyes, Sweetheart. I'm glad you're as excited as I am."

If only you knew the truth, Josh. . . .

All day long, their party's wagons had crossed the mighty Kansas River. When it was almost time for their wagon's turn, Josh answered an urgent call for medical help at the Crawford wagon. To Bethany's relief, several men volunteered to get her wagon to the other side. She'd spent the remainder of the afternoon trying to tamp down her fears. Now, they all welled up, and Josh mistook her panic for thrill.

"Away!" the burly ferryman shouted.

The raft left shore, and Bethany's breath caught. Suddenly,

the raft seemed horribly precarious. If a rogue tree snagged them, if boards slipped, if the current shifted. . .

Josh grabbed a pole and pushed a small keg away from the raft. Bethany watched in horror as it floated by. It fell off someone's wagon. What if Josh tumbled into the river? She grabbed at his shirt.

"Miss me?" he chuckled.

Bethany couldn't answer. She stared up at him as the sound of rushing water filled her ears, and the sky dimmed and swirled.

Chapter 6

"She all right?" The ferryman gave Bethany a puzzled look.

Josh cradled his limp wife in his arms and stepped ashore. Pale and clammy as could be, she'd not yet roused from her swoon. He strode toward their bright green wagon. It was easy enough to find.

Josh carefully laid Bethany in the late afternoon shade between the two wagons. She'd started to stir a bit, but he was about ready to use this makeshift privacy to loosen her clothing. Surely, she couldn't be with child this soon. He didn't think she was laced too tight, and she hadn't struck him as the fainting type, but this swoon was lasting far too long.

"Here." His sister shoved a wet cloth at him, then proceeded to wring her hands. "I feared this."

"Feared what?" He swiped at Bethany's wan cheeks and limp wrists.

"The river. It just—"

Bethany let out a small moan as her eyes fluttered open. Her brows knit as she blinked in confusion. "Where. . .what—ohh." A scant touch of color filled her cheeks as she struggled to sit up.

Josh heard his sister beat a hasty retreat. He kept his eyes trained on his bride and slipped an arm behind her shoulders to support her. "You want to tell me what this is all about?"

Her gaze dropped to her lap as she mumbled, "I'd rather not."

"I don't believe in husbands and wives keeping secrets." He tilted her face back up to his, and his heart skipped a beat when he saw how her eyes swam with tears. She tumbled into his chest, and he wrapped his arms about her.

"Bridge washed out," she said thickly into his shirt. "Mama and Daddy's carriage. . .they drowned."

"Awww, Bethy-mine." He kissed her temple and squeezed her. "Why didn't you just tell me you're scared of water?" A few minutes later, she pushed away from him, stood, and fussed with her hands. From the way she avoided eye contact, murmured something unintelligible, and hastened away, Josh knew she was still embarrassed.

"Psssst." Penny crooked a finger and beckoned him over to her wagon. Once he reached her side, she whispered, "Josh, I feel so stupid! I should have told you, but in all of the excitement, I forgot. Beth was in that carriage. The driver managed to save her, but she almost drowned, too."

He stared at his sister in shock. "Why didn't she tell me?"

"She's ashamed." Penny wrung her hands. "My guess is, she worried you wouldn't bring her along if you knew."

And she desperately wanted to be with you and Papa. . . . The instant after he thought that, Josh felt a surge of excitement. *This is how I can teach her to depend on me, to finally accept me as her protector and man. Each time we come to water, I'll be right at her side and see her through. She won't be thinking of Papa's stories or Penny's chatter at times like that—she'll need me to lean on.*

He strode off to find Bethany. The last thing she needed was to be alone right after reliving her worst nightmare. He wandered around the entire encampment and failed to find her. Frustrated as well as concerned, he glanced at their wagon and noticed how it jostled a bit.

"Bethany?" he called as he climbed inside.

She knelt atop a trunk and dusted her fingertips off on the skirt of her brown paisley dress. He'd noted she fussed with her skirts whenever she was embarrassed or uncomfortable. If ever a woman needed comforting, he was looking at her now.

Josh sat beside her and had to draw his left knee up to his chest because there wasn't enough room for both feet to hang down. He slipped his hand over hers and laced fingers. For a few moments, he sat motionless and let silence swirl around them. Finally, he said in his quietest tone, "It's not much of a home, but we've made every inch of it ours. It'll carry our goods to Oregon, and I'm going to be by your side every bit of the way—especially when we have to make crossings."

The Osnaburg canopy captured her soft gasp. She looked up at him, her eyes glistening. He wasn't sure whether it was with tears or determination. "I'm not well versed like Penny, but I have one quote by Shakespeare that I've claimed for our trip: 'Our doubts are traitors, and make us lose the good we oft might win by fearing to attempt.' I won't let my silliness hold us back."

"So my wife isn't just beautiful, she's also brave."

She bowed her head, but he still spied the single tear that slipped down her cheek. "No, Joshua. You married a coward."

"Nonsense." He tilted up her face, flashed her a rakish smile, and winked. "Clearly, you're a stalwart soul—you married me!"

"You're being too kind."

"Bethy-mine, I'm your husband. The day we took our vows, God made us partners. I'm here for you to lean on. Turn to me when you need help. I think it's about time for you to decide to do just that."

She gave him a wobbly smile. "I did determine one thing today."

"Oh?" He looked at her intently, hoping she'd show him a glimmer of trust.

"I decided how I want to spend my inheritance. I want us to drill a well and have our own pump so I won't ever have to see another stream or river once we reach Oregon."

❧

"I really do like wells," Bethany declared as she filled yet another bucket. It sloshed over and soaked her dress.

"Looks to me like wells don't like you," Emma Harris teased.

The women took turns while the men unhitched the oxen and fought to keep them from Vermillion Creek. Rawhide warned that the water wasn't good, so they were herding the huge beasts to troughs. The good grass helped keep the oxen in the roped corral after they'd been watered. It was only noon, but Rawhide declared they'd take the rest of the day and the next as "lay-bys" so the men could hunt and the women could catch up on chores.

"After I've had a drink, I've got laundry to do," Daisy Sawyer moaned as she rubbed her back with one hand and her very protuberant belly with the other.

Granny Willodene waggled a gnarled finger at her. "Time's a-comin' close for you to have that babe. You're gonna lay down in the shade and nap with the young'uns. I'll do your laundry, and your man can go look at my son's wagon. A wheel's getting the wiggle-waggles, so it's a fair trade."

"I'll never see the end of laundry," the Millberg's little maid, Katie, murmured.

Penny and Bethany exchanged a look. The Millberg women didn't do a thing. Poor Katie cooked, gathered firewood and chips, did the dishes, tended the laundry, and still had to attend to the silly and constant demands made of her. At meal-times, after she served the Millbergs, she and Dillon Trier sat apart at a small crate because they were lowly hired help.

"Why don't we all do the laundry together?" Penny suggested.

"Yes. . .and why not have a sewing circle tomorrow?" Bethany handed the bucket to Megan. "I have mending to do."

Buck Cole lumbered up and shifted his weight from one large foot to the other. "I overheard. I've got a heap of laundry to do, too. Fact is, I didn't bring enough soap, and I plum forgot Prussian blue powder. If you ladies are willing to share, I'll draw river water into your boiling pots."

No one said a word about a backwoods giant knowing about using the powder as laundry bluing. Later he grumbled, "Ain't fittin', them asking you to do this." He reached over and stole Orson Millberg's underclothes from Katie and scrubbed them himself.

Later, all of the river-rinsed clothes hung on ropes around the campground. The Sawyer's laundry was done, and the Barneses' wagon boasted a repaired wheel. Josh rode up on Tonic and swept Bethany right off her feet. She gave a surprised little yelp, and his laughter filled the air as they galloped off.

"What are you doing?"

He chuckled. "I'm kidnapping you. It's time we got away

on our own."

❧

The next morning, the men got ready to go hunting. Josh had done guard duty all night and, though he would have enjoyed hunting, decided to nap awhile first. When he awoke, he scowled at the sound of Bert Cole talking to Bethany. After his romantic abduction yesterday, Josh felt sure Bethany understood he loved her. He'd even begun to hope she loved him back. She served him flapjacks every other morning, and at least once a week, she arranged for them to share a private supper. So what was she doing, entertaining another man?

Josh hustled out of the wagon, ready to glower at his wife and blister Bert's ears, but he stopped in his tracks. Several of the women sat in a circle. Bert Cole had managed to wedge himself between Megan Crawford and Penny on a bench. A big giant of a man, he looked ridiculous with his elbows winged out and crowding the girls, stitching a button on an old shirt. "Done," he declared, then bit the threaded needle loose from the shirt.

A second later, he glanced up. "Hey, Doc! I'm done with my chores. What say you and me take a hike over yonder? I set some snares, and I'm thinking we might get lucky."

Feeling guilty for harboring unwarranted jealousy and mean feelings for the poor man, Josh rasped, "I'd like that." He reached into the wagon and got his rifle, and off they went.

"Ya know, Doc, you and me, we're the only menfolk who know how to sew."

Josh let out a crack of a laugh. "I never thought of it that way. Now that I think of it, I do a fair amount of stitching."

"Well, I never woulda thunk it, myself. I'm good at it, but it's 'cuz Ma made me learn to handle a needle and thread. With the three of us boys, we was goin' through the elbows and knees of everything we wore. Your bride—she's one dandy gal. She said you're a right fine doc—and from the way she glowed, I 'spect she's a mite biased in her opinion; but I seen how you set that busted arm and pulled two of them kids through the cholera, and I know she's not just boasting 'bout her man. Anyhow, in an emergency, your wife said she'd recommend my stitching to you iffen you needed help with suturing a body."

Well, well. Maybe I am making progress with my wife.

Unaware of Josh's musings, Bert rambled on, "I almost had to sew on all my shirt buttons, 'cuz they was in danger of all poppin' off. Right there in front of all them wimmin—and that pretty little Katie Rose—your missus said she figgers a man who can sew could stitch the gal of his choosin' right into his pocket." He patted the pocket over his heart.

"So you're carrying a torch for the Millbergs' Irish maid?"

"She shore is a beauty, but my brother helped her with some of the wash yesterday, and we might could come to blows over her, so we figured we'd best resist temptation. Besides, I seen her and Trier eating together all the time. 'Cuz I'm not a man to chase another's gal, I resolved to put her clean outta my mind."

Josh remembered those words late that night as he and Bethany snuggled under quilts beneath their wagon. They'd eaten a fine rabbit stew, thanks to the snares Bert set and Bethany's cookbook. Bethany whispered, "Penny is mad at me. When I got off the bench, Bert sat next to her. She's ordered me to protect her from his interest."

Josh snorted with laughter.

Bethany poked him in the ribs. "Shh!" She muffled a giggle

and whispered, "But the funny part is, not five minutes later, Megan yanked me aside and begged me not to let Bert near her, either. She was positive he's sweet on her. The next time Papa wants someone to recite, I think Bert ought to do a selection as Romeo!"

"Bethany," Penny grumbled from the wagon next to them, "if we were at school, Mrs. Throckmorton would make you do dishes for a week for talking after lights out."

Bethany scooted closer to Josh and whispered against his lips, "Don't ask what Mrs. Throckmorton would do if she caught us kissing."

It was the first time his wife had alluded to their closeness. Josh gathered her tight. Finally, could she be falling in love?

Chapter 7

Rawhide ranks as the cagiest old coot I've ever met," Bethany groused.

Josh stared at her. "You've been around Penny too much. You're starting to sound like her."

"Can you deny my assessment? He gave us all a day off, and now he's marching us twenty-two miles and over the Vermillion and the Black Vermillion, clear to the Big Blue all in one day."

She looked down and brushed a smudge off of her skirt and hoped he hadn't heard the way her voice cracked when she mentioned all three rivers.

Josh transferred the whip into his left hand and laced his right hand with hers. "You made it across the first with a verse."

"Judges 6:23," she quoted. " 'And the Lord said unto him, Peace be unto thee; fear not: thou shalt not die.' "

"So let's have a verse for the next river. How about Psalm 46:2? 'Therefore will not we fear, though the earth be removed, and though the mountains be carried into the midst of the sea—' "

Bethany squawked, "That's a dreadful choice!"

"Oops. Sorry."

"So am I. I shouldn't have snapped. It's horribly embarrassing to be such a baby."

"You're not a baby; you're a sensitive woman for very understandable reasons. I'll be by your side at each crossing. I'll take care of you, Sweetheart." He paused, then asked, "What about any other fears? Thunder? Lightning?"

She glanced off at a band of rapidly gathering clouds. "I'd better not have. That looks like a nasty storm brewing."

Rawhide kept the overlanders going, even when it started to rain a bit. Finally, he called a grudging halt.

Granny Willodene toddled by. She grinned from beneath her umbrella. "Saw me a gopher divin' into his hole, and two beetles follered right a-hind him. We're in for a three-day gullywasher. Best you think to make extry fry bread right quick-like."

Bethany and Penny took the old woman's advice to heart. They quickly mixed the batter and huddled under umbrellas as they struggled to light a fire. Bethany finally used four of her beautifully embossed calling cards as kindling. Once the flames started, they worked constantly to keep a fire going long enough to brew coffee, make the bread, fry some side meat, and prepare corn mush.

Josh got into their wagon and rearranged things. He slid a sheet of waterproof gutta-percha between the ribs of the wagon and the canvas to try to keep the worst of the water from dripping on their heads. Bethany lifted the food in to him. "Josh, some of the families are pitching tents."

"Rawhide suggested it for those who can't spend a couple of days in a wagon. The families have no choice." His voice dropped several notes. "And I'm not about to spend all of that time sharing you with Papa and Penny in a stinking tent."

The possessive quality of his voice pleased her, but she didn't have time at the moment to analyze just why.

"Rawhide said we'll be stuck here due to mud for a day or two after the storm. I'm just as glad the Sawyers have a good tent. Babies have a habit of picking stormy nights to make an appearance, and Daisy is close to term."

Bethany steeled herself with a deep breath. "I don't know precisely what to do, but if you need my help with her. . ."

"Granny Willodene and Nettie Harris already offered to assist with the delivery. I have no doubt that I'll need your help one of these days, but this birthing is covered."

Bethany let out a relieved sigh.

"Hey, you just told me you're not afraid of anything but water. Did the notion of tending a birth scare you?"

She bit her lip and shrugged. "I don't know what is involved, Josh. I'm trying my best to learn how to cook out here and be a wife. I'll do my best to fill in—you know that by now. You can't ask more than that." She fought tears as she turned away and tightened one of the ties holding the bonnet over the wagon's hooped ribs.

Long arms came around either side of her and retied the bow. In a carefully modulated voice, Josh said, "I know there have been a lot of adjustments. I'm proud of how well you're doing."

"I'm not doing well at all," she confessed in a choked tone. "The mush is lumpy and I singed my sleeve when I took the coffee off the fire."

He turned her around. "Did you burn yourself?"

"No, but I've ruined this dress."

"Dresses mend." He calmly unbuttoned what was left of her

cuff and turned back the sleeve. "Your arm looks a bit tender. A little salve will help. You sit tight while I finish tying everything down, then I'll get some for you."

The wind howled and rain came down in sheets. After eating the lumpy mush and sipping tepid coffee, they decided to bed down for the night. Josh had grouped the trunks and crates together; then Bethany put towels in the dips to even it out as best as she could. Together, they spread their feather bed across the not-quite-level heap and exchanged a wry grin.

"It's no worse than the rocky spot we slept on last night," Bethany said.

Josh slipped his arm around her waist, brushed a stray lock from her cheek, and kissed her. "I'd offer to pitch a tent, but we'd have company as soon as the last stake went in the ground. I relish the notion of being crowded in here with you for a few days."

A short while later, Bethany wiggled to find a less uncomfortable position, and Josh grunted. "Sorry. I can't sleep."

"Neither can I."

Bethany sat up, curled one leg beneath herself, and yanked his black leather bag onto her lap. Embarrassed by her emotional outburst earlier, she tried to sound composed. "Instead of moaning, why don't we make good use of our time?"

By the flickering light of a single candle, Bethany watched as he deftly pulled out each instrument, held it in his strong, capable hands, and identified it. She repeated the names of each item after him: scalpel, clamp, probe, retractor, lancet, tourniquet, burr, bone saw. . . .

A long while later, as the rain turned to sleet, he opened her trunk and helped her put on a second dress. He donned another shirt. Then, they huddled beneath a quilt and talked between the ear-splitting rumbles of thunder.

During that time, something deep inside Bethany shifted. Josh had fallen asleep with his chest pressed against her back, his arm wrapped about her, and his breath ruffling her hair. Even in his sleep, he managed to settle into one position and stay put, solid as an oak. For the first time ever, she felt like she truly belonged. Ever since Mama and Daddy died, she'd been so very alone. Here, beneath a linseed-coated, double-thick canopy that leaked, in the middle of a sleet storm, she felt safe and secure in her husband's unyielding arms.

She'd started out with stars in her eyes and big hopes and plans for a perfect life as a good wife. *I was in love with the idea of being in love.* She nestled a tiny bit closer to Josh and felt an odd mixture of elation and serenity as she realized, *But now I'm in love with you, my dearest Joshua. Whatever battles lie ahead of us, I'll march by your side and depend on God's leading so we can make any obstacle crumble just as Joshua in the Bible did to Jericho.*

"Doc! Doc!"

"What is it?"

It took a moment for Bethany to realize that the light was a lantern, not lightning. Josh had already turned loose of her and was tucking a quilt back about her.

"Daisy—she's needin' you!" Zach Sawyer shouted at him. "It's time for the babe to come."

Groggily, Bethany sat up.

"I'll be right there, Zach," Josh said as he gently pushed her back down.

As the lantern light disappeared, Bethany shoved the quilts off and groped in the dark for his bag. "Can I get you anything?"

Josh yanked on his boots and muttered under his breath.

"What's wrong?"

"My lace broke."

"Pull on the other." She hastily lit a candle and fumbled to tie the ragged ends of the leather thong together. "There."

A streak of lightning illuminated his smile. "I'm set. You bundle up and go back to sleep, Sweetheart. I don't want you to catch a chill."

"I'll be fine. Do you want some bread? I can heat up more coffee—"

He gave her a quick kiss. "I've got all I need. Pleasant dreams."

After Josh scrambled out into the rain, Bethany scooted under the covers, yawned, and smiled sleepily. They'd worked well together tonight. She hadn't really done much, but he knew she was willing to do whatever would help.

The first days of their marriage, she'd let herself get swept up in her husband's romantic ways and their fairy-tale adventure. In truth, that reflected honeymoon thinking. Really, this was a foretaste of what their marriage would be like—burned biscuits, blisters, and bad days all were part and parcel of a normal life. As a doctor, he'd get calls at all hours. She wanted to support him in every way possible—not just because that was what a good wife did, but because she loved him.

Chapter 8

Josh looked at Bethany and felt a surge of pride. She was an absolute wreck. Her hair hung in damp straggles and her skirts drooped in soggy clumps around her ankles. Dark circles shadowed her eyes, but she wore an angel's smile as she cooed and bathed the babe.

He turned back and spooned into Daisy the small dose of ergot he'd calculated. "You folks have cause to praise the Lord. Zach, your strapping son is as healthy as they come. Mrs. Sawyer, you stay abed and do nothing but feed him."

Bethany brought the baby over and tucked him in next to his mama. "He's got his daddy's husky build, but he favors you with his blond fuzz. I'll bring supper as soon as it's ready. I have some meat biscuits that turn into a rich stew when I boil them."

"That's right kind of you," Zach beamed, "but the Crawfords already offered tonight's viands. You folks did more than enough."

Josh pulled on his jacket and wrapped Bethany's cloak about her shoulders. "I'll check in on you tomorrow. Call if you need anything." He slipped out of the tent, hurried Bethany back to their wagon, and lifted her inside.

The birthing hadn't gone according to plan. Nettie Harris

tried to help out, but she sheepishly admitted to suffering from *la grippe* and scuttled back to her own bed. Spry as Granny Willodene was, by midday, the rains proved too much for her old bones. Bethany had already slipped over to provide some of the savory stew she'd made from those odd meat biscuits, countless pots of coffee, and her own special brand of encouragement. When Granny hobbled away, Bethany volunteered to help. "I can ask Mrs. Green or Idabelle Barnes if you're uncomfortable."

To Josh's surprise, Bethany turned her head to the side and rasped something about Jericho that a rumble of thunder drowned out. By the time he could hear again, she'd pushed past him and knelt by Daisy's side. Bethany ended up doing far more than hold Daisy's hand and brew squaw vine tea to ease the pains; she'd actually assisted him with the difficult delivery. She'd done a fine job, too.

Partners. Yes, they'd been a true team, working together. He thought to praise her, but the words died on his lips. She'd taken off her cloak and promptly fallen asleep. He pulled off her wet boots and frowned at the way her damp skirts and petticoats stuck to her ankles. Still, it would be a shame to awaken her; and with a few more days of rain and mud ahead, every last garment they owned was bound to get wet. He took off his jacket and outer shirt. His warmth clung to the fabric. He swaddled her feet and calves in it, then curled around her and drew up the quilts. Before he fell asleep, his last thought was that God had blessed him far beyond his dreams by giving him such a dear wife.

"It's a disaster!" Penny sat on a bench just a few yards from the clothesline Josh had strung between their wagons. Even the sound of the wind luffing the rain-soaked quilts couldn't muffle her wail.

The storm had taken a toll on everyone's nerves and possessions. Though inclined to agree, Bethany pasted on a bright smile. "You said the same thing last week when your hem caught fire while we made the beans, but that handsome Dillon Trier patted it out before you got burned. Looked to me like it was a pretty clever way of you asking him to join us for supper."

Penny blushed prettily, but she wasn't to be dissuaded. "This is a trouble too great to be borne!"

"Mrs. Throckmorton warned us to be careful about what we prayed for. You always fretted about how dismal your section of the garden grew, but now. . ." She let her words trail off as she tipped her head toward the soggy sack of flour at Penny's feet. Scores of tiny, green sprouts poked out of it.

"It's all my fault. I bought middlings instead of finely milled flour."

"You were trying to be a good steward and economize. That's admirable. It's not really a disaster. Josh and I have plenty, and we can always stock up on everything once we reach Fort Kearney."

"But I can't accept charity—"

Bethany jolted and stared at Penny in utter dismay. "How could you possibly say such a terrible thing? You're my sister. That's not charity; families are supposed to work together."

Penny brushed a wisp of her golden hair back under her sunbonnet. "Thomas Jefferson said, 'It is in the love of one's family only that heartfelt happiness is known.' "

Leaning closer, Bethany said, "You know what's truly astonishing? I'm starting to feel like many of the folks on this train are family. The Cole brothers are like big, bumbling brothers, and Anna Schmitt is the sour-faced aunt who never has a kind word to say. Megan and Emma tend to be watching the children, but they are dear as can be."

Just then, Lavinia stepped in a mud puddle. "Daddy, *do* something! This is horrid! These boots were from *Paris!*"

"They've got mud in Paris, Girl," Granny Willodene barked. "Stop havin' such a hissy fit. I swan, you're useless as antlers on a duck. Shake off the mud and help little Katie hang out the bedding."

"I may be muddy, but I'm not a lowly maid!" Lavinia huffed off.

Bethany turned away and grimaced. "I'm going to have to pray to have a charitable spirit, because I certainly don't want to claim Lavinia as family!"

"Good." Penny tapped her foot with emphasis. "If the Millbergs were part of your family and we're sisters, that would mean they'd be my relatives, too. I couldn't bear such a disaster."

"See? It put everything in perspective. Now, the silly flour doesn't seem like such a catastrophe."

Josh returned from checking on Daisy Sawyer. He set his black leather bag on the wagon seat and playfully nudged Bethany. "I agree. Her Paris boots were no loss. I could have told her my discriminating wife suffered a far greater tragedy when she lost her Italian slippers."

Bethany tugged a long strip of leather from her pocket. "Speaking of shoes, Zach Sawyer made this replacement for your boot lace."

"Thanks, Sweetheart."

"Oh, it's all part of being one big family on the trail," Penny chirped. "As if we aren't enough, Bethany is adopting nearly everyone."

Josh scowled. "Being friendly is fine, but you're going to have to draw some lines. There isn't enough time and energy to spend on everyone."

Chapter 9

Two days after the storm, Rawhide decided the mud wasn't enough to greatly hamper their progress, so he pushed the train ahead. The Vermillion loomed ahead. Josh watched as Bethany's face grew pinched and pale. By the time they reached the banks of the twenty-foot-wide river, he knew he had to do something to give her comfort. He stood behind her, commandingly turned her around, and wrapped her in a tight hold. "I'm here with you."

"Did Rawhide make it across?" Her voice shook almost as much as she did.

Josh stared intently at their guide as he dismounted midstream and held on to the saddle horn. He and his mount swam the rest of the way across. Rawhide had told the men that if he stayed mounted, they'd ford the river; if he had to swim, the storm swelled the river deeper than four feet, and they'd have to raft across.

"He made it, Sweetheart. With God's help, we will, too."

Previous trains used the nearby oaks to fashion rafts. Once Rawhide declared those rafts sound, the party started crossing. Each day, the front wagon dropped to the back of the line.

Though their wagon sat midway in the train, Josh decided his wife couldn't withstand the strain of waiting. He gave her a swift kiss and strode ahead.

"Fellows, I know my wagon's not first, but—"

"Say no more, Doc." Zach Sawyer slapped him on the shoulder. "You and your missus just hustle right on up here."

"Much obliged." Josh went back to his wife. "I've got just the spot for you, my Beth." He cupped her waist and swung her up into their prairie schooner. "Scoot over."

Bethany shimmied over and Josh took his place beside her. One of the Cole brothers soothed an ox that seemed a bit fractious, then led the team until they were at the river's edge. Men unyoked the team and sent them across while others pushed the wagon aboard the raft. Part of Josh wanted to help the men, but Bethany needed him. He promised himself that once they made it across, he'd help all of the others.

"Joshua." Bethany buried her face in his shoulder.

He slipped an arm under her knees and pulled her onto his lap. "First Samuel 22:23 says, 'Abide thou with me, fear not: for he that seeketh my life seeketh thy life: but with me thou shalt be in safeguard.' " He kissed her brow. "Now you say it."

"I don't know it." She trembled.

"It's a fine one to learn. Come on, Sweetheart. 'Abide thou with me. . .' "

They made it across with her stammering each phrase after him. Pale and shaken, she looked up at him once their wagon hit ground. "We did it."

"Yes, we did. You can always rely on God's help, and you can depend on me, too, Bethy-mine."

"Thank you," she whispered as she slipped her hand around

his neck and grazed a kiss on his jaw. His heart sang. Instead of paying attention to everyone else or swooning from her fears, she'd depended on him and appreciated his strength. Though he wasn't glad of her fear, gratitude for the opportunity to earn her trust and love filled him.

As Josh pitched in to help all of the others across, a verse flitted through his mind. *"In our weakness is he made strong."* Suddenly, a new sense of God's love and willingness to support and protect His children overwhelmed Josh. Just as he didn't mind Bethany's weakness and wanted to do all he could to give her succor, God willed to do those same things for him.

Someday, if God blessed them, Josh would be that same way with their own children.

❧

Twelve feet of water fell in joyous abandon into a crystalline pool. Bethany sat at the edge and soaked her feet. Being barefoot felt decadent, but all of the women were doing it together after finishing laundry.

Rawhide ordered the men to top off all of their water barrels. Fresh and sweet as it tasted, most men completely emptied their barrels, rinsed, and refilled them at an adjacent pool. Chafed by having to wait for the train ahead of them to cross the Big Blue, Rawhide paced between the men and women, spitting tobacco and grumbling under his breath.

"Alcove Springs." Emma Harris read the eight-inch-high chiseled words aloud. "One of my books says the Donner Party—"

"Hush!" Rawhide rasped. "No one mentions them. Bad luck. Bad luck." He shook his head, scowled, and stomped off.

Noticing her friend's crestfallen look, Bethany swept her

left foot in the water and splashed her. "You're going to have to read different material. I have something new—a thing by Beadle called a dime novel. It's the very first one, written by Ann Stephens, *Malaeska*. I read it during the storm. Would you like to borrow it?"

"Oh, I'd love to!" Emma's eyes shone.

"It's a dashing story," Penny chimed in.

"Humpf," Lavinia sniffed. "I've seen you reading *Arabian Nights*. That was bad enough. A novel? And it cost a measly dime? Why, I would never read such trash. It's obviously morally inferior."

Irritated by Lavinia's judgmental ways and airs, Bethany pursed her lips, then perked up. "There's Parson Brewster. Perhaps we could ask his opinion on the matter."

The parson listened, then rubbed his chin for a moment before saying, "I'm a firm believer in bettering the soul. If you've spent generous time in Bible reading and devotions, though, I trust the Lord wouldn't frown upon His children improving their minds or lightening their hearts with either educational or pleasure reading."

"Thank you, Parson Brewster," Bethany and Penny said in unison.

After he walked off, Lavinia pulled her feet out of the water, stood, and stuck her nose up in the air. "I don't care. I refuse to sully my mind."

"At least she's consistent," Penny muttered. "She didn't like sullying her boots, either."

Bethany flopped backward and dissolved into guilty laughter. "Oh, Penny! That was much nicer than what I was thinking. I wondered if she really has much of a mind at all!" After she stopped laughing, she shielded her eyes from the sun and moaned, "Lavinia might be right: I'd better spend more time reading my Bible. It's much too easy to be catty."

Granny Willodene wandered past with some laundry over her arm. She chuckled. "Never thought that honesty was a sin. Does a woman good to speak her mind sometimes. We're taught always to be nice. Turn the other cheek. Grin and bear it. Well, seems to me that Christ got mighty hot at the temple when folks were doing wrong. He didn't mince His words with them Pharisees, neither. Choose your battles, and keep a kind heart; but don't let the sourpusses like Lavinia spoil your joys, because if you do, you'll turn into someone just like her. Find happiness in the ordinary—it makes for a pleasant life and a serene heart."

❧

Bethany clung to Josh as they took the Independence Crossing over the Big Blue River. "Where to next?" she groaned once the train started moving again.

"We'll travel along the east side of the Little Blue."

She gave him a disgruntled look. "Who named all of these places 'Blue?' "

"Someone with no creativity," Josh quipped. When his lighthearted attempt fell flat, he wrapped his arm around her shoulders. "Not to rub in the word, but are you feeling blue today?"

Suddenly, the spot on the hem of her apron demanded her full attention. Josh watched as she tried to smear away the smudge. He tilted his head forward to see past the brim of her sunbonnet and noticed her cheeks carried an unexpected flush. "Bethany? What is it?"

"You've mentioned children." She paused, then blurted out, "Not this month."

He stayed silent for a few moments, then stroked her upper arm. "We have plenty of years ahead of us. The next months are going to be difficult on everyone—speaking both as your husband and as a doctor, I'm just as happy for you not to be in the family way yet."

She gave him a stricken look. "I thought you wanted children!"

"I do. I'm looking forward to a houseful of them, and you'll be a wonderful mother. For now, it's nice for us to have time together, alone."

"Oh."

He couldn't interpret her reaction. Was she simply surprised, or was she disappointed? Before he could pursue the issue, Penny came over and started to tag along, just like she had when she was a five-year-old pest. She chattered about Anna Schmitt gossiping about Megan Crawford and how Megan was a really nice girl who promised to teach them a new crochet stitch that night. Within seconds, Bethany livened up.

Josh withdrew his arm. Bethany didn't even seem to notice.

Chapter 10

They traveled along the east side of the Little Blue and halted for a day at the Hanover Pony Express stop. "Can you imagine?" Rawhide switched his wad of tobacco to the opposite cheek and continued, "The day after we left, the first Pony Express reached Caly-forny. They're a-running slick as cain be."

Papa brightened. "Excellent. It'll be no time at all before we'll have dependable mail service back to Boston so I can correspond with other scholars."

Everyone took advantage of the mail delivery and wrote letters home. Most sent several letters to friends and relatives. Bethany sent a single missive to Mrs. Throckmorton. The next day, they traveled fifteen more miles to the Holenberg station. Again, folks sat around chewing on pencil stubs and scribbling notes to loved ones. Bethany used some of her Baker's chocolate powder and Rumford baking powder to make three cakes.

"Sweetheart, wouldn't you like to send a letter to your uncle?"

She wrinkled her nose. "Last I heard, he planned to tour Europe. I have no idea where he is."

"I'm sure he'd welcome a letter waiting for him when he gets back."

She shook her head. "I wrote him faithfully for years. He never responded."

"Never?"

"Well, I did get one letter." She scooped more coals onto the Dutch oven so the cakes would bake evenly. "When I told him of your proposal, he sent the note that he'd instructed one of his workers to acquire the wagon and oxen for us. When that man delivered them, he mentioned Uncle would be out of the country."

He tipped her face up to his. Instead of saying a word, he gave her a soft-as-spring-rain kiss. Her whole life had been devoid of gentle love and affection. He was more than willing to shower her with all of the care and attention she needed.

When they reached Rock Creek Station, Josh didn't bother to ask Bethany if she had anything she wanted to mail home. Instead, he sat beside her as she sewed. He'd learned if she curled one leg up beneath herself, she was content. He'd come to share the bench with her and smiled to himself as he watched her absently slip into that catlike position. "What are you doing?"

She bit a length of white thread from a spool and spoke slowly as she concentrated on threading her needle, "Your shoulders are getting broader. I'm letting out your shirts."

"We can buy some supplies here, if you need anything."

Her eyes sparkled as she whispered, "Rawhide warned us not to. Mr. McCanless watches who spends a lot or dresses well. Then, he charges more as they cross his toll bridge."

Though he'd heard the same, Josh enjoyed her animation, so he asked, "How much more could he charge?"

"Anywhere from ten to fifty cents per wagon!"

"That's quite a range. Then again, the stage comes here."

"I heard. Eloise Bearnoo is going back East on it instead of heading on to California. She says she's sick of being dirty, thirsty, and tired."

"You're heartier than that." He gave her an approving grin. "Tell you what: You might not be able to get some of the items later on the trail that they sell here. Go on in and get whatever we need. We've been out of eggs for awhile. Get as many as you can."

She perked up. "Putting them in the cornmeal kept them from breaking 'til I used them up. I can do that again."

"Sure enough. Buy as many as they'll sell. Maybe get a little something special for Papa since his birthday's next week. I'll go speak with Mr. McCanless."

That afternoon, Orson Millberg blustered as he paid a full dollar to get both of his wagons across the bridge. Bethany scooted so close, she was practically inside Josh's shirt as he drove their wagon across. McCanless waved them, Papa, the parson, and the Coles' wagons across without asking for a dime.

As they stopped for the night, Parson Brewster walked up and shook Josh's hand. "That was kind of you—unnecessary, but kind."

"Appreciate your fine sermons. Seems like the least we could do."

Moments later gunfire sounded. Everyone gawked as Bert and Buck Cole wandered over to the Rogerses' wagon carrying five writhing rattlesnakes. "We reckon we'd like to repay your generosity today. We brung supper."

Rattlesnake, Josh decided that night, was a fine meal. It

didn't taste half bad. Better still, as Bert fried it in two big pans, Bethany refused to leave Josh's side. To her relief, she hadn't found a recipe for preparing snake in the *Great Western Cook Book.* Best of all, Penny couldn't even sit at the supper table; and after the meal was done and folks left, Josh got to spend the rest of the evening just how he wanted to: without Penny or Papa hovering, completely alone with his wife.

❧

Bethany shoved her bonnet back and wiped perspiration from her brow. Mrs. Throckmorton would be mortified to see any of her young ladies in such a deplorable state. When they'd learned about the trail, some of the more basic truths got left out—like the fact that the Platte River was so shallow and muddy, they hadn't had fresh drinking water in days. . .so bathing and laundry were impossible. Add to that, she'd eaten rattlesnake twice in the last week, and Josh seemed to be losing his wits because he raved over what a delicacy it was.

A good wife unquestioningly follows her husband. . .but why can't Josh lead me to a big bathtub and pork chops?

As if he'd read her thoughts, he said, "We ought to make Fort Kearney late tomorrow."

Bethany held out hope until she spied the fort. Instead of the orderly military installation she expected, the plot of land was dotted with the saddest collection of ramshackle buildings she'd ever seen. Most of the buildings were soddies, and the soldiers lounging around them needed haircuts, razors, and baths even more than the pioneers. Almost a dozen men in patched uniforms went from wagon to wagon, offering, "I'll pay ya a dollar fer a half pint of whiskey."

The wagon train before them bought out most of the

supplies at the store, so the stop barely seemed worthwhile. Upset that she'd find no respite here, Bethany tried not to reveal her feelings. Josh sat beside her and gave her a searching look. "Don't be so upset, Sweetheart. We're doing fine—especially since you stocked up back at Rock Creek."

She bit the inside of her cheek to keep from crying and bobbed her head in agreement. Later, as she tried to hide her tears, the biscuits burned again.

"Wait a second. I need that bucket." Bethany ran up to Josh before he watered the oxen. She leaned over the bucket and carefully slid two eggs into the water and held her breath. Both bobbed beneath the surface, and she let out a sigh.

"Fresh or spoiled?"

She plucked them out of the water and didn't even mind getting her cuffs wet. It helped cool her off a bit. "Neither. They'll do for baking, though."

"We can't spare much water," he warned.

"I know. I'll use a can of Borden's condensed milk and fix custard."

Josh started to water the oxen. "I'm not keen on you using that canned milk. The Millbergs got sick on their canned lobster and East India sweetmeats."

"I already promised Papa I'd make it."

Josh slammed the empty bucket onto the sandy soil. "Does it ever occur to you to consult with me?"

Hurt, Bethany stepped backward and stared at him. He continued to glower at her, so she figured he expected an answer. "You took guard duty last night, and this morning, you paid a call on Jeremiah to take off his cast."

His jaw jutted out as he shifted his gaze toward the rolling sandy hills. "Fine. Keep your word."

The rest of the day played out in silence. Papa and Penny raved about the custard. Josh and Bethany barely swallowed a bite. The rest remained in their bowls, and she finally scraped it out for the dogs.

"*Let not the sun go down upon your wrath.*" The verse played through Bethany's mind. She couldn't very well go to bed and sleep next to Josh with this dreadful tension between them. She summoned her nerve and went to speak to him.

"Josh?"

"What?" he snapped as he smeared grease on the axles.

"I thought maybe we ought to talk—"

"Hey, Doc?" Rawhide strode toward them. "Some of the kids in the Caly-forny group are getting croupy. Can you go see to 'em?"

"Sure." He climbed into the wagon, grabbed his bag, and stomped off.

Bethany scrambled into the wagon and whispered tearfully to herself, "He didn't even kiss me good-bye."

Josh was gone all night. The next morning, the party prepared to cross the Platte. Less than a foot deep, its sandy bottom could give way and cause a wagon to tip. Men carefully took poles and staked out a passage across the mile-wide river. Bethany kept watching her husband, but he never once looked back at her.

❧

Weary beyond belief, Josh could hardly wait to tumble into the quilts. Two nights without sleep rated as a challenge back when he practiced medicine in Boston. Here, with hard physical labor all day, it tested his mettle. He plopped down at the supper table and barely tasted whatever kind of meat Bethany and Penny cooked.

"Music tonight, don't you think, Josh?"

He lifted his head and blinked at Penny.

She waved her hand dismissively at him. "Never mind. I'll just take Bethany with me. Mr. Green plays the fiddle divinely."

"I'd be pleased to escort you ladies," Papa said gallantly. "Penny and I will go get wraps and be back momentarily."

Josh waited until they left and shoved away from the table so forcefully, the bench he'd been sitting on fell backward. "So are you going?"

Bethany's eyes widened.

"Well?" he demanded.

"I–I guess so." She climbed into the wagon to get her shawl.

He followed her and found her hunched over her trunk, muttering. "What're you grousing about?"

"I don't know. I'm tired and dirty and can't even cook anything you like. You're mad at me, and I don't know why. I'm trying so hard to be a good wife."

"No." He bit out the word and shook his head emphatically. "You're not."

His harsh words nearly tumbled her into the trunk. She slammed down the lid and turned back to him. "I mend and wash your clothes. I make decent meals. I'm kind to your family. I've helped you with patients. I don't know what you want! Tell me what you want!"

"I want you!"

"I don't know what you mean."

"If you don't know, then this conversation is pointless."

She placed her hands on her hips. "Josh!"

He jammed his fingers through his hair in a single, vicious swipe. "Forget it. Just forget it. I'm too tired to deal with this."

"But—"

"Just go listen to the music. I need to sleep." He grabbed a quilt, climbed out of the wagon, and bedded down. As exhaustion claimed him, he could hear the plaintive notes of Homer Green's fiddle.

Chapter 11

"Granny?" Bethany drew her shawl closer and whispered in the old woman's ear, "Could you spare a moment?"

Granny passed the child on her lap to her daughter-in-law and stood. Neither of them spoke as they walked away from the campfire and music.

Barely a note of the music reached Bethany's ear. She'd been sitting there, pondering Joshua's words and the anger behind them. None of it made sense to her; but since she hadn't grown up in a family or around men, his behavior baffled her. "*Seek wise counsel.*" The words from Proverbs threaded through her mind, and she'd chosen the one older woman in the group she trusted.

Granny led her past the circle of wagons, waved off Homer Green as he strode his night watch, and settled into a sandy bank with a muffled grunt. Bethany joined her.

"You and your man havin' a set-to?"

Instead of feeling embarrassed, Bethany felt a surge of relief. "Yes. I don't know what to do."

Granny stared up at the stars for a few minutes, then asked, "So what do you think the trouble is?"

"I don't know what the problem is. Josh is mad, and he won't talk to me."

"Men are a closed-mouth breed, Child. Best you learn that straight off. He ain't said nothing a-tall?"

"He's weary, Granny. I've tried to make allowances for that, but he's gotten snappish over silly things like me promising to make custard for Papa without asking him. Tonight, he told me—" she swallowed hard and whispered, "he told me he wants *me*. I've been his wife completely, so that can't be the problem. I just don't understand."

Granny nodded and hummed sagely. "You sure you wanna listen to an old woman whose words have to cut so's the hurt will heal?"

"It can't hurt any more than knowing something is wrong."

"Well then, put your hand in mine." As soon as their hands joined, Granny prayed, "Lord, You're the Source of wisdom and love. We'd be grateful to You for an extry measure of both tonight. Amen."

"Thank you, Granny. I don't have a mother or a mother-in-law to go to, and Penny—" She spread her hands in a gesture of helplessness.

"Good thing you didn't go to her. I'm 'bout to speak some truths, 'cuz you've asked." She looked Bethany straight in the eye. "It's time you put being a wife first."

Stunned, Bethany stared at her.

"Your man loves you. He protects you, provides for you, and treats you tenderly. Is it any wonder he wants the same commitment and consideration?"

"I do his laundry and keep the wagon neat and cook his favorite things. Mrs. Throckmorton always taught us the way to a man's heart was through his stomach, so I've tried hard to—"

"You're not getting the point." Granny leaned closer. " 'Member that sign on the rear of your wagon on the day we left Indy?"

"Tied the knot and un-afray-ed?"

"Well, Darlin', he tied the knot, but you're at loose ends. He wants to hold fast to you, to be complete with you. The Good Book says a man shall leave, and the woman should cleave. Instead of cleaving to him and pulling the knot tight and secure, you keep snagging. You've lassoed his sis and pa into your lives, and the poor man is desperate for you to treat him like he's all you need to fill your heart. Instead of showing him your full loyalty and respect, you treat him like he's no more important than his kin. Betcha he's got it in his mind that you wed him to stick with his sister instead of because he captured your heart."

Granny's words triggered memories. *God made us partners. . . supposed to dine alone. . .I'm not about to spend all of that time sharing you with Papa and Penny.* Josh's words flooded back, and a terrible realization dawned. *He was telling me that all along!*

"Oh, Granny," she cried, "what have I done?"

"It ain't what you've done—it's what you're gonna do that matters. You love him, don't you?"

"With all my heart!"

"Figured as much. Time for you to talk turkey with your man. Time to tell him straight out that you love him. Then, you're gonna have to show your devotion to him by putting everyone else a sad second. You got a big heart and wanna draw everybody in. When he tied the knot, he cut the strings to everyone else. What you need to do is put your man first.

Let him know he's special, then all the rest'll fall into place."

Bethany nodded somberly.

"Best we get back and bed down. Tomorra's gonna come all too soon." They walked back to the wagons, and before they parted, Bethany gave Granny Willodene a hug. "I'll be prayin' for you, Girl. Commit your marriage to the Lord, and it'll all come out right."

Bethany crept under the wagon, drew the quilts over herself, and snuggled close to Josh. Her chest ached with the sick feeling that she'd failed her husband so miserably. How he must have hurt to have finally spoken to her as he had tonight!

Even in his sleep, Josh rolled over and wrapped his arms around her. She pressed her ear to his chest and listened to the beat of his heart, all the while praying the Lord would reveal to her how to be the wife Josh needed.

❧

Josh crawled from beneath the wagon, yawned, and stretched. Somehow, he'd slept through the rifle shot to start the day.

"Good morning." Bethany brushed a kiss on his stubbly cheek and pressed a cup of hot coffee in his hands. "Breakfast is ready."

Papa plopped down in a chair and got an indignant look. "Where's my oatmeal? We had flapjacks yesterday."

"Josh likes flapjacks," Bethany stated as she put a small jug of molasses on the table.

Though everything else seemed the same, Josh sensed a difference in his wife. He couldn't put his finger on it. Last night, he'd been sharp with her and stopped before he lost his temper. They needed to talk, though. He'd let things get out of hand.

"Megan just finished reading *Malaeska*, so I thought we

could walk with her and Emma today and discuss the book," Penny said as she cut her food.

"Go ahead. I'll be walking with Josh today."

Josh startled a bit at his wife's announcement.

"Marching alongside the oxen in this sand is no picnic," Papa announced. "You'll get gritty."

Bethany merely shrugged as if it didn't matter. Later, as she ambled at his side, she still ignored the unpleasantness of the terrain. "Josh, I need to apologize."

He glanced at her.

She slipped her hand into his and threaded their fingers into a weave she tightened with a squeeze. Then, she turned her hand. "My wedding ring isn't shiny anymore."

"It can be polished."

"Our marriage isn't shiny anymore, either, and it's my fault. I didn't grow up in a family."

"And you married me to be part of a family." Every word fell like lead bullets.

"Yes. No. Oh, Josh. I've done it all wrong." She let out a ragged sigh.

"Do you regret marrying me?"

"Never! I worry that you regret marrying me. Josh, we scarcely knew each other, and I've enjoyed getting to know you. You've grown in my heart until you've filled it completely."

He shook his head. "It doesn't come across that way at all. You've roped my family and half of this wagon train into our lives."

"Only because I felt so secure that my heart grew and I felt free to reach out. Now, though, I know I was wrong. My allegiance to you should have been the priority, and I ought to have made it clear that you rate above any other relationship."

"Even Penny and Papa?"

"Why do you even ask?"

He felt a pang at the confession, but it was time to settle the matter once and for all. "You're always asking what they want. You even list them before me." He kicked the sand with the toe of his boot and quoted the words he'd so often heard her say, "Papa and Penny and you."

"Josh, that wasn't what I meant. I was saving the best for last!"

The surprised hurt in her tone and the explanation acted as a salve to his wounded soul.

"It's not just your fault," he said. "I've been fostering the hurt instead of discussing it with you. I let my pride hold me back, and it's put distance between us."

She turned loose of his hand and wound her arm about his waist. He curled his arm around her shoulders and held her close. "I do love you," she said tearfully. "More than I ever thought possible."

"Those are the sweetest words I've ever heard. I love you, too, Bethy-mine."

"Granny Willodene once told me to find happiness in the ordinary because it makes for a pleasant life and a serene heart. I'm thinking that's true of a marriage, as well."

"You'll never be ordinary," he chuckled. "But I've already found considerable happiness in you. Ecclesiastes 9:9 says, 'Live joyfully with the wife whom thou lovest.' I think we've both been concentrating more on the future and our destination instead of enjoying each day as the Lord gives it to us."

"So we need to take pleasure wherever we are. . .even if it's a gritty, dry stretch."

"With the love God gives us, it's an oasis."

Rawhide rode up. "Keep a-goin', folks. We'll hit Ash Hollow tomorrow. Fresh water and trees."

Bethany stopped and wrapped her other arm around Josh and hugged him tight. "Our oasis!"

❧

Ash Hollow was the first steep grade they took. Men tied logs to the backs of the wagons to slow their descent. They camped for two days among the first trees they'd seen in over one hundred miles and relished the first fresh water they'd had in weeks.

Josh sat by his wife and smiled. She'd curled her foot up beneath her, and she hummed as she stirred something in a big bowl. "What do you have there?"

She held it up. "Have a taste."

He swiped his finger through the batter and licked the sweetness off. "Mmm. Apple something."

"Apple spice cake."

"Looks like enough batter to float a boat."

Bethany smiled. "Apple is your favorite, so I wanted enough for you, then I thought to make one for Granny Willodene as a thanks for her wisdom. Penny's going to sugar glaze all of them if she can have one to share while the girls discuss their books."

"Do we have that many pie pans?"

"No." She giggled. "So I'm baking one for the Cole brothers since they're lending me two pans."

❧

After a two-day rest in Ash Hollow, the train continued. A few men managed to bag some antelope. The women followed the recipe for roast saddle of venison in Bethany's cookbook. Penny made mashed potatoes with Edward's dried flakes, Bert made biscuits by the score, and nearly everyone else contributed dishes for a big feast. In the midst of all of the activity, Granny Willodene wandered toward a chair and swiped something from Lavinia's hands. "What is this?"

"None of your business!"

Granny turned the book over and read aloud, "*Malaeska*."

"I wondered to whom my book was passed," Bethany said.

"Well, I'm gonna hang onto this until Lavinia and her mama finish washin' the supper dishes," Granny announced. "Everyone else has worked for the meal. I'm sure they want to do their fair share."

Bethany thought the day had been surprising enough, but as the Millberg women washed the dishes, Buck and Bert Cole shuffled up. "Doc. Mrs. Rogers. Would you be willing to loan that dime novel to us?"

Josh raised his brow at Bethany, read her expression, and managed to sound completely unfazed. "Just as soon as Lavinia is done with it."

"Hope she reads faster than she does dishes," Bert grumbled.

"We have a long time on the trail. I promise you'll get to read it," Bethany said as she slipped her hand into Josh's.

Two days later during lunch, Lavinia returned the book, and Bethany passed it on to Buck as the wagon train started its afternoon travel. About an hour later, a huge mound of rock with a breathtaking spire came into view.

"Chimney Rock!" someone shouted.

"One-third of the way there," Papa declared.

"Well, what do you think?" Josh asked.

Bethany studied it. "It's certainly a magnificent thing. I can see why they call it Chimney Rock. It's aptly named."

"Are you longing for a chimney of your own?" Papa asked.

Bethany shook her head and smiled. "My hearth is an open fire. I'm content to walk toward the sunset and sleep beneath a canopy of stars because God gave my heart a home in a green wedding wagon with the man I love."

CATHY MARIE HAKE

Cathy Marie is a Southern California native who loves her work as a nurse and Lamaze teacher. She and her husband have a daughter, a son, and a dog, so life is never dull or quiet. Cathy Marie considers herself a sentimental packrat, collecting antiques and Hummel figurines. She otherwise keeps busy with reading, writing, backing, and being a prayer warrior. "I am easily distracted during prayer, so I devote certain tasks and chores to specific requests or persons so I can keep faithful in my prayer life." Cathy Marie's first book was published by **Heartsong Presents** in 2000 and earned her a spot as one of the readers' favorite new authors.

A Bride for the Preacher

by Sally Laity

Dedication

To the valiant souls who braved the hardships
of the Oregon Trail and found love along the way.

Chapter 1

"Is that Oregon, Sissy?" Eight-year-old Susan pointed ahead.

Emma Harris kept pace with their family's wagon as it rumbled and creaked over the bumpy trail in the vast green valley surrounding Chimney Rock. "No, I'm afraid not. We still have a long way to go." She gazed up at the distant vista, then at the aperture that had loomed on the horizon all day like a beckoning finger.

"How long? More than a week? My feet are tired."

Mine, too, Emma wanted to say, but held her tongue. "We'll be making camp here in this valley. Perhaps Papa will let you ride on the seat till we stop."

Her sister's impish face brightened, and she skipped ahead, her blond pigtails bouncing. "Papa. Papa. Can I ride with you?"

"Sure, Pumpkin. You can sit by your pretty mama. She's resting her feet, too."

Emma watched her dad bend down to help his youngest daughter aboard before grasping the traces again.

"I don't think we'll ever, ever get to Oregon," twelve-year-old Deborah muttered, her high-top shoes clomping step for step with Emma's. "And even if we do, I won't have a single friend there. I wish we'd have stayed home in Philadelphia."

"I know," Emma commiserated. "But we'll make new friends once we're settled."

"Think so?" Shaded by the brim of her sunbonnet, eyes the same deep brown as her hair softened with hope.

"Well, we've made new friends already on the train, haven't we? And they'll all be there." Even as she spoke, her gaze focused on Jesse Brewster's wagon, directly in front of their own. He was already making the turn to form the night circle in the green meadow dotted liberally with black-eyed Susans and other late wildflowers. She couldn't spot him from this angle, but the young pastor's poignantly boyish face had been imprinted on her mind since the before-trip assembly in Independence.

Almost as quickly, she began to recognize, without a glance, that commanding voice, which held folks' attention during the rousing Sunday sermons, yet could turn amazingly gentle when singing hymns around late-night campfires or when comforting a whiny child. The tawny hair atop his head curled with wild abandon, and he had the most amazing eyes. . .eyes a deep indigo blue that seemed to see right inside a person's soul. For all his lofty idealism, the parson seemed akin to the romantic heroes Emma had read about in novels.

"At least we'll be camping in a pretty place," Deborah said, her girlish voice drawing Emma out of her musings. "I'll pick Mama a bouquet for the supper table."

Nodding, Emma concentrated once more on the surroundings, admiring the tall limestone landmark that dominated the view. It was the first of several rock formations in a misty semicircle stretching to the west. The morning sun had made them appear ever so grand in the distance; and now, closer up, with the slanting sun behind them, their starkness softened into a breathtaking magenta hue.

One thing she could not deny was the abundance of beautiful scenery since the company had embarked on what her father termed their "Great Adventure." Mama had been far less enthusiastic about leaving their successful city pharmacy and uprooting the family on a whim to go to the unknown. Nevertheless, she dredged up the optimism she'd possessed in her younger years and determined to support the husband she loved. Emma hoped and prayed it wasn't to everyone's folly.

As always, wagon master Rawhide Rawson made the rounds to make sure the prairie schooners were in position. Men, used to the routine, quickly unhitched the oxen teams and saw to the stock, while the women and girls got busy with supper fires.

Emma barely squelched a smile as she noticed Jesse Brewster hard at work tending to his rig, and she wondered which family had invited the handsome minister to share their evening meal this night. As always, the big yellow dog, Barnabas, stayed near his master.

A stone's throw away, newlyweds Dr. Josh Rogers and his wife, Bethany, fussed about their wagon. It seemed they hadn't stopped smiling since Parson Brewster pronounced them husband and wife at the onset of the trip.

"Emma, Dear, do quit dawdling," her mother scolded. "Your papa will be hungry when he gets back from looking after the animals."

"Yes, Mama." Dutifully, she removed her bonnet and got out the crates they'd use for chairs during the meal, then retrieved the sturdy tin plates purchased especially for the journey. The fancy china dishes remained packed in a barrel beneath the wagon's bowed canvas cover, along with Papa's medicinal supplies, books, equipment he'd kept from the apothecary, and the trunks filled with lovely dresses they wouldn't wear until they reached their destination. Emma yearned for the day when they would arrive at the journey's end and life would return to normal, with the family settled in a nice house filled with her mother's pretty things. With the miles passing by so slowly, though, she had to agree with Deborah. They'd never get to Oregon.

Gradually, various cooking smells drifted from individual wagons and mingled in a delectable mix that made stomachs growl. Muffled voices carried on the night air as folks gathered to partake of their supper fare, sometimes sharing with other families.

"We must've made a good fifteen miles today," Papa said, taking a healthy bite of fried rabbit leg from the creature he'd shot just before they'd started down into the valley. "Nary a mishap in the company since sunup yesterday. That must be a good sign."

"I hope so, Ambrose," Mama said, "for all our sakes. I fear the worst part of the journey is yet to come."

He gave her knee a comforting pat. "We'll just have to trust the Lord, Nettie, like young Pastor Brewster says. Trust the Lord and help each other along the way. Can't go wrong with that kind of advice. And if trouble happens, we'll deal with it the best we can."

Emma's ears perked up at the mention of the minister.

"Will we get to Oregon next week?" Susan asked, scraping the last bit of beans on her plate onto her spoon.

"No, Pumpkin. Not quite. We all have to be patient awhile longer."

She sighed, then gave an unconcerned shrug, and drained the remains of the water in her cup.

From across the grassy circle came the sound of Mr. Green's fiddle, and as a flute and a guitar joined in with the lively tune, folks began clearing away supper things and preparing for the evening's festivities.

"I'll wash the dishes," Emma offered.

"Wouldn't you and Deborah rather join the other young people?" her mother asked. "They seem to have such a grand time singing and dancing."

"Deborah can go if she wants, but I was hoping to read for awhile before it gets too dark."

"As you wish, Dear," Mama said, a dubious frown knitting the fine brows beneath her light brown hair. "But I do think you'd enjoy the trip better if you'd join in a little more. Oh, there's Idabelle. She's been wanting my recipe for camp bread." She waved to the other ladies, who were gravitating toward the cluster of people already enjoying the music. Then, she turned and headed toward them, her proper posture making her slight figure look too thin.

Papa settled back to watch after her. "Always was a pretty little thing, your mama. I love the way those hazel eyes of hers turn colors with whatever dress she has on. She's been a good helpmeet, too. I hope I'm not doing wrong, dragging the lot of you out West."

"I hear it's beautiful there," Emma said consolingly, rinsing each of their plates. "I'm sure you'll have a fine new business going in no time."

"Hope so. Well," he clapped his palms on his knees and stood, "guess I'll go get in on the singing. Sure you won't tag along?"

She shook her head. "I'd rather not. Next time, perhaps." But as he ambled away, Emma couldn't help wishing he'd have pressured her to go. She did like the songs. . .she just didn't feel at ease going over there and entering a crowd that had already gathered. She'd always felt more at home with books. Still, without forethought, her gaze scanned the gathering, trying to pick out Jesse Brewster. And trying to see which of the other girls was sidling up to him.

❧

Jesse stroked Barney's golden fur as they sat on the grass near the center of the camp, listening to the fiddle's cheerful tune. Small cooking fires slowly died out on the perimeter of the circle while womenfolk tidied up after the meal. Some were already laying out bedrolls under their wagons.

Must be nice, he surmised, *having a wife to look after life's little comforts*. But since his plans in that direction had met such a doleful end, it was obvious that God wanted him to concentrate on his mission. Probably wouldn't be much of a life for a woman anyway, saddled with the kids at home while her husband was off evangelizing sparsely settled Oregon for who knew how long at a time.

Certainly none of the young women in this company seemed suited to such an existence. His gaze meandered to Miss Lavinia Millberg, who sat, as always, attired in enough frills to drown a body. She seemed strangely out of place in this company, and she likely would have been happier if she had remained back in the comfort of the home she and her family had left. The other gals might be a bit more adventurous; but so far, they all stayed pretty much together in cheery calico clusters, giggling, chatting, and passing a dime novel around.

That is, all but one. . .

"A right purty night," wiry Frank Barnes commented as he eased himself down beside Jesse, a whittling stick in hand.

"Sure is."

"Thought I'd find me a quiet spot while the wife gets the baby settled for the night. Picked a fine time for cuttin' teeth, that young'un. Spent most of the day fussin' and frettin'."

"This, too, shall pass," Jesse quipped with a mischievous smile.

"And soon, I hope. It gets to wearin' a body out, and that's a fact."

"Maybe Doc Rogers has something to ease her through it."

"Could be. I'll ask him later." The farmer began making short strokes with his whittling knife. "That was a fine sermon you preached at us yesterday, Parson. Fine, fine sermon."

"Thanks. I'm glad you enjoyed it. I'm thinking of continuing on with the same theme this coming Sunday. We can all learn a lot from the life of King David."

"That's a fact. A pity he made such a mess of a good thing, though, with that wanderin' eye of his."

"I couldn't agree more. The Bible says that he who finds a wife finds a good thing. . .but I know the Lord didn't mean for us to look in the wrong places to do it."

"I expect you'll be lookin' for a gal of your own. Mebbe right here on this train."

"Maybe. I'm not in a hurry, though." Even as he spoke, Jesse's thoughts insisted on straying across the way to Emma Harris. Strange, how she avoided so many of the evening gatherings. She didn't give an impression of unfriendliness, but rather shyness. She did attend the Sunday services with her family and sometimes walked with some of the other gals her age along the trek.

But more often than not, she kept to herself or stayed near her mother and younger sisters, usually with her nose buried in what must be some of her pharmacist father's big, heavy-looking books.

Jesse saw no reason to divulge to Mr. Barnes how often his thoughts revolved around the dark-haired Emma with her serious nature and deep brown eyes. Or how often he took a backward glance toward her family's wagon just to make sure she was still there. Jesse didn't understand it himself, since the young woman never showed a spark of interest or encouragement. But she did make it hard for him to rein in his mental ramblings and concentrate on the subject of his next sermon. Even as he chided himself for being distracted yet again, he saw Emma hop down from the family wagon and roll out the bedding she'd held in her arm.

Beside him, Barnabas yawned and settled his muzzle down on his forepaws.

"I'm with you, old boy," Jesse muttered. "It's been a long day. Time to turn in." Rising, he gave a parting wave to Mr. Barnes and the others nearby and headed for his rig, where no one else had to be looked after, and the sleeping mat remained in readiness. Barney stretched and slowly got up, then pattered after his master, who cast one last questioning look at the Harris wagon before climbing into his own.

Bright and early after breakfast the next morning, the prairie schooners resumed the westward journey, holding to a trail along the gently sloping land rising from the marshy meadow. Emma watched the ever-changing sunlight splay delectable shades of ochre and soft pink across the ridge of knobby outcroppings beyond Chimney Rock, and she wondered where this night would find them.

When she tired of the view, she opened a book of poetry from Papa's library and pondered the lovely phrases and thoughts as she walked. Beside her, Susan and Deborah skipped along, unmindful of the dust stirred up by the wagons ahead. They gathered wildflowers for Mama, who walked with one of the other women today.

"Oh, look, Sissy," Susan called out. "A cross of stones."

Glancing up from her book, Emma saw the small but distinct grave marker mostly hidden by the tall grasses alongside the path. "Yes, well, leave it be." Normally a person who died along the way was buried right in the trail itself, leaving no mark to be discovered by scavenging Indians or marauding wolves. She saw no sense in alarming her younger sisters over what was obviously a small child's resting place. Expelling a sad breath, Emma tried to concentrate on reading again, but a vision of some young mother grieving over an unspeakable loss kept getting in the way. She swallowed and slipped the book into her skirt pocket.

The nooning stop seemed far too short, but Rawhide wanted to press on quickly, hoping to make Scott's Bluff by nightfall.

After the long, hard day of steady travel, the company did just that. From a distance of four or five miles away, what had appeared to be nothing more than a huge blue mound in the wide open country began to resemble a medieval castle. And as they came closer, its contortion of weathered towers, parapets, and gulches gradually defined themselves, rising up majestically from the beautiful valley floor.

Papa's grip on the traces tightened as his rig crawled single file after the others through knoll-filled Mitchell Pass. Deep ruts carved by prior westbound wagons added to the roughness of the route closest to the North Platte. "According to Rawhide, we're about a third of the way to Oregon, at this point," Papa called cheerfully over his shoulder when they'd finished navigating the pass.

Emma's heart sank. She'd been hoping they'd gone much farther by now.

Deborah put words to that thought. "You mean, we have to go as far as we've traveled now two more whole times?"

"Yes, Sweetie, we do. But we'll get there. You'll see."

"Then I hope you and Mama brought lots more shoes for us."

He chuckled and gave her a wink.

By the time the wagons reached a cold spring and circled for the night, barely any daylight remained. The two younger girls could scarcely hold their heads up to eat. Emma herself struggled to stay awake long enough to help clean up after the meal. The whole camp seemed more subdued. No one ventured out to sing and make music.

Just as well, Emma decided. Another long day like this one, and she'd be dead on her feet.

The trail boss rode up as the bedrolls were being unfurled. "How're you folks doin'?"

"Just fine," Papa said. "A mite weary, though."

"Just like I figured," Rawhide replied. "Thought we'd rest a day here, do some repairs, and the like."

"That's the best news we've had all day," Papa said.

"Well, just passin' the word, is all. There's a harder pull comin' up." The wiry man nodded, touched the brim of his hat, and nudged his mount forward.

Feeling considerably cheered, Emma watched him ride

toward the remaining wagons, then climbed aboard the rig to change into her sleeping clothes. A whole day to rest. . .and not even a Sunday.

She glanced to the pastor's wagon, wondering if it would be improper to offer to do his laundry tomorrow. It would be a proper exchange, considering all the sermons he'd prepared on the train's behalf. . .the Christian thing to do.

Chapter 2

Put the bedding out to dry, will you, Dear?" Mama asked after breakfast. "It's still damp from last night's shower."

"Yes, Mama." Emma hefted the bundle of blankets and pillows they had brought into the wagon at the onset of rain. After placing it near the seat, she hopped down and reached up to retrieve it.

A shadow fell across her arm. . .one that strongly resembled the curly-haired pastor. "Need any help, Miss Emma?" he asked in that pleasant, manly voice.

Hoping her skirts had kept her modest when she'd jumped to the ground in such unladylike fashion, she struggled to catch her breath. "I–I think I can manage. Thank you."

"Just seems neighborly to ask, is all." Jesse Brewster's indigo eyes warmed as a smile spread across his lips. "I reckon lots of folks had their sleep rudely interrupted when that storm blew over us."

"Indeed." Having rarely been in such close proximity to the handsome minister without the benefit of her parents' presence, Emma found herself staring at his strong features and noting how much bluer his eyes looked against the cobalt shirt he had on. And how the green and tan stripes in his vest didn't quite go with the brown-and-black-checked pattern of his brown trousers. Why, the poor man needed a wife to help him coordinate his wardrobe, if nothing else!

A warm flush enveloped her face, and she redirected her gaze elsewhere. After all, though he was handsome enough to turn a girl's head and possessive of a compelling personality, the last thing on her mind was getting married. Particularly to a minister. She had far grander aspirations for herself.

All around the camp, other folks who'd been sleeping beneath their wagons when the sudden shower hit also set about drying bedding. Blankets in a rainbow of hues lay strewn across the brush like patches in a crazy quilt. A few adorned wagon wheels and hitches, any place that would catch the breeze.

"We missed you at the evening gathering last night," Reverend Brewster said casually, drawing her attention back to him.

"I. . .was busy. Reading." With no idea why she'd elaborated, Emma shook out two of the heavier coverlets and draped each over a wheel, then unfolded the lighter blankets to spread out over desert sage.

"I've often noticed you reading a book," he remarked. "Even when the train is in motion. Is it something you find particularly interesting? Or do you just read to pass the time?" Moving nearer as she struggled to untangle one of the sheets, he peeled off two of the corners and helped her lay it out over a boulder, then did the same with the last one as well.

"Thank you," she murmured. As she straightened to her full height, her hands suddenly seemed far too empty. She rested one on her hip to occupy it. "Mostly I read my father's books, on medications and herbs and things."

"A lot of folks would find that pretty dull reading."

The mischievous twinkle in his eyes put Emma on the defensive. "It isn't to me. I find it fascinating, learning about plants or concoctions that can help heal sickness. God put a lot of thought into creating this world."

"I quite agree, Miss Emma. I meant no disrespect," he said gently. "It's just that most of the other young women in the company who enjoy books choose lighter fare. Novels and the like."

His explanation smoothed her ruffled feathers. "I read novels sometimes," she confessed. "James Fenimore Cooper is my favorite."

"Ah. The adventuresome type."

"And I also enjoy studying the Scriptures," she added, lest he think she sought only worldly pursuits. For some reason, that seemed important.

He gave an amused nod. "Always a wise choice."

Neither spoke for a moment. Emma, never accomplished at making small conversation, wracked her brain trying to think of something to say.

Barnabas ambled over to them just then, saving her the trouble. The minister smiled and bent to stroke him behind the ears. "What have you been up to, Barney, old fella?"

"He's a really nice dog," Emma said, cringing at her lack of brilliance. "Nice and quiet."

"Yeah, he's a pretty good boy," Reverend Brewster returned. "Lots of company." He glanced at her as he spoke, and the warmth in his eyes—along with something she could not define—made her heart skip a beat.

"Would you like—I mean, Mama and I will be doing some laundry while we're stopped here today. Is there anything we might wash for you?"

"Mighty kind of you to offer," he said, dazzling her with an incredible smile that deepened the laugh creases alongside his mouth. "But I pretty much took care of it at our last stop."

"Well, I'd best get to the chores," she blurted, turning to join her mother aboard the wagon.

"Will we see you at the evening gathering?" he asked.

Emma paused, one hand grasping the edge of the wagon frame. "Perhaps."

He touched the brim of his hat with his thumb and forefinger. "Miss Emma."

"Reverend." With a small smile, she climbed up into the rig.

Her mother, however, was nowhere to be seen. No wonder she hadn't come out to take part in the conversation. And to think the minister had actually come over and helped put the bedding out to dry! Emma placed a hand over her heart to calm its erratic beating. . .though why he should affect her so eluded her.

An hour later found her knee-deep in the river with some of the other young women of the company washing clothes. She and her sisters each had two sturdy cotton dresses for travel. . .one to wear, the other to wash; and despite the aprons and pinafores worn to protect them, constant travel amid dust and dirt took its toll on the hems. Particularly Susan's. The girl was forever stooping to pick flowers or examine something curious along the way. Emma gave particular attention to her youngest sister's dress, soaping each section of the bottom edge and rubbing it between the knuckles of both hands to get out the grime.

"I declare," Bethany Rogers said as she and her sister-in-law, Penny, labored at the same task a few feet from Emma. "Keeping Josh in white shirts is going to occupy a lot of my time." She brushed a lock of damp brown hair from her eyes with her wrist, then continued working soapsuds through the garment.

"I suppose doctors are a lot like ministers," Emma replied, "always feeling they must dress properly when they perform their duties."

The young bride paused with a dreamy smile. "And I do want him to look the part. Truly I do. But I fear we're fighting a losing battle, what with the constant dust along the trail."

"I wouldn't worry overmuch about that," blue-eyed Penny chimed in, tucking stray blond hairs behind an ear. "I'm sure my brother understands." She rinsed several pairs of sturdy stockings in the steady current, then squeezed them out.

Straightening her spine to ease a kink, Emma spied Reverend Brewster strolling along the river with snooty Lavinia Millberg. Though Emma had no designs on the man herself, she believed he at least deserved a woman who'd be an asset in his vocation. It peeved her to watch the way plump Lavinia fawned over him, batting those silly eyelashes and giggling after some of his remarks. The girl never had to soil her lily-white hands with something as mundane as laundry, since the family's Irish maid got stuck with all the drudgery.

Emma wrung excess water from the last of the dresses and underthings with more force than necessary, then looped them over an arm. "Looks like I'm finished. See you all after awhile."

"Yes, the celebration feast this evening should be great fun," golden-haired Megan Crawford chimed in. "The men shot some antelope today. When I left the wagon, my sister-in-law was already baking a cake."

Hearing the other girls embark on a new, livelier topic as she left, Emma couldn't help but wonder if her presence had dampened their spirits. Then again, she reminded herself, Bethany and Penny had been friends even before Bethany's marriage to Penny's brother made them sisters-in-law. It was probably natural she felt the outsider. Small comfort, but it helped a little as Emma hung the clean dresses on a clothes-line strung between the wagon wheels. Still, she couldn't help casting a curious glance back at the river and the girls who chatted so amiably.

She had observed Bethany and Doc Rogers growing closer since their wedding in Independence, noting the way their shared smiles would bring a faint blush to Bethany's cheeks. Emma wondered what it must be like to spend one's entire life with one special person. Not that she believed that would ever happen for her, since her mind had been set forever on becoming a doctor. . .or if that dream proved impossible, a nurse. Marriage might agree with some folks, but she wouldn't settle for only that. Not if she could accomplish something better with her life, something that counted.

Releasing a pent-up breath, she climbed aboard the wagon to check for any other chores needing to be done. Finding none, she settled down with a book instead.

❧

The whole company seemed in joyful spirits as they partook of a wondrous array of food that evening. In Jesse's opinion, the women had outdone themselves. He couldn't remember when he'd last seen such an abundance of delectable fare. Returning to the makeshift tables holding platters of roast antelope, stuffed sage hens, beans, stewed vegetables, biscuits, breads, and a variety of desserts, he filled his plate for the second time.

"Pretty tasty, eh, Reverend?" Ambrose Harris said, his graying mustache twitching into a smile as he helped himself to some browned potatoes.

"Sure is. It's truly amazing what the ladies can do with Dutch ovens, open fires, and deep pits. Seems they get better the farther along we are."

The pharmacist jutted his chin toward one of the baking pans. "Try some of my wife's pot pie. It's her specialty."

"Don't mind if I do." Dishing out a generous portion, Jesse sampled it. "Say, that really is good. I'll have to give Mrs. Harris my compliments." As he ate, he turned and let his gaze skim the clusters of chatting travelers seated on the grass or on barrels and crates, while they ate and visited with one another. "I've enjoyed getting to know you and your wife along this route. And those three lively daughters of yours must be great company for the two of you."

His chest puffed out a bit. "That they are. Of course, Emma, our oldest, is as happy with her nose buried in a book as she is talking. She's read about half my library already—and I'm talking pharmaceutical journals and medical texts, for the most part. But the other two keep us hopping. Our little Susie seems to be the daring one, always chasing off after butterflies or baby rabbits."

Jesse gave a half-smile. He would have liked to ask a few more pertinent questions about Emma, but thought it prudent to refrain. He easily picked her out in the crowd, standing with her mother and some of the other ladies across the circle. Her sable hair, loosed from the pins and sunbonnet that normally held it captive, hung to her shoulder blades in soft waves, glazed by the setting sun. It was hard to drag his attention away from the fetching sight.

She looked his way just then, and their gazes held for a moment before she smiled shyly and lowered her lashes.

When everyone finished the main courses, interest centered on the sweet treats the women had labored over most of the afternoon. A few ladies tended the desserts, slicing pies and cakes and doling them out. Jesse was more than delighted to discover Emma among them and quickly moved to her line.

"That apple pie looks mighty good, Miss Emma," he said, stepping up when his turn came.

"I hope you enjoy it, Reverend," she said, a reserved smile softening her brown eyes.

"Did you make it?"

"No, it's my mother's. I had other chores today."

"Well, thank you just the same. I'm sure it'll be delicious." A glance over his shoulder revealed no one behind him, so Jesse saw no need to move on. He cleared his throat. "The music and square dancing will start soon. Will you be staying around to join in?"

She shrugged a shoulder and grimaced as her gaze moved beyond him to where the other young people were gravitating toward each other. "I've never been much good at it."

"But, it's not all dancing, as you know. You've heard us singing all those favorite songs and hymns, I'm sure."

A doubtful expression appeared, then vanished as quickly, and he plunged bravely onward. "What I'm really hoping is that you might consider coming for a stroll. With me, I mean, if you weren't planning to stay around to sing. It's a wonderful evening."

This time, something entirely different clouded her eyes. He couldn't determine whether it was reluctance or apprehension.

"It's very nice of you to ask," she said softly, "but I'm afraid I'm not much company."

"Why don't you let me be the judge of that?" he countered. "You don't even have to talk, if you don't want to. I can do enough of that for both of us. . .and Barney will tag along, of course."

When her demeanor eased a fraction, he could see he was making a little progress. "I'm a pretty decent guy," he coaxed, with a less-than-serious grin.

It brought an answering smile from Emma. She glanced around at the people still eating. "I'll have to help clean up when everyone's through. But after that I'm free. . .if you don't mind waiting."

"Not at all, Miss Emma," he said. "I'll call back in awhile, then." Pie in hand, he headed toward the large campfire that dominated the center of the wagons' circle, where the men with instruments were already gathering and tuning up.

Emma watched the tall, lanky minister stride away, the evening breeze ruffling his unruly curls. She'd admired him since Independence, but since she rarely attended the company get-togethers, the longest she'd seen of him at one time were the occasions he preached the Sunday sermons. For all his lack of wardrobe sense on travel days, no one could fault him when performing his duties in his black suit and fairly crisp white shirt.

And she liked his mind, the way he put his thoughts

together when explaining particular Scripture passages. Back at home in Philadelphia, her parents had led evening devotions when the family gathered around the supper table, and often Papa would put forth questions that made one think. Sadly, that practice fell by the wayside since taking to the westward trail, because of weariness and other concerns. It might be rather interesting to hear what Jesse Brewster had to say apart from his weekly sermons.

The problem would be making sure he did all the talking. No sense in proving to him what a dolt she was or how little she had to talk about.

On the other hand, it might be better all the way around if he did discover how truly dull she was, Emma rationalized. Then he'd leave her be.

But somehow that thought was not quite as comforting as she'd expected.

All too soon, the last appetite was sated and no one made another trip to the food tables. The leftovers and desserts were collected by the various ladies who'd made them and the makeshift tables taken down and stowed. Then the women drifted over to where folks were dancing to a lively tune.

After carrying the remains of the food belonging to her family back to the wagon, Emma plucked her woolen shawl and went to the front to climb down.

"Allow me," Jesse Brewster offered, reaching up to help her.

Emma tamped down her nervousness and leaned into his hands, pleased when he respectfully set her down as if she weighed no more than a feather.

"I'm glad you agreed to come walking," he said, helping her to adjust the shawl about her shoulders.

She smiled her thanks. "As you said, it's a lovely evening. And, Barnabas," she crooned softly, venturing a friendly pat on the dog's head, "it's nice to have your company."

He licked her hand and plodded along beside them.

"You have a wonderful family," the minister began. "I've grown to respect and admire your father immensely during this trip. He's always the first to volunteer help when someone needs it. And your mother seems to offer great comfort and advice to the mothers with young children. They all speak highly of her."

"Thank you. Mama wasn't exactly eager for this experience, but she made up her mind to make the best of it." She paused. "Did you. . .leave your family behind when you decided to go out West?"

He shook his head. "I've been on my own for five years or so now. My ma died when I was about the same age as your baby sister. My pa passed on ten years later. A cholera outbreak."

"I'm sorry to hear that."

"Thanks. But I'm carrying out his wishes. He always wanted me to be a preacher. Thing was, I think he envisioned me pastoring a great church. But I felt called to go where new churches were needed to be founded, instead of staying in Ohio, where there's already an abundance."

"I'm sure you'll establish a fine church in time."

"That remains to be seen." He paused. "What are your hopes for the future, Miss Emma. . .if you don't mind my asking?"

She thought for a few moments as they strolled the dim perimeter of the camp, the strains of music drifting toward them on the night air. "If I had my dearest wish, it would be to become a doctor and help people. But Papa says women doctors will never be in much demand."

"I'm not too sure I'd agree with that. Times are changing. Why, back in Ohio, women are admitted to the college program at Oberlin College on an equal basis with men. And I seem to recall reading in the newspaper a couple years ago about a woman in New York who earned a medical degree."

Emma couldn't repress a sigh. "But that's just it. Ohio. New York. The medical schools are back east. And where we're heading couldn't be farther away from them. What hope do I have, really, of attending college? My dream will probably always be just that."

He didn't respond immediately. "Did you ever consider the possibility that God might have other plans for you?"

Stopping in her tracks, she eyed him. "So this is why you invited me to go for a stroll? So you could preach to me?"

"No, not at all," he returned. "I'm merely making conversation. I had no ulterior motives."

His kind tone immediately filled her with remorse. "Forgive me," she said miserably. "Too often I jump to the wrong conclusions. I told you I wasn't very good company."

"And I beg to differ. I'm enjoying our walk and getting to know you a little. I'll pray that God will make His perfect will known to you, and that if it's His plan for you to become a part of the medical field in the future, He'll make a way for you to do so."

"Would you really do that?"

"Of course. What are friends for, if not to help each other achieve our dreams?"

She had no answer and was still a little stunned that he hadn't tried to squelch her hopes. Maybe it wouldn't be so. . . lonely. . .traveling these endless miles, knowing he was praying for her happiness. And maybe going to Oregon didn't seem so bleak a prospect now, if he truly intended to become her friend.

Noticing they'd reached her wagon, Emma turned to him with a small smile. "Thank you for the invitation. It was. . .nice talking to you, Pastor Brewster."

"My friends call me Jesse," he said quietly. "I'd be honored to count you among them, if I may."

It was a simple request. One she saw no reason to refuse. "You may. . .but only if you drop the 'Miss.' "

He smiled.

"Good night, Jesse."

"Good night, Emma. Sleep well."

She accepted his assistance to climb aboard, then lingered just out of sight to watch as he and Barnabas strode to his rig.

The rest of the family had yet to return from the festivities, and for that she was grateful. There seemed so much to think about. While she gathered the bedrolls and laid them out beneath the wagon in preparation for the night, she pondered the interesting conversation with Jesse Brewster.

She had admired him since the first day she'd seen him. She liked his mind and his sermons. But something told her he was far more than just a handsome young minister and that it was going to be really nice having him for a friend. . .if nothing more.

Chapter 3

After leaving the rough terrain around Scott's Bluff, it pleased Susan and Deborah to no end when the wagons meandered past Kiowa and Horse Creeks, each of which had banks bright with sunflowers and patches of lavender daisies.

"Won't Mama be surprised at our nooning stop today," the younger girl said, while she and her sister darted to and fro adding to the colorful bouquets clutched in their hands.

"I'm sure she will," Emma said. "Please try not to get dirt from the stems on your dresses and pinafores, though. They're wearing out just from being scrubbed clean."

"Yes, Mother," they singsonged in unison. But paying little heed to their older sister, they dashed toward another grouping of wildflowers.

"I saw them first," Susan hollered.

"Oh, pshaw, there's plenty for both of us," Deborah countered, her longer legs easily outdistancing her sibling's. The two were soon joined by Barnabas, who obviously knew a game when he saw one.

Emma smiled despite herself and stepped around a small

velvet-gray sage bush while watching the girls romping with Jesse's dog.

The sight brought thoughts of last night's visit with the minister, and she wondered if it had taken him as long to fall asleep as it had her. She glanced ahead, but could not see him for the canvas top of his rig.

Many of the men now walked alongside the wagons, cracking bullwhips as the oxen labored over the sandy, climbing trail, raising more than the usual amount of dust. After a few hours, Emma no longer found sage an oddity. It grew in abundance, seemingly everywhere. Panting from the effort of hiking the uphill grade, she had a deep foreboding that the easy days had come to an end, and the trail would now begin to exact its toll on animals and people alike. This theory proved true when she noticed a weathered trunk half-buried by sand alongside the path and, beyond that, a broken rocking chair lying on the ground at a cockeyed angle, as if someone had tossed it there in passing.

She glanced at her family's wagon and envisioned the cargo inside. . .the ornate wooden chests full of pretty dresses and fancy dishes, Papa's books, equipment from his store. Already the oxen strained against the yokes as they plodded along the incline, tails switching periodically at flies. Would the terrain grow continually steeper until her parents, too, had to begin to discard belongings one by one? And if so, what would be left to start their new life in Oregon? Unable to consider the ominous possibility, she took a small book on herbs and plants from her skirt pocket and tried to focus on a more pleasant subject.

When they finally made camp at the end of the long day, folks seemed more eager to eat and turn in than to spend a time singing. But after supper, strains of quiet music drifted from the various wagons as the women in the company settled young children down for the night and the men examined their conveyances for needed repairs.

"I wonder if we even made fifteen miles today," Papa said on a yawn. "And this place has the poorest grass we've seen so far. Hope the cattle find enough to graze on."

"I'm sure they'll do fine," Mama said optimistically, but her troubled frown did not ease in the slightest.

"We should reach Fort Laramie in a couple days," he continued. "We'll be able to stock up on some supplies there."

"Splendid. Maybe I'll post a letter back home. . .I mean, to Myrtle Cromwell," she quickly corrected. "She must be wondering how we're faring on the trip."

The reminder of their former next-door neighbor made Emma feel a pang of homesickness for Philadelphia and all its brick houses and conveniences she had taken for granted. Maybe she'd write to her own best friend also. Likely she'd never see Cynthia Gardner again in this lifetime. That heavy thought pressed the air from her lungs as she put the freshly washed plates and utensils away for morning.

Before getting into her bedroll, she sought a moment of privacy behind one of the larger sage bushes, then returned to the wagon, where she found her two younger siblings already sound asleep.

"Another nice evening," Jesse commented, ambling over to her, his hands in his pockets. "Pretty tough walk today, though. You must be tired."

"About the most tired I've been since Independence," Emma admitted.

"How are you at handling a team of oxen?"

"I beg your pardon?"

Jesse shrugged a shoulder self-consciously. "I was just thinking that maybe I could swap with you from time to time. You could drive my rig, and I could walk."

The suggestion rendered Emma speechless for several seconds before she found her voice. "Actually, I've managed our team quite well, the few times Papa's encouraged me to take over. He felt that Mama and I should know what to do in case of sickness or. . .whatever."

"Well then, what do you think of my idea? After all, it would spell my oxen, too. You're a bit lighter than I am."

"I'll consider it, Jesse. Thank you."

"You're most kindly welcome. Just being a friend. One who won't keep you any longer, since I know you're bone weary. Good night, Emma. Sleep well."

"You, too. Good night." She watched after him as his long strides took him away. This new friendship with the pastor was growing on her quite rapidly. He would make some fortunate woman a thoughtful husband one day. . .assuming, of course, the gal was partial to ministers.

The company lingered at camp the following morning for their usual Sunday service. Emma casually spread out a blanket a little closer to the makeshift pulpit than she had on previous occasions. She and her family took seats while other folks gathered nearby on crates or logs or quilts.

Jesse, in his black preaching suit, stepped to the front, his frayed Bible tucked under his arm. "Let us bow in prayer," he said, then paused briefly. "Our dear Heavenly Father, we do thank Thee for this new day. And we thank Thee most humbly for Thy great kindness in our travels, for keeping us safe, healing our sicknesses, and giving us strength for the daily journey. We ask that we may be conscious of Thy presence every step of the way, that we might serve Thee faithfully. These things we ask in the name of Thy dear Son, Jesus. Amen."

His keen gaze surveyed the little flock of worshipers, then gentled with a smile. "Let's begin our service this Lord's Day by singing "Rock of Ages." He gestured to the men with instruments, who chose a common chord and played a short introduction before the others joined in:

"Rock of ages, cleft for me, let me hide myself in Thee. . . ."

Thankful that nothing horrid had befallen her family thus far, Emma concentrated on the lyrics and sang from her heart, appreciating the harmonious blend of voices through the remaining stanzas of the hymn. She couldn't help but note how pleasantly Jesse's strong, clear tenor fell on her ears.

"This morning," he said, opening his Bible after the final note, "I thought we'd look once again at the life of David—a man whom the Bible describes, in First Samuel chapter thirteen and again in Acts chapter thirteen, as a man after God's own heart. We know him from many angles: shepherd, poet, psalm-writer, killer of giants, king, and lastly, ancestor of our Lord. Yet along with those impressive qualifications, we find that he had obvious flaws as well. Those of liar, betrayer, adulterer, and murderer.

"Strange, isn't it, how those two lists could pertain to one individual? Yet, could it be that David was a picture of all of us? After all, we each have our good points. But we also have our flaws. We might not have made the choices David did, but who among us has not disappointed God and made wrong decisions we later deeply regretted? Fortunately for us, the Lord has not made all of *our* failures known to the world."

"Amen, Brother," one of the listeners said.

Jesse nodded and continued. "So how can it be that the Bible holds David up as an example to us? Let me refer once again to the passage in Acts where it states, 'I have found David, the son of Jesse, a man after mine own heart, *which shall fulfil all my will.'* The last phrase must certainly be the key. David though he sometimes failed, was quick to confess his sin and turn back to God, eager to do His will. Perhaps that is why we remember him and respect him for his godliness. He wanted more than anything to honor God, to do His will. Not many of us will achieve the same level of greatness he did, but we all share that weak, prone-to-sin side."

The simple, yet profound way Jesse preached drew Emma right in. She hung onto his every word as he spoke, taking the concepts to heart, thinking of her own weaknesses. All too aware of areas in her own life that did not please God, she determined to be more conscious of her words and actions in the future.

"So let us close in prayer," the pastor said at last, his voice cutting across her musings. "Dear Lord, help us to be more like Christ, to serve and honor Thee with our lives. Be with us for the remainder of this day as we again take up our westward journey. We ask these things in His holy name, Amen."

After the midday meal, Jesse encouraged Emma to drive his wagon, while he walked alongside. She noted the rig's lighter feel almost at once. Obviously the minister had fewer belongings to weigh it down, and his oxen didn't appear to be laboring quite as intently as most of the others.

When he lagged behind to chat with the men driving the cattle, she chanced a look inside the conveyance and found it surprisingly neat. Other than the typical barrels of foodstuffs and a few crates holding books, his sleeping pallet occupied most of the floor, and some articles of clothing hung on nails about the frame. Since she'd half expected to find it in total disarray, her appreciation for him went up another notch.

Two days later, the welcome sight of Fort Laramie, in a hollow near the mouth of the Laramie River, elevated everyone's spirits. The women immediately went into a frenzy of brushing dust from their dresses, tidying their hair, and making sure their children looked presentable. Then the wagons forded the swift-flowing river at an easy crossing point north of the fort.

The long, low wooden buildings comprising the bastion stretched out in a large circle, within a hollow surrounded by high bluffs dark with cedar trees. A sentry in the blockhouse above the entrance raised a big wooden gate to allow the train to enter.

Emma swallowed nervously at the sight of Indian teepees scattered about the outer perimeter, especially when some red-skinned individuals rose to their feet watching the wagons approach.

"Girls," Papa said, "you'd best climb aboard, just to be safe. Rawhide says they're harmless enough and will probably only beg for food and other essentials."

One by one, rigs to the front stopped near the Indians, who'd spread colorful blankets on the ground. Emma and her family watched as each family contributed something: coffee, sugar, beads and other trinkets, or beans. When it came their turn, Papa gave them some dried antelope jerky, which seemed to satisfy them.

Then he flicked the reins on the oxen's backs, and the wagon slowly moved into the confines of the fort. The great open area inside teemed with even more Indians in buffalo hides, squaws in bright robes, lean and rough-looking frontiersmen, mules, horses, and oxen. Emma couldn't get over the noise of the place as she took in the long barracks, which housed some of the soldiers, then noticed a store, a warehouse, corrals, and other buildings of assorted sizes and purposes.

"It appears safe enough," her father announced above the din, halting the animals. He hopped down, then assisted Mama while the girls fended for themselves. "While you go see what supplies are available, Nettie, I'll check on the latest news from back east. I'll meet you shortly."

"Susan, Deborah," Mama warned after nodding agreement to him. "Stay right by my side, you hear?"

"Yes, Ma'am," they muttered, their eyes bright with excitement.

Before Emma could decide which parent to follow, Jesse came to her side. "Almost like being back in civilization again, eh? Want to do some exploring?"

She sought approval from her mother, then smiled at him. "Sounds delightful. What all is there to see?"

"Who knows? I've never been here before. We'll make the rounds of the whole place. There are probably too many ladies at the store right now anyway. My supplies can wait until later."

Somehow, with Jesse Brewster beside her, Emma no longer felt apprehensive about the Indians or other odd-looking individuals loitering about, gawking at the travelers. That experience, an entirely new one for her, sent a surge of warmth through her being.

In the evening the women prepared another company feast, which some of the folks living at the fort attended with dishes of their own, and a great time of singing and square dancing followed. Enjoying the festivities with Jesse, Emma knew she'd be a long time forgetting the special night.

The wagon train spent an extra day at Fort Laramie to rest the animals after the long haul. But all too soon, the respite came to an end, and it was time to continue. In the chill morning air, they took their leave.

This time, they acquired a new member, one on horseback. Rather tall and sinewy, with dark hair and green eyes, he spoke in a slow drawl, announcing his name as Bernard Williams. He seemed friendly enough as he introduced himself to everyone, yet he stayed mostly to himself as he observed the travelers with more than a little interest.

The road leading west from the fort marked the beginning of the Black Hills. Emma, walking beside her family's wagon, focused her gaze on the low, ragged summits, which appeared to hold up the sky itself.

Before long they passed more discarded baggage. Strange items like anvils, bellows, and tools of all sorts. Buckets and spades, mirrors and trunks, cast aside as if of no importance whatsoever. She cast a worried glance at her papa's rig, calculating the weight of their earthly belongings. . .and once again, she felt a foreboding that the worst was yet to come.

Chapter 4

Traveling the more rugged climb west from Fort Laramie, Emma became increasingly disheartened at the number of castoff belongings littering the countryside, many of which had been burned beyond recognition. She tried to put them and the occasional skeleton of an ox out of her mind. Then she spied a cookstove and an intricately fashioned mantel clock beside the trail. Neither of them bore a speck of dirt or rain damage, so she could only conclude they had been discarded from wagons farther up front. She wondered which of the families she'd become acquainted with on the trip had been forced to part with such treasures.

Her father no longer rode in the wagon, but tramped beside the oxen, a bullwhip in his hand to prod them along. Finally he shook his head and signaled to the wagons behind before halting the animals altogether.

"What's wrong?" her mother asked, joining him, her fine features drawn with worry.

Emma held her breath, dreading the answer.

He removed his wide-brimmed hat and swiped a sleeve across his forehead. Then he shook his head. "Look at those poor beasts, sides heaving, all but foaming at the mouth. No sense in killing them just for the sake of a couple of trunks, is there?"

She paled. "But Ambrose. We've already discussed this. My dad carved those for each of the girls to be their hope chests one day."

Inside, Emma knew her mother had offered only a futile argument, but she couldn't help hoping it would somehow forestall the inevitable.

Defeat colored his tone as he raised sad eyes to hers. "I'm sorry, Love. I was hoping it wouldn't come to this, but it's the only merciful thing to do at this point."

"I'll go empty them," she said in a flat tone, tears shimmering on her lashes. One broke free and rolled down her face, leaving a moist track on her trail-dusted cheek.

"I'll help you, Mama," Emma blurted. Anything to keep from crying herself. What else would this trip cost them? She couldn't watch when her father hefted each beautiful trunk onto his shoulder and set it carefully beside the trail, along with some heavy apothecary jars and other weighty items from his store. She focused her attention ahead, watching Jesse's lighter wagon lumbering ever onward.

A short while later, Susan and Deborah stumbled upon some bushes sporting currants and chokecherries, which other folks in the party had also taken advantage of. Emma grabbed a pail from the wagon and the three girls gathered what they could to be used later in baking. . .a small blessing on an otherwise difficult day.

Their troubles worsened as they now faced a sharp descent down a steeply washed break in the bluffs, known as Mexican Hill. The wagons creaked and groaned, the oxen bawled in protest, and men exerted all their strength to keep each rig from breaking free of the restraints and charging downward out of control. When at last the final one made it successfully, they took a break and nooned at the river.

Mama barely spoke as she served the cold beans and biscuits left over from breakfast. Papa remained silent as well, though he spread a blanket out for her in the shade of the wagon where she could have a short siesta after they finished eating.

Emma took the soiled dishes to the river and stooped down to wash them.

Jesse sauntered toward her, hatless, his wild, sun-bleached curls stirring on the breeze. "I carved our initials in the Register Cliffs," he announced cheerfully.

"Are you serious?" She stood and shook the excess water from the stack.

"Of course," he answered, his blue eyes twinkling. "Someday somebody might be interested to know that J. B. and E. H., whoever we were, passed this way in 1860."

"I can imagine. We were ever so fascinating." Despite her wry tone, Emma felt strangely pleased at his action. . .and thought about it all afternoon as the train continued.

A couple of miles brought them to the most amazing cut in the entire overland road. . .shoulder-deep ruts etched into the solid sandstone, barely wide enough for a wagon. The bullwhackers and other travelers afoot had also worn narrow pathways in the rock over the years, but nowhere as deep as those carved by the wagon wheels. It felt weird, Emma thought, to be walking on higher ground than the rigs through that section.

In the evening, they camped at Warm Spring, in the canyon

of a small tributary of the Platte. Emma's gaze drank in the drift of fragile, downy fluff, shed by the ragged foliage of a grove of cottonwood trees. And it didn't take long for her and the other women to make a beeline for the warm pool occupying the middle of the grove.

"Doesn't this feel elegant?" fellow traveler Penny said on a sigh, rinsing soap from her golden hair. "First water in weeks that's been heated for us."

Still sudsing her light brown locks, her sister-in-law, Bethany, giggled. "Do you suppose uppity Lavinia will impose upon poor Katie to draw her a proper bath?"

Megan and Emma chuckled along with the others. "Thanks, Emma," the blond said, handing the soap to her now that it had made the rounds. "That rose scent is wonderful."

"You're welcome. My father used to sell it in the store."

"If we ever get to Oregon," Penny breathed, "I'm going to positively drown myself in cologne and toilet water for a month. Anything to forget the smell of dust."

"I hope that's possible," Emma mused.

"What?" Bethany said teasingly. "Getting to Oregon or forgetting the dust?"

"Both. I don't think we're even halfway there yet."

"Don't remind us!" Megan chimed in, wrapping her long hair in a towel.

Emma squeezed the water from her own, then followed suit, observing her mother as she washed her younger siblings' hair not far away. Oh, but it felt good to be clean again.

When some of the rambunctious boys in the company returned from exploring and reported the source of the pool as a refreshing spring gushing from a nearby hillside, folks gladly went there and filled their water barrels and other containers with the clean, clear water for tomorrow's journey.

❧

Jesse gave the wheels of his wagon close inspection, then liberally greased the hubs with tallow and tar. The miles covered were taking a toll on everything and everyone, and he knew it was only a matter of time before someone broke a wheel or an axle. As it was, one of his oxen had picked up a pebble in his hoof earlier in the day; but as soon as Jesse noticed him favoring that foot, he quickly pulled off to one side and allowed the remaining few wagons to pass him by while he dug the offending stone out. After the noon rest, the animal seemed fine, thank the Lord.

Finished with the nightly chores, he lowered himself to the ground beside Barnabas and reclined against one of the wheels, marveling at the great job Emma had done handling the team. And she hadn't seemed annoyed when he'd mentioned carving their initials in the soft rock of the Register Cliffs. He wondered what her reaction would be if he'd told her about the *other* set he'd carved. . .J. B. and E. B. He had to admit, "Emma Brewster" had a mighty nice ring to it. The more he got to know her, the more convinced he became that God had positioned their wagons the way they'd ended up. . . and he had a fairly good idea why. The problem was persuading Emma of that.

It struck him as ironic how weary of the endless trail so many folks had grown, while he was praying it would be long enough! He knew he had his work cut out for him.

Even as he sat there stroking Barney's stringy fur, he watched his beautiful neighbor return from the pond, her damp, brunette waves splayed about her shoulders. His fingers itched to lace themselves through those glorious tresses. But he maintained a casual expression when she caught his eye.

"You should try that water," she said airily. "It's truly wonderful."

"I'd imagine once all you ladies are through, we fellows will make our way over there. Even Barney's in dire need of a good washing."

She smiled and dropped down beside the two of them. "I'm glad today has ended. The climb, the hill." Then her expression turned serious. "We passed so many belongings. So many graves. It's hard to imagine what people had left—if anything."

"Maybe that's why the Lord encourages us not to set our hearts on earthly treasures," he said gently. "Nothing is forever here."

Emma met his gaze, her own troubled. "Do you think we'll ever really make it to Oregon?"

"Well, I'm sure hoping we will. God's been pretty merciful to us so far. The weather's been mostly pleasant, even now with the cool nights and frosty mornings. And only a few folks have gotten sick. Nobody's had a major breakdown with a wagon, either."

"But there's still such a long road ahead."

"We don't have to travel it all at once, remember. Just a day at a time. Let's just leave the future in God's hands."

Her sable eyes turned to his for an eternal moment, and she smiled. "Somehow, put that way, it doesn't sound quite so hopeless." She paused. "Would you care to have supper with us tonight?"

"Are you sure it's no trouble?"

"Of course."

"Then, I'd be honored."

"And I'd best get busy, in that case. Thanks for the visit." Scrambling to her feet, Emma gave Barney a parting pat, then hurried to her family's wagon.

❧

Even as Emma peeled the young potatoes and carrots they'd acquired at the fort, her mind refused to let go of Jesse Brewster. She'd never known a minister so near her own age before. . .or one so sensitive and thoughtful. Having heard a number of his sermons, she had no doubt that he was a true man of God. And having spent extra time with him aside from his official duties, she felt he had also become a true friend.

She dreaded the thought of his wagon rotating again to the back of the line, knowing that for an entire day, she would have no one to talk to until their wagon joined his once more.

And how sweet, his having carved his and her initials in the rocks for future travelers to see. What an amazing man.

"The meat is browned now," Mama said, lifting the lid on the pot. "You can add those vegetables to the water anytime."

"Yes, Ma'am." She shoved the potatoes, onions, and carrots off the cutting board into the pan. "I've invited Jesse to supper this evening. Do you mind?"

"Not at all. He's a fine, personable young man. Certainly an asset to this company." Her mother tipped her head and eyed her. "You've been spending quite a lot of time with the pastor, I've noticed."

"He's nice to talk to, is all," Emma hedged. But even as she answered, she knew deep inside there were a lot of things about Jesse she liked besides his talking. And the list was growing by the day. That realization stunned her. Maybe it wasn't such a good idea to become too attached to someone who'd be setting off for parts unknown soon after reaching Oregon.

On the other hand, if she stayed focused on her own goals, perhaps it wouldn't hurt to enjoy this friendship, however temporary, as long as it lasted. She could deal with the loss when the time came.

Half an hour later, the pastor made his appearance, scrubbed clean, his wild hair damp and slicked back. He'd changed to navy trousers and a green checked shirt, with the sleeves rolled partway up. "Evening," he said simply, and his smile made Emma's heart skip a beat.

"Good evening." She took in his broad shoulders and sun-browned forearms. . .and decided he looked like anything *but* a minister. In fact, she had to instruct herself to refrain from gaping like a lovesick schoolgirl. Strange, that his presence would suddenly affect her so. This would never do. Never.

"We're so glad you could come to supper, Reverend," she heard her mother say as she stepped forward.

"It's an honor to be invited, Mrs. Harris," he replied. "And I'd prefer being called Jesse." He held out a wedge of cheese. "Thought I might contribute."

"Why, thank you. That's very thoughtful." She turned to Susan and Deborah, standing near the barrel topped by nailed-together planks of wood, which served as their table. "Girls, go tell your papa that supper is ready, will you?"

"Yes, Ma'am," they chorused and ran off toward where he chatted with men tending the cattle.

Moments later, everyone took seats on the upended crates they used as chairs. The parents faced each other across the makeshift tabletop, the girls occupied one side, and Emma and Jesse the other. Emma suppressed her silly nervousness and did her best to relax.

Papa's mustache widened into a smile. "Would you do the honors, Jesse?"

"Certainly. Dear Lord, we thank Thee for Thy presence day by day and Thy bountiful goodness to us. Please bless this wonderful meal and the hands that prepared it. May we be faithful to do Thy will. In Christ's name, Amen."

"Amen," the others echoed.

Mama stood, ladled portions of stew into each bowl, and passed them around.

"Mmm. Looks as delicious as it smells," Jesse commented. "Tastes even better," he added after digging in.

Mama beamed. "Thank you."

"So, Jesse," Papa began. "What are your plans once we arrive at Trail's End? Is there a church waiting for you there?" He took a spoonful of the rich stew.

"No, Sir," Jesse replied candidly, helping himself to a golden biscuit. "I'm not entirely certain yet what the Lord's plans are. I only know He's called me to go out West, so that's what I'm doing. I figure when I get there, He'll show me the next step."

"But he hopes to build a great church in time," Emma chimed in. Setting her water cup down, her arm accidentally brushed his, and a maddening flush of warmth flooded her neck and slowly rose upward.

He didn't seem to notice her discomfort. "That's true. But only if it's God's will for me."

"From that fine preaching we've heard these past Sunday

mornings," Papa said, "that shouldn't be a problem. Good churches are sorely needed now that the West is filling with new families."

"I only hope there's one within traveling distance of where we'll be living," Mama ventured. "I have no idea of what to expect, really."

"That's what makes this such an adventure," Papa said cheerfully. "Everything will be new."

Emma caught her mother's ambiguous expression and related to it completely. If the two of them would have had their preference, they'd still be living in that stately brick house in Philadelphia, within easy traveling distance to church, school, stores, and even a college or two. But it was far too late for looking back now. They could only wait and see what the future held.

"Do try some of Emma's pan cookies, Jesse," Mama offered, once everyone had finished the last drop of stew. "The currants the girls found were just the right touch."

"We picked almost every one that was left on those bushes," Deborah said proudly.

"But we shared some with Granny Willodene, since she said her bones were too old to go chasing off into pickery places," Susan added.

"That was the Christian thing to do," Jesse said. "God is pleased when we share with others. And I don't mind a bit trying one of Emma's creations," he went on, bestowing a warm smile on her.

"I did my best," she said lightly. "Things don't always turn out right when cooking outside."

He took one from the plate and bit off a chunk, chewing

slowly, thoughtfully. "They are very good, I must say. Very good, indeed."

Emma smiled her thanks.

"Well," Jesse said after finishing his coffee and another cookie, "I thank you for this wonderful meal, Mr. and Mrs. Harris. It was a real treat not to eat my own cooking."

"We've enjoyed having you," Mama said. "Emma, Dear, the girls and I will clean up this time. You two young people go and have a nice walk before it gets chilly out."

Jesse looked rather pleased by her mother's suggestion and offered an arm as he stood to his feet. "Shall we?"

"All right," Emma said hesitantly. She hadn't planned on this, but she did enjoy being with him. Rising, she drew a calming breath and slipped a hand through the crook of his elbow.

The evening truly was pleasant, but without the sun's warmth, the temperature hinted at approaching coolness while they started around the encampment.

"We probably shouldn't stay out long," Emma suggested. "It's been a terribly hard day."

"Yes. Folks always seem to stick close to their wagons after a troublesome time on the road. Not much energy left for singing and frolicking." He paused. "I surely do enjoy your family. It's easy to see where you obtained many of your own fine qualities."

"What a flattering thing to say," Emma breathed, awed at how he could put her at ease.

"I didn't mean it as flattery. You truly do have some fine qualities, Emma," he said quietly, gazing down at her with those soul-searching eyes of his.

She had no idea how to respond. Her awareness of him

was too new. Should she encourage him? Not encourage him? End the friendship here and now? "So do you," she finally said. "I'm glad we're. . .friends."

He took the hint and focused ahead once again. "Well," he said as they approached her family's wagon, "sleep well, Emma. Thanks for the invite."

"You're most kindly welcome," she said and clapped a mental hand over her mouth before she said something she might regret later. She had some deep thinking to do. And some praying.

Chapter 5

After contaminated water along the Platte caused a few queasy stomachs and the loss of two oxen, the Black Hills seemed like heaven. Sweet-scented herbs and sage permeated the air of its hills and valleys, and pure water uplifted the spirit and strengthened the weak. Mountain cherries and currants grew in abundance, along with luxuriant tangles of wild roses in sheltered spots; and broad brush strokes of larkspur, blue flax, and wild tulips streaked the slopes with breathtaking color. Solitary buffalo bulls roaming the ravines provided variety to the sameness of everyone's diet.

The frequent rains that washed through the hills slowed travel considerably, however, increasing wheel breakage and causing tempers to grow short.

Beyond Horseshoe Creek, where the road climbed to the crest of a dividing ridge, the emigrants had an inspiring view of Laramie Peak. They crossed several little mountain streams that day. But the rocks of this section were particularly abrasive and wore the animals' hooves to the quick, laming several. Bickering began among the weary travelers.

When folks assembled for the Sunday service, the sullen

expressions that met Jesse's gaze seemed as dark as the clouds churning overhead. He felt the awesome weight of the responsibility he'd taken on as the company preacher and prayed that God would give him the right words to soothe, encourage, and comfort the people he had grown to know and care about.

"This morning's text is taken from Ephesians, the fourth chapter, verse thirty-two," he began. " 'And be ye kind one to another, tenderhearted, forgiving one another, even as God for Christ's sake hath forgiven you.' "

More than a few folks dropped their gazes to the ground, and square-built farmer Homer Green rubbed a sheepish hand over his grizzled face when his wife, Geneva, elbowed him in the ribs.

Nonplussed, Jesse plunged on. "Despite the hardships of this past week—and I know they've been many—it would benefit us to remember we are in God's loving hands. He has led us these many miles and protected us from all sorts of misfortunes commonly endured by people who've gone this way before. We may have lost a few animals, a broken wheel has delayed us now and again, but so far we're all still present and accounted for. That in itself is a blessing, is it not?"

A few grudging nods made the rounds, and he observed a noticeable softening of demeanors in the crowd. Encouraged, he glanced down at his notes to check his next point.

Emma drew her woolen shawl more closely about herself in the cool breeze and glanced up at the sky every few minutes while Jesse preached, wondering if the storm would hold off until he finished. She'd never seen clouds of that peculiar greenish hue before and could tell from other people's expressions that they, too, found the color eerie.

"And so, dear friends," Jesse was saying, "in closing, remember the God to Whom we belong. Think about your own personal failures He has so lovingly forgiven, and then endeavor to be patient with each other, just as you were at the beginning of this trip. Do whatever possible to support the neighbor traveling in front and in back of you. Encourage rather than criticize, help rather than ignore, bearing in mind that you, too, may soon find yourself in need of help from your fellow travelers. Showing the love of Christ to one another will smooth the distance yet to be covered. Now, let us pray."

The first sprinkles dotted Emma's faded skirt before Jesse's final amen. And within mere seconds, pelting rain sent folks scattering for shelter.

Emma and her family barely made it to their wagon before the downpour turned to hail. . .dreadful hail larger than oxen eyes. The cruel ice balls lashed at wagons, plummeting through sun-weakened spots in the bowed canvas tops and ricocheting off the hard surface of the seats in a cacophony of unbelievable clatter.

"Everyone down on the floor," Papa hollered above the unearthly racket, and he quickly drew extra canvas coverings from the barrels and positioned himself over them all as they huddled together with their arms around each other.

Chills raced along Emma's spine at the distant sounds of women and children screaming. . .and worse, the animals out in the open, bawling with no way to escape the brutal torture. Once during the onslaught, she even heard Barnabas howl in pain and prayed that Jesse was safe, that his beloved dog hadn't been seriously injured.

After an indeterminate time, the merciless pounding ceased, leaving the breathing of her dear ones as the only sound within the confines of their temporary haven.

Icy balls clunked onto the floor when Papa raised the canvas to peer out from under it, and they stared slack-jawed at the jagged tears in the wagon's bonnet, the accumulated hail near the front already melding together in globs of white.

"I wonder if anything's broken," Mama said, getting up from her cramped position, her voice strained.

"Time will tell," Papa replied. "Is anyone hurt?" At the collective shaking of heads, he gave a resigned nod. "Then I'd best check the oxen, see how they fared."

While Deborah and Susan started collecting chunks of ice and tossing them outside, Emma surveyed the number of torn spots in the canvas top and knew she and her mother would be busy mending and patching for awhile.

The two of them looked up at the sound of approaching hoofbeats and saw the trail master's leathery face peer into the wagon. "Anybody hurt here?" Rawhide asked around the wad of tobacco in his leathery cheek.

"No, praise the Lord," Mama replied.

He nodded. "Well, a few of the company suffered a blow or two, and there's a few oxen down. We'd best use the rest of today for repairs, see if we can get on the road again in the morning."

"Fine," she said with a thin smile, then turned to her brood as he rode on. "Well, girls, looks like we're going to have a busy day. Susan, Deborah, check to see what bedding and clothing need drying out. Emma, let's see if we can remove the wagon's bonnet without your papa's help. Likely he'll have his hands full elsewhere for awhile."

❧

Relieved to find only one small tear in his wagon's top, Jesse checked Barnabas over thoroughly and gave him a hug. "That sore bump will get better pretty quick, old boy. Soon as I get rid of the hail in here, I'd better put this morning's sermon into action."

Hopping down, moments later, he followed his heart to Emma's wagon. Her younger siblings were hard at work draping bedding over the wheels to dry, while she and her mother panted with the effort of removing the canvas top. "Need a hand?" he asked and climbed aboard to give assistance.

Emma's grateful smile did crazy things to his insides. "How's Barney?" she asked, stepping out of his way.

"He got conked on the head once or twice before scrambling out of the fray and has the lumps to prove it, but other than that, he seems okay. Here, Mrs. Harris, I'll get that for you."

"Why, thank you. Did your top stay intact?"

"All except one small spot near the back."

"As soon as Emma and I finish mending this one, we'll see to yours."

"I'd appreciate that. Once I get this off, I'll move my stuff out of your way."

By the end of the day, thanks to a cooperative effort from the menfolk, all major repairs to the wagons were finished, and the nimble-fingered women had set the bowed covers to rights.

An ox belonging to the tall, rawboned carpenter, Zach Sawyer, had suffered mortal wounds and was immediately butchered to feed the camp. But no one displayed the wherewithal for gaiety around the campfire while they ate the tough beef. Jesse decided a special prayer meeting might be more beneficial. At the conclusion of the meal, everyone joined hands in a circle and thanked God for seeing them through the trial, then lifted individual needs to the Lord. . .but with Emma's small hand dwarfed in his, Jesse had all he could do to concentrate on praying.

❧

Emma felt the warmth and strength of Jesse's grip even after he released her hand. She gazed up at him as he said a few parting words to stragglers who lingered to talk. And even though she had no reason to stay, she couldn't seem to make her feet walk away. She found the calming effect the pastor had on troubled hearts fascinating to observe.

Finally, only the two of them remained. Jesse focused those dark blue eyes on her and smiled. "I do believe the Lord comforted a few souls this day. I, for one, feel more conscious of His presence, His hand."

"You truly have a way with people," Emma said, thinking aloud. "You always seem to know the right words to help them."

His smile relaxed a bit. "I try. Sometimes those who are weary and at the end of themselves just need someone to bolster them again. To keep their hope alive. Oft times it's a soul rather than a body that's sick and in need of a touch, a smile, a helping hand. There is any number of ways for us to do something of worth with our lives. Think about that for awhile, will you?"

Not entirely certain where the conversation was leading, Emma had no immediate answer.

Jesse brushed a fingertip along the curve of her cheekbone, his gaze never leaving her face. "You have a wonderful heart, Emma. One God can use in more ways than you can imagine. . . if you'll allow Him to do so."

Her whole being tingled from his touch. "I. . .I'm afraid to let go of my dreams. It's like standing on the edge of a precipice and having no idea where the next step will lead."

"But if your hand is in His, there's no reason to fear. That's where trust comes in. The step is not hidden from Him."

"I don't know if I'm ready to do that," she murmured as he offered an arm and started with her toward her family's wagon.

"Well, God isn't going anywhere, my friend. He'll wait for you to commit your future into His keeping. Sometimes," he added, an impish spark in his eyes, "His plans turn out to be far better than our own."

But it certainly didn't feel that way to Emma. By honoring her parents, she was being taken far away from the possibility of fulfilling her dreams. Yet she couldn't quite relinquish the last ounce of hope of becoming a doctor. Nothing else could hold a candle to that pursuit.

Arriving back at her father's wagon, Emma fully intended to take out another of his books and read for awhile. But she saw her mother hurrying toward her, out of breath.

"Emma, have you seen the girls?"

"No, not since the prayer service. Perhaps they went looking for more berries or flowers."

"Well, I hope they come back soon. I worry when they go off without telling me where they're going. It gets dark early here in the mountains."

"I'll go look for them, if it'll make you feel better," Emma suggested.

"And I'll keep your daughter company," Jesse quickly assured her.

"Oh, would you? I'd sorely appreciate it."

After making the rounds of the camp without success, Emma and Jesse headed into the surrounding countryside, searching the rocky contours and outcroppings for any splashes of color that might stand out against the earth's hues.

"How about over there?" Emma asked, looking off into the distance, where two husky young boys were playing leapfrog in a bowl-like meadow.

"No, looks like Homer Green's kids," Jesse told her. "They might know something, though. Let's find out." Taking her hand, he quickened his pace, and they reached the lads a few moments later. "Either of you seen Susan and Deborah Harris?" he asked.

Two freckled faces grew serious as they stopped their play. "Nope," one of them said.

"Well," the other added, "awhile back we was playin' Hide-and-Go-Seek with 'em, but they got tired of it and wanted to do somethin' else."

"Which way did they go?" Emma asked, alarm racing through her.

He pointed farther up the next rise. "They was lookin' for flowers to make a crown or somethin', they said."

"Thanks." Jesse gave the closest boy a pat on his shoulder. "You two should head back to camp now, before your folks decide to come looking for you."

"Yes, Sir," they chorused and dashed off.

"Where could my sisters be?" Emma moaned in despair. "What if darkness falls before we find them?"

"It won't. There's light aplenty left, if we hurry. Come on. Deborah!" he hollered. "Susan!"

Emma added her voice to his and called out their names at

the same time, hoping the extra volume would help.

Following what appeared to be an Indian trail, they finally heard Deborah's voice answer one of their calls.

Relief flooded through Emma. "When I lay my hands on those two, I'm going to shake them till their teeth chatter," she said and broke into a run.

Jesse easily kept up.

Rounding one of a series of boulders, they caught a glimpse of the girls standing stiff as broomsticks and huddled together.

"Hurry!" Deborah cried. "Please, hurry. Please!"

Panic flooded through Emma. She would have sprinted the rest of the way, but Jesse stayed her with an arm.

"No. Wait. I'll go. I'll holler if I need you."

An uncanny foreboding rooted her to the spot. Her pulse increased as she watched him approach the rocky clearing where the girls stood. She couldn't understand why he was moving so slowly, so cautiously. Hadn't Deborah pleaded for him to hurry?

Very slowly, she saw him pick Deborah up into his arms, then just as slowly set her down again on his other side. The girl immediately darted toward Emma. He then bent to pick up Susan.

The child's piercing scream tore through the air.

Jesse held her tight and bolted up the rise.

"Is she all right?" Emma cried anxiously as Deborah collapsed, sobbing, into her arms with a single word. "S–s–snakes."

"She's fine," Jesse said, an odd expression on his face.

"The snake!" Susan cried. "It struck at me, but Mr. Jesse didn't let it get me. It bit him instead!"

Emma felt the blood leave her face as she watched the pastor turn ashen and sink to his knees.

"No!" she screamed. "No! Please, please, be all right." Then reason seized her. "Girls. Run for help. As fast as you can. Get Doc Rogers. Papa, too. Hurry!"

"I'm. . .okay," Jesse said, not quite managing a smile. But his complexion said otherwise.

"What can I do?" Emma asked, her mind going blank as she knelt down beside him. "Where did you get bitten?"

"My right leg. Just above my boot."

"Tourniquet. We need a tourniquet," she muttered to herself. She had no apron on today; her petticoat would have to do. Tearing a strip from the bottom edge, she tied it tightly below his knee. "Do you have a pocketknife?"

"Usually," he said, his voice strangely weak. "But not today."

Emma searched helplessly about for something—anything—sharp. Nothing. *Please, God, bring help fast. Please, don't let Jesse die. We need him. I need him.* Not knowing what else to do, she put her arms around him and held him close.

Chapter 6

In between frantic, wordless prayers, Emma rocked her friend in her arms. "It'll be all right, Jesse. You'll see. Just hold on. Please, hold on." But already he was drifting in and out of consciousness and moaning, and she didn't like his coloring at all. She finally eased his head down onto her lap and waited for help to arrive.

When her father and dark-haired Josh Rogers came running, the young physician wasted no time in slitting Jesse's pant leg to the knee, while her pa carefully tugged off the pastor's boot, revealing the angry-looking fang marks in Jesse's rapidly swelling limb. The doctor made two slices across the wound, then sucked out as much venom-tainted blood as possible, spitting it off to the side. His expression revealed little as he worked, but Emma could see the concern darkening his blue eyes.

"He'll be okay, won't he?" she had to ask.

Doc Rogers opened a bottle of spirits and doused the injury, then met her eyes. "He belongs to God, Emma. We'll just have to do our best and trust that His will be done."

"I hate it when people say that," she muttered, gazing down at Jesse and stroking his hair. It felt silky and soft, and the tawny curls lay against his face as he slept, making him look especially vulnerable and young. So young.

"I've brought some hartshorn," Papa said, holding out a small vial. "It often helps this kind of thing."

"We'll try everything we've got," the doctor said. After applying some of the ammonia preparation, he took a roll of bandage out of his medical bag and wrapped Jesse's calf. "We'd best get him back to the wagon now and keep him as quiet as possible. I'll stay with him through the night. Longer, if needed. After that, even if he pulls through, he'll need someone at his side all the time for awhile."

If he pulls through. Emma dismissed that statement immediately. He'd pull through if she had anything to say about it. "I'll stay with him," she blurted. "I've been driving his wagon for days."

"I don't know if that's such a good idea, Sweetheart," her father protested. "Folks might get the wrong idea."

Emma raised her chin. "Folks? We're supposed to care about *other folks* at a time like this? When Jesse might be—" She swallowed the hateful word. "When Jesse has no one to care for him? You and Mama would be right behind me."

He released a slow breath. "I see your point. But first we're going to have our hands full just getting him through the long hours ahead." He turned to the doctor. "I'll assist you, Josh, all during the night if you need me."

"Thanks. But right now we'd best get him back to camp." Stooping over, he slid his arms under Jesse's limp ones and raised his torso, while Papa picked up his legs. "Mind bringing my bag, Emma?" the doctor asked.

Not trusting her voice, she gave a nod and plucked up the

medical kit and Jesse's boot. Then she walked beside him throughout the slow trek back to his wagon.

By the time they arrived, the entire camp had heard the news. Emma pictured Deborah spreading the tale of her and Susan's harrowing experience. She looked from one grim face to the next as the company clustered around Jesse's rig.

"How is the dear pastor?" Lavinia Millberg whispered, twisting a silk handkerchief in her hands, her plump face contorted with anxiety. It was the first time Emma had ever seen the pampered brunette concerned for someone besides herself.

"Dr. Rogers has done all that's possible for now. We can only wait. And pray." Even as she spoke the words, Emma straightened her shoulders and faced the crowd. "Earlier this evening," she said in a voice everyone could hear, "the pastor held a special prayer meeting to pray for us. Now we must gather together and pray for him."

"Is that our shy Emma?" she heard her father ask as he and the doctor gently eased Jesse up into his wagon.

But she paid his comment little mind and maintained her focus.

"Of course, Dear," her mother said, and others nodded in agreement.

A circle took shape as the folks from the surrounding conveyances joined hands.

"I'll begin," Emma went on, "and any of you who wish to add a prayer of your own, please feel free to do so." She bowed her head. "Our precious Heavenly Father, we bring Your loyal servant before You at this time. He suffered a grave wound while bravely saving two defenseless children, and now he needs Your healing touch. Please remember his faithfulness to You, the way he has shared the truth of Your Word with us during our journey. And please, please heal him. We need him so." Her voice broke on the last phrase, and she couldn't hold back her tears.

Others quickly took up the petition, and to a person, everyone pleaded for Jesse's life to be spared, even the lean newcomer, Bernard Williams, who'd joined the company at Fort Laramie. Later, after the final amen died away and they'd sung a hymn of assurance, they drifted back to their own wagons.

Rawhide, however, moved quietly among them, spreading the word that the train would be laying by for at least a day.

In her bedroll, Emma barely slept a wink between praying and all her tossing and turning. At first light, when the men rose to tend the animals, she slipped to Jesse's wagon, which glowed from the lamp Doc Rogers had kept burning through the night. She gave a comforting pat to Barnabas when he raised his head and blinked his sad brown eyes, but it was her father's face she sought.

He looked up with a grave smile. "He's still with us," he said softly. "But it looks pretty bad. His entire leg is horribly swollen, and he's still unconscious and feverish. Doc and I are trying to bring his temperature down with cool cloths. Maybe you could get us some more water."

"Of course," she whispered. Taking the bucket he held out, she hurried to the river and filled it, praying all the way that the doctor's treatment would work, that God would intervene, that Jesse would make it.

But even though camp activity was subdued out of respect, he showed no improvement at all. Emma called another prayer meeting that night.

Rawhide was leery of holding the train up any longer, so the following morning, the procession of wagons moved out again, with Emma driving her family's wagon, her father taking over Jesse's, and Doc Rogers maintaining his bedside vigil. His bride, Bethany, handled theirs. Emma no longer took any delight in the passing scenery and, in fact, didn't even notice it, concentrating intently on the rig ahead.

At the noon stop, Papa hopped down and came straight to her. "Jesse's fever seems to have broken. He's still pretty sick, and there's a lot of swelling yet, but the doc thinks he's seeing some improvement."

At that news, Emma drew her first real breath since the incident happened. "Thank You, God," she murmured, then opened her eyes once more. "Can I see him?"

"I don't know if he's quite ready to receive visitors just yet, Sweetheart. But he mentioned your name quite often in his delirium. Let's give him at least until tomorrow."

Reluctantly, she agreed, but drew hope from knowing that even during such a difficult trial he'd thought of her.

During the noon stop the following day, Doc Rogers finally decided it was safe to leave his patient and return to his pretty wife, whose face lit up at the sight of him as she flew into his open arms. The tender embrace they shared touched Emma deeply, awakening new yearnings in her own heart. She cast an impatient glance toward the pastor's wagon.

Papa beckoned to her from the opening!

Her pulse pounding in her throat, Emma went over and climbed aboard, barely aware that he took his leave at the same moment.

Her eyes adjusted quickly to the dim canvas-covered interior.

She caught Jesse's gaze and weak smile from where he sat propped up on his sleeping mat, pillows and rolled blankets behind his back. Noticeably gaunt and pale, he wore a nightshirt, open at the throat. A sheet covered him from the waist down. So much emotion clogged Emma's throat, she didn't dare attempt to speak.

"Well, if it isn't the gal who saved my life," he said, his voice barely half what it normally was.

"Saved your life?" she choked out. "I've done nothing but pray since you got bitten. Pa and Doc Rogers wouldn't let me anywhere near you."

A faint smile lifted a corner of his mouth. "Nothing better than prayer. But I'm talking about the tourniquet." He paused momentarily from the effort of talking and drew a labored breath. "Doc says if not for that, I'd be greeting weary travelers at heaven's gates now."

"Oh, Jesse," she whispered, sinking to her knees at his side. "We—*I*—don't know what I'd have done if I'd lost you. I once thought I was the one standing on a precipice. . .but that was nothing compared to what you've been through. I see so many things differently now."

He gave a slight nod, but when he blinked, she could see his eyelids growing heavy. She took his hand in hers, shocked at how utterly lifeless it seemed. "I know you need to rest to get your strength back. I'll bring you some broth later. Don't worry about anything. We're looking after Barnabas." *And I'll look after you,* her heart added as he dozed off.

❧

"Driver. Driver!" Jesse called out. "Take it easy, will you?"

"What do you mean?" Emma asked ever so innocently over her shoulder.

He snorted. "What good is saving a fellow's life if you're gonna shake his bones to pieces on this rough road, I'd like to know?"

"Complain, complain," she singsonged. "How quickly we forget our blessings."

"Yes, well, I'll tell you a thing or two about blessings when we make camp this eve, Emma-girl."

"Be still, my heart," she countered.

But Jesse knew from her tone she was as thankful as he that the Lord had spared him. She'd devoted herself to helping him regain his strength, bringing nourishing food at every meal, driving the wagon, tending to Barney and the oxen. He could feel life slowly returning to his bones. . .and love for Emma Harris growing ever deeper in his heart.

She sat with her back to him, handling the traces as the oxen plodded along, and his eyes devoured the sight of the shining sable hair trailing from beneath her sunbonnet, her slim form, her determination. He'd purposely avoided expressing his feelings as yet, but once he regained his normal strength, he fully intended to question her about the statement she'd made days ago. Somewhat fuzzy in his brain, he seemed to recall her saying something about seeing things differently. And he glimpsed a most radiant glow in her eyes whenever she looked into his. Jesse hoped it meant what he'd been praying for.

She'd told him about the difficult sections of the trail he'd missed due to his unconscious state. He had a hard time envisioning infamous Rock Avenue, with its hideous stretch of deformed rock strata jutting up from the earth to torture the feet of travelers and animals, or the alkali swamps, steep hills, odorous mineral springs. Now he had even more respect for the pharmacist's stalwart daughter for managing his rig so competently.

Tonight, he allowed Emma and her father to help him off his sleeping pallet so he could enjoy the music around the campfire. For days he'd been staring at the bowed top, just as a prisoner must ogle iron bars, and felt desperate to breathe air that didn't smell like medicine. But the effort required to make his rubbery legs function had him bathed in perspiration before they even got him to the rocking chair someone had thoughtfully provided. Emma brought along a blanket, however, to ward off the chill mountain air and wrapped it about him.

"How's our patient doing this evening?" Doc Rogers asked, strolling toward him with a doting Bethany on his arm.

"Looks like I'll live after all. Thanks to God, Emma and her father, and you. And," he added, including the encampment, "everyone's prayers, of course. I don't think I'll willfully attempt to go face-to-face with a rattlesnake in the near future."

The doctor clamped a hand on his shoulder. "We're just glad you're still with us, Parson. As it is, we've missed one rousing sermon. Hope you're up to preaching again by Sunday."

"I'll do my best. I'm afraid it's a little hard to concentrate just now."

"That's to be expected. That old rattler pumped everything he had into that leg of yours. But it shouldn't take too much longer for the effects of the venom to be out of your system, I'd wager."

"Hey!" someone shouted. "The Reverend's back!" And for the next half hour, a steady stream of fellow travelers came by to greet him and offer wishes for his complete recovery. The strain of that excitement wore him out royally, and he slept until noon the next day, despite the bumping and jarring of the wagon.

❧

"Jesse, come take a look," Emma urged. "That must be Independence Rock in the distance. We'll arrive in time to celebrate the Fourth of July." She moved to one side so he could join her.

"Well, I'll be," he remarked and eased himself onto the wagon seat. "There've sure been some incredible sights along this journey. God didn't spare the beauty when He fashioned this great country."

She nodded, suddenly aware that his gaze centered on her and not on the faraway landmark. She slanted him a gaze and smiled. "Feeling better today?"

"Much. I'm on the verge of being ravenously hungry."

"That's a good sign. I'll see if I can whip up a buffalo for you when we stop."

"You probably would, too." He shook his head in wonder and reached for the reins. "Tomorrow I'll take over this chore so you can get back to your reading. I've imposed upon your good nature far too long."

"I. . .haven't felt drawn to my father's books lately, for some reason," she confessed. "They just don't seem all that important anymore."

"What does seem important, Emma?" he asked quietly.

She didn't answer immediately. Unsure of how to put words to concepts that seemed the direct opposite of the goals she'd clung to for so long, she finally shrugged a shoulder. "Not trying to outguess the Lord, for one thing," she began. "Giving Him the freedom to close old doors and open new ones. Then having the courage to step through them. Being willing to accept His will, even when it differs from mine."

"You haven't given up the desire to make your life count, have you? To help people?"

"Not at all. But now I see that help comes in many forms."

"I think you've proven that these past couple days. I couldn't have managed if you hadn't stepped into the breach. In fact," he added huskily, "I don't know how I'll do without you when you return to your family. I've grown quite used to looking up and seeing you, hearing your voice. . .feeling your touch on my brow when you thought I was sleeping. . . ."

Emma didn't quite suppress the warm blush that flooded her cheeks. "Who says I want to go back?" she whispered, shocked at her own boldness. Surely he'd think her a hussy.

But Jesse's face glowed with heaven's light. A slow smile played across his lips as he covered her hand with his and searched her soul with those heart-stopping eyes. "I might as well tell you, I'm in love with you, Emma Harris. Have been for some time."

Hearing the words she'd never really expected anyone to say, she saw no reason to hedge. Not when the handsome pastor had just laid his very heart at her feet. "I nearly had to lose you before the Lord finally got through to this hard head of mine. But I know now that I love you, too, Jesse."

"Enough to marry a poor preacher when we reach Trail's End? When I've got my strength back again and can court you proper?"

"No," she said in all candor. "Enough to marry you tomorrow. Seeing how very fragile life is, I don't want to waste a day of it. . .not when I can share every moment with you."

His eyebrows hiked high on his forehead and his jaw gaped in pleasant shock. "How do you think your parents will feel about that?"

She smiled. "Let's just say I doubt they'll be surprised."

"Well *I* am, my sweet Emma. But there's one thing I must do before we break the news."

"And what is that?"

"Just this." He put an arm around her and drew her close; and when she raised her gaze to his, he lowered his head and gave her a kiss so tender, so reverent, it left her breathless.

Chapter 7

At the crack of dawn on the Fourth of July, the men of the encampment fired off small arms and raised the flag. Then everyone circled the flagpole and sang "The Star-Spangled Banner" in honor of the occasion.

"Three cheers for Old Glory!" someone yelled, and the exuberant crowd gave their all.

"Feel up to reading the Declaration of Independence, Reverend?" Emma heard Rawhide ask. "Somehow it seems more fittin' if you'd do the honors."

She looked up at the too-thin man of God standing beside her and smiled.

"I'll do my best." Accepting the sheaf of papers from the trail master, Jesse cleared his throat and began reading:

" 'In Congress, July 4, 1776. The unanimous Declaration of the thirteen united States of America. When in the Course of human events, it becomes necessary for one people to dissolve the political bands which have connected them with another. . .' "

Amazed at how much stronger his voice sounded this morning, Emma's heart swelled with pride and concentrated on the words while he continued.

" 'We hold these truths to be self-evident, that all men are created equal, that they are endowed by their Creator with certain unalienable Rights, that among these are Life, Liberty and the pursuit of Happiness.' "

Noticeably hoarse by the time he reached the end of the historic document, he grinned as another rousing cheer sounded. Then, charges of gunpowder in the cracks of Independence Rock were set off.

"Now listen up," Rawhide hollered. "We'll be restin' here for the day while all able-bodied men go hunting. No doubt the ladies of the company are eager to cook us all up a royal feast for the celebration. But we're thinkin' beyond today. We need as much meat as can be found. There's a hard stretch facin' us ahead. And," he added, casting a peculiar glance toward Emma and Jesse, "I hear tell I'll be performin' a weddin' later today. The preacher's takin' Miss Emma Harris for his bride, and you're all invited."

A chorus of *oohs* and *ahhs* sounded, and all the young women flocked to Emma's side with a raft of hugs and suggestions.

"How wonderful," Megan Crawford crooned. "He's a fine man. He'll take good care of you."

"I'd love for you to use my veil," the doctor's wife, Bethany, offered. "To supply the traditional something borrowed."

Not to be left out, thick-waisted Lavinia Millberg edged closer. "I'm sure I have a gown you'd be welcome to wear. Of course, you'd have to tie the sash a bit tighter."

"And I have a bouquet of dried flowers you can carry," Penny Rogers chimed in, "just in case your sisters already picked all the wildflowers in the area yesterday."

Emma didn't know which one to answer first. "Thank you.

All of you. You're truly sweet. I'd be honored to borrow your veil, Bethany, and to carry Penny's flowers if Susan and Deborah can't find any. But I have a dress of my own to wear. Just be at our wedding, please. Jesse and I would appreciate your support and good wishes, and we want everyone to share in our happiness."

As the group gravitated back to their own wagons, her betrothed came to her side. "How would you feel about taking in the spectacular view they say one can see from up top?"

Emma's mouth gaped. "After just barely surviving being bitten by a snake, you want to attempt climbing a big rock?"

He flashed a sheepish grin. "It's not reported to be a hard climb. . .and we do have all day. We can go slow. Besides, it's a once-in-a-lifetime opportunity. You wouldn't expect me to leave here without carving a very special set of initials for all the world to see. I'm sure no one would expect my beautiful bride-to-be to soil her pretty hands on mundane chores on her wedding day. How about it?"

Emma cast an incredulous glance at the granite mound, which occupied a good twenty-five acres of ground, and another at her husband-to-be. "I suppose this'll be only the first of many challenges I'm going to face, being married to you."

"Spoken like the gal who's stolen my heart."

"Well, let's get to it, then."

Hand in hand, they started up the gray mass, the sun's rays reflecting off particles of red and white feldspar and mica in the granite. They picked their footing as had so many others, ascending slowly enough to read the many names and dates left by previous visitors, along with scores of initials and messages. Some had been carved into the soft surface, others written in buffalo grease or powder. Emma paid close attention to the sound of Jesse's breathing, intending to stop this foolish scheme should it prove too much for him. But he seemed only slightly winded and grinned like a kid, so she relaxed.

A strong wind whipped about their clothing and hair when they gained the top. Jesse tightened his hold on her hand, and they turned a slow circle, devouring the panoramic vista that spanned twenty miles in every direction, truly a sight to remember. They pondered the meandering trail they'd already navigated through the Sweetwater Valley and surveyed the handful of alkali pools below, which some of the men patrolled to make sure the animals didn't drink from them. Then, turning, they observed another grouping of rugged rocks jutting up from the ground a short hike away. And beyond them all, the snowcapped tops of the Rocky Mountains, with its chill winds announcing a preview of what lay ahead.

"Here's the spot we'll record our visit," he said, taking out his pocketknife and kneeling down. "Maybe I'll put our first names, since they're both short."

"As you wish." Amused at his mettle, she dropped down beside him and sat with her arms wrapped around her knees while he painstakingly carved the letters.

"There." Standing, he offered a hand and helped her up. "How's that? Jesse loves Emma, 1860."

He had etched a heart around their names, which she found particularly sentimental. She smiled, wondering what other fascinating things she would discover about the man she loved. "It's beautiful."

"So are you, my love." He cupped her face in his hands and kissed her soundly as the wind cavorted around them.

Going down, they soon found out, presented more difficulty

than going up, but they finally succeeded, their slow jaunt having used up a good portion of the afternoon.

"I have one more thing to show you," he said, a mysterious spark in his eye. "In the wagon. A wedding gift for my bride."

"How could you possibly have acquired a present for me?" she asked, completely baffled.

"I have my ways."

Without the slightest inkling of what to expect, Emma allowed him to lead her to the rig she would soon share with him and accepted his assistance aboard.

"It's in the back," he said, his lips quirking into a hopeful grin. He threw aside a heavy canvas cover and stood aside.

"My hope chest!" Emma gasped, her eyes misting with tears. She brushed her fingertips across her name, carved so lovingly by her grandfather in times past. "But how did you ever—I mean, Papa left it beside the trail miles and miles ago!"

"I know. When your sister Deborah bemoaned that sad fact, I pulled off the road and rescued it. I needed to tend the hoof of one of my oxen at the time anyway. I figured it wouldn't be too heavy for my wagon, and I knew you'd want it."

"Thank you, Jesse. Thank you." Emma moved closer and hugged him. When she raised her lashes and met his gaze, she almost drowned in the love she saw there. "You are incredibly special, do you know that?"

"I try," he said with nonchalance.

Her mother rapped on the wagon just then. "Emma? You need to change for your wedding. Everything's in readiness, and we'll be having a grand feast after the ceremony."

"I'm coming." A last lingering glance at her betrothed, and she hurried away.

Getting ready took less than half an hour. She donned one of her Oregon dresses. . .an ivory tulle with a spray of tiny pearls and sequins accenting the bodice. Mama helped pin her hair up into a tumble of soft curls with some loose tendrils along her cheeks and neck. Then she added the exquisite veil provided by Bethany Rogers.

"Oh, you do look lovely, Daughter. My baby, a bride. I can't believe it."

"I know, Mama. It was the last thing I expected to have happen on this journey. But I know this is God's will and that Jesse is God's man for me."

She nodded. "If your father and I didn't share that sentiment, we would not let go of you so easily." She smiled and hugged her, then straightened. "Come. Your groom is probably already waiting."

Susan and Deborah, all curled and beribboned in their own pretty Oregon dresses, held out a bouquet of fresh wildflowers as Emma stepped down. "We picked these special ones for you."

"I hope you were careful to watch out for snakes," she said, admiring the prairie roses and other pastel blooms. She gave each of her sisters a hug.

A row of heavily laden tables sat to one side of the grounds within the circled wagons. Emma could smell a delicious assortment of mouth-watering dishes as she and her mother approached, and she surmised there'd be an array of food similar to what they'd enjoyed at Fort Laramie, complete with baked desserts.

She spied Jesse at the front of the company, standing tall and straight in his Sunday preaching suit, his hair slicked back. His eyes softened as she moved into view, and the crowd, seated on blankets and upturned kegs awaiting the ceremony, smiled their approval.

Emma's siblings preceded her to the front one at a time, while Papa blinked moisture from his eyes and proudly escorted her to her groom's side.

Rawhide Rawson, in the one worn and scruffy outfit that made up his wardrobe, harrumphed and stepped to the center, a small black book in his grip, the usual wad of tobacco missing from his cheek. "Dearly beloved," he read in a flat tone, "we are gathered here to join together this man and this woman in holy matrimony. . . ."

Emma scarcely heard the words as she lost her gaze in Jesse's, so very thankful for God's goodness. Rawhide's voice, the people around her, the lovely day, the smells of supper, all faded to a misty blur.

All too soon the vows had been spoken, and the trail master pronounced them husband and wife. "You may kiss your bride, Preacher."

Jesse smiled and drew her into his embrace, then lowered his lips to hers. Twice.

Granny Willodene gave a hoot and a holler. "Supper's on," she announced. "No sense wastin' the rest of daylight, nor all these good vittles, when folks're starvin' to death. Let's allow the newlyweds to head up the line, then the rest of us will traipse by with our good wishes once our plates are dished up. Parson, we'll have you say grace."

He nodded. "Dear Lord, we thank Thee for Thy wondrous faithfulness in guiding and protecting us day by day. We ask Thy blessing upon this food and those who labored so long to prepare it. Make us strong to do Thy will. And Emma and I give special thanks for Your bringing us together and allowing us to share the remainder of our lives together. In Christ's name, Amen."

Emma felt him squeeze her hand, and she glanced up to meet his gaze.

"After you, Mrs. Brewster." A most endearing twinkle glinted in his eye.

"Thank you, Reverend," she replied. Somehow she sensed this was but a foretaste of years to come. . .being honored along with God's man and moving to the front of the line, waiting for him to ask the blessing over this feast or that, among this crowd or some future gathering. Being at his side to help him and help others. Laborers together for the Lord.

If she lived to be a hundred, she could ask for nothing more.

SALLY LAITY

Sally spent the first twenty years of her life in Dallas, Pennsylvania, and calls her self a small-town girl at heart. She and her husband Don have lived in New York, Pennsylvania, Illinois, Alberta (Canada), and now reside in Bakersfield, California. They are active in a large Baptist church where Don teaches Sunday school and Sally sings in the choir. They have four children and fourteen grandchildren.

Sally always loved to write, and after her children were grown she took college writing courses and attended Christian writing conferences. She has written both historical and contemporary romances, and considers it a joy to know that the Lord can touch other hearts through her stories.

Having successfully written several novels, including a co-authored series for Tyndale, nine Barbour novellas, and nine **Heartsong Presents**, this author's favorite thing these days is trying to organize a lifetime of photographs into Memory Pages.

Murder or Matrimony

by Pamela Kaye Tracy

Chapter 1

Megan Crawford knew more about keeping secrets than a woman her age had a right. Today she added one more. She crawled out of bed while a faint darkness still canvassed the too-early morning. Lately, nothing seemed to disturb Alison, but Megan needed to be a bit more careful as she eased over Rebekkah's sleeping form.

Sticking her nose over the wagon's awning, she took a deep breath. This nightmare had been tame compared to some of the others. Still, sweat trickled down her chest and forehead. At best, she could claim an uneasy sleep.

The lingering scent of last night's dinner fires added a smoky edge to the cloying aroma of garden larkspur. As much as she hated leaving the comfort—and warmth—of the crowded pallet on the prairie schooner's floor, she did enjoy the peace the predawn afforded. Squinting, she could just make out Independence Rock. Even Allie had roused long enough to add her initials. Megan figured only she and Larson Schmitt had stayed with the wagons while the majority explored the giant, gray, granite outcropping. She just couldn't catch the excitement of the others. Mr. Schmitt no doubt stayed behind because it required effort to climb the towering rock; and as far she could tell, the man never made a move that might break him into a sweat.

The Greens had reached the milestone first, hooting and hollering as if it were Christmas. What a family! Megan had never seen such an unorganized, noisy bunch. Now they were, thankfully, asleep, and the circle of the wagon train sheltered an almost tangible silence impossible to imagine during the hectic daytime hours. The sun peeked over the mountain, barely showing. Would it make an appearance? Hide behind a cloud? Later, would it bear down so unrelentlessly that the back of Megan's dress would stick to her skin with an uncomfortable, damp heat?

She took one last look around. It was too early to get dressed. Even the Greens, who were early risers, still slumbered. Just thinking about the Greens inspired Megan to scoot backwards toward the trunk she shared with her brother's family. The Greens had foiled her predawn plans before. She needed solitude. Today a promising prairie wind blew from the south. If not for the new blister on the bottom of Megan's left foot, maybe later she'd skip or do a little dance of happiness. She shook that thought off. She didn't deserve the joy that a random romp in the dew-kissed grass brought. Frolicking, without a care, was something the old Megan would do, the Megan who'd been the belle of Cedar County, Illinois. Why, Megan would never forget the time Caroline and. . .

Caroline.

Megan's hand clenched tightly. The simple cotton nightgown she clutched didn't protect her palm from feeling the halfmoon impression of nails that needed filing. She closed her eyes, dizzy, for a moment. Opening them again, white dots danced across her vision. She crawled back to the wagon's opening and took a deep breath. *Think about something else.*

She'd even awakened before the wagon captain. Usually she caught a glimpse of Rawhide or that vagabond Mr. Williams as they rode their horses to scout the area. No matter the time, Mr. Williams always seemed to prowl somewhere nearby, usually close enough to bump into the one woman in camp who wanted nothing to do with him—namely herself. The man just didn't take a hint.

Maybe this morning she would manage to elude him. Well, that would be one good thing about her ridiculous early morning rising. The only good thing.

Glad for the privacy of a still-sleeping family, she crawled past thc bag of cornmeal and opened the trunk she shared with her brother's family. Quickly, she changed into her none-too-clean brown wool frock. Allie and Rebekkah nestled close to each other. They had no idea just how early Megan left their company. Flossie, Rebekkah's doll, did. Megan regularly managed to smush the doll's moss-filled body as she tried to maneuver past the tightly packed sleeping figures.

She climbed from the back and snuck under the wagon. Without a sound, she relieved Jeremiah of yesterday's treasure. She had to pry a few fingers away. He held on to the jar as if sheer willpower would hinder any mishap. He murmured unintelligible words. Still, he'd had a restful night. His arm healed and the memories of the accident faded. Until last night, he'd regularly climbed into the wagon to sleep with the women. Now that made a tight fit. Why he thought they provided more safety than under the wagon with his pa, Megan didn't understand. Louis shrugged his shoulders in bewilderment, too. Still, Jeremiah was a brave soul, Megan thought, as she brushed a lock of hair from his eyes. Her foot slipped on the dry, brittle ground as she left the underbelly of the wagon. Wiping the dirt from her fingers, she clutched the jar to her chest and headed away from camp.

A wooden cross, simply engraved with the words "Baby Girl" blocked her path. A broken-down wagon came next. Megan would forage it for firewood later. A guard, Beau Cole, leaned against a tree in the distance. She had to admit, the guards weren't easy to spot unless you knew where to look. His twin brother, a distance away, imitated a turkey call. Megan could only wish there were turkeys in this area. They'd seen her. Both were well aware of the habits of the Crawford Kid. That's what they called her, after she rebuffed their advances. They figured she must be a kid if she didn't recognize their many valuable qualities, their manly gifts. She ignored them and stepped near a particularly heavy patch of prickly pear, opened the lid of the jar, and bent down.

A twig snapped. Megan hit the dirt and lay flat, hoping she couldn't be seen. The Indians they met up with since Fort Laramie had been friendly, but fear remained at Megan's side, an unrelenting companion for well over a year now.

"Looking for toads?"

It was that insufferable Mr. Williams, appearing from nowhere—or so it seemed. Since he'd joined the camp back at Fort Laramie, he'd somehow always managed to be around when Megan did something she'd rather keep private.

"If I were looking for toads, then I'd be real disappointed since the only thing I've managed to find is a snake." She glared at him as she scrambled to her feet. Brushing grass, dirt, and bits of twig from her dress, she gave him a look that anyone else would have read as dismissal. Not Bernie. Taller than most of the other men, he was what her mother would call a tall drink of water.

He made her uncomfortable and never called her the Crawford Kid.

❧

Megan Crawford's cheeks were turning a healthy shade of pink. She clutched an empty jar in her hand. Bernie figured she wouldn't mind knocking him atop the head with it. Well, he'd been hit in the head before and by a pretty lady. He'd almost welcome some show of physical spunk from this girl. She had gumption, of that he had no doubt. He'd seen her deal with the Cole brothers, always in a nonconfrontational way, but he didn't buy the quiet, unassuming act. Almost daily he noted her clenched fists. Anger, or something else, boiled just below the surface. He wanted to know what motivated her. Even more, he wanted to know the truth behind the haunted look in her eyes.

"You need some assistance?" Bernie had spotted Megan well before she reached the tall grass more than a few yards away from her family's wagon. Thanks to Buck's turkey call. Truthfully, he'd been too busy admiring Megan to span the distance between the Greens' wagon and her in a reasonable time.

"I'm perfectly capable of taking care of myself." Her chin went in the air.

She had the bluest eyes he'd ever seen.

"Mr. Williams, are you all right?"

He'd been staring. This woman put him on edge, and he

didn't like it. "I told you to call me Bernie. On the trail, there's no need for formalities."

She shook her head, reminding him ever so much of the Sunday school teacher, more than fifteen years ago, who'd expected more of him, too. He'd exasperated Megan, and he wondered why. Maybe that was his problem. He spent so much time annoying her, she didn't trust him.

Now that was another problem. Usually by the time he annoyed a woman, she knew she was quarry. Megan hadn't a clue. She was annoyed by his very existence, and it puzzled him. He'd done nothing to raise her hackles. Why was she so wary of him. . .of men in general? What did she suspect?

He removed his hat and bowed to her retreating form. She'd turned tail and walked away with a dignity that let him know, although he'd not witnessed the gesture, that he'd been thoroughly dismissed.

The top of her head just might brush against his shoulder, if he ever got close enough. Even after weeks on the trail, her hair—at least what peeked out from under her bonnet—attracted the glare of the sun and shone in a way that made a man's fingers itch to explore.

"Williams!" Orson Millberg looked as though he smelled something sour. The large man sat both awkward and haughty in the saddle. Orson's expression reminded Bernie of Ronald Benchly, a sometimes-partner who had a constant stomach ailment.

Ronald had no patience for men such as Orson. Self-important snobs who tossed blame on others rather than dealing with a problem. Orson's horse even managed to look pained as he paused next to Bernie. The Tennessee walker, ribs showing, blew out a gust of air and pawed restlessly, sending a billow of dust to settle on Bernie's boots.

"Williams, you bothering Miss Crawford?"

Bernie wanted to laugh, not that humor was an option in his line of work. "Not as much as you're bothering me."

Orson's eyebrows inched toward each other. His lips compressed. Bernie figured that only the fact that Orson considered him as possible son-in-law material kept the man from continuing his harangue. With her conniving, simpering ways, Lavinia Millberg had managed to alienate all of the single men on the wagon train. Having only recently joined the train, Bernie rated as the new man in town. He'd not been off his horse but ten minutes before recognizing Lavinia Millberg as trouble. Too bad she wasn't who he was looking for.

The Cole brothers made disappearing an art when Lavinia came nigh. Bernie needed to learn their technique. For three burly men to evaporate into thin air was no small feat. They gleefully informed Bernie that *he* would be perfect for Lavinia. After all, she came with a dowry a poor man could surely use. It bothered the Cole brothers to listen to Bernie's pretend dreams about becoming an Oregon rancher. They wanted him to wear a felt hat, and have a supply wagon, and lead a good strain of horses. They didn't understand the concept of heading west with only a horse and two saddlebags

The women were much easier. After reading the little novels they had passed about, they all imagined him building an empire out of nothing and sweeping one of them off her feet.

It wouldn't be Lavinia.

Bernie Williams wasn't looking for a wife. He was looking for something else. It wasn't in Oregon, either. He despised the

Oregon Trail and all it stood for. Just his bad luck to pull this particular duty.

Orson carefully took off his hat, slapped it against his leg to free it of dust, and then cleared his throat. "Rawhide says there's some elk to the west. Thinks it'd be a good idea to bag a few."

Years had taught Bernie to guard his tongue. Today's adversary might be tomorrow's witness. "How many?"

The way Orson's lips curled, Bernie knew he'd figured right. Rawhide had suggested Orson go hunting, not that Orson could. The man couldn't shoot a tree. Well, the man could shoot a tree, but he'd be aiming at something else.

"Two should do it." Orson Millberg huffed, then pursed his lips before offering. "You want some help?"

Men who'd taken him up on the offer seldom made the mistake twice. Not even getting pleasure from watching the pompous man fumble was worth the danger of accidentally getting shot when Orson closed his eyes and pulled the trigger. Why Beau Cole swore he once saw a buffalo snicker at Orson's antics with a gun.

Claiming to be an entrepreneur looking for opportunities, Orson's talk around the campfire mimicked a jack-of-all-trades but a master of none.

Bernie shook his head and turned his back on the man. It wasn't until he was halfway back to his own horse that he realized his retreat parroted Megan's.

Did she feel about him the way he felt about Orson?

Megan. He had to keep his mind on Megan and quit letting the daily needs of the wagon train divert him. Bernie went back to where they'd been standing. Why had she walked out this far? What was in that jar? It was too small to be a slop bucket. He bent down and carefully pushed aside a clump of prickly pear, then another. Nothing. With a backward glance at the immobile wagons, he went to his knees and patted the ground. He spent a few more minutes picking through the foliage. Bugs crawled up his wrists and burrs dug into his palms until he finally gave up. One thing for sure, he didn't want anyone on the train—especially Megan—to look over and see him rearranging prairie grass and think he'd gone loco.

Or maybe he should let her know he was watching her. He needed to somehow get past her wall of mistrust; and to do that, he didn't need to feel concern about emotions, neither his nor hers.

It was the day-in and day-out repetition of the trail that put the burr under Bernie's saddle. He worked alone. He'd always worked alone. Even when he dealt with a partner, like Ronald, they'd had their own assignments. The partners were never together for more than clandestine meetings to exchange information. On the trail, he was forced to see the intricate working of family life. On the trail, not only did he have to fill a role, but people were depending on him because they thought he was a vital link in the quest for survival. That put him smack dab in the middle of family life.

Family life. Bernie felt his mouth dry. The trail robbed families; it didn't build them. Against his will, Bernie wondered if his father had traveled this very road.

❧

"Whither thou goest, I will go." Idabelle Barnes plucked a thread from her feed-sack dress and stared off at the distant Rocky Mountains. They'd been walking uphill for hours.

"What?" Megan felt guilty, as if she'd invaded the privacy of the other woman's thoughts. Idabelle probably didn't even realize she'd spoken aloud. The farmer's wife often fell in step beside Megan. They enjoyed a comfortable relationship either sharing small talk, usually about novels, or just walking in the silence of each other's company.

"Oh, I didn't mean to say that. I was just thinking about something Pastor Brewster said during meeting yesterday."

Megan nodded, unsure as to what her friend needed to hear. Clearly Idabelle had some doubts as to what Oregon might offer. Brewster's sermon had been about God's promises. The men had nodded, save Bernie Williams, who smirked—no doubt thinking about their glorious futures. Most of the women had offered weak smiles. The female exceptions were, of course, Geneva Green—nothing bothered her—and Pastor Brewster's new wife, who looked like she could blaze a new trail to Oregon at the side of her husband. Emma took to being a wife like a cat took to cow's milk. Megan thought Emma radiated satisfaction.

A small bead of jealousy flared. Megan suppressed it.

Oh, and Bethany Rogers smiled eagerly, looking at each day as adventure. Bethany, though, even smiled when the wheel on their emerald green wagon cracked thanks to a hidden stump that had no business in the middle of a much-traveled trail. Megan could almost read Bethany's thoughts that day a fortnight ago. The young bride had admired her husband's ability to repair wood. Repair wood!

Megan longed to be that naive again.

"Why are you heading for Oregon?" Idabelle put a hand on Megan's shoulder, hopped up and down twice, and successfully slipped off her much-too-big, simple leather shoe to empty it of yet another pebble.

No one had asked that question, not in all the weeks they'd put between five and thirty miles a day on the soles of their shoes. Megan's shoes were heavy soled, with copper toes. Her papa had purchased them before packing his only daughter off for the brutal West. He wanted only the best for the belle of Cedar County, even when she was no longer the belle.

"I'm helping Louis and Allie." Megan wasn't lying, she was only saying the words everyone else on the trail took for granted.

"Not good enough, although your sister-in-law surely needs your help. How is she?"

"Better." Megan didn't know what else to say. The once vivacious Alison Crawford was using sleep to escape reality and even after a month hadn't ceased from her sorrow.

"Hmm," Idabelle said and tactfully went back to her previous topic. "That sermon last night set me to thinking. I mean, I know why I'm leaving behind my friends and family in Iowa. Mr. Barnes thinks that we'll be walking into 160 acres, free from the government, in the Willamette Valley. Me, I have my doubts; but I'd follow that man clear to the edge of the world if he crooked his finger. You're not following anybody, are you?"

Megan forced a chuckle. "I'm following the Greens, that's what I'm doing."

"Mother!"

In a division containing more occupants than the Cedar County Spelling Bee, the word *Mother* turned quite a few heads; but Idabelle was already heading toward her own wagon, where Frank Barnes waited with a newly awakened daughter in his arms.

Megan watched Idabelle's retreating figure. Frank called; Idabelle responded. Men led; women followed. Jasper lied; people believed. And a few wagons ahead, Megan could hear Orson Millberg berating his wife. Megan closed her eyes. The Millberg women were the best-dressed women on their train, but Megan wouldn't change places with them for all the money in the world. No wonder Lavinia considered every single man a temptation. The other girl wasn't looking for love; she was looking for escape.

"Why don't you ride a spell?" Mr. Williams's lips were so close to her ear that she could feel a faint trace of the heat of his breath.

The hair at the back of her neck prickled. She shook away the memory of her last year in Cedar County. It annoyed her that she hadn't heard the man. "Don't sneak up on me like that."

"I didn't sneak. I walked up just like I walk up to everybody."

"Why don't you go walk up on Lavinia?" Megan wanted to accent the suggestion by adding a wave in Lavinia's direction, but the other girl was in her wagon. Lavinia was dressed in a pink serge skirt and a beige cloth shirt. Her feet didn't boast copper-toed shoes, nor did her hands prove by their calluses the work she did on the trail. Megan figured she could count, using the fingers on one hand, the miles Lavinia had walked. And at least half of those miles had been while she tried to lure Pastor Brewster away from Emma.

Megan felt sorry for the girl, but she still didn't like her.

"Because I'd rather talk to you." The slow grin didn't quite reach Bernie's eyes.

He was playing with her, and she didn't quite know why.

"What are you thinking?" He spoke the words softly, his

green eyes promising an interested audience.

Why all the questions today? Was it just a year ago that Megan would have welcomed attention from such a handsome stranger? Was it just a year ago when she'd had nothing to hide from an acquaintance like Idabelle?

The problem with questions, Megan decided, was that the ones she least wanted to answer were the ones so often asked.

Why arc you heading to Oregon? *To escape Caroline's memory.*

What are you thinking? *That there is no escape.*

Chapter 2

For the fifth day in a row, Bernie watched Megan take the jar and dump the contents. He almost looked forward to these early morning wanderings. She might very well be the most beautiful woman he'd ever seen. Megan Crawford rubbed sleep from a face that would look at home on an angel. In many ways, her pretense of innocence made him all the more suspicious.

He waited for her to busy herself so he could find the spot and do a thorough search. She was good at pretending she was just an ordinary traveler on the Oregon Trail. No matter how long the day, how bad the water, how tough the travel, he'd never heard her utter a word of complaint. Often her behavior made him curious. She'd ignored the view from the Devil's Gate gorge. When they'd come across a group of Mormons pushing handcarts, she had kept to herself instead of using the opportunity to engage in conversation.

Women were supposed to lean toward social gatherings.

Why did she avoid them?

He found the spot she'd just left and got down on his hands and knees. Searching was a bit easier here at the pass.

She'd not chosen a grassy area but had instead found a crevice where a tiny cedar grew. He scoured the area. There had to be something, some hint as to what the woman was doing. But, no, only a garter snake witnessed the search for nothing.

What was the woman getting rid of? Why did she choose to empty the jar a little at a time instead of all at once? Why couldn't he find any evidence of what she was hiding?

Bernie had always been an early riser, but if there were awards to be given for greeting the morning, Megan had him beat. He'd given up sleep for naught. The jar remained a mystery. Megan's secret still needed to be unearthed, and this morning the only new information he gleaned about the members of the wagon train had to do with Homer Green and Anna Schmitt. Homer was a master pack rat, Bernie discovered. The Green family had stumbled across a deserted wagon, just a few feet off the trail. Essentials like wheels, yoke, and the like were already picked clean. Homer made sure nothing was left. Rusty hooks and drawstrings were pulled from the torn canvas.

While Homer's particular gift hadn't been a surprise, Anna Schmitt was. Who'd have guessed such a sour-faced, brick wall of a woman could create such incredible drawings. He'd watched her yesterday, as a hesitant sun cast yellow and orange hues onto the trail. She'd climbed from the wagon, her large hands clutching a tattered, brown leather satchel. Probably didn't want to disturb her deadbeat husband. Larson Schmitt managed to avoid any of Rawhide's assigned duties. Larson made Orson look like a hard worker.

What was it Granny Willodene had said about Larson? Handsome is as handsome does. The womenfolk agreed Larson Schmitt was a fine-looking man. Most of them also recognized him as a lazy good-for-nothing. Granny's words, not Bernie's. Bernie didn't care what Larson did.

Anna made her way into the prairie, wearing boots two sizes too big, and trampled a path in a sea of chamiso flowers Bernie had just scoured for clues. He almost hadn't followed, figuring the woman needed privacy. But the way she gingerly held the satchel grabbed his interest.

She found a secluded spot. If Bernie hadn't been following her, she'd not have been seen. She was a natural at picking out a private area. After finding a bit of shade and laying down a blanket, she took out charcoal and a drawing pad. Years of experience let him sneak up, undetected. He'd almost been discovered, though, when, after drawing a realistic likeness of an early morning wagon train amidst the craggy cliffs, she'd plucked yellow and orange chalk from her satchel and added a sunrise so realistic that Bernie could feel the distant, golden rays. Male instinct was to let out a whistle of appreciation. Bernie was a master at suppressing his instinct and instead just nodded.

He'd watched her far too long, mesmerized by the likeness of Rawhide appearing next to the wagon. By the time she'd signed her initials at the bottom of the paper and he'd rejoined the wagon train, Rawhide had spit a plug of chew and yelled, "Let's move out." The company was lumbering to a fresh beginning. All were in jovial moods. From the front of the train to the end, the immigrants were sucking on ice. A boggy marsh, known as the Ice Slough, provided an oasis where ice dwelt in muck. Never before had Bernie seen anything like it.

Granny Willodene had reached one hand in and pulled out a piece. "Well, I'll be!" Those three words brought the hordes running. Even the cows were given chunks to lick on.

From the corner of his eye, Bernie watched Anna return to her wagon. He located the Crawfords. They were near the end of the line, which made Bernie's job easier. Megan often traveled alone; and, as last wagon, a parade of travelers would not hinder his view.

His grand plan for surveillance wasn't to be. Not today. Come to think of it, not this week and not since they'd entered the Sweetwater. He really wanted to get near enough to listen in on thc conversation Megan was having with Bethany Rogers. Something had transpired in the last week, and suddenly most of the young women near Megan's age wanted to walk with her, even if their wagon was a good distance from hers.

Megan looked none too happy about the attention.

Watching as the oxen in the lead wagon shuffled into movement, Bernie started toward Megan only to be hailed by Rawhide to come talk to a man leading a wagon train back East. These were not the first returning immigrants they'd encountered. Bernie hurried to his bedroll, still under the wagon Dillon Trier drove. He quickly composed a letter to the Chicago office, and ten minutes later, he and most of the others sent messages homeward.

And right when Bernie least wanted it, Pastor Brewster stood in the way. He put one foot on the wheel of the wagon Bernie intended to drive for the next four hours. When the wagon stopped for nooning, Bernie would turn the reins back to Dillon Trier.

For the most part, Bernie didn't trust pastors. Jesse Brewster was trying his hardest to become the exception. "You got a minute?" Brewster wanted to know.

To Bernie's mind, a pastor who cared so little if his clothes matched maybe wanted the masses to think he spent his time caring for his flock.

Bernie couldn't figure that out, and he'd seen the like before.

Then, there was the dog. Sitting at his master's feet, Barnabas's tongue lolled as he looked at his owner with adoring eyes. Pastor Brewster had the love of a good woman *and* the loyalty of a good dog.

Bernie couldn't figure that out, either. But Brewster, and a long-ago Sunday school teacher, would claim it had something to do with faith.

"I notice you've been attending the Sunday service, yet you never speak up." Jesse absently scratched behind Barney's ear.

Bernie knew the ploy. Pretend indifference, then the quarry will feel free to offer information. He'd often played the game. He knew the rules. Why, he'd even contributed some of them. "Nothing better to do."

Brewster looked up. "Name one thing more important than your soul."

"Can't."

"Then you believe in God."

A grave, no wooden marker, just piles of rocks to keep the occupant safe from animals, was just left of Pastor Brewster's foot. *Had that person believed in God*, Bernie wondered? *Had his family?* Bernie blamed the Oregon Trail for not only the death of so many irresponsible travelers but for putting him in position for so many too-personal questions.

"I do," Bernie allowed. "I also believe it's time to head out, then I need to go fishing. I'm sure there's a nearby stream full of trout just waiting for a visit from the likes of me."

Brewster nodded and headed back toward his wagon, the dog loping beside.

As Bernie urged an oversized ox into action, he convinced himself that there really would be a later need for trout. No, Bernie Williams wasn't just going fishing to keep himself from having told a lie to a pastor.

❧

She tried not to watch him. He finished speaking with Pastor Brewster, turned his team over to Dillon Trier, and then jumped on his horse heading north. Mr. Williams wore freedom like a badge, and lately she'd been thinking about him way too often.

It was wrong to have feelings for him. And, for the life of her, she couldn't quite put a finger on what her feelings were. On one hand, he scared her. Just watching the broad expanse of his back, the strength in those hands as they took off the wheels of a wagon, one at a time, and dipped his fingers into a bucket of grease to rub the axles. The cords of his forearms bulged, and Megan almost understood Bethany's fascination with watching her husband.

On the other hand, he puzzled her. No one had ever watched her the way he did. Not even Jasper during the early courting days, when she didn't know the vulnerability between men and women.

"He is a good-looking man." Bethany Rogers changed the subject, but Megan had the feeling she'd just left the frying pan for the fire. Maybe the topic of why Megan traveled the Oregon Trail was safer than speculation about Mr. Williams.

"Who?"

"Who?" Bethany chuckled. "Why our wild Mr. Williams. I'd like to know his past same as I like to hear about yours."

"I've told you my past. Cedar County, Illinois, was not exciting. I have parents, seven brothers, and now I'm heading to Oregon to help Louis and his wife. I'm not interested in marriage. I have my family, and I have God. That's all I want or need."

Bethany nodded, her lips pursed in an "I'm not finished with my inquiries, but I'll let it go for now" sort of look. Guilelessly, she suggested, "Tell me more stories about the trouble you and your brothers got into."

Megan searched her memory. She needed to think of something good to keep Bethany from returning to the admiration of Mr. Williams.

Megan liked Bethany. The doctor's wife had a gentle manner, which made it easy to confide. Many of the women, too bashful to share a personal malady with a male physician, used Bethany as an intermediary. Since leaving Missouri, Bethany had bloomed. She greeted each day with a prayer and a word of thanks for her blessings. It made Megan intensely aware of how she'd lately laid only her burdens at God's feet, forgetting to acknowledge His blessings.

The greatest blessing of all, Bethany claimed, was her husband, Joshua, and the prospect of her own little family.

Megan could almost believe in happily-ever-afters, if Joshua and Bethany were an example. But Megan had also seen the flip side, the *not*-so-happily-ever-afters. She'd seen the "till death do us part." Shuddering, Megan tried to focus on Bethany's words. Megan traveled the Oregon Trail to start anew, but she finally understood the meaning of Matthew 9:17.

She felt like an old wineskin and mistakenly she'd thought that the fresh change of the Oregon Trail would free her of past mistakes. Unfortunately, even though she'd put herself in a new surrounding, she was still the same inside.

Bethany Rogers was a good example of a new wineskin. She'd taken to marriage and every day found something good to be thankful for. Now the doctor's wife was intent on getting Megan married.

"Did I tell you about Gramma and the rabid dog?" It had been years since Megan had thought about Gramma Milly and the rabid dog. That day all the brothers had been out helping Pa, even Louis, who announced daily he had no intention of becoming a farmer. Mama had been over at a sick neighbor's.

Bethany's eyes widened. Her thirst for books kept the young women on the Oregon Trail entertained. She loved a good story.

A few sentences into the telling of the event, Megan realized the true story would be over far too quickly to keep Bethany from returning to the subject of Mr. Williams. Years of entertaining Jeremiah and Rebekkah brought fruition. Megan took a breath and wove a tale that would have made Gramma Milly proud.

A half hour later, Bethany raised an eyebrow. "You made that up. There's no such thing as a rabid cow."

Megan laughed, surprised at how good it felt. "You're right. What gave me away?"

"The part about your riding through the forest yelling 'Giddy-up' while aiming the gun with one hand and picking mulberries for your supper with the other."

"I do get carried away, don't I?" Megan's heart felt lighter. She'd been trying to think of a way to push aside a conscience that whispered *Liar*. Almost as an answer to a silent prayer, the story turned into a tall tale that not even her niece would believe. And little Rebekkah had once believed that Flossie, her doll with the milky white china head, could fly, thanks to a series of good-night tales Megan had made up right before they'd left for Oregon.

"Maybe you ought to write a dime novel," Bethany suggested, her expression half serious.

Before Megan could answer, Jeremiah, Megan's ten-year-old nephew, skidded to a stop, barely missing the two girls. "Papa wants to know why you haven't gathered any firewood."

Standing next to him, Henry Green kicked at a good-sized rock and kept his head bowed while he offered, "I'll gather wood fer ya, Miss Megan."

"I'd appreciate that, Henry. Only, I don't see any wood. Why don't you gather up some sagebrush for me? And you can help him, Jeremiah."

Jeremiah's teasing face turned to a scowl. Henry turned bright red and scampered ahead, picking up pieces of sage not even a robin would, or could, line her nest with. Jeremiah gave Megan a dirty look, marched toward Henry, took the tiny shards from his hand, and led the way to a better cache. A few minutes later, he dashed back to the wagon for his jar. Jeremiah had little patience with his best friend's crush on Megan, but he did love to explore the underbrush.

"It don't make no sense," Jeremiah declared at least fifteen times a day. He was probably telling Henry that right now. Megan couldn't hear her nephew's mutterings, but she could guess at their content. Megan might feel sorrier for Henry if she hadn't known that Henry was already asking Jeremiah to name Megan's favorite type of sage. He'd also want to know what type burned the best and how high smoke rose.

"You've certainly got an admirer there." Bethany stooped to pick up a bunch of sage. Although their noon meal was still a tangible memory, gathering fodder for the evening chores never ended. Jeremiah's reminder actually was a blessing.

"There are benefits," Megan admitted. "Louis says he hasn't shot a single game hen since we left Nebraska. It's a mystery how one somehow finds its way, dead, to our campfire each night."

"Have you actually witnessed Henry leaving you the hen?"

"No," Megan said. "The kid's actually pretty sneaky. Sometimes we find the hen tied to the side of the wagon. A couple of times, Henry has thrown it in the back." She made a face. "It always lands on my side, but luckily, no one's been hurt by a flying fowl. Our pallet has been full of feathers, or even worse, a bit more often than we like, but it's a small price to pay for free food." She chuckled. "Once, the kid even managed to sit it on the buckboard. It looked ever so much like a small passenger enjoying the view. It gave Granny Willodene quite a scare. Of course, the real giveaway was when Henry asked if I thought there might be baby game hens missing their mama."

The girls giggled, and then Bethany headed back to take over the driving of her wagon so Joshua could stretch.

"You've not gathered enough sage to cook a gnat." Mr. Williams fell into step beside her, carrying an armful of firewood.

Megan sniffed.

The bachelor had yet to cook for himself, always being welcome at the Millberg campfire. Megan wondered if Mr. Williams noticed the way Mr. Millberg bossed his wife, but Megan doubted another man would care. Mr. Williams looked suspiciously just like Louis did when he wanted something.

"You need something, Mr. Williams?"

"I need an invitation for dinner tonight."

"I've heard my brother invite you more than once."

"Yes, but I'd like an invitation from you."

"Whatever for?"

"Could be I'm interested in your company?" His green eyes could only be called imploring. One hank of brown hair fell down in such a way that Megan considered brushing the offending strands away from his eyes.

No, this man had an easy way with the women. All of them cooed when he stopped to chat. Penny Rogers glowed. Lavinia Millberg giggled. Even Emma Brewster simpered, and her so newly married that the ink hadn't dried on the record page of the family Bible.

Megan didn't trust Mr. Williams. Really, outside of family, she didn't trust any of the men, save Pastor Brewster. Oh, and Henry, who now watched Mr. Williams with all the symptoms of a little boy about to throw a rock.

"Mr. Williams—"

"Call me Bernie."

"Mr. Williams, if you need a meal, my family is always willing to share."

He thrust the firewood at her. "And what about you, my lovely Megan, why won't you share a little time, as well as nourishment, with me?"

She took the firewood, mostly because she knew he expected her to refuse it. "Some people," she said slowly, "just aren't hungry."

"And some people," Bernie said easily, "can't tell the difference between the taste of the finest seafood from the toughness of one of Frank Barnes's oxen." He touched his hat. "I'll be along about seven." He backed up, a wicked grin on his face. "Oh, and I don't need a meal." He took his hand from behind his back. "I have a meal." Four trout, hooked to a line, proved his words. "I just need someone to share it with, and I want that someone to be you."

He was a year too late. Megan Crawford didn't want a beau, no matter that the memory of Bernie's eyes kept her awake at night and he looked like he could protect her from the world.

Looks were deceiving. No one could protect Megan Crawford from the world, especially not a good-looking man.

Chapter 3

"Oomph." Henry Green groaned as he rolled an oversized rock so that it stood three feet from his earlier oversized rock endeavor. He'd questioned Megan often about her mealtime habits, and he finally figured out Megan's favorite dinner table configuration. Now, and for every meal, he strove to recreate what she wanted.

"Thank you, Henry. I love setting a good table." Megan lay a plank across the rocks and spread the red-and-white-checked tablecloth. Back in Illinois, Megan's father claimed that Megan set such a great table to compensate for not being able to cook.

Henry turned a bright red and disappeared just long enough to fetch the wild berries he'd gathered earlier. It looked like Henry, as well as Mr. Williams, would be joining them for dinner. Geneva Green never noticed when one of her brood failed to show for a meal; and truthfully, Henry had provided so many game hens for the Crawford family, that whenever she baked something special, like service berry pie, Megan always made sure Henry was nearby.

Megan took a towel and lifted the coffeepot from the fire.

Coffee she could do. The trout crackled in the frying pan not quite ready to serve. Her favorite meal, trout; but back in Cedar County, Megan would have seasoned it, or at least tried. Truthfully, her mother always seasoned the trout while Megan watched. Louis hadn't stocked enough herbs and spices. They'd run out months ago, and Louis hadn't been willing to barter with any of the white traders they encountered on the journey.

Taking a deep breath, Megan thought about feigning a loss of appetite. Anything to not feel beholden to Mr. Williams. Three days straight of jackrabbit had her mouth watering for a change. That Mr. Williams had provided trout, of all things, only made her more nervous. It was as if the man knew her. Knew her better than her own family.

"I hear you make the best coffee in camp." Mr. Williams held out his cup.

She filled the cup and set the coffeepot on the table. "That's a rumor I started myself. It's not true."

"I doubt that." Bernie followed her as she fetched some pickles.

He really didn't follow all that close, but Megan felt a tangible presence. He took her breath away and not because the July sun beat down so relentlessly. Never had her body been so aware of the opposite sex. She tried to ignore him. Maybe if she went about her business and didn't fawn over him, he'd think she wasn't interested and go off and visit with Louis. That was the best thing to do, the safe thing to do.

Taking a sharpened willow stick, she spread slices of bacon over the trout, then she rescued the overdone bread from the coals. Mr. Williams had distracted her. It had been days since she'd last burned bread.

"I like it well done." Mr. Williams shooed away a fly and grinned as he took the plate from her and set it on the table.

"A gentlemen would refrain from remarking about the cook's flawed efforts." There'd been a time when Megan's tongue was sweet. Years of instruction by a proper mother created a proper lady. It had taken Jasper Mapes only seven months to destroy a lifetime of example. Megan looked Mr. Williams straight in the eye. "Especially a gentlemen who invited himself to dinner."

"I've never claimed to be a gentleman; but if you like, I can easily take my trout and go elsewhere."

Allie chose that moment to climb from the back of the wagon. "Do I smell fish?" Raising a delicate nose, Allie sniffed. A bright smile spread across her face. The first smile evident in weeks—could it really be months? Megan was trapped by both her sister-in-law's first display of interest and her own love of fish.

"Dinner ready?" Louis finished caring for the horses and now took his place sitting cross-legged on the ground. Allie and the children took one side. Mr. Williams sat across from Louis, leaving Megan and Henry the remaining space.

Louis said the prayer.

Henry sat strangely quiet, not asking questions.

The only reason Megan didn't scold Mr. Williams for leaving his eyes open during the thanks was because he would, in turn, accuse her of having open eyes as well, since she caught him.

Mealtime around the Crawford fire seldom meant conversation anymore. Louis was too tired from a hard day's driving. Allie stared off into space, trapped in her own little world, not even acknowledging Jeremiah's chatter about the day's adventures. Rebekkah usually huddled close to Megan, but not this meal. Megan's niece didn't even touch the trout, although it was her favorite meal, too. Instead, Rebekkah stared at her hands.

Mr. Williams changed the Crawford's dinner routine, at least where Louis was concerned. Taking a bite of bread, Mr. Williams shot Megan an appreciative look and then asked her brother, "Whereabouts are you settling in Oregon?"

"Wife and I are going to look for the most likely town to set up shop in. I've been a traveling salesman." Louis beamed. "Bibles. I've got more than fifty in the false bottom. I sell a few other books besides. Wanted to be a preacher but didn't have the patience. Allie's been hoping for more children, and she'd like to lay down roots so the children can have friends."

"So you've traveled quite a bit?" Mr. Williams took a bite of pickle. His eyes closed, and he gave a sigh of contentment.

Allie stopped eating. Megan knew why her sister-in-law had stopped. She wondered if Louis realized what he'd unwittingly said.

Reaching for a second pickle, Mr. Williams paid no attention to the tension surrounding the Crawfords' table. Megan wondered if the man even knew why pickles were so important. Allie packed quite a few items to help prevent scurvy. The pickles were for special occasions. Megan tried not to analyze why she'd served the delicacy the first time Mr. Williams joined them. His presence wasn't a special occasion and never would—never could—be.

Louis grabbed a pickle, too. "For the last six years, Allie and I've seen all the East Coast. She loves the ocean. Maybe when I get her there, she'll feel some better. She hankers for a home facing the waves. I'll get it for her, too. Just see if I don't."

Mr. Williams looked disappointed, Megan noticed. Was it her food? Maybe he didn't like pickles. Surely, he wasn't envious of the vagabond life her brother lived.

"Megan travel with you often?" He obviously expected Louis to answer, but he looked at Megan, his green eyes accusing instead of curious.

"No, Megan's the only girl in our brood and the baby. She's Pa's favorite. I'm amazed he let her come with us." Louis smiled. "Truthfully, I've no idea why she wanted to join us. She's been a great help." Louis reached over and patted Megan's hand. "She's gone from pampered daughter to a working woman without much preparation."

Megan curled her fingers, ashamed of the broken, dirty nails.

"I don't know what we'd have done without her," Louis finished.

"So," this time Mr. Williams expected Megan to answer—she could tell by the way he leaned toward her, "you really wanted to leave Cedar County and fast."

It wasn't a question; it was a statement. Mr. Williams made her so nervous that she stopped eating.

He knew it, too.

❧

For four days straight, Bernie managed to find time for a little fishing. He and his trout sat at the Crawfords' table. Just when he thought he'd sprout fins and breathe underwater, Rawhide led them to the area that had once been Fort Bridger and, since it was Sunday, he declared a day of rest. It took awhile to find a campsite that hadn't been picked clean of grass and firewood; but as Rawhide said, it didn't do the cows any good to travel without a break. Most times they just took a half day. Bernie figured the wagon master was getting closer to religion than ever before. Why, if Emma Brewster had her say, soon Rawhide would be giving up tobacco. That's what women did, if you gave them a chance: They started looking for ways to change you.

Bernie climbed out from under Dillon's wagon and glanced over at the Crawfords. Miss Megan was gathering up the laundry, looking ever so ordinary, like all of the other women her age on the trail. No, not looking like all the others. She looked like an angel. An angel with brown hair and golden streaks. She had a stubborn tilt to her chin that made him want to antagonize her.

Calling Jeremiah over, he gave the boy his laundry. Time to get closer to Miss Megan. He wanted her to be thinking about him.

Frank Barnes saddled up, ready to hunt fresh meat. Bernie's mouth watered. "Okay, we'll go, Samson." As if sensing an easy day, Bernie's horse pranced eagerly.

"I'd join you," Orson said as he rode up, "but as you can see, my horse is doing poorly." The man seemed to get bigger as his horse decreased in size. Horses were fine on the trail. Often they saved the pioneers time and money; but a Tennessee walker didn't belong here. Orson Millberg didn't belong here. Bernie Williams didn't belong, either. Too much time was passing. He needed to take care of business and head back to Chicago.

"Maybe you should turn him loose and let him graze," Bernie suggested.

"Can't. I've got important things to do." Orson wheeled the horse around and took off the way they'd come.

Bernie watched for a few moments. He'd lay odds that Orson would avoid contact with his fellow travelers. He'd want the womenfolk to think he was hunting, and he'd want the men to imagine him gainfully preoccupied elsewhere. He fooled no one.

Bernie watched the activities of the Crawford family until he located Megan. Her skirt swayed in the wind as she sashayed toward the water hole with the other women.

He'd just nudged Samson into a trot when Jeremiah ran up beside him. "Can I go with you? I know Pa would let me. I can ride our horse."

Bernie had made a huge effort to win over the boy. Children were honest in a way adults couldn't be. Bernie could learn more about Megan from listening to Jeremiah talk than he could from the lady herself. Truthfully, children made Bernie uncomfortable. They had runny noses. They made strange sounds, especially boys.

"Sure, Kid. I'll wait a minute."

Jeremiah returned faster than Bernie thought possible. Brown hair stood straight up and freckles dotted a white face. The kid bounced in his saddle, excitement evident in his every movement. "Pa said no gun, but I can watch if I stay out of the way."

"Stay behind me."

Jeremiah immediately prodded his horse to follow. "Pa says you're the best shot on the train. Is that true?"

It was, but Bernie hadn't realized anyone else recognized the fact. "No, I'd say Rawhide can outshoot me. Frank's pretty good with a gun and so is Dillon Trier. I've just been lucky lately."

"I'd like to learn to shoot, but Pa says I have to be thirteen."

"Thirteen is a good age."

"Yup, Pa wants Grandpa to teach me. He says Grandpa handles a gun a lot like you. Grandpa taught all his children how to shoot when they turned thirteen."

Bernie nudged his horse away from Frank. He scanned the distance for a sign of moose or any other worthy target. Seldom did information just fall in his lap like this. "Does your aunt Megan know how to shoot?"

"She can shoot better than Pa, but Mama says I'm not supposed to mention that."

"I won't tell."

Instead of smiling, Jeremiah clutched his horse's mane. "Can you solve secret problems?"

Looking at the trust in the boy's eyes, Bernie felt the first stirring of conscience. Here he was, using Jeremiah to glean information about Megan, and instead the boy looked at him as some type of hero.

"Sometimes. What's wrong?"

Tears shimmered in the boy's eyes, but they didn't brim over. The Crawfords were a tough bunch, thought Bernie, even the children.

"Maybe I can help," Bernie offered. Just because Megan Crawford deserved his scrutiny didn't mean little Jeremiah shouldn't deserve a little bit of guidance. Might be good for the boy.

"It's about snakes."

Forget the honesty of children, Bernie thought. *Kids are just plain unpredictable.*

"Are you afraid of snakes?" Bernie had a feeling he wouldn't be pleased with the outcome of this conversation.

"Oh, no. I like um."

Bernie nodded, waiting while Jeremiah looked from side to side, making sure no one could overhear. "It's my ma who's afraid of them."

No surprise there, Bernie thought. Allie Crawford looked to be afraid of her own shadow. She lived in the almost-barren wagon—her husband wanted to save the weight allowance for his Bibles—and slept most of the day away.

Unlike Megan, who seemed to only fear Indians.

"Why is your mother's fear of snakes a problem? Lots of womenfolk are afraid of creepy, crawly things."

"Yes," Jeremiah agreed in a whisper, "but Ma doesn't know about *all* the snakes."

"*All* the snakes?"

Jeremiah nodded.

"Give me a little more information," Bernie encouraged.

"I've been collecting snakes, or at least trying to," Jeremiah admitted, "in my jar."

Jar?

Now the tears shimmered closer to the surface. "And they're getting loose. Why, I bet there are near about ten snakes loose in Mama's wagon. She's gonna see one or something! What if it makes her even more sick?"

Laughter, the deep-bellied kind, made its presence known. Bernie's stomach hurt as he fought to keep it inside. Coughing, to mask an escaped chuckle, Bernie reined his horse and smiled reassuringly at Jeremiah. "I'll tell you what. I'll find time to search your wagon, and I'll make sure those snakes find a new home."

Jeremiah's eyes grew big and his mouth opened in apparent awe. *So this is what it feels like to bask in a child's admiration*, Bernie thought. Plus, if Bernie got caught in the Crawfords' wagon, he'd have the perfect excuse. Then Bernie heard the rustle behind him and Frank's light murmur. They'd spotted game. Just in time, Bernie stopped Jeremiah from charging forward.

❧

Every bone in his body ached. After returning from the hunt, most of the men had pitched in to help Anna Schmitt fix the axle of her wagon. Larson stood behind them, hands in his pockets, offering no advice. Orson, too, stood behind them, giving ridiculous orders and getting in the way. The repair took at least an hour longer because of the man's interference.

Bernie yawned. He couldn't remember so black a night. The stars receded in the sky as if not wanting to assist Bernie Williams in his quest. He lit a well-used tallow candle, smoothed out the blanket, and after lying down, took a folded piece of paper from his back pocket.

Before opening it, he looked down the line of wagons. It appeared that the Crawfords were all in bed, including his new best buddy Jeremiah, who'd wanted to sleep under the Trier wagon with Bernie. Dillon had pulled guard duty for the next four hours; Bernie would spell him. Oh, but he wanted to search Megan's wagon for "snakes." He couldn't believe it. He'd spent two weeks on his hands and knees looking for whatever Megan had been disposing of. Come to find out, he'd seen it—more than once. Noticing that this part of the trail seemed to have an overabundance of garter snakes hadn't given him any clue as to Megan's activities. All this time, she'd been setting free Jeremiah's snakes. Probably so her sister-in-law wouldn't come across one. Still, the comedy of errors had led to his getting permission to search the Crawfords' wagon. If he could just arrange the time. Allie only left the privacy of the canvas walls for short periods.

The light of a small candle sent a wavering shadow on the piece of paper. The Wanted poster had changed from a crisp vellum likeness to a soft, wrinkled one. Across the top, in bold, black letters, were the words: WANTED FOR MURDER. Down below, it said: $1000 REWARD. In the middle, Megan Crawford's face stared at him.

Chapter 4

Unknown Female, case number 41, drew her last breath on April 3, 1854. A ticket from the mighty Illinois Central Railway proved Megan Crawford had been a Chicago-bound passenger on April 2. A witness tied the two women together. A witness who disappeared after supplying a description.

Without the witness, they needed a bit more proof. Smoothing out the Wanted poster, Bernie studied the few words under the picture. He wondered who A.S. was. Someone had cared enough about Unknown Female, case number 41, to contact the Pinkerton agency at Washington and Dearborn Streets. Allan Pinkerton himself took the case. A.S. offered the reward, which explained the initials. Bernie hated initials. He'd rather have a full name or at least some type of identity. *Sheriff of Dodge County* was a good signature. *Sons of John Smith* was another good signature. A.S. was as big a mystery as the dead woman's name!

When Bernie took on the case, two days after the murder, Ronald Benchly hadn't come up with any connection between the two women; but since neither woman had a criminal past nor seemed to even have any criminal connections, very little was known about their histories. Ronald headed for Cedar County, Illinois, to dig into Megan's old life. Bernie joined the westward movement to keep track of her new one.

Ronald had discovered that Megan's brother, Louis, failed to meet his sister at the station. Caught in a massive spring storm, he and his family holed up in a small town outside Evanston until roads cleared. Megan had left a note with the stationmaster; and although the man suggested a nice hotel in the area, Megan had ignored his advice and rented a room on the wrong side of town.

Either she'd made a mistake, thinking she knew more than the stationmaster about the unfamiliar town, or she'd picked the shady part of town because she had shady business. No one admitted seeing her leave her room after check-in. As beautiful as she was, and on that side of town, somebody would have noticed her. In an area frequented by only down-and-outers and "women of the evening," Megan Crawford would have been as obvious as a rose amidst a mile of skunk cabbage.

Unless she disguised herself.

Could she successfully dress as a male?

He couldn't fathom such a possibility. Still, Bernie pulled his journal out of the saddlebag and wrote a note to himself: *Check clothing stores; show Megan's picture.* Later, if he needed evidence, this might be proven an avenue.

So far, his scribblings over Megan Crawford amounted to about a hundred questions. Most of them, even after a month on the trail, remained unanswered.

By far, the most damaging evidence, besides the missing witness's account, was her ability to shoot.

Unknown Female, case number 41, took one bullet to the heart. The shooter had been standing close and had used a pillow to muzzle the sound.

Guns were not the weapons of choice for most women. Would Megan really be an exception? Could she cold-heartedly pull a trigger?

Bernie kept going back to *why*—why had Megan been in the slum area of Chicago? A woman of her rearing should have followed the stationmaster's advice. But then, a woman of her rearing should have fainted the minute the cab turned onto Lower Gallagher Street.

Another unanswered question had to do with why Unknown Female, case 41, had been there. Neither female belonged. The fact that both had all their teeth, kept clean fingernails, and looked free of the pox declared their presence in the shantytown district as suspect. The victim's clothes weren't the quality of Megan's, not quite as expensive or clean; but they were neither the fancy do-dads of a tart nor the ragged filth of a squatter.

Bernie figured both Megan and Unknown Female, case 41, were out of their natural environment. Entirely out of character for Megan. He'd wait to form a hypothesis about Unknown until he had more information about her past. Someone had to be missing her. And why was she worth a reward to A.S.?

A twig snapped in the distance. Either Dillon had made a poor choice of guard location or something was amiss. Bernie held his breath as he patiently listened to the night sounds. He heard no more and settled back with Megan's picture.

He preferred hunting male perpetrators. The female killers, and there'd only been two he'd come in contact with, were hard-as-nails women who likely had never owned a pair of white gloves or cared overly much for clean hair. Megan proved an interesting quarry. For the most part, Bernie believed there were only two motives for murder: money or love, not necessarily in that order.

Megan didn't need money.

Love? Why would love bring Megan to Chicago?

Unknown had been married. A pale mark circled her ring finger. Why would Megan remove the ring after shooting the woman? Or maybe the ring had been removed before Megan pulled the trigger.

What kind of man could inspire Megan into such a lover's triangle? Was she thwarted? Jilted?

Could Megan Crawford be traveling the Oregon Trail to rendezvous with a man?

Wait! Maybe the man was already a member of their party! Who were the single men? The Cole brothers? Beau had seemed interested. Megan's rebuff could have been for show. Then, there was Dillon Trier, although Bernie hadn't noticed the two exchange more than a stray sentence. But with Dillon, Bernie thought he detected—and he wasn't a Pinkerton agent for naught—an attraction for Penny Rogers.

Maybe the man traveled with a different section of the train? That had to be it! And it certainly explained the rebuff of the Cole brother. Bernie nodded, folding the likeness of Megan and putting it back in his pocket. It also explained the even more puzzling issue of why Megan seemed immune to the charms of Bernie Williams.

Putting the notes on the Crawford case back in the saddlebag, Bernie glanced one more time over in Megan's direction.

Yeah, that explained it. To think Bernie wasted valuable time worrying about why the woman wasn't taken with him.

Vanity, vanity, saith the Lord. Bernie pushed that thought away. He'd been spending too much time listening in on Pastor Brewster's sermons when he was supposed to be watching Megan.

Watching Megan? Sometimes he thought he could watch her for eternity, then he reminded himself of why he was watching her. By far, she was the most interesting quarry he'd ever trailed. And as for leaving a trail of evidence, she hadn't. She was the most innocent acting criminal he'd ever trailed. She never even looked longingly at any of the single men. He had no clue who the other man could be. Bernie almost wanted to rescue her, and he didn't know from what.

It must have something to do with a challenge, Bernie thought, as he lay his head on the saddle and drew a blanket over his shoulders. Because no way was he allowing himself to become smitten with one of his cases.

Why, that would be downright unethical. And Bernie Williams learned ethics at an early age. Of all the lessons his Sunday school–teaching mother and strict father had taught, the sense of right and wrong had taken seed in young Bernie's heart and rooted deep.

Bernie stretched and turned over. Time to start thinking about Megan as more than just a simple criminal. She was a murderer.

Yet, Bernie Williams couldn't stop thinking about Megan Crawford as a woman.

❧

Megan couldn't believe they were taking an extra day of rest just because Mr. Millberg lost his hat.

Back home Megan owned over ten hats; she didn't miss them.

It seemed the hat that blew off Mr. Millberg's head had been hand-tooled, especially for him, by a master craftsman in Europe.

"Why didn't Orson pick it up when it blew off?" Louis asked over a breakfast of bacon and bread.

"Claimed he saw Indians." Mr. Williams had appeared, with his laundry in tow, in time to eat. Megan wondered how many meals it would take before their trout debt was paid.

Louis shook his head, picked up a plate, and loaded it with more food than Allie could possibly eat, even on a good day. He'd stoically ignored his wife's state of mind until Rebekkah started acting the same way. Now he walked slowly toward the wagon and carefully climbed in. Megan gave up on propriety and strained to listen. She couldn't hear the words, exactly, but she knew Louis wanted his wife to eat. For Louis, he was acting firm. As the gentle Crawford brother, he'd taken lots of ribbing for not having a temper. Funny thing was, he always got what he wanted.

Jeremiah's shout told Megan that he was still chasing butterflies with Henry. Rebekkah sat on a stump and watched them. *Why isn't she playing?* Megan wondered.

By rights, her breakfast table should be ready for clearing. Instead Mr. Williams sat there, legs outstretched, and such a look in his eyes that Megan shivered. He wanted something. What was it? He never asked her to go for an evening walk, like Jesse had Emma. He didn't woo her with words like Joshua had Bethany. No, instead the man invaded her space without permission and didn't have the good manners to say why.

"Your brother says you spent some time in Chicago. I've been there myself. What did you think of the town?" He had the longest legs Megan had ever seen. They went on forever. Now he crossed them at the ankles, and they became even more of a blockade she'd have to cross if she wanted to avoid his questions.

Chicago?

She'd thought the nightmares would end in Chicago.

The man wanted to know about Chicago.

Harumph. Chicago had only proved how inept she was at taking care of herself. "I liked Chicago just fine. I even purchased a new hat."

"Louis said you arrived there by train."

It was idle conversation, yet stilted. Did Mr. Williams really want to know about the stifling trip from one end of Illinois to the other? Miles when Megan longed to stretch but couldn't. Soot would have ruined her shoes and hems. The aisles were narrow and the mostly male passengers looked too appreciative of the young female's traipsing. Just before Megan boarded the train, her mother had advised, "Find an older woman, a grandmother type, sit by her."

Good advice, had there been someone fitting that description on the train. Instead there'd been a sour-faced mother with two screaming children. The open seat available in their section remained empty. The only other woman on the train must have worn all the clothes, unwashed, she owned. Megan might have been able to overcome that and the smell of onions, but the tears flowing down the woman's face increased even as Megan watched.

Megan took a seat across from her. She'd been a silent crier. Megan wasn't. Had she taken the adjoining seat, she'd have joined in the woman's sorrow. Homesickness and guilt were powerful foes tugging at the heart of a girl leaving home for the first time. Mr. Williams didn't need to know all that, so Megan said, "I liked the train, except it ruined my gloves."

Bernie raised an eyebrow. "And how did you manage that?"

"All the soot. My gloves turned black within hours."

His gaze dropped to her hands. He had green eyes, like a cat. She wanted a dress of the same color. She felt a powerful attraction to this man. She didn't know why. All she could figure was, every time she turned around, there he was. It took all her will to keep herself from hiding her hands behind her back. A year ago, had her hands and skin been in such pitiful shape, she'd have hidden inside and combined the soaking of lemon juice and wrapping of certain plant skin for a month.

She wasn't interested in him. Could not be interested in him.

She had the feeling the conversation wasn't what he wanted, but she didn't care. "Mr. Williams, I need to clean up. Would you like some more coffee before you go?" Megan pointedly surveyed the area. Around their campground, women were doing the chores they'd put off for too long. Men were repairing harnesses and doing the things men do. Even Mr. Millberg was busy convincing a small group of men to help him backtrack his movements and locate the missing hat. Only Mr. Williams lounged, unoccupied.

Bethany waved. Megan returned it. No doubt her friend figured the wild Mr. Williams was doing some courting.

"No thanks." Mr. Williams set his cup on the plank and stood. He looked like he wanted something more.

Picking up Louis's dirty plate, Megan said firmly, "Goodbye, Mr. Williams."

❧

So seldom did the grown-ups have time to play, Rawhide indulged Penny Rogers's request to have an early evening potluck. The women pulled together, each intent on providing a dish superior to the offerings of their nearest neighbor. Granny Willodene made her famous fritters. Megan's mouth watered. Even Anna Schmitt joined the women, something she hadn't done since the onset of the journey. She contributed coffee, a staple they all owned, but no one neglected to say a thank-you. Strong bonds were sometimes forged over the feeblest of overtures.

Butterflies lost their attraction to Jeremiah. Now he and some other boys sat at Rawhide's feet and learned the fine art of whittling. Rebekkah was a permanent shadow at Megan's side. The little girl had donned her mother's apron and pretended to be older. Megan might have been touched at Rebekkah's aping had it not been for the forlorn expression on her niece's face.

They prepared beans with a dash of molasses, a dish cooked often by the Crawford women. Back in Illinois, Megan had failed at culinary attempts. When she'd first accepted Jasper's proposal, most of the reason had to do with a certainty that they'd always employ a cook.

Leaving Rebekkah to stir, Megan climbed in the wagon, careful not to disturb Allie. Penny wanted something tatted and lacy. It took Megan only minutes to unearth the tablecloth that had once belonged to her grandmother, also a Megan. She and her husband, Liam, crossed over from Ireland and settled in the beautiful rolling hills of Illinois. Megan's memories of

Granny Meg were few, but most had to deal with food. Megan should have paid more attention to Granny Meg and her cooking advice. No matter how often Mr. Williams claimed to enjoy her meals, Megan refused to believe it. Besides, the man had a silver tongue and was more than willing to use it.

As Megan rejoined the women, she wondered where he'd gone. He hadn't followed Mr. Millberg's brigade. She certainly hoped he wasn't trout fishing. Why, the red-and-white tablecloth might never clear the smell of fish, thanks to Mr. Williams. Also, the pond where they'd done laundry this morning had more mud than the Mississippi. Any fish coming from such waters would taste of it. Of course, if any man could pull a sweet-tasting trout out of—

Stop thinking about him.

She handed the tablecloth to Penny. The doctor's wife had big ideas about how to put on an Oregon Trail potluck, but her sister-in-law knew how to throw a party. In a matter of hours, she was putting together entertainment worthy of a Friday night social. Megan had no clue what role her tablecloth would play; she just hoped to get it back in one piece.

Then, she heard the shout from the lead wagon. To the west, Indians, on small, painted ponies, rode toward them. One wore Orson's hat.

"Rebekkah, Jeremiah, over here. Now!" Megan forced herself to walk slowly toward their wagon so as to not scare the children. Her brother followed her gaze and took up his rifle.

Her niece and nephew, plus Henry Green, gathered close. Allie poked her head from inside the wagon, where she'd been sleeping. Seeing the Indians, she immediately disappeared inside, leaving Megan to deal with the children, not that they were scared of the Indians, not a bit.

"What kind of Indians do you think they are?" Henry whispered.

"Nothing to worry about." Rawhide rode up beside them. He spit and glanced at Megan, and she wondered if he recognized her unreasonable fear. "Them Indians and their pinto cayuses won't hurt us."

"Miss Megan, there really ain't nothing to worry about," Henry said. "Papa says Indians is just people. Be nice to them, and they'll be nice to us."

"It's true, Megan." Mr. Williams joined the crowd of people witnessing Megan's fear. Someday, if she ever had a parlor, she'd reenact this scene, and it would be a comedy.

"I'm not scared." Megan forced her hands to still.

Rawhide kicked his horse and rode ahead. Mr. Williams waited a moment, his eyes studying Megan, and then he followed the wagon master.

Although she didn't want to, Megan couldn't stop watching Rawhide and Mr. Williams deal with the Indians.

Rebekkah stayed nestled close. "Aunt Megan, what do you think they're doing?"

"Probably just bartering for food." Megan touched Rebekkah's shoulder, noticing her niece's white face and fidgeting fingers. Funny, Rebekkah wasn't a nervous child. Indians had been a blight to the wagon train since Illinois. Never had Rebekkah even blinked. The girl had always stared, fascinated, at the brightly colored clothes and often painted horses.

It wasn't the Indians. Maybe her mother's strange behavior was having some effect. No, the hard routine of the trail kept the children from dwelling on their mother's strange behavior.

They accepted their father's word and simply thought Allie was sick.

There was something else. Something different about Rebekkah.

"What's bartering?"

She needed to be there for Rebekkah until Allie got better. Taking a breath, Megan forced her voice not to waver. "Making some sort of trade. They leave us alone, and we give them a cow."

"Not our cow!" Rebekkah's eyes widened, and she looked back at Moo. Named by two young children, Moo didn't realize that her name caused more chuckles than admiration.

"Moo's safe. Don't worry." *Easier said than done*, Megan thought to herself even as she said the words.

Rebekkah's hand grasped Megan's. Tiny fingers worked their way into a clutch. "I won't worry if you won't worry."

"Sounds like a deal to me," Bernie returned, silent as ever.

"I like to worry," Megan announced. "It gives me something to do."

"Then you need something more to do." It looked like he intended to keep talking, but an already quiet wagon train came to a deeper hush as the Indians rode away.

Megan watched as most of the women left the shelter of their wagons. Geneva Green marched straight. The sight of Indians hadn't bothered her a bit.

"God's will," she said about each and every struggle.

Henry took off to follow his mother, Jeremiah at his side. Rebekkah stayed plastered against Megan, both arms wrapped around her aunt. Both arms.

"Rebekkah, where's your doll?"

Rebekkah didn't answer. Instead she bowed her head and in a whisper said, "She's gone."

"When did you lose her?"

"Two days ago."

"Why didn't you tell me?" Megan couldn't believe it. Her niece's prized possession. The doll had blinking eyes and was the size of a real baby. One arm hung limp, thanks to Megan's early morning mushings, and there was a crack from the top of the doll's forehead to an ear, thanks to Jeremiah and a short-lived slingshot; but Flossie remained a much-beloved doll, forever in Rebekkah's arms.

"Where did you lose her, Honey?" Mr. Williams's tone was sincere. Megan's stomach dipped as she looked up at the man. His smirk had disappeared, and instead of looking cocky, he looked concerned.

Tears ran down Rebekkah's cheeks. "She's gone. That's all. I need to go be with Mama."

Silently, Megan and Bernie watched the child climb into the wagon. Louis shrugged and tapped the whip on the back of the oxen. With a clumsy lurch, they continued.

"When was the last time you saw her with the doll?" Bernie said as Rebekkah disappeared inside the canvas.

"I'm trying to remember, but that doll is such a part of her, I no longer even notice."

"Tell you what, I'll backtrack some. I've got time before this shindig starts. If that doll's on the path, I'll find her."

❧

Even the flies accommodated Penny Rogers's gala and must have found someplace better to go. Megan's molasses beans hadn't even needed to be covered, thanks to the absence of the winged pests, or maybe the flies had heard about her cooking. The sun set early, and twinkling stars gave an ethereal light to the festivities.

Megan found an unoccupied corner and leaned back against a wheel. She watched as her brother and his wife did a slow dance around the fire. He'd gotten Allie, wheedled her, actually, from her bed. The man fiddling stopped, and Louis and Allie sat on a log, scooting over to make room for Doc Rogers.

Rebecca didn't play with the other children. She moped, going from her mother's side to Megan's lap and, finally, to her own secluded corner.

It was so nice to just sit. Megan's eyes drooped. Had today really been that much busier than the preceding? Truly, she'd never felt this tired.

Sleep. She needed sleep, and maybe as fatigued as she felt, there'd be no nightmares.

"You okay?" Mr. Williams stood over her. His shadow loomed, huge. Was he really that big? Three slow, popping noises sounded in the background. She started to stand.

"Megan," he said again. Why was he talking so slow? And he didn't look like he was backing away, so why did he sound so distant?

"I towld yooou. Call me Missss. Cawft."

The last thing Megan heard before the black velvet of unconsciousness completely enveloped her was Orson Millberg's voice as he bellowed, "Who shot my horse?"

Chapter 5

Rawhide, the wagon master, galloped up to where Bernie rode point. The captain didn't look harried, given the events of the last two days. This was his fifth trek—his second time with their trail guide—across the Oregon Trail and nothing seemed to surprise him, especially about people. Bernie figured that Rawhide had almost enjoyed listening to Orson Millberg demand justice. The ex-banker was now shy one hat and one horse. He, alone, had been victim to the Shoshone visitors. They were responsible for the loss of his hat. Bernie knew they'd been lucky not to lose more to the Indians. Wars had been started over less than the theft of good headgear.

The Tennessee Walker had been a fine—no, a great horse until Orson subjected him to the trail. Walkers were known for their temperament. They were not meant for the Oregon Trail. Orson thought more of how a horse looked than how a horse worked.

Bernie's own horse was a five-year-old Appaloosa. He'd have gone after it himself had the Shoshones made off with it. Most of the men felt the same way about their horses, although the wisdom behind that way of thinking was debatable. After all, the Shoshones hadn't made off with Orson's horse. Anna Schmitt had shot it.

Terrified by the shadows playing outside her wagon, victimized by a husband who did little or nothing to make her feel safe, Anna had heard strange noises. Bernie hadn't realized that Anna apparently feared Indians as much as Megan. And since Anna didn't have the type of husband who might investigate a curious noise, she took his gun and started shooting.

Some in their company thought the loss of Orson's horse far outweighed the loss of Larson Schmitt. No one even mentioned how Anna shot a hole in Granny Willodene's water barrel. That Anna had shot her own husband was news enough.

Bernie'd shot more than one man, but never anyone he loved. He figured Pastor Brewster had his work cut out for him, but Anna refused to talk to the man of God. Bernie, Dillon, and Pastor Brewster dug the grave late at night, hoping to spare Larson's wife the sight of the freshly turned dirt. There were three neighboring graves: two children and one unidentified. Granny Willodene said it was a shame to get this close for nothing.

The next morning, as Pastor Brewster gave the eulogy, Anna had stared straight ahead. Some of the women tried to comfort her, but Anna Schmitt would have none of it. After the final amen, she headed for her wagon, hitched it herself, and then stood, lips pressed together in irritation, and waited for Rawhide's shout to begin.

As for Anna, she trekked on. Larson's death hadn't changed her world one bit, outwardly. Bernie hadn't noticed any tears, nor had she commented when Rawhide mentioned that more people had died on the trail from gunshot wounds than they had from sickness or Indians.

Pastor Brewster had plenty of sheep to care for. He devoted plenty of time to both Anna and Megan. The dog must be getting downright dizzy what with his master's goings back and forth. Neither woman acknowledged the man's efforts. Anna muttered to herself, and Megan slept.

With the curious events, the company felt vulnerable, and guards had been doubled. Bernie doubted he'd spend much time spelling weary drivers. Rawhide, without realizing it, had given Bernie duties reserved for second in command, mainly riding far front to see what might be coming their way. Just when he wanted to be near Megan the most, he'd be farthest away.

Some Pinkerton agents felt free to divulge their identity to a limited number of bystanders. Bernie'd always played his cards close to the hip. There were plenty of personal questions he wanted to ask the captain about Megan. Instead, he simply said, "She still asleep?"

Rawhide nodded. "Three days. Doc's going wagon to wagon and trying to figure if it might have been something she ate."

"That's a good thought; but if it had been food, there'd be more people complaining. And food sickness doesn't make you sleep."

Rawhide made a face; clearly he'd eaten his share of spoiled vittles, too. "Doc says the same thing, but he's wondering if she's allergic to anything."

"Her sister-in-law slept quite a bit. Could there be a connection?"

Rawhide shook his head. "Doc says no. Sounded pretty sure."

Bernie couldn't remember being so scared in his life. Once,

he'd taken a bullet to his leg, thought he'd lose it. Off hand he couldn't name any one-legged Pinkerton agents. He'd once crossed a river, only to lose his horse, his possessions, and for a moment, he thought he'd be pulled under, too, in a current stronger than it looked. He'd met Indians who wouldn't think twice about putting an arrow in his back. But he'd never been as scared as when he watched Megan Crawford slink to the ground in an unnatural sleep.

It hadn't been a faint. Bernie's mother had fainted often, but then she wore a corset so tight that breathing was a luxury. Thank goodness the women on the trail, save Lavinia, traded their sense of style for common sense. No, when Megan Crawford fell at his feet, he'd thought for sure she'd died.

It had only taken him a moment to react. He'd scooped her up and ran toward the doc's wagon without even hearing the shouts of concerned neighbors.

She'd weighed less than his saddle. And smelled much better.

"Orson thinks it was the Indians." Rawhide urged his horse up the steep hill they were climbing.

"Orson thinks when he gets to Oregon, he'll find pigs already cooked with forks and knives in them."

Rawhide nodded. "There was a full moon last night. Nothing good happens under a full moon."

Bernie doubted the full moon did anything but help the travelers see better. It had certainly aided him, when just minutes before finding Megan, he'd searched their wagon. He'd not found one shred of evidence linking Megan to the death of Unknown Female, case 41.

He'd not found any snakes, either. Jeremiah would be pleased, if Bernie remembered to tell him.

The Crawfords were a thrifty bunch. The five members shared one trunk. Although advised to take three dresses, the women had two. No wonder Megan was so devoted to laundry. Most of the wagon's space was taken up by Louis's trade stock. The man not only sold books but did taxidermy on the side. A good second occupation. There were limited cooking utensils, and they hung outside. Someone had sewn pockets onto the sides of the canvas. Bernie's exploring proved that most of the pockets were filled with a belonging that could be traced to Louis. Obviously the man figured to make enough money to purchase the niceties of a home that women find so appealing.

Very little belonged to Megan, besides her clothes. She didn't keep a journal, at least not one he'd found. He'd never observed her writing in one, either. Even needlework, a mainstay of the trail women, belonged to Allie instead of Megan. It was as if Megan decided on the spur of the moment to head for Oregon.

Which made sense if she'd decided to commit murder.

Had she known she would murder the woman when she left Illinois?

Or, somewhere in Chicago, did the belongings of Megan Crawford wait for discovery? No, she'd always known she was meeting Louis in Chicago to head west. Or had that been a ploy as well? Maybe she had told friends and family she would be meeting Louis, but she really planned on meeting someone else.

Wait! Were her belongings in somebody else's wagon? Maybe the man who inspired her to commit murder? Bernie let out a low whistle. Their train was miles long. He'd set his sights on this one division. The accomplice, if there was one, might be in a division so far ahead that it would take weeks to even pinpoint a likely suspect.

Touching his hat in farewell, he nudged Samson back toward the Crawfords' wagon. His attendance at their mealtime was now a given. He had secured a role as trusted friend. It almost shamed him that his actual goal, the reason he sat by their fire every evening, was to make sure an unconscious girl didn't escape.

At least he kept telling himself that was his main goal.

The train couldn't wait for Megan's recovery and, as if prodded into action by an unseen finger, Allie Crawford took back her role as caretaker of the Crawford family. How Louis stayed sane was a mystery to Bernie. He'd endured one hardship after another since leaving Nebraska.

"God's will," Mrs. Green said. Louis nodded and sold Mrs. Green a new Bible.

Bernie didn't think God could be blamed for all the calamities. He figured man had some hand in the goings-on of the Crawford family.

Doc said Megan'd either wake up or fade no matter if they stayed still or moved. Ahead, sections of the train scattered. Some pointed their wagons in the direction of Salt Lake City, but more than half headed northwest toward Muddy Creek.

Rawhide claimed that up ahead lay better water, better game, and better passage. With Megan unable to function, Allie Crawford picked a sensible time to slowly start her journey back into normalcy. She nodded as he walked toward her.

Bernie had to give his mother due; she'd always claimed there was a bright side to every situation. Far as Bernie could tell, the positive side to Megan's ailing was her sister-in-law's return to reality. She'd probably been a fine-looking woman at one time. Maybe she still was. A good bath and some sun might be beneficial. Her husband didn't seem to notice the circles under her eyes, how peaked she looked, or how often she paused to rest; he was just happy to have his wife back. Chewing on the noon meal of bread and bacon, Bernie had to agree with Jeremiah's earlier declaration—"When Aunt Megan remarked that she wasn't a cook. . .she wasn't joking."

Jeremiah took seconds for the first time, Bernie noticed. Louis did, too. Only Rebekkah seemed fretful at the change. The little girl stayed close to the wagon, checking often on her aunt Megan.

Bernie managed to snag the last piece of bacon just as Doc and the preacher walked up. They had a few more moments before their division started again. Doc, medicine bag clutched tightly in one hand, climbed into the back of the wagon; Allie went with him. Rebekkah started cleaning the plates while Jeremiah helped his pa with the animals.

The preacher had a look on his face that Bernie'd seen before. Fishermen often got it when there came a faint tug on their line. Women got it when the right man reached for their hand. If possible, Bernie might claim later that the dog even looked expectant. Pastor Brewster took a biscuit and sighed. "I am indeed glad that Mrs. Crawford's feeling better. I sorely missed her fresh bread."

"She's a fine cook," Bernie agreed.

"I notice you've been taking your meals here quite often. Since it's not on account of *Miss* Crawford's cooking, I'm assuming you've got other interests—say, courting—on your mind?"

Bernie almost choked. He supposed to the casual observer, it did look like courting. And, although he hated to admit it, it did sometimes feel as such. "I'm not in a position to take on a wife."

"I doubt if any man feels ready for that responsibility. I certainly didn't. Yet, I know true happiness now. The good Lord knew in the beginning, back in Genesis, when he said: 'It is not good that the man should be alone; I will make him an help meet for him.' Are you sure you don't need some counseling? Miss Megan walks with Jesus. I cannot imagine her feeling comfortable with your lack of commitment."

"You're overstepping the bounds of friendship." Weaker men had stepped back from Bernie when he used that tone of voice.

Brewster didn't even flinch. "I think I'd feel more like I was intruding if I hadn't seen you riding over here just awhile ago."

"What does that have to do with anything?"

"Well," Pastor Brewster said, finishing up the last bite of biscuit, "I know what a man looks like when he's praying."

"I—"

"You were praying, Mr. Williams."

"I—"

"As it says in James: 'And the prayer—' "

" '—of faith shall save the sick .' Chapter five, verse fifteen."

Pastor Brewster's eyes lit up. "You do know your Bible."

"My pa was a preacher." It had been more than ten years since Bernie'd said those words. They felt dry, like what you'd get from an empty well. And although he'd stopped going to church, Bernie had never stopped praying. *Must be habit, this talking to God.* Sometimes, Bernie had the feeling God listened.

Oh, yes, Bernie did think God listened. Bernie just didn't believe that God often answered.

"Williams?" The inquisition look left Pastor Brewster's eyes and speculation took its place. "A common enough name. Your father wasn't by chance Horace Williams?"

It was the Oregon Trail. It had taken his father far from home, never to return. A simple plea from the Methodist *Christian Advocate*. They weren't even Methodist! Horace Williams hadn't read the *Christian Advocate* before. How it found its way into his hands, Bernie and his mother never knew. But Horace felt the calling and answered it. He went to convert the Indians. Gertrude Williams didn't know how or why or even when he died. After four years of waiting for her husband's return, she'd given his clothes to a needy family. She packed their few belongings, for preachers were rich in salvation but poor in investments, and moved Bernie and herself into her father's home.

Bernie's maternal grandfather hadn't approved of the marriage between his daughter and a lowly circuit rider. Grandpa attended a hell-and-brimstone kind of church, while Bernie's father had preached more about love. A once-happy home became an empty home. Bernie's mother died, maybe of a broken heart, and Bernie ran away when he was fifteen.

Bernie blamed the Oregon Trail for taking his father; he blamed God for taking his mother.

No one had mentioned Horace's name in years. "He was my father; and if you don't mind, I'll be checking on Miss Crawford now."

The preacher had a look of awe on his face. Bernie knew had he stuck around, Pastor Brewster would have waxed poetic on some of Horace Williams's published sermons, or perhaps Brewster had even heard him speak. Horace Williams had been a circuit preacher with a vast area he claimed his own.

Allie was crawling out of the wagon as Bernie started up.

"She's looking better," the woman whispered.

Before Bernie could hoist himself in the wagon, Henry Green tugged on his shirt. Not in all his days as a Pinkerton agent had Bernie had so many obstacles present themselves in the form of do-gooders. Megan seemed surrounded by champions. The preacher had interfered more than once and now this boy. With his left hand, Henry clutched Bernie's shirt. He held something behind his back with the other.

Bernie forced himself to count to ten. He knew the Green boy had a crush on Megan. He also knew the Green boy asked more questions than the pastor. Right now, Bernie just didn't have the time. "What can I do for you, Henry?"

Henry took a bunch of wildflowers from behind his back and thrust them at Bernie. "Do you know what kind of flowers these are, Mr. Williams?"

"No."

"Me, either, and you don't appear to be having much luck. My pa says flowers always work. I thought I'd help you out." Henry kicked at the dirt. "Jeremiah says Megan's sweet on you an' I might as well give up."

"Thank you." Bernie took the flowers. He didn't know how he'd explain the flowers. Maybe he should just give them to Doc Rogers.

"I think I'll be sweet on Miss Rebekkah now anyway," Henry admitted. "She likes candy. I can tell. She also knows all the names of the presidents. Maybe if you asked Miss Megan—"

Before the boy could offer any more advice or ask any more questions, Bernie swung himself into the wagon. Doc Rogers had somehow managed to get cross-legged in the small space left in the Crawford's wagon. Words seemed to fly off his pen as he scribbled notes in a thick journal.

"Them flowers for me?" Doc said without looking up.

"Would you believe it if I said yes?"

"No."

Bernie hunkered down beside the doctor, wishing the prairie schooner came in a bigger size. Trying to read the man's chicken scratch was a study in futility. Bernie gave up. "You got any ideas, Doc?"

"Yes, and none of them are good."

"Want to run them by me?" Bernie offered.

Doc still didn't raise his head. "Very few ranchers I know have any medical knowledge unless it has to do with their horses. You an exception?"

"No."

"No one else is sick. There's not even a high fever nearby. If I were Pastor Brewster fixing a sermon, I'd call that a miracle."

"Is she going to make it?" Bernie's words were in a whisper—why, he couldn't say. There was no reason not to voice the question normally. Yet the choking, hard-to-swallow, dry-well sensation had returned.

"I think so. She's young, she's strong, and she's made it this far."

She barely made a bump under the covers. Sweat beaded just under her hairline. A white nightgown, which had seen better days, bunched up by her neck. If the doc had turned away or closed his eyes, maybe Bernie might have straightened out the bedclothes. Megan deserved to be more comfortable. Suddenly the wildflowers made perfect sense. Bernie lay them on her pillow. No, that didn't work. Made him think of death.

"Stick them in one of the pockets," Doc suggested.

The closest, accessible one required Bernie to lean over Megan. He balanced his hand on her pillow, too close. He could feel the heat from her body. A few wisps of hair fanned across his hand. Come to think of it, he'd never seen her without her bonnet before. He'd known she had golden brown hair, but he'd not guessed the length of it.

Three days without even a sponge bath and she still rated as the most beautiful woman he'd ever seen. "So you have some ideas?" Bernie urged. He needed to leave the closed space, get away from her, clear his head.

"I have a few," Doc admitted.

"What are you thinking?"

"I'm thinking someone tried to kill her."

❧

"Who's Caroline?"

Megan's mouth tasted of medicine. She stuck her tongue out a few times and tried to rid herself of the bitterness. "Water."

Mr. Williams quickly left the wagon and returned with a dipper. She drank thirstily and long. She didn't ask but expected him to willingly make three trips to refill that dipper. He did. And then he asked, "What happened to Caroline?"

"Why are you in my wagon?" Megan croaked the words. She had always thought the wagon small with her niece and sister-in-law taking up space. Mr. Williams reduced the wagon to doll size. She tried to swallow, but couldn't. Even her ears hurt from the effort.

"Megan!" Allie climbed in, a wet towel over her wrist. After placing it on Megan's forehead, she said, "Mr. Williams is the one who carried you here after you fainted. He might have saved your life by finding you so quickly. He's been as worried as the rest of us, what with you being out so long."

"How long was I sick?"

"You've been out for four days."

Megan sat up so fast that she lost the blanket covering her. Although her nightgown was more than decent, she grabbed the blanket and held it to her. The wet towel landed on Mr. Williams's boot. Now he had one clean spot. She wanted to ask this man, no, demand of this man that he leave, but she had a feeling he had more answers than Allie.

"Was it cholera?"

Bernie shook his head.

"Brain fever?"

Allie shook her head.

"Well, then, what was wrong with me?" Her voice gained strength as anger built. It didn't make her feel any better, but it sure made her sound in control.

"Doc doesn't know." Mr. Williams took advantage of the situation and straightened the bed coverings.

Megan wanted to throttle him, but weakness kept her arms at her side, and the drumming of a monster headache made her close her eyes.

"Maybe we should let her rest," Allie suggested.

"Good idea." Mr. Williams said the words, but his tone disagreed with them.

Megan heard the gentle swish of her sister-in-law leaving the wagon. When had Allie returned to coherency? Mr. Williams lingered. He smelled of tobacco. No doubt, he'd been riding with Rawhide. She felt his hand on her forehead. It was scratchy but firm, and for some reason, it soothed her even more than the return of the wet towel.

"Tell me what you were doing right before you fainted."

Megan opened her eyes. "I don't faint, Mr. Williams."

"All women faint."

He said it so matter-of-factly, like all women fit in some nice neat bundle to be carted around as the male wished.

"How many women do you know?" she demanded.

"Bernie." Doc poked his head through the back of the wagon. "It's time for Miss Crawford to rest."

Allie crawled past the doctor, balancing a bowl of soup.

Four days, Megan thought as she allowed her sister-in-law to spoon-feed her. She felt hungry, but the food had no smell or taste. Well, there was a bitter taste in Megan's mouth, but it could not have possibly resulted from Allie's cooking.

Mr. Williams lingered. One leg over the edge of the wagon, the other planted firmly inside. He didn't want to go, Megan realized, oddly pleased with his intrusion.

Four days passed, and I didn't even realize it.

Four days without nightmares.

"Auntie Megan, I missed you." It was Rebekkah. Mr. Williams lifted the tiny girl into the wagon. She clutched a pale blue blanket, a baby's blanket, and blinked back tears.

"I know," Allie whispered. "It's okay. I gave her the blanket. I need to tell my children the truth so they don't worry."

Rebekkah knelt beside Megan and tucked her hand in her aunt's. "I said a prayer about you. God answered it."

Mr. Williams made what sounded like a choking noise.

Who's Caroline? he had asked.

And for some strange reason, Megan wanted to tell him.

She fell asleep instead.

Chapter 6

Baby blanket dolls are just as good as china dolls," Megan insisted. For the first time since getting off the Chicago-bound locomotive and meeting up with Louis, she'd spent days sitting. She'd rather be walking. Every time the wheels went into a rut, the whole wagon lurched, sending Megan's stomach into a type of roll not even the wheels could imitate. Walking would have been easier, but Doc said *no*. Never before had Megan so looked forward to the nooning. Funny, even when the wagon ceased moving and she stepped outside, the motion stayed with her, making her dizzy and more than a little nauseous.

Rebekkah didn't notice that her aunt often turned green. Her whole attention focused on the loss of her blanket. She'd trustingly turned it over to Aunt Megan, but now the little girl looked doubtful as she stared at the forming piece of art. "Dolls are not blue."

"Who says?"

"Henry Green says. He saw that you were sewing, and he asked me what you were making, and then he laughed."

Megan chuckled. If Henry Green intended to be a farmer,

then he should know more about how ugly ducklings can turn into swans. The Oregon Trail appealed to farmers, maybe because they could see the difference from when they left the overcrowded East and traveled to the barrenness of the Big Sandy, where water either was nonexistent or tasted of alkali; and they could appreciate the change into this lush green land. The changing of the seasons, Megan compared it to.

The Bear River Valley followed a healthy stream. There was plenty of clean water, more fish than Megan ever wanted to see again, and the rich soil actually had the farmers sniffing at the air. They edged forward with more energy than they'd had since Fort Laramie. Henry had perked up along with the scenery. He brought Rebekkah flowers every day. Megan might have suspected that he'd taken to reading one of Bethany's novels, except Henry couldn't read.

Where was Henry? He usually nooned with them and then stuck around asking questions and seeing if they had some chore for him to do. He liked feeling useful. Megan glanced around, finally locating the boy following Jeremiah and Mr. Williams.

Harumph. Maybe Mr. Williams was reading a novel aloud to Henry. That would explain the cluster of dead flowers that Megan kept in the pocket closest to where she slept. Why had he brought her flowers? Outside of his being there every time she turned around, he'd not said one romantic word. She should throw the flowers away. She really should.

Mr. Williams had been on her mind constantly since she'd awakened. Megan tried to tell herself it was because she'd seen him, first thing, when she opened her eyes. Those flowers would be pressed and kept as soon as she could convince her brother to part with a heavy book. Louis always grumbled when he found plant resin stuck between the pages of a book.

She'd watched Mr. Williams so often this past week that she knew exactly where he parted his hair—an intriguing discovery, considering how seldom he took off his hat. She knew how his eyes crinkled when he started to smile. Megan even knew that his socks needed darning, but she could thank that finding to Jeremiah.

As she knotted the thread, Megan allowed herself the luxury of pretending that someday she might darn Mr. Williams's socks. She'd be sitting on a rocking chair in a warm room. Maybe a baby would be sleeping nearby. On that day, maybe she'd called him Bernie instead of Mr. Williams. A few of the women on the trail called their husbands by their given names. Megan liked the sound of it. And, from what she could see, those husbands and wives had a togetherness she envied.

Bernie.

Such a handsome-sounding name. Strong. Dependable.

Not like Jasper.

Dare she depend on that?

Rebekkah touched the top of the blanket. "Mama 'splained to me about the little baby."

The needle pricked Megan's finger as she missed the tiny hole in one of Louis's buttons. She'd been working on the eyes and had been so lost in a Bernie-created fog, she'd almost forgotten Rebekkah's presence.

The button fell to the ground, blending with the dirt. Rebekkah retrieved it without a word. Megan swallowed. Just how much explaining can you do to a child? It was easier to concentrate on the shirt. Louis had brought two good blue cambrics.

Now both of them were missing the bottom button, but Louis was too happy about his wife's improved state of health to care. Megan almost believed that, had Allie requested a sudden return to Illinois, Louis would say yes without blinking an eye.

Return to Illinois?

Was that the answer?

No, not at the moment. She had Rebekkah leaning against her knee. "So," Megan asked gently, "you understand why your mama was so sick?"

"Yes, she went to bed for a long time because she was so sad about losing our baby brother."

Megan had no clue as to the gender of the child. What should she say? These weren't her children. They'd sure felt like it, though, since Nebraska. Gathering her niece close, Megan said, "Everything's all right now. You don't need to worry."

"Yes," Rebekkah agreed. "Mama's good. You're good. Everyone's good, except. . ." Her eyes dropped to the strange-looking doll taking shape in Megan's hands.

"Honey, you'll like this doll. Give it a chance."

Rebekkah nodded, although she still didn't look convinced. Behind their wagon, Allie finished the noon dishes. Rebekkah scampered over to help. She'd timed it well; Allie finished the last plate as her daughter joined her. A mother's touch had given the girl back her vitality; but the loss of the doll still kept her from complete happiness. That was no surprise. Grandpa Crawford had given her the doll last Christmas. He'd told her to keep it always and remember he loved her.

What he hadn't said was that they'd probably never see each other again. Although a good many of the Oregon-bound did return east, Louis had stars in his eyes about the future, and Louis had made true every one of his dreams so far. In a family where the sons had roots so deep they reached China, Louis, alone, was a creeping vine.

Oh, they'd probably return someday for a visit, Megan acknowledged, but would her father still be alive? She was the youngest of eight, born of her mother's old age. At least that's what her mother had always claimed. Her father was twenty years past that, he'd often joked.

I was wrong to run away, Megan suddenly realized. *I can never live up to a new wineskin until I get rid of the old wine.*

Megan started to stand, intent on finding Rawhide and seeing about the likelihood of a lone female finding passage back East. If she returned, would Mr. Williams even notice? Instead, she sat back down as Doc Rogers straddled Rebekkah's recently vacated stump.

"May I join you?" Doc sat before she could answer, which meant a *no* was out of the question, besides being rude. He eyed the doll with some suspicion.

Why did everyone look at her as if she was doing something sneaky? First Mr. Williams and now Doc.

"I'm making Rebekkah a blue doll," Megan said, as if she needed to explain. Actually, crocheted dolls weren't all that uncommon, especially out West. And having a blue doll just meant it was special.

"I can see that." Doc looked a little nervous.

Megan *felt* nervous. During the four days she'd been unconscious, she'd obviously mentioned Caroline. Enough to pique Mr. Williams's interest. What all had she said in front of Doc Rogers? She put the doll down, better not to have a needle if he started asking about Caroline.

"Is there something you'd like to tell me?" Doc urged softly.

Megan squirmed.

"As your physician, I'm only asking so I can be of help. If you're not comfortable talking with me, Bethany would be more than willing to listen."

Tell Bethany? No, impossible. If anything, Bethany favored Caroline. Both women were gentle souls intent on happiness. Bethany chose well with this doctor husband of hers. Caroline had made the greatest mistake of her young life, accepting Jasper Mapes's proposal.

"Okay, I'll be blunt," Doc said. "Did you enter my wagon during the potluck back at Fort Bridger?"

"What?" The doll slipped from Megan's lap and fell on the grass.

"There are at least five doses of laudanum missing. I need to know: Did you try to take your own life?"

❧

Bernie figured it was past time to find out what Megan discussed with the doc. They'd sat, the two of them, until the train started; and then, even though Doc told her she had to ride, they walked together for more than an hour. Bernie'd have missed their rendezvous had he not returned to the wagon train to spell his horse. Samson picked up a stone. Even after Bernie had taken his knife and sent the stone flying, Samson favored the hoof. Time to let the horse walk without a burden. Bernie returned to the train in time to gain an insatiable curiosity. For a woman who claimed she didn't faint, she'd certainly been white after her conversation with the doc.

Should he go to Megan? And do what? Ask what? His job centered around asking questions. He should be the one asking questions! Why wasn't he asking questions?

"Mr. Williams, do you know how to make moccasins?" Henry was of a different breed than Jeremiah. Since giving Bernie permission to court Megan, Henry had decided to keep Bernie in sight at all times. Now Bernie had two boys traipsing at his heels.

Henry asked more questions than a lawyer—make that more questions than *two* lawyers. "What kind of tree is that?"

Did it escape the child's notice that Bernie seldom bothered to answer?

"What's laudanum?"

Now Henry had Bernie's attention. "Where did you hear that word?"

"From Doc Rogers."

"He told you about laudanum?"

"No, he was looking for his laudanum. I saw him out searching in the box attached to his wagon. I asked him what he was looking for and that's what he said. I told him I would help him find it if he just told me what it was. He told me he was too busy to explain and to come back later. What's laudanum?"

Bernie figured the boy deserved something—a prize of some sort for giving him the first new piece of information he'd had in days. "It's a type of medicine."

"What does it do?"

"It makes you feel better." Bernie slowed his steps so that they matched Henry's. "Why don't you go find me some more flowers for Miss Megan. I still need the help."

Henry nodded. "I can find the best flowers."

There goes a future Pinkerton agent, Bernie thought. *He's asking the right questions of the right person and showing me up.*

Doc Rogers sat beside his wife on the buckboard as their oxen grunted toward Soda Springs. He held a basket in his lap and sorted what looked to be different types of leaves.

"Got a minute?" Bernie could tell by the intense look on the doctor's face that something bothered the man.

"You feeling okay?" Doc asked.

"Yes."

It took Doc a minute to figure out that Bernie wasn't in the mood to have a discussion in front of Bethany.

"Okay," the doctor said, setting the basket down.

There were too many people around. Never before had Bernie noticed how loud came the sound of men shouting orders at their animals; women shouting advice at their children; and the Green youngsters shouting just for the fun of it. A normal day for everyone else. Pinkerton agents seldom knew normal days. They knew about criminals, and theft, and deceit.

They knew better than to become personally involved with a woman whose face graced a Wanted poster.

The people in the surrounding wagons would be more than surprised to find out they had a murderer in their midst.

Many would not believe it.

For the first time, Bernie had trouble believing in the guilt of his quarry. His gut told him Megan was innocent.

A Wanted poster said otherwise.

Oxen pounded the dirt and somewhere in the distance birds screeched loud enough to drown out Bernie's thoughts. He wished he could enjoy the day like everyone else.

The Oregon Trail stole his father; it would steal Megan from him, too. When the trail ended for the pioneers, it would end for him and Megan in a much different way. Maybe, after he turned her in, he would become a rancher, all alone, somewhere near the Willamette Valley.

Alone, where no one could disappoint him.

Or he, them.

"You want to talk, or we just gonna walk in silence?"

The sounds Bernie'd been focusing on suddenly weren't as loud or as important. Doc had a concerned look on his face. "You sure you're feeling all right?"

"Yes, it's not me I'm worried about. I need you to tell me what's going on with Megan Crawford and why you're looking for laudanum. "

"Preacher said he thought you were interested in Miss Megan," Doc said with a grin. "How much you been talking to her? What kind of help do you need?"

"I'm not here because I'm spooning with her."

"Oh. Then, just what are you here for?"

"What's wrong with Megan? Did she try to kill herself?"

The grin disappeared from Doc's face. Gone was the boyish expression that at first made Bernie think the Doc looked too young to be a man of medicine.

"I'm not just being nosy," Bernie said. "You said you thought someone was trying to kill her. Now I hear you're looking for laudanum. I want to know what's going on."

"Megan is not suicidal, if that's what has you worried."

Bernie's relief was so intent, that he audibly let out a sigh of relief.

Doc stopped. He waited as long seconds ticked by. "You want to tell me, since you're not courting, why you think Megan Crawford is any of your business?"

Reaching in his back pocket, Bernie took out the papers

that identified him as a Pinkerton agent. He handed them to the doc and then waited while the man read the words.

"Okay, what does your being a Pinkerton agent have to do with Miss Megan? Do you think someone is trying to kill her?"

Bernie passed over the Wanted poster. "No, she killed somebody, and I'm trying to prove it. You say she didn't try to kill herself. Can you prove that?"

"No, I can't." To the doc's credit, his mouth didn't drop open as he stared at Megan Crawford's likeness. "I don't believe it. Quite frankly, I'm surprised you do. I'd heard you Pinkerton boys were supposed to be intelligent."

"What were you two talking about this afternoon?"

"You'll have to get that bit of information from the young lady. As her physician, I'm bound not to repeat confidentialities."

Most of the time, Bernie felt no qualms about using force to gain information; but this time, on this never-ending Oregon Trail, he felt too close to those involved. Maybe that's why he felt the attachment to Megan. The proximity. He stuffed his hands in his pockets. "Surely the law supersedes the binding."

"Not a bit. Here's what I can tell you. Someone relieved me of five doses of laudanum. I'm convinced they somehow managed to drug Megan." The doc put a steadying hand on Bernie's shoulder, like a father would a son. "So, while I believe you're looking for a murderer, and while I believe there is someone on the train willing to take the life of another, I don't think that person is Megan. I think whoever it is, is quite willing to take Megan's life."

Megan's life.

He'd spent this long depending on others to provide the proof that would mean Megan spent a life behind bars. Time to go to the source. He'd not let anyone harm Megan. Given time, maybe he could hire the right lawyer. Megan could pay for her crime. After all, his father, Horace Williams, claimed that to err is human, to forgive divine. Or was that from the Bible?

It was almost like Bernie could hear his father talking, giving words of comfort on the hated Oregon Trail.

It was time to get to the truth.

There was no place for Megan to run. He'd arrest her, proof or not. At least that way if someone was trying to quiet it—maybe the man she'd killed for—then at least Bernie could keep her safe.

For the first time, Bernie wondered if Megan might be afraid.

She was in the wagon. He'd spell Louis; that way he'd be alone with Megan and no one would bother them. He managed to take two steps.

"Mr. Williams?"

Rebekkah tugged on Bernie's sleeve. For a moment, Bernie feared that hanging around with Henry had inspired another child who wanted too many questions answered.

"Mr. Williams, my brother says you can solve secret problems." This Crawford did cry. Tears started at long lashes and slowly made their way down Rebekkah's chubby cheeks.

Chubby cheeks that reminded him of Megan.

"I solved one problem," Bernie said gently. "I've not had much luck since."

"I have," she hiccupped, which only let the tears flow harder, "a problem."

"Can you tell your pa?"

"No."

"Your ma?"

"No, Jeremiah said to tell you. He wanted me to tell him, but I couldn't, and he said you were a good solver of secret problems."

A secret problem she couldn't go to a family member with. How many secrets did the Crawfords have? At this point nothing would surprise Bernie. Maybe Rebekkah collected snakes, too. Bernie didn't dare hope little Rebekkah could tell him about Caroline. For a moment he was tempted to ask. Ronald Benchly would have.

"What is your problem?" he asked.

She tugged on his sleeve a little, and he realized that she wanted to whisper in his ear. He'd been riding since early morning. He'd skipped noon meal. His knees were on fire, and he had at least two inches of trail dirt in his throat.

He wanted a bath; he wanted Megan; and he wanted to head back East. He wasn't sure of the order. Instead he went down on one knee.

Rebekkah's hand was hot and damp as she cupped it behind his ear. "It's about my doll."

"The one you lost or the blue one?"

"I didn't lose it."

"You didn't? You know where it is?"

Rebekkah nodded. "Anna Schmitt has it."

He had to stop thinking he couldn't be surprised. Not in a month of Sundays had he suspected Anna of doll theft. "Why does she have your doll?"

"I saw her drawing people; and when I asked her to draw me, she got mad because she doesn't want people to know she can draw."

Why would anyone with talent like that be so intent on keeping it a secret? Bernie scratched his chin. "So, she took your doll to keep you quiet?"

"She said she'd draw Flossie. She said if I didn't tell, she'd make a beautiful drawing that would last me forever and ever. I've waited and waited, but, I don't think she's really going to draw Flossie. I'm scared to go ask. She looks at me like she hates me. I want my doll back. Will you go get her for me?"

Now that wouldn't be fun. The woman just shot her husband, was grieving in a most particular way, and Rebekkah wanted him to walk over and ask for a doll.

"I'll try."

Before Bernie had time to hail Louis and volunteer to drive, Rawhide sent one of the Coles back to say they'd found the perfect campground. An hour later, Bernie was eating fish again. Jeremiah caught two, and Henry caught three. The Greens joined them for supper, and Bernie couldn't find an opportunity to draw Megan aside. She stared at him but avoided him so skillfully that he couldn't get near her. On the other hand, Rebekkah wouldn't leave him alone. He'd seen her journal, complete with misspellings and one comical drawing of him. He'd been shown her favorite books, the only two her pa let her bring along. She'd sung for him, and right now he wore a necklace she'd found back at Fort Bridger. It was made of shells, and Rebekkah just knew it had once belonged to an Indian chief.

Up ahead, in a division so removed from theirs that they hardly knew the travelers, a fiddle started up. It carried on the wind and set Bernie's foot to tapping. There was a festive feel to the air. Mr. Green fetched his fiddle and clamored in with the same tune.

Bernie pushed himself up. Megan did dishes. This time she wore her dark green wool. It complimented her eyes.

"Go for a walk, Miss Megan?"

She blushed. "I told you to call me Miss Crawford."

"I seldom do what I'm told. Now was that a *yes* or a *no*?"

"Go." Allie took the towel from Megan's hand.

"Go." Louis gave her a gentle push.

Before she had time to answer, Bernie took her by the elbow and directed her toward an open patch of tall grass blowing in the breeze. Flies buzzed but seemed content to leave the young couple alone.

He had more questions than time, but he hated to start. The minute he brought up Caroline, she'd change the subject and most likely clam up. Maybe he should use the preacher's technique: pretend indifference and gain her trust.

No, he'd wasted too much time already.

He opened his mouth, desperately trying to decide which question to ask first.

"I like your necklace," she said, grinning.

He didn't want to ask questions. He wanted to kiss her.

So, he did.

Chapter 7

The Sunday morning sermon on forgiveness couldn't have come at a better time. Many on the trail outwardly demonstrated the need. Frank Barnes wasn't speaking to Rawhide. The farmer claimed he'd been doing an unfair share of tasks. Rawhide joked, cajoled, reasoned, and finally spit tobacco on the farmer's shoe. Tempers were high. The Cole brothers had come to words over whose cow went lame. Pastor Brewster painted stripes on the cow, dividing it into three parts, and offered to slice it up so they all could have their section. The parable worked as well for Pastor Brewster as it had for Solomon. Orson Millberg harangued his wife to such a degree that Pastor Brewster finally pulled the man aside.

Megan thought it was easier to forgive others than it was to forgive oneself. Idabelle Barnes had refused to walk with Megan for two days now since Megan refused to divulge her feelings about Bernie Williams.

How could Megan divulge when she wasn't sure herself? After Bernie kissed her, he'd taken off faster than a tornado. Now he avoided her and spent more time with Doc! And never had she thought she was the type to relive a kiss over and over. Mr. Williams hadn't asked for permission. He hadn't inquired about her dreams, beliefs, or even about the weather. He overstepped the bounds of good manners, and she wished he'd do it again.

But right now she sat listening to Pastor Brewster list some steps to take to feel the spirit of forgiveness. Megan mentally started making a list herself.

Rawhide had laughed over her idea of wanting to return east alone. She should have known better than to go to the man. It might take a few years, but she'd get home. She needed to talk with Caroline's parents and sister. It might not do any good, but she needed them to know how sorry she was. They might slam the door in her face or they might think she'd exaggerated, like her own father had, but sometimes the truth needed to be known.

There were other, more immediate things she could do. First of all, she could stop feeling sorry for herself and start giving. The boys on the trail experienced adventures galore, but the little girls were fewer in number and had done boy stuff just to get along. Megan decided to form a girls' social club. She'd do a little bit of Sunday school teaching and a little bit of school teaching—none of the Green children could read—and do some crafts. Why soon, maybe the whole train would be carrying blue dolls.

After Pastor Brewster finished preaching, two hymns were sung, and the final prayer was given. Megan then searched out Idabelle Barnes and worked in an apology while asking for help with the girls' social club.

Yup, forgiving others worked. Idabelle even had blue yarn.

Megan looked over at the Schmitts' wagon. Anna seldom left

the seclusion of her own little space. Maybe Megan should invite the woman for supper. Allie had invited both the Schmitts to share a meal back in Nebraska. They'd said no. Others had made overtures to no avail. Anna Schmitt probably needed a friend. Megan took two steps.

"Miss Megan, my wife says you've been looking for me." Pastor Brewster fell in step beside her.

Taking a deep breath, Megan said, "I was."

"Well, what can I do?"

Megan clasped her hands together, tightly. "Doc thinks I should talk to you and tell you what's been bothering me."

"I won't lie. I've known something was amiss. Sensed it for a long time. Does it have anything to do with Bernie Williams?" The minister smiled, no doubt believing that everyone deserved the happiness he himself had found.

"Not directly." Megan slowed her steps. Her hands started shaking, even in the tight clasp. She'd given Doc only the briefest of explanations. In some ways, the men on the trail were easier to approach than the men back in Cedar County. She'd have lost her voice if anyone had asked her to talk to the pastor or doctor from her childhood.

She'd done a poor job of talking to her father. He hadn't believed her. Today, for the first time since telling her father, she was about to tell the truth about Caroline.

Her best friend.

Dead now almost seven months.

"Go ahead," Pastor Brewster urged.

She told herself to talk fast, get it over with, before she had second thoughts and shut right up. Doc said it wasn't good to carry such guilt inside. Megan began, "Pastor, I promised myself

I wouldn't ever fall in love. I thought I didn't believe in it. But, I'm really having serious feelings for Mr. Williams. You're right about that."

Brewster nodded.

"You see, last year at this time I was engaged. He was older, already nearing forty. He purchased the farm next to ours and was quite wealthy. I figured my life would be easy. Looking back, I'm ashamed of how 'immature' I was."

Brewster didn't say a word; he only continued nodding.

Megan took another breath. "About a month before we were to be married, he got real mad at me—I don't remember why—and grabbed my arm so tight that I had marks left from his fingers. It surprised me. None of the men in my family ever touched a woman in anger, but I thought maybe he hadn't meant it or that I bruised easy. Then, a few days later, coming home from a Friday night social, he missed a turn; and when we tried to go back around, his buggy stuck in the mud. I thought it was funny, so I giggled. Pastor, he slapped me so hard I tasted blood."

Brewster still didn't say a word, but his eyebrows drew together making one line. "Go on."

"I gave him back his ring the next day. Two of my brothers went with me. It took a few weeks, but both James and Johnny made sure to remind him to leave me alone. I was frightened. I thought he'd hurt me, but he did something worse."

"What?" Pastor Brewster stopped. The train kept going, breaking around them.

"He started courting my best friend. I told Caroline, Pastor, really I did; but she said I was just jealous because I'd lost him. Jasper made sure they didn't go to places where he knew I'd be.

He told her to avoid me. Within a month, they were married. It happened so quick. I think if there'd been more time, I could have convinced her. We'd been best friends all our lives. She married him, Pastor, and two months later they found her. . . They found her. . ."

Pastor Brewster pulled her toward him, patting her on the back and offering a prayer, the words so softly spoken that she couldn't make them out.

Megan wanted to pray, too, but the words kept pouring out. "I should have stopped the wedding. I should have shot that man. I should have been able to convince my father to stop the wedding, but he said I was overreacting and that it was his fault that, as the youngest and only girl, I was so spoilt."

"I watch you, Megan. The way you cared for your niece and nephew when Allie was sick. I watched how carefully you treaded on young Henry's feelings when he laid his child-heart at your feet. The whole train watched that and admired you. You are a good woman, and what that man did was horrible, but it was not your fault. God said in Mark, the seventh chapter, that evil comes from inside. There was no way for you to battle that."

"I'm afraid, Pastor Brewster. I'm having feelings for Mr. Williams, but I'm worried that what happened with Jasper Mapes will be such a memory that I'll never trust a relationship. With the exception of my brothers, I don't know if I can ever completely trust a man."

"You trusted me enough to tell me."

"You're a man of the cloth."

"Which doesn't make me perfect, either. Give Mr. Williams a chance. I think you'll be surprised." Pastor Brewster squeezed her hand. "Read Mark, chapter seven. Read it every day as often as possible."

Trust, Megan thought, as Pastor Brewster walked away. She'd spent most of her life trusting everyone. One man had reduced her to trusting no one. Could she trust again?

It took her until the next morning to make her decision.

Allie and Rebekkah both snored; they claimed Megan did, too, but she knew better. The Greens were still asleep. Megan hurried and dressed. She felt wonderful, free. Carefully, she climbed out of the wagon.

Jeremiah had grasshoppers in his jar. Megan left them alone.

Since Mr. Williams seemed so intent on avoiding her, maybe it was time to make her presence known. She hadn't seen him even once yesterday. He'd missed the Sunday morning sermon and he hadn't shown up for meals. He'd been scouting the area. The man did sleep; she knew that. And he usually bunked under Dillon Trier's wagon.

He wasn't there, nor was his horse tied behind. He did have a scattering of laundry. She could take that. Why, she'd be the first to reach the riverbank this morning. When she finished, she could hand deliver his clothes and use them as an excuse to find out why he'd kissed her.

She bundled up his shirt and pants. Seven brothers had taught her one thing. Clean out the pockets. She wouldn't look. It felt a little like trespassing to empty a knife, some coins, and a stash of papers. As she sat them down on his blanket, the biggest of the papers unfolded.

She'd seen Wanted posters before.

Just not one with her face on it.

Chapter 8

Anna Schmitt's wagon was dirty. All the wagons were dirty, for that matter, but the grim despair that clung to this one was tangible. Bernie found the doll. It was tucked behind a hope chest. He'd had to move some drawings aside. She'd drawn quite a few trains. Bernie recognized two Chicago-based ones. From more recently, there was the serious face of Joshua Rogers as he scribbled a note. Another drawing showed Katie, the Millberg's Irish maid, as she bent over an open fire. Then there was one of Orson Millberg sitting on top of his horse. As Bernie looked at the one of Geneva Green, he could almost hear the words "God's will" coming out of her mouth. Anna was gifted, no doubt, and she'd studied somewhere.

Flossie's captivity hadn't been kind. Some kind of brown fungus grew on the doll's fingers and inside her eyes. Bernie would clean it off before returning it to Rebekkah.

What a strange woman the Schmitt woman was. Bernie's father, the preacher, had often been suspicious of artsy folks, but had said to love them anyway.

Larson and Anna had been mismatched. Gorgeous men seldom married plain women unless there was money involved.

Maybe the woman made money as an artist? Why on earth would they be traveling west? The Oregon settlers had little money to spend on art. Was Anna hoping to make drawings and then return east?

The wagon certainly didn't look like it belonged to a moneyed couple.

The early morning sounds of birds and gurgling water and even a few toads croaking in the distance serenaded Bernie as he left the wagon. Anna probably was drawing near Soda Springs. Riverbanks appealed to artists for some reason.

Bernie wondered whose likeness she'd concentrate on today.

He stopped. Did he have an answer as to why such a talented woman hid her gift? What kind of woman would kidnap a little girl's doll just to keep the child from talking?

Anna could shoot a gun.

She could shoot laying hens, water barrels, and even a husband.

He'd never liked initials.

Bernie started running. Not only had Anna hired the Pinkertons to find Megan, she'd drawn the Wanted poster herself.

❧

It wasn't every day that water boiled right in a river. Megan figured she'd have really done the laundry justice if she'd really been looking for a watering spot. Instead, Megan came looking for Mr. Williams and stumbled across somebody else.

"I didn't know you could draw." Megan stepped closer.

Anna Schmitt's pencil stilled. "You've been a pest since the beginning."

"What?" Megan held the Wanted poster behind her, wishing she'd ignored the sight of Anna drawing. There were better things to do, like find Mr. Williams and demand an explanation. The back of Megan's neck prickled.

"What Anna is saying—" Mr. Williams appeared, without making a sound. He stood by a tree, his eyes never leaving Anna. "—is that I should have arrested you and headed back East more than a month ago. Isn't that right, A.S.?"

"Yes." Anna's initials were already on her current drawing. The likeness of Bethany Rogers leaned against her husband, book in hand, smile on face. Anna snarled, "But you pussyfooted around. A pretty face always does it." Anna dropped her charcoal into her pocket and took out a gun.

Megan stood too close. The gun stopped not even an inch from her forehead.

"Get rid of your weapons, Mr. Williams." Anna moved the gun closer, closer. It touched the skin above Megan's right eye.

"Now. All of them. And I've been drawing Wanted posters for years. I know exactly how many guns a Pinkerton agent carries."

Megan watched as Mr. Williams emptied his pocket, and both holsters, and a knife from under his pant leg.

"What's going on?" Megan was surprised that she could even manage the words. A gun was being held against her head. A gun!

"Who did you kill in Chicago, Anna?" Mr. Williams took a tiny step but backed up when he heard the click.

"Whoa," Megan said. Maybe she was the type of woman who fainted; but if she fainted now, would it all the more inspire Anna Schmitt to shoot her?

"I didn't kill anyone in Chicago." Anna's tone didn't change and the gun didn't wobble.

"Then why are you holding a gun on Megan?"

Anna snatched the Wanted poster out of Megan's hand. "This. I'll get the reward. Her parents will be more than grateful that I found their daughter's killer."

"There's still no proof," Mr. Williams said. "You were hoping I'd find something. Weren't you?"

Anna laughed softly. "Some Pinkerton agent you are. I'd hate to be the one to send you to an early grave not knowing that a *woman* outsmarted you. There is proof. The wedding ring. It's still in the Crawford wagon. In the same pocket as those stupid flowers you gave her. I can't believe you didn't find it. Too busy thinking about a pretty face, no doubt."

"But—" Mr. Williams began.

"I'll shoot you," Anna said, nodding, "and say it was Megan. I've got the Wanted poster right here. You were threatening to arrest her, and here all along she thought you loved her."

"I do love her," Mr. Williams said quickly. "And she doesn't have a gun."

"How sweet." Anna snarled again. "I have a gun. She took it."

He loves me.

Megan no longer felt like fainting. She had questions, though; and anger started to bubble. "Why am I on that Wanted poster?" Funny how she could move her lips without moving her face. Megan felt frozen. Time stopped, and she couldn't even hear the noises from the train. Surely people were waking up. Surely her brother would miss her.

"After I killed Larson's wife, I needed to blame somebody." Anna spoke quickly, as if getting a burden off her chest. "And there you were, right in the same broken-down hotel. It was perfect."

"But you're Larson's wife," Megan said.

"No, I was his mistress, but I wanted to be his wife. Trudy wouldn't give him a divorce. He didn't love her."

"So you killed her." Mr. Williams tried a tiny step. Anna frowned, so he stayed put. "And what about the witness?"

Anna laughed, a bitter sound. It scared Megan almost as much as the gun.

"I was the witness. I'd done enough posters for that sheriff so when I showed up with the one I did of Megan, he believed that somewhere there was a witness. I made up a phony description and he started looking. He was a bit puzzled as to why a witness had been sent to me without him knowing it, but he had no reason to doubt me. After I get rid of both of you, no one will have reason to suspect me."

"Why are you heading west?" Mr. Williams asked.

"To make sure you arrest her."

"If you loved Larson enough to kill his wife," Mr. Williams said, "why did you kill him?"

"He didn't love me," Anna whispered. "He never loved me."

And then, a gun sounded.

Megan hit the ground. Her knees hurt from the force. Sand, damp from the nearby river, went into her mouth. Her eyes closed tightly, and she tried to figure why she still breathed.

"Nice shot, Dillon. I'd help you up, Megan, but if you open your eyes, you'll see we have Miss Schmitt, and she no longer has a gun. Dillon shot it right out of her hand."

Only Megan heard his next words, so softly were they spoken.

"God answered this prayer."

Chapter 9

I don't want you to go back East, Aunt Megan." Rebekkah carried two dolls now. Flossie didn't seem to mind her new blue sister.

"I'll miss you, too, but I have some things to take care of." Megan figured Rebekkah didn't need to know about escorting Anna Schmitt to the nearest fort to turn her over to the authorities. That could be explained when Rebekkah got older and the tales of this journey were bantered again and again by the adults.

Megan looked back at Bernie. He was busy assuring the Cole brothers that he did, indeed, know the proper belongings a future rancher should carry across the Oregon Trail. Bernie intended to resign from his Pinkerton position. But first he wanted to find the family of the late Trudy Alexander. Finding relatives shouldn't be difficult now that they had a name. Larson's last name had not been Schmitt. It had been Alexander.

The crying woman on the train. Megan wished now that she'd sat by Mrs. Alexander, comforted her, anything. Mrs. Alexander had lodged on Lower Gallagher Street in order to meet with her wayward husband. Megan had been there because of a mistaken address for an aunt.

Megan shuddered. Since the time of Cain, man had raised weapons against brother when consumed by greed. Women could raise weapons, too. Megan didn't understand how, but watching Bernie guard Anna Schmitt taught her that trust was a glorious thing and possible.

"Bernie and I will come to Oregon next summer. He'll be a rancher." Megan grinned. This was Bernie's way of compromising. He'd not been happy at all when Megan suggested the idea of a husband and wife Pinkerton team.

So I'll be a writer, Megan said to herself while opening her new journal. Louis sold more than Bibles. He'd parted with this book and not even charged her.

Megan didn't put in a date. She started by writing the dedication:

To Caroline.

It would be a grand gesture to dedicate a dime novel to Caroline.

Well, maybe Megan would dedicate the second dime novel to Caroline.

Megan carefully scratched out the only two words she'd written in three days.

She tried again.

To my beloved husband.

PAMELA KAYE TRACY

Pamela is a new bride living in Arizona, where she teaches at a community college. Pamela had her first novel of inspirational fiction published in 1999 by Barbour Publishing's **Heartsong Presents** line. She has been a cook, waitress, drafter, Kelly girl, insurance filer, and secretary; but through it all, in the back of her mind, she knew she wanted to be a writer. "I believe in happy endings," says Pamela. "My parents lived the white picket fence life." Writing Christian romance gives her the opportunity to let her imagination roam.

Bride in the Valley

by Andrea Boeshaar

Dedication

In memory of my father, Roy L. Kuhn,
February 1932 – September 2002,
known as "Papa" to his nine grandchildren. . .
you will be missed.

Chapter 1

Early morning colors of pink and gray were painted across the horizon. To Penny Rogers, they looked like strokes from the Master's brush. On the other hand, if she tilted her head and squinted her eyes just right, the sky became flowing yards of dusky silk with a rosy sash to match. Perhaps it was an evening gown that she would wear to the reception after a lovely symphony. In Penny's mind's eye, her handsome escort's face appeared; and he just happened to resemble Mr. Dillon Trier, the Millbergs' driver.

Penny sighed dreamily. Wouldn't he look dashing in a dark jacket, crisp white shirt, and black necktie?

"Miss Penny, are you all right?"

Inhaling sharply, she whirled around at the sound of the familiar voice. She heard that voice everyday—mostly in her daydreams.

"Mr. Trier. . .yes, I'm quite all right." She felt herself blush.

"You had your face all scrunched up. I thought maybe you'd taken ill."

"Um. . ." Penny sucked in her lower lip, not wanting to divulge her fanciful behavior just now, especially since Dillon Trier was a part of it.

Suddenly, and without warning, he took hold of Penny's upper arms and pulled her against him. With her hands splayed across his broad chest, she gazed up into his face, thinking her most wonderful imaginings had just come to pass. However, Dillon's next words brought her back to reality in a flash.

"Miss Penny, you almost started your skirts on fire." Releasing her, he removed his worn, leather gloves, leaned over, and began to swat at her hems. "Campfire is still smoldering as far as I can see."

"I'm so clumsy. . . ."

Straightening to his full height of over six feet, Dillon gazed down at her, wearing a warm smile. "Well, now, I wouldn't say that. Clumsy isn't a word I'd use to describe you."

"Really? And what word would you use, Mr. Trier?" Penny could hardly wait to hear it.

"Ah, well. . ." Dillon appeared suddenly uncomfortable. Lowering his strong chin that held the most delightful little cleft, he studied his boots for a long moment. "I'm not too good with words," he admitted at last.

"That's quite all right," Penny replied, deciding she shouldn't have put the poor man on the spot. It's just that she'd been wishing for so long. . .hoping and praying. . .

Glancing over her shoulder, she frowned at the smoking pile of charred buffalo chips. "You're not too good with words, and I'm not too good with campfires." She looked back at Dillon. "Guess we're even. One would presume that after all these months on the trail, I would have learned to cook over an open flame, but—"

"Miss Penny," he said with an earnest expression, "I reckon you're too hard on yourself. You're doin' fine, and I never did eat a more tasty breakfast than the one you served up this morning."

"But I burned the biscuits. . .again. And the coffee was much too strong."

"Can't ever make coffee too strong," Dillon said in his Missouri twang that never ceased to fascinate Penny. This somewhat introverted man, who kept to himself much of the time, seemed to always be around whenever disaster struck. True, he wasn't a learned man, not a scholar like Papa; but he was intelligent, hardworking, strong, and brave. Best of all, he knew the Lord Jesus Christ.

However, that's about all she really knew of him—even after all these months.

"Miss Penny? Your breakfast was good. Real good."

She smiled up into Dillon's deep brown eyes. "Thank you, Mr. Trier. You're awfully kind to say so."

He shrugged, lowering his gaze and suddenly examining the hard-packed dirt under his feet.

With a little smile, Penny hunkered down and gathered her cooking utensils. Dillon's occasional bashfulness stirred her heart all the more. "I'm ever so thankful that it was Beau Cole who married the Millbergs' maid and not you."

A pause.

" 'Scuse me?"

Penny swallowed hard, realizing her folly. She'd spoken out of turn again! Would she ever learn?

Embarrassed, she peeked up at Dillon, only to find him wearing a confounded expression.

"The Millbergs' maid. . .Katie and me?" His gaze darkened. "Now, why would you think something like that?"

"I've offended you, haven't I?" Penny stood. "I certainly didn't mean to. Please forgive me. I have this terrible habit of saying what's on my mind before thinking it through first. My former headmistress at school, Mrs. Throckmorton, was forever reprimanding me for my outspokenness."

Dillon lifted his gaze and looked past her. "That's all right. Easy mistake to make, given the fact that Katie and I are of a like social standing. We're both Millberg hirelings and nothing more."

"On the contrary, Mr. Trier. Social class had nothing to do with it. Besides, Katie is a Cole now and not in the Millbergs' employment. And she's. . .well, she's quite lovely."

"I didn't rightly notice."

"You didn't?"

"Well, now, don't act so surprised. Beauty is in the eye of the beholder."

"How very true." Penny smiled. "And you said you weren't good with words. . . ."

"I'm not."

"I beg to differ."

Dillon exhaled a long breath. "Differ all you like, but I'm still curious how you came to the conclusion about Katie and me."

"Oh. That." Penny frowned. "Well. . .it was a misunderstanding, really. You see, my sister-in-law and best friend, Bethany. . .well, we noticed you and Katie eating together at mealtime. We just figured the two of you were romantically involved. So when Lavinia Millberg told us that their maid was getting married—"

"You assumed it was to me."

Penny swallowed hard, praying he'd understand. "Beth and I were obviously mistaken."

"Seems so."

"Yes, and I apologize for the wrongful assumptions on my part."

Dillon nodded. "Apology accepted. But lemme get this straight. All these long months on the trail, you thought I'd set my cap on Katie O'Neil?"

Penny managed a weak nod.

"Hmm. . ." He furrowed his brows. "Reckon that explains a lot."

"Whatever do you mean?"

"Nothing." He shook his sandy brown head, and the muscles in his jaw seemed to relax. "Nothin' at all. . .just that I'm not now, never have been, nor ever will be sweet on Katie."

Penny tried to stifle her smile. "I'm glad to hear it." Realizing how forward she must sound, she quickly changed her tone. "Ah. . .I mean. . .I'm glad to hear it for Beau Cole's sake. After all, we can't have two grown men fistfighting over a woman."

Dillon chuckled softly and donned his wide-brimmed leather hat. "No, Ma'am. We sure can't have that." He seemed thoroughly amused, much to Penny's chagrin. "I'll see you at noontime, if it's still all right that I partake of the midday meal with you and your family."

"Of course it's still all right." Penny looked around him to where the two Millberg women were floundering in Katie's absence. "We can't have you starving to death, now that Lavinia and her mother are doing their own cooking."

Still smiling broadly, Dillon gave her a parting nod. Then, as if in afterthought, he leaned toward her and whispered, "Their cookin' is why you didn't hear one complaint out of me about burned biscuits."

With that, he chucked her under the chin and strode away, heading for the overcrowded wagon he'd been hired to drive.

Penny whirled around and sighed. "Be still my foolish heart. . . ."

Women. Dillon sure couldn't figure them out. Especially that little blond with eyes so blue they rivaled the sky on a perfect summer day.

Penelope Rogers. Her name was branded on his heart for good, it seemed. But that she thought he was interested in the Millbergs' maid all this time proved he hadn't done a good job in letting his intentions be known. And just what were his intentions anyway?

Marriage.

A home.

A family of his own.

He envisioned Miss Penny helping to make his dreams come true. But would someone like her, someone so beautiful, educated, and refined, ever seriously consider a man like him? It appeared she liked him. . .did he dare to hope?

Seeing as he was the fourth son in a family of six boys and three girls, Dillon didn't stand to inherit his father's farm in Missouri. Worse, since he hadn't established himself in Oregon yet, as he planned to once he arrived, he was as poor as Job's turkey! He had nothing to offer a woman like Penelope Rogers. In truth, he had no business even thinking along the lines of courtship.

Except he couldn't seem to keep his distance.

Dillon heaved an exasperated sigh as he readied the Millbergs' second wagon. Fool thing. He should have never agreed to drive this overstuffed rattletrap all the way to Oregon. However, he needed the money and a way to get out West. This job seemed to supply both needs. But if this monstrosity, known as the Millbergs' piano, didn't make it to Willamette Valley in one piece, Dillon was out of both a job and his pay. That was the deal.

"Good morning, Mr. Trier."

He cringed, hearing the simpering voice of the Millbergs' daughter. Then, after a quick glance in her direction, he nodded politely. "Miss Lavinia."

"We missed you at breakfast this morning."

"Thank you, but I ate with the Rogerses."

"Yes, I saw that."

Doing his best to ignore the young woman, Dillon concentrated on his present task of securing the wagon. His gut feeling said Lavinia Millberg was up to no good. . .as usual. Dillon didn't trust her—spoiled and pampered as a queen's house cat, with a temperament to match. In fact, if he were a betting man, he'd wager that the thick-wasted brunette was, at this minute, trying to work her wiles on him so he'd be fired. Mr. Millberg had warned him that his hirelings were not to consort with his daughter—not that he had a mind to. But Miss Lavinia seemed the type who liked to watch people fail as a direct result of her actions. He'd seen in the past how she'd tried to come between Josh Rogers and his sweet bride, except the doc was quick to recognize a scheme from a mysterious virus. And she bore false witness against Megan Crawford to that Pinkerton detective. . .of course, Bernie wound up marrying Miss Megan, which ruined Lavinia Millberg's sordid plans. Furthermore, Dillon had personally witnessed Miss Lavinia's shameless flirtations with the preacher after last Sunday morning's service—with his new wife by his side, no less! Of course, the preacher handled the situation in a manner befitting his station.

Yessiree, Lavinia Millberg was up to no good.

"I can cook, you know," she stated defensively. "I'm just not accustomed to such. . .such primitive means."

"Yes, Ma'am." Dillon wasn't about to argue the point.

"Shall I expect you at noon?"

"No, Ma'am. . .but I thank you for the offer."

When no reply was forthcoming, Dillon assumed she'd stomped off in one of her usual huffs. But when he turned to fetch more rope, he found her staring at him, her head tilted in a calculating manner.

"Don't tell me you're sweet on Penny Rogers."

Dillon couldn't help a small grin. "I ain't 'sweet' on anyone, Miss Lavinia," he drawled. "Sweet don't describe anything about me."

"Humph. Well, that's good. I would hate to tell Daddy that you're distracted by a silly blond who quotes Shakespeare incessantly and, therefore, you're unworthy of your position as his driver."

Gritting his teeth, Dillon pivoted and finished tying down the wagon's tarp. "No, Ma'am. Wouldn't want you to have to tell your daddy anything of the kind."

Moments later, he heard Lavinia's swishing skirts and, glancing over his shoulder, he saw her walk away. He let go a frustrated sigh.

Lord God, I'm sorry I took this job—sorrier than a Mississippi flood in springtime. I only ask that You see me to Oregon. Leastwise I won't make it. Dillon scowled. *And neither will this here piano.*

Chapter 2

"All set to pull out?"

Penny swiveled and stared up at the wiry wagon master. She gave him a nod. "We're ready to go."

"Where's your pa?"

"He's returning some rope to one of the Cole brothers, but he'll be back in no time."

"Just see that he is, cuz we're leaving. I hope to make Salmon Falls by this evening."

"Yes, Mr. Rawhide."

He smirked, his left cheek bulging with chewing tobacco. "How many times do I hafta tell ya that I ain't no 'Mister'? I'm plain ol' Rawhide."

Standing beside the wagon, Penny felt herself blush. "Yes, Sir. I'll try to remember that."

"See that you do." The grizzled man with sharp whiskers and leathery skin that matched his name turned and spit out a dark brown wad. "And I ain't no 'Sir,' neither."

"Yes, Si—I mean, Mis—I mean. . .Rawhide."

"That's better, little lady." With that, he spurred his horse on to the next wagon and the next, making sure the entire train was ready to break camp.

Penny sighed with relief when he was gone. The man scared her—always did. His fierce presence caused her to feel all flustered and tongue-tied, a trait that didn't exactly belong to Penny.

Suddenly Dillon's light brown head peered around the Millbergs' wagon just up ahead. "You all right back there?"

Embarrassed, Penny lifted her chin. "Of course I am!" Instantly, she regretted her harsh tone. "I'm fine, but. . .well, I'm just a bit uneasy around Mr. Rawhide."

"Only for the last four months," Dillon said with a charming grin. "In fact, I'd say you're downright petrified around the fellow."

"Oh, go on with you," she replied, waving a hand at him. "The last thing I need is teasing. You're as bad as my brother Josh."

To her shock and surprise, Dillon jumped from his perch. In several great strides, he was standing right in front of her.

He removed his hat. "My humble apologies, Miss Penny. I'd never have a laugh at your expense."

She looked into his eyes and saw only sincerity, no mockery or ridicule. "Apology accepted."

"Thank you." Donning his wide-brimmed hat, he added, "Don't be afraid of Rawhide. He might be as hard and worn as the buckskin he wears, but he's a decent man."

"I appreciate you telling me that, Mr. Trier. I feel ever so much better now."

He grinned. "Maybe I should've told you that back in Independence and saved you some worry."

Penny returned the smile, unwilling to share the fact that Bethany had been saying much the same thing. Besides, Dillon's boyish charm and rugged gallantry touched her heart for the umpteenth time, causing him to seem more believable than her friend, precious as she was. After all, Bethany's experience around men was nearly as limited as Penny's—well, until she married Josh, anyway.

In the next moment, a cloud of dust kicked up by horse hooves settled down upon them. "You gonna stand there and make moon eyes at each other, or are you two gonna get these wagons rolling?"

Penny peeled her gaze from Dillon and looked over at their frightful wagon master. Then, before she could utter a sound, Dillon took hold of her wrist and led her to the front of the wagon. His hands moved to her waist, and he hoisted her up so that she could easily climb into the seat.

"Th–thank you, Mr. Trier," she said somewhat breathless.

He nodded, handing her the reins. Turning to Rawhide, he said, "We're set to go."

" 'Bout time," came the clipped reply.

"Papa!" Penny called, seeing her father casually strolling toward their wagon. "Papa, hurry! We're leaving."

The older man quickened his pace, climbing onto the seat just as Dillon began to roll out the Millbergs' wagon ahead of them. Penny gladly handed over the reins.

"Lovely morning, isn't it, Penny-lo?"

"Yes, Papa, it is."

"And just look at this landscape! Makes me wish I were a painter like Leonardo da Vinci."

Penny glanced over at her father and noticed how his billowy white hair stuck out from beneath his leather cap.

"As magnificent as this area is," Papa continued, "it'll be rough going through the rock and the sagebrush until we reach the Snake River."

"Who said that?"

"The Cole brothers. Just this morning, in fact."

Penny let out a weary sigh and forced herself to look forward to the noon hour when they would stop to eat and rest. Then she could talk to Dillon again. . . .

"Papa, I think I'm in love."

"With one of the Cole brothers? Heaven help us! Which one of them?"

Penny laughed. "No, Papa, it's neither of the Coles. I'm in love with—"

"Wait. Don't tell me. Let me guess."

"He's tall, handsome, brown eyes, courageous chin. . . ."

"No more hints. I'll guess. I'll guess."

"Shouldn't be terribly difficult."

"I know. I know. . . ."

Papa took the rest of the morning to ponder his first guess—which was incorrect. The noon meal and rest time proved equally as disappointing since the Millbergs kept Dillon so busy that he barely had time to grab a couple of the charred biscuits left over from breakfast before the wagons pulled out onto the trail again. But, nine miles later, when they stopped for the night and made camp, Papa declared he knew the one who had conquered Penny's heart.

"John Wentworth."

"Who?" Penny furrowed her brows.

"John Wentworth. He's with the other circle of pioneers."

"Oh, yes, of course. Mr. Wentworth."

"I took the liberty of inviting him to share our meal this evening."

"You. . .what?"

"Here he comes now!"

Penny glanced over her shoulder in time to see the strapping young man headed their way. True, he wasn't unpleasing to the eye, but in Penny's opinion, he couldn't hold a candle to Dillon.

"Papa, I'm not in love with him," she muttered under her breath.

"No?"

"No."

"Oh dear. . ."

Penny rolled her eyes before looking at Bethany. Her friend was hard-pressed to contain her giggles. Then, lifting her gaze, Penny spotted Dillon making his way toward their camp. What would he think with Mr. Wentworth here? Would he assume incorrectly, as her father did, that she was interested in him?

"This is a fine mess, Papa."

"What mess? We're just being neighborly." He stuck his right hand out in welcome. "John! Glad you could join us."

"Yes, Sir, I'm grateful to have been asked." He shook Papa's hand. "Not often that I get a decent meal. My cousin and I have been taking turns, but he's a worse cook than me."

"Well, go fetch your cousin. He can eat with us, too."

"He can?"

"Certainly. The more the merrier."

By now Dillon had reached them, and Papa gave him a friendly slap between the shoulder blades. "We might make our first crossing of the Snake River sometime tomorrow."

Dillon grinned at the older man. "With all due respect, Sir, I think it'll be another two days."

"Why do you say that?"

"Because we're not traveling as fast as Rawhide anticipated

on account of a woman giving birth over in the other circle of wagons." He turned to Josh. "They said they'd call for you if they need you. She's got her mother and sister helping out."

Joshua nodded. "Very well."

Penny stepped toward him. "And how is it that you're privy to all this information, Mr. Trier?"

He smiled down at her, causing Penny's heart to flutter in the most unusual way. "I reckon I'm just a good listener."

Penny matched his smile, and they stood there in adoring regard until Bethany cleared her throat loudly.

Penny turned to her friend.

"Will you help me with our meal?"

"Of course, Beth." She glanced back at Dillon. "Please excuse me."

He gave a single but courteous nod.

Following Bethany to the end of the wagon, she began to help form the baking soda biscuits.

"I pray I won't burn these again. I want to impress Mr. Trier with my culinary skills."

"I'll take care of the biscuits," Beth said. "I have finally learned the secret, thanks to Granny Willodene."

"Well, her secret didn't work with me. I still burn them every time." Penny looked over her shoulder to see if her father and Dillon were engaged in conversation. They were, along with Josh. Moments later, John Wentworth and his cousin joined them.

"Imagine Papa thinking I was in love with Mr. Wentworth. Anyone can see who I'm really crazy about."

"And he's crazy about you, too."

Penny stopped forming the dough. "Really? Do you really think so?"

"Yes, and I've told you that a million times, if once at all.

Whenever are you going to listen to me?"

Penny did her best to look contrite.

"I knew all along that Mr. Trier didn't have eyes for Katie O'Neil—er—Cole. Katie Cole."

"You were right. He admitted as much."

"He did what? When?"

"This morning." Penny shifted uncomfortably at having to confess her blunder. But at last she divulged this morning's conversation with Dillon.

"You said you were. . .thankful that he didn't marry Katie? Oh, my soul! You are too bold, Penelope Rogers!"

"I didn't mean to be. But you know how I am, Beth. I couldn't help it. The words just tumbled out of my mouth."

"Mrs. Throckmorton would be shocked."

"It's a good thing she's not here."

"I'll say!"

Then Penny began to laugh, imagining their starchy headmistress traveling like a primitive pioneer along the Oregon Trail. She laughed so hard, in fact, that she nearly knocked over the pot of venison stew.

"Honestly, Penny. Mind your manners. We have hungry men to feed."

Penny, as usual, ignored the scolding. "Oh, Beth, can you see it? Mrs. Throckmorton cooking biscuits over a campfire? Bathing in a river wearing nothing but her chemise?"

"Or how about coming face-to-face with a rattlesnake like Mr. Rawhide said he once did?"

"Pity the snake!"

At that, the two burst into a fit of giggles and, once again, the biscuits were burned.

Chapter 3

Dinner was served and, thanks to Bethany's catering skills, the ladies were able to disguise the blackened biscuits by splitting them on each plate and ladling over a portion of hot stew. The men raved about their supper, and even Penny didn't think it tasted all that bad.

Dillon approached her as she was collecting empty plates. "Meal was delicious. Thank you."

"You're welcome," she said with a pleased smile.

Josh kissed Bethany's cheek. "Sweetheart, how about a little stroll around camp before we turn in for the night?"

"Yes, I'd enjoy that." Looking at Penny, she asked, "Would you mind cleaning up tonight? I'll take on the chore tomorrow after breakfast."

"I don't mind a bit. The two of you go on."

Penny stood there watching her brother and her best friend walk away, but she was very much aware of Dillon still standing beside her. Would he ask her out for a stroll, too?

"Miss Penny?"

She whirled around at the sound of John Wentworth's voice. He now stood on the other side of Dillon.

"Much obliged for the supper tonight." He handed her two empty plates and then scratched his scraggly light brown beard. "My cousin, Paul, and me ate two helpings each."

"Glad you enjoyed it, Mr. Wentworth."

"Oh, you can call me by my given name. I'm not fond of formalities and such."

Penny smiled a reply, feeling suddenly very uncomfortable. Where was Papa? Glancing in between the two men, she saw him conversing with Orson Millberg.

"Would you care to take a little walk with me, Miss Penny?"

She looked at Dillon. "What?"

"I said. . .would you care to take a walk with me?"

Slowly, she turned to John. To her disappointment, it was he who did the asking, not Dillon.

"It's a nice evening," John persisted, his hazel eyes sparkling with hope.

"Thank you, but no," Penny said. "I. . .I have to clean up."

"Here, I'll give you a hand."

She swallowed hard and glanced at Dillon only to find him studying the toes of his dusty boots. Couldn't he speak up? Couldn't he come to her defense in some way? Perhaps he didn't care at all.

Penny set a forestalling hand on John's arm as he reached for the dirty dishes. "I appreciate your offer, Mr. . . .I mean. . . John, but my father has a list of chores for me that's a mile long and I'm afraid they're women's work and nothing I'd allow a man to help with, if you know what I mean."

Judging by his puzzled expression, he didn't. But, to Penny's relief, he didn't press the matter.

"Maybe another time."

She just smiled. She didn't want to take a walk with him "another time." She wanted to take a romantic stroll with Dillon. She wanted to hold onto his arm and gaze up at him beneath the moonlit sky. . . .

"Well, I guess I'd better leave you to your chores, Miss Penny," John said. He looked over at Dillon. "How 'bout a game of cribbage, Trier?"

"I'd like that. Thanks."

"Come by our wagon when you're ready."

"Will do."

Grinning like a boy, John strode away, while Penny felt the wind leave her lungs. *He'd rather play a board game than take a stroll with me?*

"I've got a bit of a problem," Dillon said softly. He took a step closer to Penny. His hat in his hands, he worked its brim in a circle as he spoke. "While I'm in the Millbergs' employ, my life is not my own. Orson Millberg made it clear that he won't pay me if I. . .well, if he senses that I'm 'distracted' from my job."

"I see," Penny replied, although she wasn't sure that she really did.

"I'm counting on the money from Millberg to pay for the supplies I'll need to start a ranch in Oregon. Without it. . ." He looked at her, meeting her gaze straight on. ". . .without it, there'll be no ranch and I won't be able to support a. . .a wife and family."

Penny wet her suddenly parched lips. Did he mean her? He wouldn't be able to support her as his wife? Was he really thinking along those lines?

"Do you want a wife and family, Mr. Trier?" She couldn't

help but pursue the question.

He smirked in a charming way. "I reckon it's high time you called me Dillon, and. . .yes, I do want a wife and family. But I'm not in a place where I can even court a lady proper-like." He glanced over his shoulder. "If Millberg catches wind of my interest in a. . .a certain lady," he said with an intensity darkening his brown eyes, "he's liable to fire me on the spot."

Protest rose up in Penny. "Then who would drive his wagon?" She smiled. "I think you've got the upper hand."

"No, Millberg would find someone. He already hired a girl to cook for him, his wife, and Miss Lavinia."

"Really? Who?"

"Martha Buckley. She's about twelve or thirteen, and she's traveling with her family in one of the other wagons. I heard her pa say they needed the money, so he hired her out to the Millbergs."

Penny felt a little sorry for the girl.

Dillon chuckled softly. "But I sure wish I had your tenacity."

"Oh, nonsense. You have it and more. You're so brave and courageous. I've watched you all the months we've been on this trail and I've seen your daring in action. Why, I have no doubt you could stand up to Orson Millberg or anyone else." Penny sighed. "And yet I do understand your precarious situation."

He gave her a rueful-looking grin.

"However," she said with a coquettish look, "a certain lady can't wait forever."

She watched Dillon's face fall with disappointment, and she smiled.

"But I'm sure she can wait until we reach Oregon!"

His head snapped up, and Dillon narrowed his gaze. "Miss

Penny, I believe you're something of an imp."

"I believe you're right, although Papa and Josh have another name for it."

Dillon laughed, and Penny thought it was a nice, rich, healthy sound. She wished he would laugh more often. But at that very moment, she saw Mr. Millberg's calculating gaze settle on them.

Stepping back, she whispered, "You'd better go now. The very troll we're speaking about is watching us."

Dillon hesitated before slapping his leather hat against his knee in obvious frustration. "Thanks again for supper."

"You're welcome."

Penny pivoted and carried the plates to the wash bucket. Once safely out of Mr. Millberg's sight, she watched Dillon's retreating form. The poor man. . .he just needed some encouragement. How dreadful to be enslaved by the fear of one's employer. And yet, Penny understood Dillon's apprehension to some degree. She had dreaded Mrs. Throckmorton's disappointment and wrath at school.

"Lord, God," she began to pray, "I ask You to give Dillon wisdom in his dealings with the Millbergs and I ask You to somehow soften their hearts of granite." She exhaled a weary breath. "I also ask that You temper my impatience. In a roundabout way, I told Dillon I'd wait until he was in a position to court me; and now Oregon seems farther away than ever!"

❧

After a lively game of cribbage, Dillon meandered back to his respective campsite. He shook his head, thinking of John and his cousin, Paul. Their wisecracks reminded Dillon of his brothers back home in Missouri, and suddenly a cloud of homesickness enveloped him like fog.

Lord, what if I made a wrong decision in coming out West?

He passed Doc Rogers's wagon and came upon Penny's—

"Dillon."

He paused. Was he hearing things? Like a whisper upon the wind, he just imagined he heard Penny calling his name. It sounded nice coming from her lips, too.

"Dillon!"

He whirled around, realizing it wasn't his mind playing tricks on him after all. Penny's blond head stuck out of the back of her covered wagon and, with a white nightdress-encased arm, she beckoned him to come closer.

"What are you doing awake at this time of night?" he asked, stepping toward her.

"Shh," she warned. "Papa's asleep in his tent right over there."

He looked at her askance. "You should be sleeping, too."

"I know, but I was waiting for you. Here," she said, thrusting a folded piece of parchment at him, "take this. It's a letter I wrote to you."

He accepted it, but narrowed his gaze suspiciously all the same. "What kind of letter?"

"Well," she whispered, "I realized that there are so many things I want to tell you about my family and me, but I can't because of that old troll Mr. Millberg and his ridiculous rules."

With a smirk, Dillon glanced at the paper in his hand.

"So, I decided I'd write down all the things I wanted to say. And I thought you could write back to me. That's how my brother and Bethany first got to know each other. Here. . ."

Dillon took the ink and pen she handed him. Next came a journal.

"I had planned to write my memoirs on this trip," she said in a hushed tone, "but I haven't even filled up my first diary yet. . .and I brought along three."

Dillon mulled over the idea she proposed.

"Of course, I might be acting much too forward. If that's the case—"

"No, no. . .that's not it." He looked up at her, meeting her gaze. "I'm just not much of a writer, Miss Penny."

"Oh. . ."

Her obvious regret tugged on his heartstrings.

"But, for you, I'll give it my best shot," he quickly amended.

He saw her smile in the shadows and felt glad he could please her in this small way.

"I'm not saying my penmanship is the best, mind you."

"I understand. Good night, Dillon."

"G'night."

With that she vanished into the wagon, and Dillon found himself feeling mildly disappointed. Turning, he made the rest of the trek to his tent and bedroll, which were situated beside the piano-laden wagon he drove by day. Then, lying prostrate near the canvas flap, he carefully unfolded Penny's letter.

Beneath the light of the moonbeams, he read—

Dear Dillon,

I must say that I am intrigued by your given name. It is one I have never heard before. My given name is after my father's favorite aunt—Penelope Rogers. While I am honored to bear her name, I do not intend to follow her example in life as she was a spinster. . . .

Dillon grinned, thinking this letter-writing business might prove downright entertaining.

He quickly read through the rest. Penny wrote of her salvation testimony, then about her deceased mother, whom she still missed. She went on to describe how she was sent to boarding school, where she met her best friend, who wound up marrying her brother. She had no other siblings, but she hoped to have nieces and nephews soon! She ended the letter with *Truly Yours, Penelope Anne Rogers.*

Dillon rolled onto his back and gazed up into the darkness of his tent. *I wish you were truly mine, Penny Rogers,* he thought. Moments later, he realized he'd have to do more than wish in order to make that a reality. Just like his dream of owning a ranch and livestock. It had become apparent to him last year that he'd never attain his goal by staying in Missouri and keeping it a mere wistful longing. That's why he was headed to Oregon.

Tell her that! his heart seemed to say.

Rolling onto his belly again, Dillon opened the ink bottle and journal, figuring that would be a good place to begin. He dipped his pen and wrote: *Dear Miss Penny. . . .*

Chapter 4

Gracious me, Papa! How could you ever think such a thing? Mr. Rawhide? Never!"

Beside her as the wagon bumped along on the trail, Penny's father chuckled. "All right, now you guessed every man in this wagon train except the one I'm sweet on."

"Dillon Trier."

Penny sighed. "Finally!"

Again, her father laughed. "I knew that all along, Penny-lo. I would have to be blind not to notice."

"I was beginning to wonder," she quipped. She studied Papa's profile, his straight nose, the laugh lines around his intelligent eyes. "So? What do you think?"

"I think Mr. Trier is a fine Christian man."

"Good."

"But I don't know much about him."

"Neither do I. That's why we started writing to each other. Look, Papa," Penny said, pulling a thick letter from the apron pocket of her calico dress. "Here's my first one. Dillon gave it to me this morning. Shall I read it aloud?"

"Dillon, is it?"

Embarrassed, Penny just shrugged.

"Whose idea was it to correspond by letter writing?"

"Um. . .well. . ."

"Yes, I thought so. Now, Penny, see here. . ."

"Papa, please hold your reprimand until I explain."

He let out a huff, but acquiesced.

"Dillon would like to court me—he said so. But Mr. Millberg told him that there would be no payment if he didn't give his every attention to driving that sorry old piano to Oregon. So Dillon asked if he could wait until we reached Willamette Valley, where he can court me properly. I said yes, but in the meantime I thought we could write to each other." She looped her arm around her father's. "So you see, Papa, if I'm too bold, it's all Mr. Millberg's fault."

"Now, Penny, don't try to work your feminine wiles on me."

She withdrew her arm, feeling properly chastened.

"What's done is done," Papa said. "But I think Mr. Trier would have done himself a favor and spoken to me before approaching my daughter."

"I'm sure he plans to when the time is right."

"Humph. We'll see, won't we? But for now, why don't you read Mr. Trier's letter, and let's discover if he can impress me."

"All right," she replied, unfolding the epistle. "Just don't expect him to be another William Shakespeare."

"Indeed I won't."

"Dear Miss Penny," she began, "ever since I was sixteen, I have wanted my own land and a home to call mine. Since I'm the fourth son in a family of six boys and three girls, I knew I would not inherit my father's farm. My pa was aware of my hankering and taught me everything he knew about livestock and running the place.

"Each year I drove the cattle to market along with my brothers, but it was me who got the best prices. My pa likened me to the servant in Matthew 25 who was given five talents and doubled his master's money. I do not mean to brag. I only mean to write the truth. When I left for Oregon, my pa bawled like a new calf, which is not in his nature to do. But he sent me away with his blessing. So here I am on my way to Oregon."

Penny nudged her father. "Isn't that sweet, Papa? Dillon was so close to his father that the older man wept when his son left."

"Spare me your editorials, my dear. Read on."

"Yes, Papa." After a moment's gaze heavenward, she continued, "My mother is a good Christian woman. She taught me and my brothers and sisters about Jesus since the time we were knee-high to a milk stool." Penny giggled at the phraseology. A quick glance at Papa told her he shared her amusement.

"You asked about my given name," she read on, "so I will tell you how it came about. Ma named all us boys after upstanding members of both sides of the family, using their surnames. First comes Morgan, then Kanter, then Roth, then me, then Hawley, and last is Woodrow. Ma said she would have used first names, but some of them were the same. My sisters have less unusual names. Rebecca, Elizabeth, and Catherine.

"This is probably more than you wanted to know, so I will close. Fondly, Dillon Matthew Trier." Penny paused before reading the postscript. "P.S.—I reckon I had best speak to your pa if this is going to continue."

Penny sighed dreamily as she set the letter in her lap. "Isn't he wonderful?"

"How's his spelling?"

"Not too bad."

"Hmm. . ."

"Papa! I would have expected a better response from you."

"Well, now, Penny, I see you as. . .well, as these blue wildflowers dotting the meadow through which we're presently traversing. I can't imagine that you'll enjoy being plucked and put into a tin vase in some cabin on a ranch. You'll wither and die. Rather, I foresee you in Oregon City, blossoming at the university I hope to cultivate."

"On the contrary, I will 'blossom' on a ranch quite nicely. Best place for a wildflower."

"Best place for smelly hogs and cattle, too. As a rancher's wife, you'll have to help clean up after the animals. Are you really ready for the barnyard, Penny-lo?"

"If it's Dillon's barnyard, then yes, I am!"

"You're a sturdy dreamer. I'll grant you that much."

Exasperation bubbled up inside of Penny. "Oh, Papa. . ."

"Likewise, I don't imagine that Mr. Trier knows what he's getting into, courting a. . .a wildflower."

Penny was about to retort when rousing cheers sounded from up ahead, capturing her attention. The wagons pulled to a stop, and Rawhide came riding alongside each one.

"We'll noon on the Snake!" he shouted. "We'll noon on the Snake River."

Within minutes, the wagons rolled into their usual formation. Soon women were unpacking and preparing the midday meal. Penny noticed that Dillon stayed near the Millbergs' wagon, chewing on a cold piece of bacon. As she and Bethany served Papa and Josh, Penny wished Dillon would join them. But, to her disappointment, only John Wentworth and his cousin, Paul, sauntered over to their camp.

"We wondered if you had a few spare biscuits," John said, wetting his lips and wearing a famished grin. "They sure tasted good, and we're awful low on supplies."

"Why, certainly," Papa said cordially. He nodded to Penny, who quickly served their guests cold biscuits and jerked beef.

While the men conversed, Penny and Bethany straightened up the wagons and prepared themselves for a short rest.

"It's a hot day," Penny groused. "A swim in the river is quite tempting."

"Not to me!" Bethany declared. "And I must say I am not looking forward to crossing that river in a couple of weeks."

Penny nodded in understanding. Ever since Bethany's parents drowned in a tragic accident, she shied away from aquatic recreation of any sort—not that fording the Snake would be "recreation." Rawhide had warned them that the river was a fast-moving body of water with a swift undercurrent. His tales of crossing the Snake caused even Penny a moment's apprehension, and she was a champion swimmer, thanks to Josh, who had taught her when they were children.

"Now, Beth, don't fret. The Lord parted the Red Sea for the children of Israel. Perhaps He'll part the Snake River for us."

Bethany smiled. "Yes, perhaps He will."

Folding the blanket she and Beth had sat upon to eat, Penny lifted it into the wagon; and doing so, she happened to glance across the camp. She caught sight of Dillon just as he looked over at her. She smiled while he tipped his hat and gave her a subtle grin. Then he went back to securing the wagon.

Her smile faded, and Penny felt slighted that Dillon didn't do more than give her a polite nod. However, a heartbeat later,

Orson Millberg came around the other side of the wagon, barking all sorts of orders. Penny quickly lowered her gaze. In the next moment, she decided that while she rested this afternoon, she'd compose her next letter.

❧

Dillon wiped the grime and perspiration off his neck before stuffing his handkerchief back into his shirt pocket. It was particularly hot today, and from what Rawhide said, the heat was unusual for this part of the country. But up ahead flowed Salmon Creek, just a few miles up a bluff from the Salmon Falls. Both were tributaries of the Snake. Beside the creek was where their wagon master decided they'd make camp for the night. They'd traveled some seventeen miles today in the August heat, and Dillon felt about as ornery as an old bear. He planned to catch fish for supper, bathe, and take to his bedroll. He had no more patience for the Millbergs and their derisive daughter, who had done nothing but whine and complain all afternoon. Worse was that Miss Lavinia had bellyached about the dust from the preceding wagons so that her pompous father ordered her to ride next to Dillon, who was first in line due to this morning's rotation. Consequently, he'd heard all he could tolerate from her mouth for one day!

"As I was saying. . .I do hope Rawhide knows what he's doing."

"Rawhide knows what he's doing," Dillon grumbled.

"How do you know?"

"I just know."

"Oh, you men! You think you know everything. Why, Daddy would have gotten nowhere in life if he hadn't listened to Mama. She's gifted with a keen sense for making money—almost as good as any man. Although, I do think Mama made a mistake in coercing Daddy to travel to the Oregon Territory. This has been the most miserable trip of my life."

"You can say that again!"

"Miserable?" Lavinia, dressed in all her usual frills, cast a burning look on Dillon. "What in heaven's name are you complaining about? All you've had to do is sit in the wagon all day. . . and you're getting paid for it, too! This job has to be a far sight better than digging in dirt and milking smelly cows!"

Pulling the wagon into formation, Dillon jerked on the reins and nearly unseated Lavinia. Then he jumped down and didn't bother helping the prissy little thing alight from the bench. Ma would have scolded him for his temper fit even if Miss Lavinia and the heat of the day had provoked it.

Hot and tired, he tended to the oxen and forced himself not to glance in the direction of the Rogerses' wagons. Dillon still felt perturbed over this noon when he saw John Wentworth enjoying Penny's hospitality. The sight plucked a jealous chord in his heart. But Dillon needed to keep his distance—at least when Orson Millberg was around. The older man had questioned him again about his interest in Penny and warned Dillon that if he got "preoccupied" and didn't give his work his full attention, he would be fired. However, staying away from Penny meant that another suitor, namely Wentworth, might win her heart. On the other hand, without this job, Dillon wasn't fit to court her.

"Mr. Trier?"

Dillon whirled around to find young Martha Buckley gazing up at him with huge brown eyes that sparked with mischief.

"Miss Penny Rogers gave me something to pass on to you, but she said no one should see me give it to you."

Dillon stifled a grin and gazed over Martha's light brown head. The Millbergs appeared to be distracted by one of Lavinia's tantrums. No doubt she was telling her parents about their driver's bad manners.

"No one's looking." Dillon held out his hand, and Martha placed a folded piece of paper in his palm.

"Miss Penny said you're invited to supper. She said she's got a hankering for fresh fish and she hopes you'll feel like catching some. I'm to tell you that Doc Rogers said he'll keep you company and not to worry about the Millbergs on account that they're invited to supper, too." Martha grinned impishly. "I'm invited also, 'cept I offered to help Miss Penny and Miss Bethany fry up our meal."

Dillon smiled. Leave it to Penny to think up such a clever plan. He gazed down at the girl. "Tell Miss Penny I accept her invitation and that, after I fetch my fishing gear, I'll head to the river posthaste."

"Yes, Sir, I'll tell her." With that, Martha ran in the direction of the Rogerses' wagons.

Wagging his head in her wake, Dillon thanked the Lord that the events of the day had suddenly taken a turn for the better.

Chapter 5

A safe distance away from camp and a ways downstream from where the men fished, women and young girls stripped to their chemises on the shore of the Salmon Creek and bathed. Penny filled a pail of water for Beth, who stayed ashore and washed up. But most of the others plunged right in, Penny included.

Floating on her back, she gazed at the dusky sky. Only a couple of hours of light left and supper still had to be cooked. Even so, Penny couldn't get herself to rush with her bath as the cool water felt delightful after a day on the hot, dusty trail.

"Be careful, Penny," Bethany warned from the bank.

"I will." She righted herself and smoothed her soaking wet hair back from her forehead. "Come on in, Beth. The current isn't swift, and look how shallow the water is right here."

A few young girls splashed her and giggled, and Penny splashed them right back.

"My guess is the men have returned to camp with the fish," Bethany said, stepping into the water. She stopped when it reached her knees. "They'll need to be cleaned. . . ."

"Who? The men or the fish?" Penny laughed at her jest and

earned several chuckles from the women around her. Even timid Emma Harris—make that Emma Brewster, since she married the preacher—smiled at the quip. But seeing Bethany's head shaking in disapproval, Penny made for the shoreline.

"Oh, all right. . .but I'll say this. Since you married Josh, you've grown much too serious."

"Perhaps I've just grown up," Bethany retorted, handing Penny a towel and dry clothing. "And maybe it's time you did the same."

Penny froze. Had those words really come from Bethany's mouth? "You're sounding more like Mrs. Throckmorton every day."

Bethany whirled around and walked into the makeshift dressing area, privatized by two sheets draped from one tree to another. She dressed in a hurry. Then before Penny had even donned a fresh calico, her friend marched off.

Penny thought back on the day and tried to recall a time that she had offended Bethany, but no incident came to mind. Why did she act angry? Perhaps the heat had adversely affected her.

Brushing out her long hair, Penny knotted it in a fat braid that fell to the middle of her back. Next she gathered her wet things.

"There you are, Penny Rogers."

Looking over her shoulder, she saw Lavinia Millberg standing several feet away. Her too-wide mouth curved with condescension.

"Would you mind helping me dress? I just loathe the fact that we couldn't bring our maid. But it's just as well, I suppose. She was the laziest woman on God's green earth!"

Surprised by the request, but deciding it was her Christian

duty to help, Penny dropped her laundry. Stepping forward, she took the dress from Lavinia. It was all pink ribbons and white lace and the most impractical gown for their present circumstance—but so was the rest of Lavinia's wardrobe.

"I rode beside Dillon today," she cooed as Penny began fastening the tiny pearl buttons in back of the dress. "He is such a charmer, wouldn't you say?"

"I'm sure I wouldn't know," Penny replied, thinking it'd be just like Lavinia to try and trick her into admitting her interest in Dillon. She would most likely go straight to her father with the report, and Dillon would lose his job.

"Well, I know. That rascal had his hand on my knee for nearly a mile."

She's lying, Penny thought, but she refused to speak her mind and give her heart away to this little conniver.

"But don't say a word, Penny Rogers, because if Daddy finds out, he's liable to strangle Dillon with his bare hands!" Lavinia paused before adding, "Either that, or he'll make Dillon marry me."

With only half the dress buttoned, Penny purposely gave the fabric a hard yank. "Why, Lavinia Millberg, I believe you've gained weight. I can't fasten the rest of this dress for the life of me!"

"What?" She pivoted. "That's impossible."

"Such a shame, too," Penny drawled, fingering the lace collar.

Lavinia's eyes narrowed dangerously before she slapped Penny's hand away. "This dress fits me just fine!"

Penny sighed. "I'm afraid it doesn't. But perhaps you'll get a chance to walk off your thick waistline tomorrow."

Lavinia gasped indignantly while Penny lifted her wet underthings from out of the long grass. She folded them up in the towel with which she'd dried off.

"You'll be sorry you insulted me so!"

Penny replied with a nonchalant shrug.

However, as she made her way back to camp, she didn't feel good about her behavior. Not in the least. Instead of being a godly example, she had acted just as mean-spirited and callous as Lavinia.

Heavenly Father, please forgive me, she prayed. *I don't know what You're going to do with me. Maybe Beth is right. It's time for me to grow up. . . .*

Penny began climbing the dirt-packed bank, which, she soon discovered, had been easier to descend. A few more steps, and suddenly a large hand appeared before her. Intuitively, she took it; and when she glanced up, she found herself looking into Dillon's brown eyes.

"My hero!" Penny exclaimed blithely. She made it the rest of the way up the steep hill with little effort, thanks to his help.

At the top of the bluff, Dillon proudly displayed the bluegills he'd caught. "Your brother hooked a passel as well."

"We'll eat hearty tonight."

"Praise the Lord!"

Penny smiled. She noticed then that Dillon's clean, white cotton shirt was rolled to the elbows and that his dark slacks with their suspenders looked equally as crisp. His sandy-brown hair was wet, but parted and neatly combed. His overall appearance was a telltale sign that he'd also enjoyed a dip in the river.

"That's better," he said.

"What's better?"

"You're smiling. I never did see such a dark frown as the one you wore climbing that hill."

"Oh, it's Lavinia Millberg. Doesn't she just rattle my cage, though?"

Dillon laughed. "She rattles everyone's cage," he said as they began walking back to camp together.

"She told me that you had your hand on her knee for a whole mile and that if her father finds out, he'll make you marry her—a regular shotgun wedding."

Dillon shook his head. "He'd have to shoot me dead, that's for sure."

Somehow Penny found the facetious remark comforting.

"Well, I didn't act like a proper young lady should," she confessed. Penny chanced a peek at Dillon, hoping to gauge his reaction. He looked back at her from out of the corner of his eyes, his expression unreadable. "I insulted her. I insinuated that she's fat."

He gave a tight-sounding little cough, and it occurred to Penny that he was doing his best not to laugh.

"It's not funny, Dillon."

"You're right. My apologies."

"Accepted." On that note Penny sighed audibly. "I guess it's time for me to grow up and put childish things, like sparring with Lavinia, behind me. Papa says I'm a wildflower, but I suspect it's high time I become a rose."

"I like you just the way you are, Miss Penny Rogers."

"Papa would say that's because you don't know me very well."

Dillon chuckled. "Well, we're working on that, aren't we?" He smiled so wide, a dimple appeared in his clean-shaven cheek. "I enjoyed your last letter."

Penny felt herself blush.

They slowed their strides as they neared the wagons. "I'll try to write one back tonight."

"I'd like that."

"I reckon I oughta speak with your pa."

Penny nodded.

An awkward moment passed between them.

"I probably should, um, help Bethany with supper."

Dillon handed her the fish. "I already cleaned 'em."

"How thoughtful of you. . ."

He shrugged.

"Excuse me, Penny dear," Bethany's voice cut in.

She turned and regarded her sister-in-law, who stood just a few feet away.

"Could I have a word with you?"

"Of course." Looking back at Dillon, Penny smiled. "Please excuse me."

He nodded.

"I'm so terribly sorry for the awful things I said," Bethany blurted once they were out of earshot. "I don't know what's come over me lately."

"It's the heat," Penny said. "And we're all so weary from this journey."

Bethany nodded, but there were tears rolling down her cheeks.

"Here, now, Beth, don't cry. I forgive you. All is well." With an arm around her friend's shoulders, Penny lifted the bluegills with her other hand. "We've got fish to fry."

Bethany nodded once more.

"Besides, when you hear of what I told that haughty Lavinia Millberg, you'll laugh till your sides ache. That is, after you reprimand me for my audacity."

"Oh, no, Penny, what have you done now?"

She grinned. "I'll tell you while we prepare supper. . . ."

Chapter 6

After a satisfying supper, Isaiah Rogers took hold of his daughter's hand and fairly dragged her into the center of their camp.

"It's time, Penny."

"Oh, Papa, not tonight," she protested, but her objections went no further than those first few words. Her father seemed adamant about performing a Shakespearean classic. "I refuse to play the role of Ophelia again," she managed, loud enough for Papa to hear. "I don't feel like dying tonight."

"Very well. How about a scene from *Twelfth Night?*"

"How about *Romeo and Juliet* instead?"

"I thought you said you didn't feel like dying."

"Oh, for pity sakes, Papa, we don't have to do that tragic scene in which Juliet kills herself. How about one of the more, um. . .romantic scenes?"

"Hmm. I can't imagine who you would choose to play Romeo," Papa teased with a mischievous gleam in his eyes.

Penny gave him an impish grin.

Papa sighed. "All right. A monologue it will be." He faced the rapidly growing crowd. "Ladies and gentleman," he began, "my lovely daughter has agreed to perform a short presentation of William Shakespeare's *Romeo and Juliet.*" Leaning over, he whispered to Penny, "Which portion of the play?"

"Act three, scene two."

Isaiah nodded. Then, to his audience, he began to deliver a brief synopsis of the play. "Romeo and Juliet have fallen in love, but their families are bitter enemies. In secret, the couple marry; however, one of Juliet's relatives finds out that Romeo had attended a feast that he was not invited to. The two men get into an awful argument, and Romeo ends up killing the fellow—in self-defense, of course. Nevertheless, he is banished from the kingdom and Juliet is set to marry another man.

"But the night before the wedding, someone gives her a potion that will render her lifeless for forty-two hours. Unfortunately, there's a misunderstanding and word gets to Romeo that his dear, sweet Juliet is dead. Of course this is not true; she had only pretended death in order to avoid marriage to Count Paris.

"Devastated, Romeo kills himself. Then, when she awakens from her imposed slumber and discovers her beloved is dead, Juliet, too, commits suicide—"

"And all that tragedy could have been avoided," Reverend Brewster cut in, standing outside the circle of onlookers with his arm around his lovely wife, "if only Romeo and Juliet had obeyed God's Fifth Commandment and honored their parents."

A hearty "Amen!" sounded from several in the audience, while others chuckled.

"Those are words fitly spoken, Preacher," Isaiah affirmed, nodding to the man. "And now my daughter will perform a scene from Shakespeare's play in which Juliet is pining for her beloved Romeo. . . ," Papa glanced in Pastor Brewster's direction, ". . .in spite of her parent's wishes, the disgraceful girl!"

"Thank you very much, Papa," Penny quipped, and more laughter emanated from the crowd.

Papa gave her an affectionate wink, and Penny laughed softly. They played well off each other and always to the delight of their audiences.

"I'd be obliged to play Romeo," John Wentworth called out. "You're more than welcome to pine over me, Miss Penny."

"I'm afraid Romeo isn't in this scene, my man," Papa said quickly. Then he bowed to Penny and stepped off to the side.

"Gallop apace, you fiery-footed steeds," she began. "Towards Phoebus' lodging: such a wagoner. . . ."

Dillon scratched the back of his neck, feeling a mite confounded as he watched Penny's dramatic interpretation. Tonight, like all the other times he'd seen her perform something from Shakespeare, he didn't understand all she said. The plain truth was, Shakespeare's writing ran deeper than he cared to fish. He had studied the bard's masterpieces only briefly in school; and if he remembered correctly, he didn't earn high marks in that particular class. But from the way Penny held her right hand over her heart, he could well believe she was "pining," just as her pa said.

Dillon exhaled a long, slow breath and continued to watch Penny's theatrics. He had to admit, he took pleasure in watching her—the expression of longing reflected on her face as she looked up to the heavens, the graceful movements of her arms.

Her gaze suddenly met his and for a good half minute she spoke to him as though he were Romeo and they were the only two in the whole universe. In that brief span of time, Dillon realized that if he hadn't already fallen in love with Penny Rogers, he had now. What's more, he didn't see her single anyone else out, which told him all he wanted to know.

Folding his arms across his chest, he leaned against one of the covered wagons. He casually scanned the crowd, curious to see folks' reactions to Penny's recital. Most were smiling, especially the ladies. But the men. . .

Dillon's thoughts came to a hard stop when he found John Wentworth staring back at him. If looks could kill, Dillon figured he'd be maimed at best; but he held the other man's gaze to make a point. Finally Wentworth slapped his hat on his head and left the crowd.

Dillon grinned and returned his attention to Penny. *Good*, he thought, *one less score to settle.*

"Come, night; come, Romeo; come, thou day in night," Penny said, gazing at Dillon again. "For thou wilt lie upon the wings of night whiter than new snow on a raven's back. . . ."

Penny finished her monologue and earned the applause from her onlookers. Clapping, Dillon pursed his lips and couldn't help wondering if women really equated all those things to love. . .wings of night and new snow on a raven's back? If they did, he sure had a lot to learn.

He watched Penny curtsey and exit center stage, which was really no more than a place near the campfire. Then Professor Rogers reappeared and encouraged others to share their talent. A heavy-set woman with dark brown hair eagerly stood and announced that she'd recite a poem she'd written.

"I wrote it while on this journey," she informed the spectators. Clearing her throat, she began, "We are weary travelers on the Oregon Trail, with nothing in foresight but our oxen's swishing tail. . . ."

Dillon stifled a yawn and decided to make for his bedroll. He'd had enough prose for one night. Pivoting, he stepped around a few other folks and headed for his tent. Halfway there, he met up with Penny.

"What did you think of my performance?" she asked with a little smile.

"You did fine. Just fine."

She tipped her head, and Dillon had a feeling he was supposed to say something more.

"I'm afraid I'm not much of a fan of Shakespeare," he blurted before she could ask. "All those words you said tonight didn't make a whole lot of sense to me, but I liked watching you say them."

"Well, thank you. . .but you don't appreciate Shakespeare? I mean. . .I thought that was a very romantic scene." She put her hands over her heart. "Couldn't you just envision a young woman who's so in love that she can't wait for her beloved to return and hold her in his arms once more?"

"Well, now, Miss Penny," Dillon drawled, "if you'd said it like that, I wouldn't have missed the point."

She laughed softly.

"May I walk you back to your wagon or were you planning to rejoin the group?"

"Are you planning to rejoin the group?" Penny countered with a hopeful expression, illuminated by tonight's half moon.

At that moment, Homer Green began playing a lively tune on his fiddle. Dillon thought about going back and making merry with the others if it meant he could stay in Penny's company. However, the latter was not meant to be, since Old Man Millberg would be watching him like a hound dog.

"Reckon I'm turning in for the night."

"Guess I'll do the same."

Side by side, they ambled in the direction of the Rogerses' wagons. As they passed the tent Dillon had pitched for himself, Orson Millberg's voice thundered through the darkness.

"Trier, I want to speak to you!"

Penny gasped; and then, before he could even think, she ducked into his tent. Wide-eyed and suddenly imagining all sorts of implications, Dillon swallowed hard. What on earth was that girl thinking?

"Trier?"

"Yes, Sir?" Moving slowly around, he could just barely make out the older man's stout figure as he came closer.

"Is someone with you?"

"Um. . .no, Sir."

"Good."

Millberg closed the distance between them, and Dillon prayed Penny wouldn't cough, sneeze, or sniffle.

"About this afternoon, Trier. . ."

Dillon placed his hands on his hips. He'd known all evening that this was coming. "Yes, Sir, what about it?"

"You were inexcusably rude to my daughter."

"You're right. I was. And I apologize for it. I'm afraid the heat got the best of me."

"Your apology is unacceptable, and I have a mind to dock your wages."

Dillon wanted to protest, but with Penny so near, his pride wouldn't let him.

"Did you hear what I said, Trier?" Orson chuckled. "You're awfully quiet all of a sudden."

Dillon clenched his jaw in anger. "Do what you have to do. I was wrong and I admit it. But with all due respect, Sir, your daughter needs to mind her manners just as much as I do."

"How dare you say such a thing! Lavinia has impeccable manners. She's gone to the finest boarding schools and studied under the most sought-after instructors. No, Trier, it's you who needs to mind your manners. You're nothing but a crude farmhand, and that's all you'll ever be." With that, Millberg turned on his heel and stomped off.

Dillon fumed in his wake, hating the fact that Penny had overheard the entire conversation. Well, at least she heard the truth; he was a farmhand and that's exactly what he always would be.

Suddenly, he felt something poke his backside. Glancing over his shoulder, he found Penny holding his rifle out to him.

"Here. Shoot him."

After the momentary shock ebbed, he carefully accepted the gun. "I'm not going to shoot anyone." Taking Penny's hand, Dillon helped her out of the tent.

"Then give me back that rifle, and I'll shoot him!"

"You'll do no such thing!"

"He's a horrible man to talk to you that way, Dillon."

"I agree, but killin' him won't do any good."

Penny gasped. "I wasn't planning to kill him. Just shoot him. Afterwards, Josh can dig out the bullet—it'll serve that troll right." She reached for the gun, but Dillon held it away from her. He began to laugh. If this little darlin' wasn't the pluckiest thing he'd ever met. . .

"Give me that gun."

"I will not, either! You're a little spitfire, Penny Rogers, you know that?"

As if to make his point, she stomped her foot, and Dillon laughed all the harder.

She laughed, too. "I'm just teasing. I really wouldn't shoot someone—not even Mr. Millberg."

"You're a mighty good actress. I'll attest to that. In fact," he said, leaning closer, "I prefer you in this role rather than playing Juliet."

"Really?"

"Really!"

"Penny-lo. . .is that you?"

She spun around so fast that Dillon felt the hems of her skirts brush against his boots. "Yes, Papa, it is I."

The bushy-haired man stepped out of the shadows. "Good evening, Mr. Trier. It cooled off nicely, didn't it?"

"Yes, Sir, it sure did."

"Papa, Dillon won't let me shoot Mr. Millberg," Penny whined, causing Dillon to grin. "That troll said the most atrocious things. He called Dillon a 'crude farmhand,' and that's not true."

"Of course it's not."

Dillon felt his cheeks warm with embarrassment. Bad enough that Penny heard the insult, but now her pa knew about it, too.

"Well, don't despair, my darling," Isaiah said. "Someone is bound to shoot Orson Millberg before this journey is over."

Dillon started chuckling once more. He thought the pair was quite the comedy act; and in that moment, he decided his family would get along nicely with the Rogerses.

"Come along now, Penny, I'm sure Mr. Trier needs his rest—as do we all."

"Yes, Papa."

"Oh, um, Professor Rogers?"

"Yes?"

Dillon cleared his throat. "Might I speak with you tomorrow before breakfast?"

"Does it, by chance, concern my daughter?"

"Ah. . .yes, Sir, it does."

"Hmm. . .well, in that case, I'll have to think about it for a month or two."

"Papa!"

The older man laughed, putting Dillon at ease. Certainly Isaiah Rogers wouldn't make light of the situation if he disapproved. . .would he?

"Yes, of course, you may speak to me tomorrow, Mr. Trier, unless you would prefer we talked over the matter tonight so you can sleep. Wouldn't want you to fret all night long. Despite what Penny's told you, I'm really not a monster."

"Oh, Papa, I never said anything of the sort."

"And I never thought it," Dillon added. He glanced at his boots before looking back at Penny's pa. "I reckon tomorrow is soon enough. . .if you're agreeable."

"I am." With that, Isaiah put a fatherly arm around Penny's shoulders and led her toward their wagons. "See you in the morning, Mr. Trier."

"Yes, Sir."

"Good night, Dillon," Penny called sweetly.

"G'night."

As he watched father and daughter disappear into the night, Dillon shook his head in wonder. If he married Penny Rogers, life certainly wouldn't be dull.

But first, he'd have to convince her pa that he was worthy enough to court her.

Lord, he prayed, *You're going to have to put the right words in my mouth, 'cause this farmhand sure don't know how to persuade an intelligent, sophisticated man like Isaiah Rogers.*

Chapter 7

Papa, please, please tell me how your conversation went with Dillon this morning?" Penny begged as their wagon bumped over the volcanic-like terrain. "I haven't had a chance to talk to you since we started off after breakfast."

"I'm sure the suspense has been eating you alive," Papa teased.

Penny made a *tsk* sound with her tongue in reply and her father chuckled.

"All right, all right. . .well, Mr. Trier asked me if he could court you once we arrived in Oregon."

"And?" Penny prodded, growing annoyed.

"And I told him I would think about it."

Penny brought her chin back in surprise. "What? You didn't give him your blessing? Why?"

"Because, my dear, I'm not certain that you will be happy on a ranch. You were born and raised in a refined setting. You're unaccustomed to the rough-hewn life and all the back-breaking labor that goes with it."

"Papa, I've lived a rough-hewn life on this trail. I've adapted quite well."

"Yes, you have, and I commend you for it. But, Penny-lo,

you don't want to live like this forever, do you?"

"Sarah followed Abraham wherever God led him. She lived in a tent."

"We're not discussing the Sarah of the Bible. We're discussing Penelope Anne Rogers."

"Papa—"

"Your mother would turn in her grave if she saw what's become of us!"

Penny shook her head. "Oh, Papa, what a silly remark. Mother is in heaven, and I'm sure the Lord has kept her informed of our activities."

"If that's so, then your mother has every right to be disappointed in me. This is all my fault. . . ."

"Papa?"

Penny narrowed her gaze and considered her father's profile. He certainly behaved out of character this morning. Gone was his lighthearted outlook on life, and the sparkle in his eyes had dulled. "Papa, what's wrong?"

She placed her hand on his arm, and, at last, he gazed in Penny's direction.

"What's wrong is my little girl has grown up," he replied soberly. "What's wrong is that she isn't in love with a scholar, but a rancher."

Looping her arm around her father's, Penny laid her head against his shoulder as they bounced along. "Vocation doesn't make the man. A man's worth comes from within him. Dillon loves the Lord; he's hardworking and honest." Penny popped back up. "And to think that he put his life in jeopardy in order to help Bernie Williams capture that awful Anna Schmitt!"

"That's just my point, Penny-lo. You see only his heroics.

You're not considering the entire picture, as I am."

Penny sighed, feeling a stab of dejection pierce her heart. She wondered how she would ever change her father's mind. Almost at once, the first verse of Proverbs, chapter twenty-one, sprang to mind. *"The king's heart is in the hand of the LORD, as the rivers of water: he turneth it whithersoever he will."*

In that moment, Penny realized it wouldn't be her who turned Papa's heart. . .but God!

❧

Beneath an overcast sky, the prairie schooners nooned near the Salmon Falls. The air was heavy, causing the pioneers to feel sticky and uncomfortable in spite of the cooler temperatures.

As Penny nibbled on repast, she scanned the campsite for Dillon. The daily rotation of wagons this morning had put him at the back of the train. Finally she spotted him eating with the Cole brothers, but she couldn't catch his eye to even give him a smile.

Several hours later, they were back on the trail. They made good time and traveled an amazing forty miles.

"Quite a feat!" Papa declared after Rawhide made the announcement. "Our average has been ten to fifteen miles a day. Why, we'll reach Oregon in no time!"

Penny felt encouraged by the thought, except it was short-lived. That evening, instead of supping with her and her family, as Dillon was wont to do, he and several other men drove the animals some three miles away, where the grass grew thick and lush. Nearer to the trail, it had dwindled to almost nothing because of so many emigrants and their animals traveling this route over the last decade.

At least Lady Macbeth will eat her fill, Penny thought as she crawled into her bedroll. The cow's milk supply had all but dried up from the many months of traveling. Moreover, the poor animal had grown so thin.

As we all have, Penny added on a cynical note. Then she chided herself for not possessing a more positive outlook. But she was tired, so very tired, and she felt discouraged by her father's hesitation regarding Dillon.

"I'm so impatient, Lord," she whispered into the darkness.

Penny suddenly recalled Pastor Brewster's message last Sunday. It had been based on Isaiah's fortieth chapter, verse thirty-one. Pastor Brewster had talked about maintaining a peaceable temperament during this last leg of the journey. Everyone battled exhaustion, but looking to Christ at all times would give the Christian insurmountable endurance along with a quiet, untroubled spirit.

Penny knew the reverend spoke the truth because his words were backed by Scripture. "But they that wait upon the LORD shall renew their strength; they shall mount up with wings as eagles; they shall run, and not be weary; and they shall walk, and not faint."

Run and not be weary, she thought. *Walk and not faint.*

With those words in mind, Penny fell fast asleep.

❧

The next morning brought the first crossing of the Snake. Up until now, they had followed a crude course of the river's south bank. They had camped close to it, nooning at its tributaries; however, they had yet to cross it. Rawhide had decided to ford the Snake rather than follow the river until they reached what had once been Fort Boise. He selected a place known as "Three Island Ford"—a place where the river was divided by three small islands that could be used like steppingstones. Rawhide claimed it was the easiest passage. A mile upstream, he'd said, there was another location called "Two Island Crossing," but the river was deeper, ran swifter, and the likelihood of drowning increased. Rawhide added that in order to ford the river at Two Island Crossing, the wheels would need to be removed from each wagon so they could float across like tiny boats. The wagon master declared the task "too much of a chore." So, with the help of several Indian friends, Three Island Ford became the choice of passage.

Penny stood on the shores of the wide, rushing river, watching as the first of the wagon train prepared to cross—Josh and Bethany among that initial group.

Please, God, Penny prayed, *please keep Beth safe. She's so frightened of the water.*

"She'll be all right."

Startled, Penny whirled around and saw Dillon had come up behind her. She immediately noticed that wound around his shoulder and hanging to his waist was a cord of thick rope. "How on earth did you know what I was thinking?"

Dillon chuckled. "Wasn't hard once I followed your line of vision." He looked toward the wagons. "Everyone knows your sister-in-law is scared senseless of the water. It's only natural that you'd worry about her."

"Yes. . .yes, I am worried about her." Penny faced him once more.

"I can't rightly promise that I'll keep trouble away, but I'm going down to help and I'll do everything in my power to keep Mrs. Rogers safe. So don't fret. All right?"

Penny looked at him askance, wondering if she could keep such a vow.

"Come on, now," he coaxed with a charming grin. "Give me your word."

"I promise," she said at last, meaning each syllable. Then she smiled. "I always feel so much better when you're around. You're my hero."

The poor man actually blushed at her candid remark.

Dillon gave the brim of his hat a parting tug; and, after he began his descent off the steep bank, Penny let out a long, slow breath. Would she ever learn to curb her wayward tongue?

Onlookers gathered on either side of Penny. They all stared down at the three white-bonneted wagons making ready to cross the river. The August sunshine beat down on them and sparkled on the water like the silver heads of stick pins imbedded in flowing blue silk. Surrounding the wagons that were hitched to oxen were men on horseback—men who included Rawhide's Indian friends.

At first the half-naked, long-haired men were a fright to behold, and the majority of the wagon train opposed the Indians' help. But Rawhide made it clear that, without the aid of his practiced Indian friends, crossing the Snake would be many times more difficult. The likelihood of drowning would increase. Families chanced losing their entire belongings.

Folks soon came around to see his point.

Amidst the din of the men shouting directions to each other, the wagons made it safely to the first of the islands. Then the second. Then the third. Cheers went up around Penny, who looked to the heavens and praised the Lord. Bethany had made it across unscathed.

Maybe, just maybe, crossing the Snake River wouldn't be so problematical after all!

Chapter 8

As it happened, crossing the Snake River was a painstaking event that took nearly three days. But finally it came down to the last four wagons—the Barneses', the Millbergs' two, and Papa and Penny's.

Dillon helped Rawhide and the Indians secure the carts. When he reached the Rogerses', he smiled up at Penny.

"Are you scared?"

"Not a bit. I'm a terrific swimmer."

Dillon's brows furrowed, and he appeared none too pleased by her admission. "You're no match for the Snake River, Penny. Remember that. There's a powerful strong undercurrent that would've swept away the oxen had they not been yoked and hitched. Would've swept away the men on horseback, too, if they wouldn't have held fast to the wagons."

"Are you purposely trying to frighten me?"

Dillon's expression softened at once. "I'd do no such thing. I just want you to take care—really good care."

Penny tipped her head, gauging his reply. "Are you worried about me, Dillon?"

"Sure I am! And if I had my way, I'd be driving your wagon

with you and your pa on board instead of ferrying the Millbergs' piano across the river." He glanced down at the soft dirt beneath his boots. "I don't much like the fact that I won't be able to help you if trouble comes."

"Papa and I will manage, Dillon," Penny assured him. "You needn't worry about us—except I'm most grateful that you do."

Dillon nodded, then slapped his hat on his head. "I reckon I'd do just about anything for you."

Penny was touched to the very core of her being. "You are ever so gallant, Dillon Trier."

He shrugged, looking a tad embarrassed, but at last he handed up the reins. Penny gave him her sweetest smile in return.

"All right, ever'body, listen up!" Rawhide's gravely voice interrupted their tender moment. "The river's movin' awful fast today on account of that rainstorm last night. It's gonna be a mite harder to cross today and that means takin' extra special precautions. Understood?"

Murmurs of acquiescence emanated from the group as Dillon made his way back to the Millbergs' wagon. Papa climbed aboard theirs, took the reins from Penny, and sat beside her.

"We're as ready as we'll ever be," he muttered.

"You're not fretting over the crossing, are you, Papa?"

"Of course not."

His words, however, failed to convince her; and Penny couldn't understand all this "to do" about nothing. To Penny, the Snake didn't seem so imposing. But she'd never been afraid of water, nor had she ever been affected by a drowning tragedy like Bethany. On the contrary, Penny associated lakes, rivers, and streams with pure enjoyment; and, in her estimation, this whole ordeal was highly overrated.

The wagons pulled out slowly and rolled into the water. Deeper, deeper, they went. Penny felt the wagon shudder with the force of the current. The oxen were in up to their ears, and the men struggled to keep them from drowning. Water lapped over the edges of the wagon, and Penny suddenly recalled every terrible story she'd heard about this crossing. Suppose they were true?

In the next moment, as if she'd somehow conjured up the catastrophe, the Barneses' wagon swayed violently before tipping onto its side. Its white canopy broke away, spilling the entire contents of the wagon—including the Barneses' children!

Horror-struck, Penny stood. She barely felt Papa's steadying hand at her elbow. All she could think of was the children! The children! Why weren't the men going after them? Why were they trying to save the animals instead? Couldn't they see that the children were being swept away?

Up ahead, Idabelle Barnes cradled her bawling infant while she stood chest deep in the river, holding onto the tipped wagon for her own life. She frantically screamed Penny's exact thoughts. "The children! The children!" Granny Willodene looked soaked to the bone and hollered with all she had, but no one appeared to hear her or Idabelle. . . .

Except Penny.

Without a single thought for her own safety, Penny shook off her father's hold and jumped into the river. The initial cold shock of the water washing over her took her breath away, but it didn't stop her from swimming hard and fast downstream, keeping the boys' bobbing heads in sight.

Please, God! Please, God! Please, God! she prayed with each stroke.

Finally, she reached the two children, who were gasping for air as, time and again, the current pulled them under. Looping an arm around each one's waist, Penny tried to kick hard enough to swim back upstream, but the river was too powerful. Nevertheless, she managed to hold the boys' heads above water even if it meant she went under—and she did. Once. Twice. . .

She coughed and sputtered, and it was all she could do to keep herself afloat.

Then suddenly, they were slammed backwards into a protruding embankment, Penny taking the full force of the impact. The eight year old grabbed onto a long tree root that stuck straight out from the brown, muddy bank. And that's the last thing Penny saw before giving way to murky unconsciousness.

❧

As if in a torturous, slow-moving dream, Dillon watched the tragedy unfold before him as the Barneses' wagon overturned. He felt helpless until the women's screaming captured his attention, and he realized at once that the two Barnes kids were about to drown.

Pulling off his boots and tossing his hat into the back of the Millbergs' wagon, Dillon prepared to plunge into the depths of the Snake River, but he was brought up short by a sickening splash behind him.

Penny! She'd jumped in after the boys!

Oh, sweet Lord, he prayed, *what'd she have to go and do that for?*

As Dillon hit the water, he knew he couldn't save them all, and he prayed that God would somehow intervene. Swimming downstream, he saw Penny meet up with the two boys, and his initial alarm subsided. Now he had a good chance of rescuing them.

Thank You, Jesus!

As he swam in their direction, he could see Penny nearing a jagged, ten-foot-tall embankment. He called out a warning, only it was too late. A moment later, he witnessed the skull-splitting collision; but he reached the trio just as Penny lost consciousness and slipped beneath the water's surface.

"Is she dead?" the older Barnes boy asked, his eyes wide with impending hysteria.

"Merciful Father, I hope not!" Dillon replied, lifting her out of the water as the younger boy latched onto his one arm.

The river was shallow enough that Dillon found a foothold, although the water came as high as his elbows. Holding Penny's head between his hands, he put his cheek against her lips. A chilling fear crept up his spine when he couldn't detect a breath.

"Penny!" he cried, giving her a shake. "Breathe!"

He slung her over his shoulder, intending to somehow get her to the top of the stout cliff and onto dry land. But to his immeasurable relief, a siege of coughing wracked her slender body, and it was the best sound Dillon ever heard.

He looked at the oldest Barnes kid. "Praise, God! She's alive!"

Tears streamed down the boy's freckled cheeks. "But she's bleeding. . .look!"

With one arm firmly around her waist, Dillon carefully tipped Penny back in order to inspect the wound. But the younger Barnes kid had wrapped himself around Dillon like an anaconda, so the task proved impossible. "Doc Rogers'll have to look at it."

At that very moment, Penny's eyes fluttered open, and Dillon smiled down into their blue depths. "I'm not willing to go down in the Snake, but I'd drown in your eyes any day," he whispered against her lips.

"I must be in heaven," she muttered softly, dreamily. Then a slight frown furrowed her delicate brows. "Dillon, are you in heaven, too?"

"A semblance of, I'd say," he replied, grinning.

"You two act like Ma 'n' Pa," the older boy declared on a note of repulsion. "Yuck!"

Above them, on the edge of the embankment, five or six men appeared with ropes and blankets.

"Is anyone injured?" Doc Rogers called, his medical bag in one hand.

"Penny's hurt," Dillon said, coming to his senses. He wondered how in the world he could even think of romancing this woman while she lay impaired in his arms. He must be as crazy as a loon—

Or crazy in love.

The children were quickly plucked from the water. Dillon lifted Penny into her brother's arms, after which Bert and Buck Cole pulled Dillon from the river.

As they stood ashore, drying in the August sunshine, the men assessed nicks and scrapes while Doc Rogers examined the laceration on the back of Penny's head. Minutes later, a thunderous crack splintered the air and drew every gaze upstream. To Dillon's second horror of the day, he saw that the Millbergs' wagon—the very one which he'd been hired to drive—had tipped. The prized piano began floating upside down, moving with the current, and gathering momentum as it went. Orson Millberg's expletives followed in its wake.

Then, at the very place where Dillon, Penny, and the children had been, the piano smashed into the bank with an eerie, descanted chord. A heartbeat later, it broke into pieces that were quickly swept away.

The Cole brothers looked at each other and burst into laughter.

"If that weren't the funniest thang I ever did see!" Bert said, holding his side.

"Yah, and that was the purtiest tune that ol' pianer made this whole trip!"

Dillon stared at them as if they'd just traveled from the moon. Didn't these two fellows know that his dreams of a new life in Oregon—his future with Penny—were now as shattered and worthless as that piano?

Besides, he'd just lost everything he owned!

He closed his eyes against the overwhelming disappointment. . .until the sound of retching reached his ears.

Penny.

Shaking off his piteous thoughts, he strode toward where she sat on her haunches, doubled over. Next to her, Josh held an arm around her waist and a hand against her forehead. The grim set of his mouth told Dillon more than he wanted to know.

"It's not good, is it, Doc?"

Josh met his gaze and shook his head. "My guess is she's got a concussion."

"My head hurts so badly, Josh," Penny managed to whimper.

"What can I do to help?" Dillon asked.

"Fetch my wife. Tell her to bring some dry clothing for Penny. But, please," Josh added with a beseeching look in his blue eyes, "please don't let on that Penny nearly drowned. Beth won't take it well."

"I understand." Early on in their journey, Dillon had heard all about the tragedy that befell Beth's folks. "You can count on me, Doc. I won't say more than needs to be said."

"Good. Oh, and. . ."

Dillon paused.

"I'm eternally grateful to you for saving Penny's life."

She looked up at him, a damp blanket pressed against her mouth. "Yes, thank you, Dillon," she murmured.

Her face suddenly paled, and she turned her head away, preparing to be sick again.

An odd sense of dread coursed through Dillon's veins. "I'll get your missus," he promised Josh before sprinting toward the wagons.

Chapter 9

Dillon didn't have to go far before he met Bethany already on her way to see after her sister-in-law. In her arms, she carried a bundle of clothing and a blanket.

"How's Penny? Is she all right? I about swooned when I saw her jump into the river!"

"Your husband's tending to her right now," Dillon replied guardedly.

With a hasty nod, Bethany continued her trek toward Penny and Josh. Dillon would have followed, but off in the distance he heard Orson Millberg bellowing for him.

Squaring his shoulders, Dillon decided to face the inevitable. Now or later, he reckoned, it may as well be now.

"Trier, get your sorry hide over here!"

He felt disgusted that the man would use such language around womenfolk. As for himself, he didn't much care what Millberg had to say. It was all over. He'd lost his job.

"You no-account farmhand, I should have known better than to hire you to drive my wagon. Why you're not fit to lick the mud off my boots."

Standing just a few feet away from the older man now, a

molten-hot fury surged inside of Dillon. He took a stride forward, but Zach Sawyer and Homer Green grabbed his upper arms and held him back.

"He ain't worth even skinnin' your knuckles," Zach said.

Dillon tried in vain to tamp down his anger while Millberg continued his ravings.

"That piano has been in our family for generations, and now it's lost because of you!"

"I beg your pardon, Orson," Frank Barnes put in, "but this man saved our children."

"That's right," Idabelle said, her plump arms around the shoulders of her two sons. "Had it not been for Mr. Trier, they would have drowned."

"More's the pity," Millberg replied, wearing a scowl. "That piano was worth at least a thousand dollars."

Idabelle gasped at the insinuation.

The men at Dillon's side released their hold.

"Have at 'im," Homer said.

Millberg spit at Dillon's feet. "You're not worth the—"

Clenching a fist, he didn't wait to hear the rest of the insult. He swung and struck Millberg square in the jaw. The man spun like a top. Another blow to his midsection sent Orson sprawling backwards in the dirt.

Dillon looked down on him, his jaw firmly set. "Get up, Millberg. I'm not through with you."

"Yes, you are."

Turning, Dillon came face-to-face with the barrel of Rawhide's rifle.

"He might deserve a good beating," the gristly wagon master said from high in his saddle, "but you 'n' the others got work to do. We've wasted enough time here. We gotta get back on the trail or the Blue Mountains'll be snowcapped when we reach 'em."

Grudgingly, Dillon gave up the fight.

"You're fired, Trier!" Millberg declared, struggling to his feet.

"Can't fire me," he retorted. "I quit!"

"Can't quit, 'cause you're fired!" the man bellowed.

Rawhide cocked his gun and aimed at Millberg. "Don't make me get off this horse 'cause if I do, it'll be to pick up your dead carcass."

Millberg had the good sense to keep his mouth shut.

"You got no cause for your bellyaching," Rawhide added, lowering his rifle. "Your wagon woulda overturned whether Trier was driving it or not, seein' as it was so overloaded with that piano. Ever'one including me told you not to take that atrocious thing. What's more is you're gonna pay Trier what he earned up till today. Now, get yourself cleaned up 'cause we're heading out in one hour."

Millberg frowned just as his wife and Lavinia reached his side. He angrily pushed them away and strode for his wagon.

"I'm sorry you lost you're job, Mr. Trier," Idabelle said. Wisps of her wheat-colored hair blew across her face, and she brushed them aside. "If my boys hadn't fallen in. . ."

"Mrs. Barnes, a human life is worth far more than a piano. . . and a job. I have no regrets. Neither should you."

Tears of gratitude filled her eyes and she nodded.

Zach and Homer gave him an encouraging slap on the back as they walked away, while Granny Willodene reached up and pinched the fat of his cheek.

"You're a good boy, Sonny. God bless you."

"Yes, Ma'am. Thank you kindly." Once her back was to him, Dillon rubbed at the sore spot left by the old woman's assault. Next, he backtracked with the intention of finding out how Penny fared in the hands of Doc Rogers and his wife.

❧

As it happened, Penny didn't fare well at all. Joshua, of course, expertly sutured the laceration on the back of her head, but neither he nor Ambrose Harris could cure her brain-twisting headache. Rawhide conceded to spending one more night by the Snake River; and once Penny was tucked into her bedroll, Bethany told her about the events of the latter part of the afternoon and evening.

"Mr. Millberg has a giant bruise on his jaw from his fight with Dillon."

Penny couldn't help a little grin. "Serves him right, that troll."

"Certainly does. And now the Coles are allowing Dillon to share their wagon since they have room enough for his things."

Beth gasped, startling Penny out of her groggy state. "What is it, Beth?"

"I almost forgot to tell you. Bert and Buck Cole fished Dillon's chest out of the river. It floated downstream, but got stuck between two large stones. God is so good! And guess what else? Mr. Millberg paid Dillon through today; and, if that wasn't miracle enough, Bernie Williams said he had planned to share a portion of the reward money with Dillon once we reach Oregon City."

"Oh, that's wonderful, Beth. Tell Dillon I said it's wonderful."

"I will. I promise." Soaking the rag in cool water, Beth draped it over Penny's forehead again. "Well, that dreadful Lavinia Millberg," she prattled on, "threatened to turn Dillon in to the sheriff as soon as we reach Oregon because he dared to strike her father. But Mr. Rawhide said he'll swear on the Bible that it was a fair fight."

"Beth, can we please talk about this tomorrow?" Penny asked as a crescendo of pain gripped her. "My head is about to explode."

Penny hadn't meant to hurt her dear friend's feelings. Very simply, her body yearned for peace and quiet. Nevertheless, huge tears rolled down Beth's cheeks.

"I'm just trying to help."

"I know. . .Beth! Wait, don't go."

But it was too late. Bethany had already begun her descent from the wagon.

Feeling more than miserable, Penny squeezed back tears of her own. "Dear Lord," she whispered into the darkness of the wagon, "what's wrong with Beth lately? She cries over practically nothing. Is she just tired? Tired as I am?"

On that thought, Penny drifted into a restless sleep.

The next day proved no better. Her head still pounded like a bass drum. Penny tried hard not to complain for fear she would set the wagon train back another day. When they stopped at noon, she rested in a shady spot with a wet rag over her forehead and eyes. At last she found reprieve—but not for long. Just as soon as she began walking the trail, her headache came rushing back.

"Penny, I'm so worried about you," Bethany said that evening as Josh and Papa frowned their obvious concerns. "You need to eat something."

"I can't. I'll be sick. I just need to sleep."

Josh nodded. "Sleep's about the only cure I know of at this point."

Penny was soon snuggled inside her bedroll with another damp cloth spread across her forehead.

At breakfast the next morning, Bethany told Penny that Dillon had asked over her. "A host of others wanted to visit, too," she added, "but you were asleep."

"Yes, and thank you for making my excuses, Beth," Penny replied. "I do feel better this morning."

Unfortunately, once she began her trek on the trail, the headache returned. Riding in the wagon did little to alleviate it. In fact, it only made it worse. When the wheels hit the ruts in the worn, dirt road, Penny's head throbbed all the more.

❧

For the weeks that followed, Penny continued to battle her headaches. One evening, after crossing the Snake River for the last time, Reverend Brewster decided to hold a special prayer service. Sitting on a fallen log beside Dillon, she laid her pounding head on his shoulder. To her utter shame, she fell asleep during Pastor's preaching.

It was days before he quit teasing her about it.

On the second day of September, the wagon train rounded Farewell Bend, the place where the trail veered away from the Snake River for good. Ahead of the pioneers lay the Blue Mountains. Cheers went up when they saw that the peaks were blue and not white with snow. Rawhide exclaimed that they were practically assured an easy passage through the mountains now.

With a heavy sigh, Penny leaned against the wagon after they'd paused to take in the majestic panoramic view before them. Pressing her palms against the excruciating pain at her temples, she suddenly wondered if she'd ever reach Oregon.

"Wish there was something I could do for you," Dillon said, coming up behind her.

Turning slowly, so as not to further disturb the pain in her head, Penny gave him a weak smile. "I wish there was something you could do for me, too. I'm weary of this headache."

"I'm sure you are."

"Dillon," she murmured, searching his rugged face, "I think I'm dying."

His brown eyes widened. "Don't say such things."

"It wouldn't be so bad, really. I'd be with Jesus, and—"

"Stop, Penny!" Before she could utter another syllable, Dillon pulled her into his strong arms. "Don't you know you're scaring the liver out of me?"

"But—"

"Shh. . .no more talk. I think God wants you to just be still for a spell."

"Perhaps. That's when I feel a little better."

"Mm-hmm, and that's what your pa thinks, too. He and I've been having some fine discussions in the evenings."

With her head against Dillon's chest, Penny felt the throbbing pain at her temples ebb. "What sort of 'fine discussion' have you and Papa had?"

A rumble of laughter bubbled up inside Dillon. "I reckon you're feeling better already."

"Oh, go on with you." Penny would have liked to playfully push Dillon away, but she couldn't get herself to move a muscle. "Seriously, now, tell me what you and Papa talked about."

"I can't just yet, Penny. I gave him my word. But I'll say

this much. . .you're not dying on me now."

She laughed, then moaned as the pain hit like a bolt of lightning through her skull.

"Shh, Penny. Rest yourself and just look yonder at the wide, blue sky. The clouds seem so low I feel like I could reach out and pick one—like a man'd pick a wad of cotton. This is Oregon!" he declared, pointing off to the left. "We've all but arrived."

"But there are still mountains to pass and rivers to cross."

"Won't be nothing like what we've been through. You'll see."

Gazing across the vastness spread out before her, Penny felt a stab of doubt pierce her soul. Would she ever truly settle in Oregon?

Chapter 10

Dillon was right. The next few weeks of traveling didn't seem as bad to Penny as they had in the past. The days were warm and the nights were cool. The grass was plentiful enough for the animals to feed upon, and Lady Macbeth began producing again. For a long stretch of trail, the ragged pioneers traveled through a dense forest that Dillon said reminded him of Missouri.

Oftentimes, Papa let Dillon drive the wagon while he walked beside Penny. He encouraged her by engaging her in all sorts of games involving their knowledge of Shakespeare's plays. On other occasions, when the trail wasn't as rough and uneven, Papa allowed Penny to ride beside Dillon and didn't even balk when she set her aching head on his shoulder. Penny smiled as Dillon recounted happy memories of his childhood and spoke about his plans for the future. Papa didn't balk at that, either. He didn't even interrupt, but listened raptly as he traipsed along beside the wagon.

At one point, Penny realized she'd never heard Dillon talk so much. Why, he talked more than she did! Of course, she wasn't feeling like herself. . .yet. Even so, she felt as though a very special prayer had been answered—the one in which she'd asked that she might get to better know the man she loved.

The Lord in all His wisdom, Penny decided, must have quieted her in order to bring Dillon out of his shell and to help her listen. What's more, Penny realized she liked Dillon Trier—liked him as a friend—while, at the same time, she felt the love in her heart for him blossom into a desire to be his wife someday.

Now, if she'd only survive the rest of the journey to make that wish a reality.

❧

One starry September night, Dillon sat on the edge of a large rock, wondering over the events of the day. As the wagons had progressed at an agonizingly slow pace down a ravine this afternoon, Penny lost her footing and fell. Worse, she'd struck her head again, giving Dillon the fright of his life; and now she lay unconscious in the Rogerses' wagon.

Looking up from the cup of coffee in his hands, he saw Doc Rogers coming his way. Dillon stood. "How is she, Doc?"

"Not good, I'm afraid." The grim set of his mouth gave credence to his reply. "And while I'm glad you convinced Rawhide to stop early today, I'm unsure of whether Penny can travel tomorrow."

"Then we stop for a day or two. . .or however long it takes," Dillon said. Try as he might, he couldn't keep the vehemence from his tone. "If Rawhide and the others complain, they can go on without us. We'll catch up once Penny's better."

Josh smiled slightly and gave his shoulder a mild squeeze as he strode toward his own wagon. "We'll just have to take it day by day, prayer by prayer."

"Your concern for my daughter is touching," Penny's pa said from where he sat on a worn rug before the fire. "I'm deeply indebted to you for your kindness and help these past weeks."

"You're not indebted to me, Sir. I love Penny. . . . I–I can't help it."

In the twilight of the evening, Dillon saw the elder grin above the tracings of worry etched on his brow.

Suddenly a commotion near Penny's wagon caught his attention, and Dillon glanced over in time to see Mrs. Rogers sobbing as she ran for her husband.

"Josh! Oh, Josh. . .what are we going to do? I can't bear it if Penny dies."

"Shh, Sweetheart. She's not going to die."

Dillon watched with a heavy frown as, several feet away, Doc Rogers consoled his wife. Then he ushered her into their wagon.

"Poor, dear Beth," Isaiah said, voicing Dillon's very thoughts. "She and Penny are so close. I'm sure she feels as helpless as. . .well, as we all do."

"Yes, Sir. I'm sure." Dillon lowered himself back onto the boulder.

The professor narrowed his gaze. "And how would you handle such a thing if your, um, wife despaired over a friend in need?"

"How would I handle it?"

"Yes, I'm curious. Some women are more sensitive than others, and I know plenty of men who are impatient with their wives' tears."

"Doesn't seem Doc Rogers is impatient with anyone or anything," Dillon replied. "Especially his wife."

"I agree. But I'm not referring to either Josh or Bethany.

I'm merely inquiring over a purely hypothetical situation."

Dillon grinned. The turn in conversation didn't throw him as much as it might have many weeks ago. Ever since he'd asked to court Penny, Isaiah Rogers had been grilling him like a rabbit on a spit.

But that was all right. He respected any pa who made a man squirm when it came to giving away his daughter's hand in marriage. In fact, Dillon suspected that someday he might be harder to convince than even the professor!

❧

Penny opened her eyes and knew immediately that something wasn't right. To her left, the sun was streaming in through a window.

A window!

Slowly, she lifted herself up in the bed.

A real bed!

She felt weak and lay back down against the fluffy pillows. *Where am I? How did I get here? When did I get here? Where's Papa, Josh, and Bethany? Where's Dillon?*

She glanced around the room and its dark rough-hewn walls. She wondered if her family had abandoned her somewhere along the trail—a small settlement, perhaps, because of her headaches.

Her headaches!

Penny touched her temples. The pain was gone. "Oh, praise God!" she said in a raspy voice that was unrecognizable to even her own ears. Clearing her throat, she tried it again. "Praise God!"

There. That was better.

The door creaked open and a little boy peered in. His blond hair hung straight down on his forehead. He took one look at

Penny, gasped, and slammed the door shut.

"Mama! Mama!" she heard him call. "The lady is awake!"

Penny lay silent, straining to hear the reply.

"Why, Nathan, you shouldn't have disturbed Miss Rogers. For shame." The woman's voice sounded soft and gentle, even in the reprimand.

The door creaked open once more and a blond woman looked in. Her hair was elegantly pinned at the nape, giving her a regal appearance. "Hello," she said in a tentative tone.

"Hello," Penny replied.

The woman smiled and stepped into the room. She wore a plain brown skirt, adorned by a multicolored apron, and white blouse. Penny estimated her age to be somewhere in the late twenties. "I'm Deborah Lannon. I live here with my husband and two young sons."

"Pleased to meet you. I'm Penelope Anne Rogers. Penny, for short."

"Well, Penny, I'm sure you're wondering what you're doing in our home."

She managed a nod.

"You've been very ill, and when your family reached the Willamette Valley last week—"

"I made it to Oregon?"

"Just barely."

Penny struggled to sit, and Mrs. Lannon stepped forward to assist her. "Let me explain how you came here. Our house is the first one pioneers reach when they arrive in Oregon City. My husband is a minister; and after we traveled the trail from our home in New York, it became his fervent wish that we aid pioneers in need. Some come to us sick, others come to us with nothing but the tattered clothes on their back. Our mission is to tend to and refresh weary immigrants and get them back on their feet so they can begin their lives here in the Willamette Valley."

"That's a very charitable mission, Mrs. Lannon, and I'm forever grateful."

She smiled. "It's reward enough to see you awake and talking. You had all of us very worried. Kept us on our knees."

"My family. . .?"

"They're here in the valley, also. Your father is already pursuing his interests at the university in Oregon City."

Penny grinned.

"Your brother and his wife are in the throes of building their cabin. They're assisted by every able-bodied man available, including that nice man who seems quite taken with you," Deborah said with a twinkle in her blue eyes.

"Dillon?" Penny's grin became a smile.

"Yes, and when your brother's home is built, the team of men will help him with his cabin. That's how it's done here because families need homes by the time winter hits. Everyone tries to help each other.

"Of course, folks in town are glad that we'll now have our own doctor," Deborah added, "since your brother will settle here. And my husband and I feel so blessed," she said, flitting around the room and straightening up. "We've been praying for another pastor to help us with growing our church and ministering to our congregation. Why, when Reverend Brewster and his sweet wife came to see after your health, we knew without a doubt our prayers had been answered.

"Now, then," Deborah said, with hands on her hips and a lovely grin curving her mouth, "why don't I help you bathe and dress? I have a feeling we can expect company this evening."

The measures taken to wash and change clothes left Penny exhausted. Attired in a simple gown with her hair brushed out, she lay atop the bedcovers trying to regain what little strength she had. Worse, she felt ashamed of how she looked. Her face appeared sallow in the mirror, and the calico that once fit nicely now hung like a drape over her too-thin body. But Penny had to admit she felt glad to be a part of the living again; and she knew she had much for which to be thankful.

Just as Mrs. Lannon predicted, word that Penny had regained consciousness soon spread through the valley. By suppertime, she was reunited with her family, following which Bethany immediately blurted her good news. But she needn't have said a word; the fact appeared quite obvious.

"You're going to have a baby! Oh, Beth, this is going to be so much fun. I can hardly wait until she's born. I'm going to be the auntie who spoils her rotten."

"She?" Josh said with an arched brow. "Her?"

"Oh, did I say she?" Penny teased. "I meant little she or he. Him or her."

"Yes, I thought that's what you meant," Josh replied, wearing an amused grin. He glanced at Papa. "She seems her old self again."

Papa smiled. "Yes, she does."

"There's only a handful of lawmen around," Bernie said, "and Willamette Valley is growing by leaps and bounds."

At that moment, Dillon stepped into the bedroom, looking better than Penny had ever seen him. His tan trousers looked fresh and his cambric shirt had been starched and pressed. Penny wanted to throw herself into his arms, but Pastor Brewster and

Emma walked in right behind him and began exclaiming over her renewed health. Afterwards, the reverend led everyone in a prayer of thanksgiving.

More people flittered in, and the tiny room soon filled to capacity. The Millbergs stopped by, looking as pompous as ever, and Lavinia's pink gown with its white ruffles and satin bows had to have been brand-new and store-bought, no less. But the fact that the Millbergs even deigned to visit her at all was, Penny decided, oddly touching.

Over the next hour, as guests came and went, it was all Penny could do to make eye contact with Dillon. He stood against the far wall, waiting patiently for his turn to speak with her. Penny had a hunch he'd prefer a bit of privacy when the right time arrived, except it didn't look like that was going to happen soon since the Cole brothers had just burst into the room.

Then, all at once, Dillon seemed to have had his fill of waiting. Penny smiled with anticipation as she saw him making his way through the throng. When he reached her bedside, he nodded out a formal greeting.

"Penny."

"Dillon. . ."

She held out a trembling hand, but instead of taking it, he scooped her up into his arms and proceeded toward the doorway.

"Dillon, I don't know if—"

"I'll be careful, Doc. I promise."

"Young man, perhaps it would be best if. . ."

"Pardon me, Professor, but I've been mighty long-suffering, if I do say so myself."

"Why, Dillon!" Penny exclaimed. "Y–you skirted my family's wishes!"

"Sure did," he said, gazing down at her with an intense spark in his eyes. "But they're all well aware of my intentions."

Wide-eyed and with an arm around his thick neck, Penny could hardly believe it. Gone was that shy, uncertain man, and in his place loomed a veritable hero wrought from any imagined work of literature!

Upon hearing Papa's guffaw as they left the room, she relaxed and allowed Dillon to carry her onto the back porch of the Lannons' log home. He set her down gently in a wooden rocker and knelt by her side.

"Penny," he said, taking her hand, "I can't stand to think I almost lost you. . .except I knew God was doing something. I just didn't know what."

"Oh, Dillon. . ." His words melted her heart.

He kissed her fingers, sending delightful shivers up her arm; and Penny felt as though she might lose consciousness again—but for very different reasons.

"I love you, Penny. I love you more than words can say." He paused and swallowed hard before adding, "Just ask your pa."

"He approves?"

Dillon nodded. "He does. Gave me his blessing to court you just before we reached Farewell Bend. But I couldn't tell you then. You were too ill."

He took a deep breath and exhaled slowly, looking like he might be forming his thoughts with painstaking care. "When you had that next accident, you slipped into some sort of coma. It was like you were half with us and half someplace else. Your sister-in-law would spoon-feed bites of food into your mouth, and sometimes you'd eat. You would look at us all glassy-eyed, and we could tell you weren't really there. Some Indian folks we met along the way said your spirit had taken flight and wouldn't ever come back. But I refused to give up hope.

"Then while we were traveling the pass around Mount Hood, I told your pa that I thought our courtship had lasted long enough. I said when you woke up, I wanted to marry you. He said when you woke up, I could. Ever since, I've been waiting. . . ."

Tears of joy sprang into Penny's eyes. Such devotion she couldn't fathom; and she knew without a doubt, if she hadn't before, that Dillon Trier was the man for her.

"I love you, too."

"Well, if so, will you marry me? And the sooner the better, as far as I'm concerned."

She tipped her head and grinned. "You want to marry me in this sorry state?"

"I'd marry you in any state."

She smiled at the candid reply and placed a hand against his rough cheek. "Yes, I'll marry you. I'll be your wildflower bride, and I'll love you with all my heart and with all the breath I have in me."

Dillon's brown eyes clouded with unshed emotion. "I couldn't ask for more."

He pulled her onto his knee and wrapped his arms around her. Penny never felt so cherished and protected. As she gazed up at the immense Oregon sky, with its ribbons of scarlet and gold fastened across the horizon, she thanked the Lord for giving her this treasured moment—

This one, and those sure to follow in the lifetime ahead.

ANDREA BOESHAAR

Andrea was born and raised in Milwaukee, Wisconsin. Married for nearly twenty-five years, she and her husband Daniel have three adult sons. Andrea has been writing ever since she was a child. Writing is something she loves to share, as well as help others develop. Andrea has written twelve **Heartsong Presents** titles of inspirational romance and for the past few years has been voted one of **Heartsong's** top ten favorite authors.

As far as her writing success is concerned, Andrea gives the glory to the Lord Jesus. Her writing, she feels, is a gift from God in that He has provided an "outlet" for her imagination. Andrea wants her writing to be an evangelistic tool, but she also hopes that it edifies and encourages other Christians in their daily walk with Him.

A Letter to Our Readers

Dear Readers:

In order that we might better contribute to your reading enjoyment, we would appreciate you taking a few minutes to respond to the following questions. When completed, please return to the following: Fiction Editor, Barbour Publishing, Inc., P.O. Box 719, Uhrichsville, OH 44683.

1. Did you enjoy reading *Wildflower Brides?*
   - ❑ Very much—I would like to see more books like this.
   - ❑ Moderately—I would have enjoyed it more if ________________

____

____

2. What influenced your decision to purchase this book? (Check those that apply.)
   - ❑ Cover ❑ Back cover copy ❑ Title ❑ Price
   - ❑ Friends ❑ Publicity ❑ Other

3. Which story was your favorite?
   - ❑ *The Wedding Wagon* ❑ *Murder or Matrimony*
   - ❑ *A Bride for the Preacher* ❑ *Bride in the Valley*

4. Please check your age range:
   - ❑ Under 18 ❑ 18–24 ❑ 25–34
   - ❑ 35–45 ❑ 46–55 ❑ Over 55

5. How many hours per week do you read? ______________________

Name ____

Occupation ____

Address ____

City ______________________ State ____________ Zip ____________